There was nothing to do but surrender. To the molten fire that rolled through her. To the heaviness in her breasts, pressed hard against his chest. And to that restless, edgy, weighted thing that sank low into her belly and then pulsed hot.

Needy. Insistent.

And Kathryn *forgot*.

She forgot who he was. That she had been his stepmother for two years even though he was some eight years older than she was. She forgot that in addition to being her harshest critic and her bitter enemy, through no fault of her own Luca was now going to be her boss.

She forgot everything but the taste of him. That harsh, sweet magic he made…the way he commanded her and compelled her—as if he knew the things her body wanted and could do when she had no idea. When she was simply lost—adrift in the fire.

USA TODAY bestseller and RITA® Award-nominated author **Caitlin Crews** loves writing romance. She teaches her favourite romance novels in creative writing classes at places like UCLA Extension's prestigious Writers' Programme, where she finally gets to utilise the MA and PhD in English Literature she received from the University of York in England. She currently lives in California, with her very own hero and too many pets. Visit her at caitlincrews.com.

Books by Caitlin Crews

Mills & Boon Modern Romance

At the Count's Bidding
Undone by the Sultan's Touch
Not Just the Boss's Plaything
A Devil in Disguise
In Defiance of Duty
The Replacement Wife
Princess From the Past

The Chatsfield

Greek's Last Redemption

Scandalous Sheikh Brides

Protecting the Desert Heir
Traded to the Desert Sheikh

Vows of Convenience

His for a Price
His for Revenge

Royal and Ruthless

A Royal Without Rules

Scandal in the Spotlight

No More Sweet Surrender
Heiress Behind the Headlines

Self-Made Millionaires

Katrakis's Last Mistress

Bride on Approval

Pure Princess, Bartered Bride

Visit the Author Profile page
at millsandboon.co.uk for more titles.

CASTELLI'S VIRGIN WIDOW

BY
CAITLIN CREWS

Published in Great Britain 2016
By Mills & Boon, an imprint of HarperCollins*Publishers*
1 London Bridge Street, London, SE1 9GF

© 2016 Caitlin Crews

ISBN: 978-0-263-92100-7

Our policy is to use papers that are natural, renewable and recyclable
products and made from wood grown in sustainable forests. The logging
and manufacturing processes conform to the legal environmental
regulations of the country of origin.

Printed and bound in Spain
by CPI, Barcelona

CASTELLI'S VIRGIN WIDOW

To my wonderful editor Flo Nicoll
for our fantastic year together!

Thank you so much for taking such great care of me—
and my books!

CHAPTER ONE

"Please tell me this is a bad attempt at levity, Rafael. A practical joke from the least likely clown in Italy."

Luca Castelli made no attempt to temper his harsh tone or the scowl he could feel on his face as he glared across the private library at his older brother. Rafael was also his boss and the head of the family company, a state of affairs that usually did not trouble Luca at all.

But there was nothing *usual* about today.

"I wish that it was," Rafael said from where he sat in an armchair in front of a bright and cheerful fire that did nothing at all to dispel Luca's sense of gloom and fury. "Alas. When it comes to Kathryn, we have no choice."

His brother looked like a monk carved from stone today, his features hewn from granite, which only added to Luca's sense of betrayal and sheer *wrongness*. That was the old Rafael, that heavy, joyless creature made entirely of bitterness and regret. Not the Rafael of the past few years, the one Luca greatly preferred, who had married the love of his life he'd once thought dead and was even now expecting his third child with her.

Luca hated that grief had thrown them all so far back into unpleasant history. Luca hated grief, come to that. No matter its form.

Their father, the infamous Gianni Castelli, who had built an empire of wine and wealth and brusque personality that spanned at least two continents, but was better known around the world for his colorful marital life, was dead.

Outside, January rain lashed the windows of the old Castelli manor house that sprawled with such insouciance at the top of an alpine lake in Northern Italy's Dolomite Mountains, as it had done for generations. The heavy clouds were low over the water, concealing the rest of the world from view, as if to pay tribute to the old man as he'd been interred in the Castelli mausoleum earlier this morning.

Ashes rendered ashes and dust forever dust.

Nothing would ever be the same again.

Rafael, who had been acting CEO of the family business for years now despite Gianni's blustery refusal to formally step aside, was now indisputably in charge. That meant Luca was the newly minted chief operating officer, a title that did not come close to describing his pantheon of responsibilities as co-owner but was useful all the same. Luca had initially thought these finicky bits of official business were a good thing for the Castelli brothers as well as the company, not to mention long overdue, given they'd both been acting in those roles ever since the start of their father's decline in health some years back.

Until now.

"I fail to understand why we cannot simply pay the damned woman off like all the rest of the horde of ex-wives," Luca said, aware that his tone was clipped and bordering on unduly aggressive. He felt restless and edgy in his position on the low couch opposite Rafael, but he knew if he moved, it would end badly. A fist through a wall. An upended bookshelf. A broken pane of glass. All highly charged reactions he did not care to explore, much less explain to his brother—given they smacked of a loss of control, which Luca did not allow. Ever. "Settle some of Father's fortune on her, send her on her way and be done with it."

"Father's will is very clear in regard to Kathryn," Rafael replied, and he sounded no happier about it than Luca felt. Luca told himself that was something anyway. "And she is his widow, Luca. Not his ex-wife. A crucial distinction."

Luca nearly growled but checked it at the last moment. "That's nothing but semantics."

"Sadly not." Rafael shook his head, but his gaze never left Luca's. "The choice is hers. She can either accept a lump settlement now, or a position in the company. She chose the latter."

"This is ridiculous."

It was something far worse than merely ridiculous, but Luca didn't have a word to describe that gnawing, hollow thing inside him that always yawned open at any mention of his father's sixth and final wife. *Kathryn*.

The one who was even now in the larger, more formal library downstairs, crying what appeared to be real tears over the death of a husband three times her age she could only have married for the most cynical of reasons. Luca had seen them trickle silently down her cheeks, one after the next, as they'd all stood about in the frigid air earlier, giving the impression she could not manage to contain her grief.

He didn't believe it. Not for a second.

If Luca knew anything, it was this: the kind of love

that might lead to such grieving was rare, exceedingly unlikely and had never made a great many appearances in the Castelli family. He thought Rafael's current happiness was perhaps the only evidence of it in generations.

"For all we know, Father found her hawking her wares on the streets of London," he muttered now. Then glared at his brother. "What the hell will I do with her in the office? Do we even know if she can read?"

Rafael shifted, the dark eyes that were so much like Luca's own narrow and shrewd. "You will find something to keep her busy, because the will assures her three years of employment. Ample time to introduce her to the joys of the written word, I'd think. And whether you like her or not is irrelevant."

Like was not at all the word Luca would have used to describe what happened inside him at the mention of that woman. It wasn't even close.

"I have no feelings about her whatsoever." Luca let out a laugh that sounded hollow to his own ears. "What is one more child bride—acquired solely to cater to the old man's ego—to me?"

His brother only gazed at him for a moment that seemed to stretch on for far too long. The old windows rattled. The fire crackled and spat. And Luca found he had no desire whatsoever to hear whatever his older brother might say next. He'd preferred Rafael when he'd been lost in a prison of fury and regret, he told himself, and unable to concentrate on anything outside his own pain. At least then he'd been a known quantity. This new Rafael was entirely too insightful.

"If you are determined to do this," he said before Rafael could open his mouth and say things Luca would have to fend off, "why not set her up with something in Sonoma? She can get a hands-on experience at the vineyards in California, just as we did when we were boys. It can be a delightful holiday for her, far, far away."

From me, he did not say. *Far, far away from me.*

Rafael shrugged. "She chose Rome."

Rome. Luca's city. Luca's side of their highly competitive wine business. The marketing power and global reach of the Castelli Wine brand were, he flattered himself, all his doing—and possible in large part because he'd been left to his own devices for years. He had certainly not been required to play babysitter for one of his father's legion of mistakes.

His father's very worst mistake, to his way of thinking. In a lifetime of so very many—including Luca himself, he'd long thought. He knew his father would have agreed.

"There's no room," he said now. "The team is lean, focused and entirely handpicked. There's no place for a bit of fluff on sabbatical from her true vocation as an old man's trophy."

Rafael was his boss then, he could see. Not his brother.

And entirely pitiless. "You'll have to make room."

Luca shook his head. "It may set us back months, if not years, and cause incalculable damage in the process as we try to arrange the team around such a creature and what are sure to be her many, many mistakes."

"I trust you'll ensure that none of that happens," Rafael said drily. "Or do you doubt your own abilities?"

"This sort of vulgar nepotism will likely cause a riot—"

"Luca." Rafael's voice was not loud, but it silenced

Luca all the same. "Your objections are noted. But you are not seeing the big picture."

Luca tried to contain the seething thing within that pushed out from the darkest part of him and threatened to take him over. He thrust his legs out in front of him and raked a hand through his hair as if he was languid. Indolent. Unbothered by all of this, despite his arguments.

The role he'd been playing all his life. He had no idea why it had become so difficult these past couple of years to maintain his profoundly unconcerned facade. Why it had started to feel as if it was more of a cage than a retreat.

"Enlighten me," he said, mildly enough, when he was certain he could manage to speak in his usual half bored, half amused tone.

Rafael did not look fooled. But he only picked up his glass from the antique side table and swirled the amber liquid within.

"Kathryn has captured the public's interest," he said after a moment. "I shouldn't have to remind you of that. *Saint Kate* has been on every cover of every tabloid since the news of Father's death broke. Her grief. Her selflessness. Her true love for the old man against all odds. Et cetera."

"You will excuse me if I am skeptical about the truth of her devotion." At least he sounded far more amused than he felt. "To put it mildly. The truth of her interest in his bank account I find a far more convincing tale, if less entertaining."

"The truth is malleable and has little to do with the story that ends up splashed across every gossip site and magazine in existence," Rafael said, and there was the hint of a rueful smile on his face when he looked at Luca again. "No one knows this better than me. Can we really complain if this time the coverage is not exactly in our favor?"

Luca wasn't sure he found his latest stepmother's obvious manipulation of the press to be in the same realm as the stories Rafael and his wife, Lily—who also happened to be their former stepsister, because the Castelli family tree was nothing if not tangled and bent back on itself—had told to explain the fact she'd been thought dead for five years.

But he thought better of saying anything.

After a moment, Rafael continued, "The reality is this. Even though you and I have been running things for years now, the perception from the outside is very different. Father's death gives anyone and everyone the opportunity to make grand claims about how his upstart, ungrateful sons will ruin what he built. If we are seen to shun Kathryn, to treat her badly, that can only reflect negatively on us and add fuel to that fire." He set his glass down without drinking from it. "I want no fuel, no fire. Nothing the tabloids can sink their dirty little claws into. You understand. This is necessary."

What Luca understood was that this was a directive. From the chief executive officer of Castelli Wine and the new official head of his family to one among his many underlings. The fact that Luca owned half of the company did not change the fact he answered to Rafael. And that none of this sat well with him didn't alter the fact that Rafael wasn't asking his opinion on the matter.

He was delivering an order.

Luca stood abruptly, before he said things he wasn't

sure he meant in an effort to sway his brother's opinion. Rafael stayed where he was.

"I don't like this," Luca said quietly. "It can't end well."

"It must end well," Rafael countered. "That's the whole point."

"I'll remind you that this was entirely your idea when it becomes a vast and unconquerable disaster, sinking the whole of Castelli Wine in the wake of this woman's incompetence," Luca said, and started for the door. He needed to *do* something. Run for miles and miles. Swim even farther. Lift very heavy weights or find a willing and eager woman. Anything but stay here and brood about this terrible new reality. "We can discuss it as we plummet to the bottom of the sea. In pieces."

Rafael laughed.

"Kathryn is not our Titanic, Luca," he said, and there was a note Luca did not like at all in his voice. Rafael tilted his head slightly to one side. "But perhaps you think she's yours?"

What Luca thought was that he could do without his brother's observations today—and on any day, should those observations involve Kathryn, who was without doubt the bane of his existence.

Damn that woman. And damn his father for foisting her upon his sons in the first place.

He left Rafael behind in the private library with a rude hand gesture that made his brother laugh, and headed downstairs through the grand old hallways of the ancient house that he hardly noticed the details of anymore. The portraits cluttering the walls. The statuary by this or that notable Italian artist flung about on every flat surface. It was all the same as it had been before Luca had been born, and the same as it would be when Rafael's eldest son, Arlo, was a grandfather. Castellis endured, no matter the messes they made.

He imagined that meant he would, too, despite this situation.

Somehow.

He heard Lily's voice as he passed one of the reception rooms and glanced in, seeing his pregnant sister-in-law, some six months along, having one of her "discussions" with eight-year-old Arlo and two-year-old Renzo about appropriate behavior. Luca hid a grin as he passed, thinking the lecture sounded very similar to ones he'd received in the very same place when he'd been a child. Not from his mother, who had abdicated that position as quickly as possible following Luca's birth, or from his father, who had been far too important to trouble himself with domestic arrangements or child rearing. He'd been raised by a parade of well-meaning staff and a series of stepmothers with infinitely more complicated motives.

Perhaps that was where he'd learned his lifelong aversion to complications.

And to stepmothers, for that matter.

Luca had grown up in the midst of a very messy family who'd broadcasted their assorted private dramas for all the world to see, no matter if the relentless publicity had made it all that much worse. He'd hated it. He preferred things clean and easy. Orderly. No fusses. No melodrama. No theatrics that ended up splashed across the papers, the way everything always did in the Castelli family, and were then presented in the most hideous light imaginable. He didn't mind that he was seen as one of the world's foremost playboys—hell, he'd cultivated that role so no one would ever take him seriously, an asset in business as well as in his personal life. He didn't break hearts—he simply didn't traffic in the kind of emotional upheavals that had marked every other member of his family, again and again and again. *No, thank you.*

But Kathryn was a different story, he thought as he made his way to the grand library on the ground floor and saw the slight figure standing all alone in the farthest corner, staring out at the rain and the fog as if she was competing with it for the title of Most Desolate. Kathryn was more than a mess.

Kathryn was a disaster.

He wasn't the least bit surprised that *Saint Kate*, as she'd been dubbed around the world for her supposed martyrdom to the cause that was old Gianni Castelli and his considerable fortune, was all over the papers this week. Kathryn did *convincingly innocent* and *easily wounded* so well that Luca had always thought she'd have been much better off dedicating her life to the stage.

Though he supposed she had, really. Playing the understanding mistress and undemanding trophy wife to a man so much older than her twenty-five years was a performance all its own. What Luca couldn't understand was why an obvious trollop like Kathryn made his skin feel too tight against his frame and his hands itch to test the smoothness of hers, even now. It didn't make any sense, this stretched-taut, heavy *thing* in him that nothing—not time, not space, not the odious fact of her marriage to his own father, not even the prospect of her polluting the refuge of his office in Rome—ever eased or altered in any way.

He glared at her from the doorway, down the length of the great room with so many books lining the floor-to-ceiling shelves, as if he could make it disappear. Or barring that, make *her* disappear.

But he knew better.

It had always been like this.

Luca's father had made a second career out of marrying a succession of unsuitable younger women who'd let him act the savior. He'd thrived on it. Gianni had never had much time for his sons or the first wife he'd shunted out of sight into a mental institution and mourned very briefly after her death, if at all. But for his parade of mistresses and wives with their endless needs and worries and crises and melodramas? He had been always and ever available to play the benevolent God, solver of all calamities, able to sort out all manner of troubles with a wave of his debit card.

When Gianni had arrived back in Italy a scant month after his fifth wife had divorced him with his sixth wife in tow, Luca hadn't been particularly surprised.

"There is a new bride," Rafael had told him darkly when Luca had arrived in the Dolomites as summoned that winter morning two years ago. "Already."

Luca had rolled his eyes. What else was there to do?

"Is this one of legal age?"

Rafael had snorted. "Barely."

"She's twenty-three," the very pregnant Lily had said reprovingly, her hands on the protruding belly that would shortly become Renzo. She'd glared at both of them. "That's hardly a child. And she seems perfectly nice."

"Of course she seems nice," Rafael had retorted, and had only grinned at the look Lily had thrown at him, the connection between them as bright and shining as ever, as if Castellis could actually make something good from one of their grand messes after all. "That is her job, is it not?"

Luca had prepared himself for a stepmother much like the last occupant of the role, the sharp blonde creature whom Gianni had inexplicably adored despite the fact she'd spent more time on her mobile or propositioning his sons than she had with him. Corinna had been nineteen when she'd married Gianni and already a former swimsuit model. Luca hadn't imagined his father had chosen her for her winning personality or depth of character.

But instead of another version of fake-breasted and otherwise entirely plastic Corinna, when he'd strode into the library where his father waited with Arlo, he'd found Kathryn.

Kathryn, who should not have been there.

That had been his first thought, like a searing blaze through his mind. He'd stopped, thunderstruck, halfway across the library floor and scowled at the woman who'd stood there smiling politely at him in that reserved British way of hers. Until his inability to do anything but glower at her had made that curve of her lips falter, then straighten into a flat line.

She doesn't belong here, he'd thought again, harsher and more certain. Not standing next to his old, crotchety father tucked up in his armchair before the fire, all wrinkles and white hair and fingers made of knots, thanks to years of arthritis. Not wringing her hands together in front of her like some kind of awkward schoolgirl instead of resorting to the sultry, come-hither glances Luca's stepmothers normally threw his way.

Not his *stepmother*.

That thought had been the loudest.

Not her.

Her hair was an inky dark brown that looked nearly black, yet showed hints of gold when the firelight played over it. It poured down past her shoulders, straight and thick, and was cut into a long fringe over smoky-gray eyes that edged toward green. She wore a simple pair of black trousers and a cleanly cut caramel-colored sweater open over a soft knit top that made no attempt whatsoever to showcase her cleavage. She looked elegantly efficient, not plastic or cheap in any way. She was small and fine boned, all big gray eyes and that dark hair and then, of course, there was her mouth.

Her mouth.

It was the mouth of a sulky courtesan, full and suggestive, and for a long, shocking moment, Luca had the strangest notion that she had no idea of its carnal wallop. That she was an innocent—but that had been absurd, of course. Wishful thinking, perhaps. No *innocent* married a very rich man old enough to be her own grandfather.

"Luca," Gianni had barked, in English for his new wife's benefit. "What is the matter with you? Show some manners. Kathryn is my wife and your new stepmother."

It had filled Luca with a kind of terrible smoke. A black, choking fury he could not have named if his life had depended upon it.

He hadn't been aware that he was moving, only that he'd been across the room and then was right there in front of her, looming over her, dwarfing her with his superior height and size—

Not that she'd backed down. Not Kathryn.

He'd seen far too much in those expressive eyes of hers, wide with some kind of distress. And awareness—he'd seen the flare of it, followed almost instantly by confusion. But instead of simpering or shifting her body to better advantage or sizing him up in any way, she'd squared her slender shoulders and stuck out her hand.

"Pleased to meet you," she'd said, her English-accented voice brisk. Matter-of-fact. The sound of it had fallen through him like a hail of ice and had done nothing to soothe that fire in him at all.

Luca had taken her hand, though he'd known it was a terrible mistake.

And he'd been right. It had been.

He'd felt the drag of her skin against his, palm to palm, like a long, slow lick down the length of his sex. He should have jerked his hand away. Instead, he'd held her tighter, feeling her delicacy, her heat and, more telling, that wild tumult of her pulse in her wrist. Her lips had parted as if she'd felt it, too.

He'd had to remind himself—harshly—that they were not only not alone, she was also not free.

She was something a whole lot worse than *not free*, in fact.

"It is my pleasure, *Stepmother*," he'd said, his voice low and dark, that terrible fire in him shooting like electricity all through his limbs and then into her. He'd seen her stiffen—whether in shock at his belligerence or with that same stunned awareness that stampeded in him, he'd never know. "Welcome to the family."

And it had been downhill from there.

All leading him here. To the same library, two years later, where Kathryn stood like a lonely wraith in a simple black dress that somehow made her look fragile and too pretty at once, her dark hair clipped back and no hint of color on her face below that same inky fringe that kissed the tops of her eyelashes.

She was gazing off into the distance through the windows that opened up over the lake, and she looked genuinely sad. As if she truly mourned Gianni, the man she'd used shamelessly for her own ends—ends that, apparently, included forcing herself into Luca's office against his will.

And it enraged him.

He told himself that was the thing that washed over him then, digging in its claws. *Rage.* Not that far darker, far more dangerous thing that lurked in him, as much that terrible hunger he'd prefer to deny as it was the familiar companion of his own self-loathing.

"Come, now, Kathryn," Luca said into the heavy quiet of the book-lined room, making his voice a dark and lazy thing just this side of insulting, and taking note of how she instantly stiffened against it. Against him. "The old man is dead and the reporters have gone home. Who is this maudlin performance for?"

CHAPTER TWO

LUCA CASTELLI'S TRADEMARK GROWL, his English laced with an undercurrent of both his native Italian and that particular harsh ruthlessness that Kathryn had only ever heard directed at her, jolted through her like an electric shock.

She jerked where she stood near the library window, actually jumping in a way he'd be unlikely to miss, even from all the way on the other side of the long, luxurious, stunningly appointed room.

Well done, she thought, despairing of herself anew. *Now he knows exactly how much he gets to you.*

She didn't expect that anything she did would make this man *like* her. Luca had made it clear that could never happen. Over and over and over again, these past two years. But she wanted him—*needed* him—not to actively hate her as she started this new phase of her life.

Kathryn figured that was better than nothing. As good a start as she could hope for, really. And her mother certainly hadn't raised her to be a coward, despite how disappointing she knew she'd always been. Rose Merchant had never let hardship get between her and what needed to be done, as she'd reminded Kathryn at every opportunity. Forging ahead into the corporate world the way Rose hadn't been able to do with a child to raise all on her own was, truly, the least Kathryn could do to honor all of her sacrifices.

And to assuage the guilt she felt about her marriage to Gianni—the one time "honoring her mother's sacrifices" had allowed her to do something purely for herself, too. But she couldn't let herself think about that too closely. It made her feel much too ungrateful.

Kathryn straightened from her place at the window, aware that her movements were jerky and awkward, the way she always seemed to be around this man, who noticed every last embarrassing detail about her and never hesitated to use each and every one of them against her. She nervously smoothed down the front of her dress. Nervously and also carefully, as if the dress was a talisman.

She'd agonized over what to wear today because she'd wanted to look as unlike the gold-digging whore she knew the family—*Luca*—thought she was as possible. And still, she was terribly afraid she'd ended up looking rather more like a poor man's version of an Audrey Hepburn wannabe instead. The papers would trumpet that possibility, call it *an homage to Audrey* or something equally embarrassing, and Luca would assume it was all part of a deliberate campaign toward some grim end he believed she'd been angling toward since the start, rather than simply riding out the attention as best she could. The cycle of his bitter condemnation would continue, turning and turning without end…

But she was delaying the inevitable. She'd always wanted a chance to prove herself, to work on the creative side of a corporation and try her hand at something fun and interesting like marketing or branding instead of the deadly dull figures at which she was utterly hopeless. She'd spent her whole marriage excited at the prospect of working in the family company with Luca and his creative genius.

Even if, other than that corporate flair of his, he was pretty much just awful. She assured herself powerful men often were. That Luca was run-of-the-mill in that sense.

Kathryn took a deep breath, resolutely squared her shoulders and turned to face her own personal demon at last.

"Hello, Luca," she said across the acres of space that separated them in this vast room, and she was proud of herself. She sounded so calm, so cool, when she was anything but.

For any number of reasons, but mostly because looking at Luca Castelli was like staring directly into the sun. It had been from the start.

And as usual, she was instantly dizzy.

Luca moved like a terrible shadow across the library floor, and tragically, he was as beautiful as ever. Tall and solid and impressively athletic, his rangy form was sculpted to lean, male perfection and was routinely celebrated in slick, photo-heavy tabloid exultations across at least five continents. His thick black hair always looked messy, as if he lived such a reckless, devil-may-care life that it required he run his hands through it all the time and rake it back from his darkly handsome face as punctuation to every sentence—despite the fact he was now the chief operating officer of the family company.

Even here, on the day of his father's funeral, where he wore a dark suit that trumpeted his rampant masculinity and excellent taste in equal measure, he gave off that same indolent air. That lazy, playful, perpetually relaxed state that only a man cresting high on the wealth of generations of equally affluent and pedigreed ancestors could achieve. As if no matter what he was actually doing, some part of him was always lounging about on a yacht somewhere with a cold drink in his hand and women presenting themselves for his pleasure. He had the look of a man who lived forever on the verge of laughter, deep and whole bodied, from his gorgeous mouth to his flashing dark eyes.

Kathryn had seen a hundred pictures of him exactly like that, lighting up the whole of the Amalfi Coast and half of Europe with that irrepressible *gleam* of his—

Except, of course, when he looked at her.

The scowl he wore now did nothing to make him any less beautiful. Nothing could. But it made Kathryn shake deep, deep inside, as if she'd lost control of her own bones. She wanted to bolt. She might have, if that wouldn't have made this whole situation that much worse.

Besides, if she'd learned anything these past two years, it was that there was no outrunning Luca Castelli. There was no outmaneuvering him. There was only surviving him.

"Hello, *Stepmother*," he said, that awful dark thing in his voice wrapping around her and sinking hot and blackened tendrils of something like shame into every part of her body, so deep it hurt to breathe. He seemed unaffected as ever, sauntering toward her with his usual deceptively lazy deadliness and those dark eyes so burning hot she could feel them punching into her from afar. "Or should we concoct a different title for you? *The Widow Castelli* has a certain gothic ring to it. I think. I'll have it engraved on your business cards."

"You know," Kathryn said, because she was still entirely too light-headed and not managing her tongue the way she should, "if you decided not to be horrible to me for five minutes the world wouldn't *actually* screech to a halt. We'd all survive. I promise."

His face was like stone, his full lips thin with displeasure, and he was closing the distance between them much too fast for Kathryn's peace of mind.

"I have no idea why you feel you need to bring this particular performance of yours into an office setting," he said as he drew closer. "Much less mine. I'm certain there are any number of hotel bars across Europe that cater to your brand of desperation and craven greed. You should have no trouble finding your next mark within the week."

That he could still hate her so much should not have surprised her, Kathryn knew, because Luca had been remarkably consistent in that since the day she'd arrived in Italy with Gianni two years ago. And yet, like that cold winter morning when he'd charged at her across this very same floor, dark and furious and terrifying in a way she hadn't entirely understood, it did.

Though *surprise* wasn't really the right word to describe the thing that rolled inside her, flattening everything it touched.

"I suppose the world really would end if you accepted the possibility that I might not be who you think I am," she said now, straightening her spine against the familiar rush of pointless grief that was her absurd response to the fact this angry, hateful man had never liked her. Kathryn channeled that odd, scraped-raw feeling into temper instead. "You'd have to reexamine your prejudices, and who knows what might happen then? Of course a man like you would find that scary. You have so many of them."

The truth was that she hardly knew Luca, despite two years of having forced, unpleasant interactions with him. What she did know was that he'd taken an instant and intense and noticeable dislike to her. On sight. Why she'd subsequently spent even three seconds—much less the whole of her marriage to his father—trying to convince him that he was wrong about her was a mystery to her. It no doubt spoke to deep psychological problems on her part, but then again, what about her relationship with this family didn't?

But she did know that poking at him was unwise.

Kathryn had a moment to regret the fact she'd done it anyway as Luca bore down on her, striding across the expanse of polished old floors and priceless rugs tossed here and there below rows of first editions in more languages than she'd known existed, all as smug and wealthy and resolutely untouchable as he was.

"This is as good a time as any to discuss the expectations I have for all Castelli Wine employees who work in my office in Rome." Luca's voice was dark. Cold. And as he moved toward her he regarded her with that sharpness in his eyes that made her feel…fluttery, low in her belly. "First, obedience. I will tell you when I am interested in hearing from you. If you are in doubt, you can assume I prefer you remain silent. *You* can assume that will always be the case. Second, confidentiality. If you cannot be trusted, if you are forever running off to the tabloids to give whining interviews about the many ways you have been wronged and victimized, *Saint Kate*—"

Kathryn flinched. "Please don't call me that. You know that's something the tabloids have made up."

Her mum had sniffed at the name and the image more than once, then reminded Kathryn that *she* had given Kathryn everything and received little in return, yet had never been called a saint by anyone. She'd even suggested that perhaps it had been Kathryn who'd come up with that name and that obnoxious storyline in the first place. It hadn't been.

That wasn't to say she hadn't played to it now and again. She'd always been fascinated with a good brand and widespread global marketing.

The fact that no one believed she hadn't made it all up herself, however, she found maddening. "*Saint Kate* has nothing to do with me."

"Believe me," Luca said in that quiet, horrible way of his, "I am under no delusions about you or your purity."

An actual slap would have hurt less. Kathryn blinked, managed not to otherwise react and forced herself to stay right where she was instead of reeling at that. Because his opinion of her aside, this was her chance to do something she really, truly believed she'd be good at instead of what other people thought she *ought* to be good at. She knew he hated her. She might not know why, but it didn't matter in the end. Kathryn had never wanted status or jewels or whatever the stepmothers before her had wanted from Gianni. She'd wanted this. A chance to prove herself at a job she knew she could do, in a company that had international reach and a bold, bright future, and to finally show her mother that she, too, could succeed in business. *Her* way, not Rose's way. This was what Gianni had promised her when he'd persuaded her to leave her MBA course in

London and marry him—the opportunity to work in the family business when the marriage was over.

This was what she wanted. She knew that if she did what every last nerve in her body was shrieking at her to do and broke for the door, she'd never come back, and Luca, certainly, would never give her another chance, no matter what it said in Gianni's will.

Her mother would never, ever forgive her. And the lonely little girl inside Kathryn, who had never wanted anything but Rose's love no matter how out of reach that had always been, simply couldn't let that happen.

"Luca," she said now, "before you really warm up to your insults, which are always *so* creative and comprehensive, I want to make sure you understand that I have every intention—"

"May the angels save me from the intentions of unscrupulous women." He was almost upon her, and one of the most unfair parts of this was that she couldn't seem to keep herself from feeling something like mesmerized by the way he moved. That impossible, offhanded grace of his he didn't deserve, and she shouldn't *notice* the way she did. It made her limbs feel precarious. Uncertain. "Third, my father's will says only that I must accommodate your desire to play at an office job, not what that job entails. If you complain, about anything at all, it will get worse. Do you understand?"

She felt a dark, hard pulse inside her then. It felt like running. Like fright. It gripped her, hard. In her temples. In the hollows behind her knees. In her throat.

In her sex.

Kathryn didn't have any idea what was happening to her. She struck out at him instead.

"Oh, what fun." She stared back at him when his

scowl edged over into something purely ferocious, and she made no attempt to rein in her sarcastic tone. Gianni was dead. The gloves were off. "Are you planning to make me scrub the floors? Let me guess, on my hands and knees with a toothbrush? That will teach me… something, I'm sure."

"I doubt that very much," he gritted out. He stopped a few feet away from her. *Too close.* Luca stood there then, in all his male fury while that dark thing that had always flared between them wound tighter and tighter around them and stole all the air from the graceful room. "But if I ask you to do it, whatever it is, I expect it to be done. No excuses."

Kathryn forced herself to speak. "And what if it turns out you're wrong about me and I'm not quite as useless as you imagine? I'm guessing abject apologies aren't exactly your strong suit."

His hard mouth—that she shouldn't find so *fascinating*, because what was wrong with her? She might as well find a shark cuddly—shifted into a merciless curve that was entirely too harsh to be a smile. "Have I ever told you how much I hate women like you?"

That word. *Hate.* It was a very strong word, and Kathryn had never understood how everything between them could feel so *intense.* She wasn't any clearer about that now. Nor why it scraped at that raw place inside her, as if it mattered deeply to her. As if he did.

When of course, he couldn't. He didn't. Luca was a means to an end, nothing more.

"It was rather more implied than stated outright," she replied, fighting to keep her voice even. "Nonetheless, you can take pride in the fact you managed to make your feelings perfectly clear from the start."

"My father married ever-younger women the way some men change their shoes," Luca said darkly, as if this was news to either one of them. "You are nothing but the last in his endless, pointless game of musical beds. You are not the most beautiful. You are not even the youngest. You are merely the one who survived him. You must know you meant nothing to him."

Kathryn shook her head at him. "I know exactly what I meant to your father."

"I would not brag, were I you, about your calculating and conniving ways," he threw back at her. "Especially not in my office, where you will find that the hardworking people who are rewarded on their merits rather than their various seduction techniques are unlikely to celebrate that approach."

Luca shook his head, judgment written in every line of his body in that elegant suit that a man as horrible as he was shouldn't have been able to wear so well. *Seduction techniques*, he'd said, the way someone might say *the Ebola virus*. It offended her, Kathryn thought.

He offended her.

Maybe that was why she lost her mind a little bit. He'd finally pushed her too far.

"I spent most of my marriage trying to figure out why you hated me so much," she bit out, heedless of his overwhelming proximity. Not caring the way she should about that glittering thing in his dark eyes. "That a grown man, seemingly of sound mind and obviously capable of performing great corporate feats when it suited him, could loathe another person on sight and for no reason. This made no sense to me."

She was aware of the grand house arrayed behind him, its ancient Italian splendor pressing in on her from all sides. Of the crystal clear lake that stretched off into the mist and the mountains that rose sharp and imposing above it. Of Gianni, sweet old Gianni, who she would never make laugh again and would never call her *cara* again in his gravelly old voice. Even this rarefied, beautiful world felt diminished by the loss of him, and here Luca was, as hateful as ever.

She couldn't bear it.

"I'm a decent person. I try to do the right thing. More to the point—" Kathryn raised her voice slightly when Luca made a derisive noise "—I'm not worth all the hatred and brooding you've been directing at me for years. I married your father and took care of him, the end. Neither you nor your brother had any interest in doing that. Some men in your position might *thank* me."

It was as if Luca expanded to fill the whole of the library then, he was so big, suddenly. Even bigger than he already was. So big she couldn't breathe, and he hadn't moved a muscle. He was simply dark and terrible, and that awful light in his eyes burned when he scowled at her.

"You were one more in a long line of—"

"Yes, but that's the thing, isn't it?" He looked astonished that she'd interrupted him, but Kathryn ignored that and kept going. "If you'd seen the likes of me before, why hate me at all? I should have been run-of-the-mill."

"You were. You were sixth."

"But you didn't despise the other five," Kathryn snapped, frustrated. "Lily told me all about them. You liked *her* mother. The last one tried to crawl into bed with you more than once, and you laughed each time you dumped her out in the hall. You simply told her to stop trying because it would never happen with you—you didn't even tell your father. You didn't hate *her*, and you *knew* she was every single thing you accuse me of being."

"Are you truly claiming you are not those things? That you are, in fact, this unrecognizable paragon I've read so much about in the papers? Come now, Kathryn. You cannot imagine I am so naive."

"I never did anything to you, Luca," she hurled at him, and she couldn't control her voice then.

There were nearly two years of repressed feelings bottled up inside her. Every slight. Every snide remark. Every cutting word he'd said to her. Every vicious, unfair glare. Every time he'd walked out of a room she entered in obvious disgust. Every time she'd looked up from a conversation to find that stare of his all over her, like a touch.

It was true that on some level, it was refreshing to meet someone who was so shockingly *direct*. But that didn't make it hurt any less.

"I have no idea why you hated me the moment you saw me. I have no idea what goes on in that head of yours." She stepped forward, far too close to him and then, no longer caring what his reaction would be, she went suicidal and poked two fingers into his chest. Hard. "But after today? I no longer care. Treat me the way you treat anyone else who works for you. Stop acting as if I'm a demon sent straight from hell to torture you."

He'd gone deathly still beneath her fingers. Like marble.

"Remove your hand." His voice was frozen. Furious. "Now."

She ignored him.

"I don't have to prove that I'm a decent person to you. I don't care if the world knows your father forced you to hire me. I *know* I'll do a good job. My work will speak for itself." She poked him again, just as hard as before, and who cared if it was suicidal? There were worse things. Like suffering through another round of his character assassinations. "But I'm not going to listen to your abuse any longer."

"I told you to remove your hand."

Kathryn held his dark gaze. She saw the bright warning in it, and it should have scared her. It should have impressed her on some level, reminded her that whatever else he was, he was a very strong, very well built man who was as unpredictable as he was dangerous.

And that he hated her.

But instead, she stared right back at him.

"I don't care what you think of me," she told him, very distinctly.

And then she poked him a third time. Even harder than before, right there in that shallow between his pectoral muscles.

Luca moved so fast she had no time to process it.

She poked him, then she was sprawled across the hard wall of his chest with her offending hand twisted behind her back. It was more than dizzying. It was like toppling from the top of one of the mountains that ringed the lake, then hurtling end over end toward the earth.

Her heart careened against her ribs, and his darkly gorgeous face was far too close to hers and she was *touching* him, her dress not nearly enough of a barrier to keep her from noticing unhelpful things like his scent, a hint of citrus and spice. The heat that blazed from him, as if he was his own furnace. And that deceptively languid strength of his that made something deep inside her flip over.

Then hum.

"This, you fool," Luca bit out, his mouth so close to hers she could taste the words against her own lips. She could taste *him*, and she shuddered helplessly, completely unable to conceal her reaction. "This is what I think of you."

And then he crushed his mouth to hers.

CHAPTER THREE

HE DID NOT ASK. He did not hesitate. He simply *took*.

Luca's mouth descended on hers, and Kathryn waited for that kick of terror, of unease, of sheer panic that had always accompanied any hint of male sexual interest in her direction before—

But it never came.

He kissed her with all that lazy confidence that made him who he was. He took her mouth again and again, still holding her arm behind her back and then sliding his free hand along her jaw to guide her where he wanted her.

Slick. Hot.

Deliciously, wildly, stunningly male.

He kissed her as if they'd done this a thousand times before. As if the past two years had been leading nowhere but here. To this hot, impossible place Kathryn didn't recognize and couldn't navigate.

There was nothing to do but surrender. To the molten fire that rolled through her and pooled in all the worst places. A heaviness in her breasts, pressed hard against his chest. And that restless, edgy, weighted thing that sank low into her belly and then pulsed hot.

Needy. Insistent.

And Kathryn *forgot*.

She forgot who he was. That she had been his step-mother for two years, though he was some eight years older than she was. She forgot that in addition to being her harshest critic and her bitter enemy through no fault of her own, he was now going to be her boss.

She forgot everything but the taste of him. That harsh, sweet magic he made, the way he commanded her and compelled her, as if he knew the things her body wanted and could do when she had no idea. When she was simply lost—adrift in the fire. The greedy, consuming flames that licked all over her and through her and deep inside her and made her meet every stroke of his tongue, every glorious taste—

He set her away from him. As if it hurt.

"Damn you," he muttered. Followed by something that sounded far harsher in Italian.

But it seemed to take him a very long time to let go of her.

Kathryn couldn't speak. She didn't understand the things that were storming through her then, making her blood seem like thunder in her veins and her skin seem to stretch too tight to contain all the *feelings* she didn't know how to name.

They stared at each other in the scant bit of space between them. His face was drawn tight, stark and harsh, and it still did absolutely nothing to detract from his sheer male beauty.

"You kissed me," Kathryn said, and she could have kicked herself.

But her lips felt swollen and she had the taste of him in her mouth, and she didn't know how to process that hot and slippery feeling that charged through her and then concentrated between her legs.

If possible, that dark look on his face got blacker. As if he was a storm.

"Don't you dare try that innocent game on me," he gritted out.

"I don't know what that means."

"It means I know the difference between a virgin and a whore, Kathryn," Luca said, the fury in him like a brand that pressed into her, searing her flesh, and she didn't understand how she could feel it the same way she had that desperate kiss. "I can certainly taste it."

She realized she had absolutely no idea how to respond to that.

"Luca," she said, as carefully as she could when her entire body was lost in the tumult of that endless kiss. When she had no idea how she was even capable of speech. "I think we should chalk that up as nothing more than an emotional response to a very hard day and—"

"I will not be your next target, Kathryn," Luca told her, a frozen sort of outrage in his voice and pressed deep into the fine lines of his beautiful face. "Hear me on this. *It will not happen.*"

"I don't have targets." She blinked, the room seeming to shimmer everywhere he was not, as if he was a black hole. "I'm not a weapon. What kind of life do you lead that you think these things?"

He reached over and took her upper arm in his hand, pulling her close to him again, and that fire that hadn't really banked at all blazed. Fierce and wild. Almost knocking her from her feet.

"I don't want you in my office," he growled. "I don't want you polluting the Castelli name any more than you already have. I don't want you anywhere near the things that matter to me."

Kathryn's teeth chattered, though she wasn't cold.

"That would probably be far more terrifying a threat if you weren't touching me," she managed to point out, though her voice wasn't nearly as cool as she'd have liked. "Again."

Luca laughed, though it bore no resemblance to that carefree, golden laughter that had helped make him so beloved the world over, and released her. If she didn't know better, if he'd been some other man with the usual collection of weaknesses instead of a monolith where his heart should have been, she'd have thought he hadn't meant to grab her in the first place.

"I will never lower myself to my father's discards," he told her, horribly, his gaze hard on hers in case she was tempted to pretend she hadn't heard that. "Nor will I allow you to corrupt the good people in my office with your repulsive little schemes. Your game won't work on me."

"Right," she said, and maybe it was because this was all so out of control already. Maybe that was why she couldn't seem to keep herself in check any longer around him. What was the point? She'd tried to *rise above* him for two years, and here they were anyway. "That's why you kissed me, I imagine. To demonstrate your immunity."

Luca went very still.

So still that Kathryn stopped breathing herself, as if the slightest noise might set him off. His dark eyes were fixed on her as if she was the kind of target he'd mentioned before, and she'd never felt more like one in her life. Between them, that spinning, tightening, desperate and dangerous electric band seemed to wrap tighter, pull harder. So hard it pulsed inside her, insistent and rough. So lethal she swore she could see it stamped across every tightly held, hard-packed muscle on his sculpted form.

Rain clattered against the windows behind her, and off in some other part of this massive house, little Renzo let loose one of his ear-piercing toddler screams that could as easily be joy as peril.

Luca shook his head slightly, as if he'd been released from a spell. He stepped back, his expression shifting from whatever that harsh, hard thing was to something far closer to disgust.

"You will regret this," he promised her.

She swallowed. "You'll have to be more specific. That could cover a lot of ground."

"I will make sure of it," Luca told her, as if she hadn't spoken. "If it's the very last thing I do."

His voice had the ring of a certain finality, and it clanged inside her like a gong. She stood there, stricken, her mouth still aching from his kiss and her body lost in its own strange riot, and watched as he simply turned and began to walk away from her.

She wanted nothing more than to forget all about this. To take the lump payment Rafael had offered her and disappear with it. She could have any life she wanted now. She could be anyone she wanted, far away from the long shadow of the Castellis where she'd lived for so long.

But that would mean the past two years of her life had been for nothing. That she'd simply thrown them away for cash. It would mean she was exactly the woman Luca thought she was—and that all her mother's sacrifices would have been for nothing in the end. That there was nothing to Kathryn's own life but guilt and falling short.

And Kathryn could bear a lot of things. She'd had no choice, given what a failure she'd turned out to be in her mother's eyes. She simply didn't have it in her to make it that much worse. There was that part of her that was convinced, after all this time, that if she tried hard enough she could make her mother love her. If she could just do the right thing, for once.

"I'm so glad we had this talk," she called after him, directing her not-quite-sweet tone straight toward the center of his tall, broad back. He wanted to play target practice? She could do that. "It will make Monday so much better for everyone."

He didn't turn back to face her, though he slowed. "Monday?"

If she was the good person she'd always believed herself to be, Kathryn thought then, surely she wouldn't take *quite* so much pleasure in this tiny little moment, this almost pointless victory.

"Oh, yes," she said, with deliberate calm and that triumph right there in her voice. "That's when I start."

He should never have touched her.

He should *certainly* not have tasted her.

But he had always been a fool where that woman was concerned, and in case he'd been tempted to doubt that, she haunted him all the way back to Rome.

Luca drove himself into the city from the family's private airfield, risking death in an appropriately sleek and low-slung car that made Rome's famously chaotic traffic a game of wits and daring and delicious speed. And he regretted it when he arrived at the Renaissance-era villa that housed both his business and his home, because playing games with his life at high speeds through the streets of the ancient city he loved was far preferable—and much less dangerous—than letting himself think about Kathryn.

Though he supposed both edged into that same dark place inside him, as if he was as much of a damned mess as every other Castelli in history down deep, beneath all the controls he'd spent his life putting into place to prevent exactly that.

He tossed his keys to the waiting attendant in his garage and stalked into the building, only to find himself standing stock-still in his own empty reception area, his head filled with those damned *eyes* of hers, turned a dreamy slate green after he'd kissed her, and that sulky mouth—

Luca muttered a chain of curses. He raked both his hands through his hair as he headed into the offices that sprawled across the first two levels of this lovingly maintained building in Rome's Tridente neighborhood, a mere stone's throw from the Spanish Steps and Piazza del Popolo.

His office. His one true love. The only thing he'd ever loved, in point of fact. The only thing that had ever come close to loving him back, with one success after the next.

He lived in the penthouse that rambled over the top two levels, and that was where he headed now, taking his private lift up into the rooms he'd furnished with steel and chrome, wide-open spaces and minimalist art, the better to play off the history in every bit of stone and craftsmanship in the walls and the high, frescoed ceilings and every view of gorgeous, sleepless, frenetic Rome out of his windows. He tore off his clothes in his rooftop bedroom of glass and steel before making his way out to the pool on the wraparound terrace that surrounded the master suite and offered a three-hundred-sixty-degree perspective on the Eternal City.

If Rome could stand for more than two and a half thousand years, surely Luca could survive the onslaught of Kathryn. She had no idea what she was setting herself up for. Luca was a tough boss at the best of times, demanding and fierce, and that was what the loyal employees he'd handpicked said about him to his face. What could a former trophy wife know of the corporate world? She might have some fantasy of herself as a businesswoman, but it was unlikely she'd last the week.

Of course she won't be able to handle it, he thought with something a great deal like relief—how had he failed to realize that earlier? He was called upon to indulge her whim, not alter the whole of his carefully controlled existence. The sooner she understood how ill suited she was to a life that involved more work than play, the sooner she'd drift off to find her next conquest. The problem would take care of itself.

Luca still felt edgy and entirely too messed up, despite the chill of the winter evening and the kick of the wind. Out of control. Jittery and appalled with himself. He told himself it must be grief, though he hadn't been close with his father. He might have wished, from time to very rare and sentimental time, that he'd had a better understanding of the man whose shadow had fallen over him all these years—but he never had.

Perhaps the funeral had hit him harder than he'd realized.

Because he could not understand why he'd kissed Kathryn. What the hell was the matter with him?

How could he—a man who prided himself on always, *always* keeping his life clean and trimmed down and free from anything even resembling this kind of emotional clutter—have no idea?

He dived into the pool then, cutting into the heated water and then pulling hard as he began to swim. He lost himself in the rhythm of his strokes, the weight and rush of the water against him and the growing heat in his body as he kept going, kept pushing.

Lap after lap. Then again.

He swam and he swam, he pushed himself hard, and it was no good. She was still right there, cluttering up his head, reminding him how empty he was everywhere else.

Wide gray eyes. All that dark hair and that fringe that made her seem more mysterious somehow. All of her, wedged in him like a jagged splinter he could never remove, that he'd never managed to do anything but shove in that much farther. She worried at him and worried at him and he had no idea anymore who he was when he was near her. What he might do.

Luca stopped swimming, slamming his hands down on the lip of the pool, sending water splashing everywhere.

He did not dip his quill in his company's ink, ever. He knew better than to throw grenades like that into the middle of his life. He did not touch his employees, and he certainly did not avail himself of his father's leftovers. He had been a loud, angry child often abandoned by his single living parent for months at a time in the old manor house because of the trouble he'd caused. He'd gotten over that kind of behavior while he'd still been a child. This kind of mess was precisely what he'd spent his adult life avoiding.

This was a nonissue.

Luca climbed out of the pool and wrapped himself in one of the towels his staff kept at the ready, and then made his way back inside, hardly noticing the way the sun had turned the rambling old city orange and pink as it sank toward the horizon. Not even when he stood at one of the high windows that looked out over the winding, cobbled streets that led toward Piazza di Spagna and the famous Spanish Steps, where it seemed half of Rome congregated some evenings.

He saw nothing but Kathryn, dressed in her funeral clothes like some waifish fairy tale of a widow, and it had to stop. She'd already had two black marks against her before today. Her marriage to his father in the first place. And the unpalatable fact of her tabloid presence, the endless canonization of *Saint Kate*, nauseatingly described as the plucky English lass who'd bearded any number of dragons in his twisted old-Italian family.

It repulsed him. He told himself she did, too.

That kiss today was the third black mark. He couldn't pretend he hadn't started it, hauling her to him with the kind of heedless passion he'd been so certain he'd completely excised from his life. How many times had he seen this or that foolish longing lay his father low? How often had he rolled his eyes at his brother's enduring anguish over Lily? How many times had his own pointless emotions bit him in the ass as a child? He'd promised himself a long time ago that he would stay clear of such quagmires, and the truth was, it had never been particularly difficult.

Until Kathryn. And the truth remained: he'd been the one to kiss her. He accepted that failing, even if he couldn't quite understand it.

The problem was the way she'd kissed him back.

The way she'd melted against him. The way she'd opened her mouth and met him. The way she'd poured herself into him, against him, until he'd very nearly forgotten who and where they were. That she was his stepmother, his father's widow, and that they'd been standing much too near the family mausoleum where the old man had only just been interred.

Luca was sick, there was no doubt about that—and the fact he was hard even now, at the mere memory of her taste, proved it.

But what game had she been playing?

She was good, he could admit it. She'd tasted like innocence. He still had the flavor of her on his tongue.

That was the most infuriating thing by far.

And Luca vowed, as the last bit of winter sun fell down behind Rome's enduring skyline, that he would not only make this little corporate adventure for his father's child bride of a widow as unpleasant as possible—he would also do much worse than that.

He would take Saint Kate's halo and tarnish it. And her.

Irredeemably.

By the time Kathryn made it to the ornate Castelli Wine offices in one of the most charming neighborhoods in Rome that Monday morning at exactly nine o'clock sharp, she'd prepared herself.

This was a war. A drawn-out siege. She might have lost a battle in that library far to the north in all those forbidding, foggy mountains, but that meant nothing in the scheme of things. It was a small battle. A kiss, that was all.

The war was what mattered.

The receptionist greeted her in icy Italian and pretended not to understand Kathryn's halting attempts to speak the language—then picked up the phone and spoke in flawless English, staring at Kathryn all the while. Her expression was impassive when she ended the call, but Kathryn was certain she could see triumph lurking there in the depths of the other woman's haughty gaze.

She ordered herself not to react.

"How lovely," Kathryn said, her own tone cool. "You speak English after all. Please tell Luca I'm here."

She didn't wait for the other woman's response. She went and sat in one of the rigid antique chairs that lined the waiting area and pretended to be perfectly comfortable as she waited. And waited.

And waited.

But this was a war, she reminded herself. And it had occurred to her at some point over the weekend that for all his bluster, Luca had no idea who she was or what he was dealing with. All he saw was his image of her as the gold digger who'd snared his father. That meant, Kathryn had decided, that she had the upper hand. So if he wanted to leave her stranded in purgatory all morning, cooling her heels in his waiting room as some childish gesture of pique and temper, let him. She wouldn't give him—or his receptionist, for that matter—the satisfaction of looking even the slightest bit impatient.

She kept her attention on her mobile, keeping her expression as smooth as glass as she dutifully emailed her mother to let her know she'd started work in Castelli Wine as planned, then thumbed through the news. For an hour.

When Luca finally appeared, she sensed him before she saw him. That dark, thunderous, electric thing that made every hair on her body leap to attention, filling the whole of the great cavern of a waiting room that had until that moment been bright with the Rome morning, light pouring in from the windows to dance across the marble floor. She forced herself to take her time looking up.

And there he was.

He was even more devastatingly gorgeous today, in a more casual suit than the one he'd worn at the funeral, the open white collar of his shirt offering her a far too tempting glimpse of the expanse of his olive skin and the hint of that perfect chest she knew—from the tabloid pages dedicated to him and that one Castelli family outing to Positano that had involved a boat and Luca without his shirt, God help her—had a dusting of dark hair and all those finely carved ridges in his abdomen.

She told herself she was starting to find that scowl on his face almost charming. Like a love song from an ogre.

"You're late," he said.

That was astoundingly unfair at best, but Kathryn didn't have to look to the smug receptionist to understand that there was no point arguing. Besides, Luca had warned her not to complain. She wouldn't. Kathryn stood, smoothing out her skirt as she rose.

"I apologize. It won't happen again."

"Somehow," Luca replied, sounding very nearly merry—which was alarming, "I doubt that."

Kathryn didn't bother to reply. She walked toward him, telling herself with every click of her heels against the hard floor that she remembered nothing from last week in that old library up north. Not his taste. Not that thrilling, masterful way he'd simply *taken* her mouth with his. Not the searing, impossible heat of his hand against the side of her face and that deep stroke of his clever tongue—

She hadn't dreamed those things. They hadn't kept her wide-awake and gasping at the ceiling, not sure how to handle the riot all those searing images and memories had caused inside her. *Certainly not.*

Luca's expression was unreadable as she drew close to him, and she hated that she had no idea what was going on behind his gleaming dark eyes as he ushered her deep into the heart of the Castelli Wine offices. She thought she felt him glance over her outfit, a pencil skirt and a conservative silk blouse that could offend no one, she was sure, but when she sneaked a look at him, his attention was focused straight ahead.

He stopped at the door to a large glassed-in conference room and waved a hand at the group of people sitting around the table inside. *My coworkers*, Kathryn thought—with what she realized was an utterly naive surge of pleasure when she realized not a single one of them was looking out at her with anything approaching a smile on their faces.

She froze beside Luca, who already had his hand on the door.

"What did you tell them?" she asked.

"My people?" He sounded far too triumphant, mixed in with that usual hint of laziness that she was beginning to suspect was all for show. "The truth, of course."

"And which truth is that?"

"There is only the one," Luca said. Happily, she thought. Again. "My father's petulant trophy wife has insisted she be given a job she does not deserve. We do not have jobs hanging about without anyone to fill them, so there was some reshuffling required."

"I assumed you'd be giving me janitorial duties." She arched a brow at him. "Wasn't the idea to make sure this was as unpleasant for me as possible?"

"I made you my executive assistant," Luca replied smoothly, his dark eyes glittering. "It is the most coveted position in this branch of the company." He shifted back slightly. Relaxing, she realized. Because he was obviously enjoying himself. That sent a shiver of ice straight down her spine. So did his smile—which she was close enough to see did not reach his eyes. "It is second only to me, you see. That's quite a bit of power to wield."

She frowned at him. "Why would you do that? Why not make me file things in some basement?"

"Because, *Stepmother*," Luca said in that slow, dark way of his that should not have gotten tangled up in all her breathless memories of that kiss, not when it was clearly meant to be a blow, "that would only delay the inevitable. I am quite certain you won't make it the allocated three years. But if you leave after three days? Three weeks? All the better."

She stiffened. "I won't leave."

He nodded toward the group of people inside, all eyeing her with ill-disguised hostility.

"Each and every person in that room was handpicked by me. They earned their positions here. They function together as a tight and usually congenial team. But I have informed them that all of that is a thing of the past, as you must be shoehorned in whether we like it or not." He turned his gaze on her. "As you can see, they're thrilled."

Kathryn's stomach sank to her feet, because she understood what he'd done. Her pathetic little fantasies of distinguishing herself somehow through hard work in some forgotten corner of the office where she could quietly shine crumbled all around her.

Her mother would be furious. She'd claim that this was exactly what had happened when Kathryn tried to defy her and strike out on her own. Kathryn felt a sinking feeling in her gut, as if maybe Rose was right.

And maybe it was hideously disloyal, maybe it made her a terrible person and an ungrateful child, but Kathryn really, really didn't want that to be true.

"You painted a target on my back," she said now, her lips feeling numb. "You did it deliberately."

This time, Luca's smile reached his eyes, but that didn't make it any warmer. Or this situation any better. "I did."

Then he pushed open the conference room door and fed her straight to the wolves.

CHAPTER FOUR

THREE HARD WEEKS and two days later, Kathryn boarded the Castelli family private jet on the airfield outside Rome, this time in her capacity as the most hated employee in Luca's office. She marched up the folded-down stairs with her back straight and her head high—because that title, of course, was an upgrade compared to her previous role as the most hated stepmother in Castelli family history.

She thought she had this being-loathed thing under control.

It was all about the smile.

Kathryn smiled every time conversation halted abruptly when she entered a room. She smiled when her coworkers pretended they didn't understand her and made her repeat her question once, then twice, so she'd feel foolish as her words hung there in the air between them. She smiled when she was ignored in meetings. She smiled when she was called on to answer questions about past projects she couldn't possibly know anything about. She smiled when Luca berated her for allowing unrestricted access to him and she smiled brighter when he let his people in and out the side door of his office himself, so he could do it all over again.

She smiled and she smiled. The benefit of having been splashed across a thousand tabloids and held to be *so good* and *so self-sacrificing* was that she found she could use *Saint Kate* as a guide through each and every one of her chilly office interactions. Especially because she was well aware that the less she reacted, the more it annoyed her coworkers.

Luca, of course, was a different issue altogether.

She ducked into the plane and made her way into the upgraded living room space, smiling serenely as she took her seat on the curved leather sofa that commanded the center of the room. Luca was already sprawled out at one of the tables to the side that seated three apiece in luxurious leather armchairs, one hand in his hair as usual and the other clamping his mobile to his ear.

He eyed her as he finished his conversation in low Italian, and didn't stop when it was done.

"You're still here," he said. Eventually.

She smiled brighter. "Of course. I told you I wouldn't leave."

"You can't possibly have enjoyed these past few weeks, Kathryn."

"You certainly went out of your way to make sure of that," she agreed. She showed him her teeth. "Much appreciated."

He frowned, and she smiled, and that went on for so long, she was tempted to turn on the big-screen television and ignore him—but that was not how an employee would behave, she imagined.

"You were at the office when I arrived this morning," he said gruffly.

"Every morning."

"I beg your pardon?"

"I'm at the office when you arrive *every* morning," Kathryn said mildly. "Your assistant can't be late the way I was that first day, can she? It sends the wrong message."

She didn't expect him to admit that he'd deliberately kept her waiting that day, simply so he could chastise her for tardiness. He didn't disappoint her, though there was a gleam she didn't quite understand in his dark eyes as they remained level on hers.

"Surely you have other things to do with your time." He waved a hand at her, as if she was displaying herself in a tiny string bikini rather than wearing another perfectly unobjectionable blouse and skirt, chosen specifically to blend in with everyone else and be unworthy of comment. "Trips to the places rich men frequent, the better to identify your next target, for example."

"I had that all planned for this weekend, of course," she said in her sweetest, most professional tone, "but then you scheduled this trip to California. I guess the gold digging will have to wait."

He didn't speak to her again until the plane reached its cruising altitude and the single, deferential air steward had set out trays of food for their dinner on the dark wood coffee table that sprawled in the center of the jet's deeply comfortable and faintly decadent living room. Kathryn's stomach rumbled at her, reminding her that she'd worked through lunch. And breakfast, for that matter, not that her dedication ever seemed to make a difference in Luca's slippery slope of an office, where she literally could do no right.

You're used to that, aren't you? a voice inside her asked—but she shoved it away. Her mother's disappointment in her hurt, yes, but it wasn't invalid. Kathryn was well aware of her own deficiencies, and not only because she'd heard about them so often.

If she hadn't been so deficient, she reminded herself, she wouldn't have found marrying Gianni to be such a perfect option for her. She'd have excelled at her MBA the way she'd been supposed to do.

"Tell me the story," Luca said after they'd eaten in silence for a while, surprising her.

He had a plate on the table before him and was lounging in his leather armchair as he picked languidly at it, but his seeming nonchalance didn't make her heart beat any slower. Nor did it help matters that they were trapped in a plane together, and Kathryn couldn't seem to make herself think about anything but that. All the gilt edges and wood accents and noncommercial setup and decor in the world couldn't change the fact that she and Luca were suspended above the Atlantic Ocean in the dark, with no buffer between them.

Alone.

That hit her like a punch then slid down deep into her belly and pulsed there, as worrying as it was entirely too hot.

She had never actually been alone with Luca before.

There had always been someone else around. Always. Gianni. Some other member of the Castelli family. Staff. All the people in his office, especially because they all lived to catch her out in a misstep as she muddled her way through her first weeks on the job. Rafael and his family the week of the funeral, never more than a room or two away, liable to walk in at any moment.

This was the first time in over two years that it had ever been just the two of them.

There's a pilot, she told herself as her heart slowed, then beat too hard against her ribs. *You're not* really *alone.*

But she knew even as she thought it that it didn't mean anything. Neither the pilot nor the air steward would disturb Luca unless he summoned them himself. She might as well have stranded herself on a desert island with the man.

That, she reflected helplessly, her mind suddenly full of images of a half-naked Luca gleaming beneath some far-off tropical sun, *is not a helpful line of thought.*

And there was a certain hunger in that dark gaze of his that made her think he was entertaining the same rush of images that she was.

"What story?" she asked, and hated how insubstantial her voice was. And the way his dark gaze sharpened at the sound, as if he knew why.

"The lovely and touching fairy tale of how an obviously virtuous young woman like yourself fell passionately in love with a man who could easily have fathered your parents, of course. What else?"

That was meant to insult her, Kathryn knew. But he'd never asked her that before. No one had. The entire world thought they knew exactly why a younger woman had married a much older man—and that wasn't entirely untrue, of course. There were reasons, and some of those reasons were financial. But that didn't mean it had been as cold or as calculated as Luca was determined to believe.

"It wasn't a fairy tale," she told him, tucking her feet up beneath her on the butter-soft leather sofa and smoothing the edges of her skirt down farther toward her knees. She frowned at him. "It was just…nice. I met him very much by accident at a facility that caters to seniors and people with degenerative health challenges."

He didn't *quite* snort at that. "How touching."

"Surely you know that your father wasn't well, Luca." She shrugged. "He was visiting a specialist. I was in the waiting area and we got to talking."

"You were there, one assumes, to gather some extra polish for your halo and crow about it to the tabloids?"

Kathryn thought of her mother, and the way her body had betrayed her, growing so old and knotted before her time. She thought of the gnarled hands that had scrubbed floors to give Kathryn every possible chance—*I had plans for my life, Kathryn*, Rose had always said in that sharp way of hers, *but I put them aside for you.*

How could Kathryn do anything less than the same in return for her?

"Something like that," she said now, to this man who didn't deserve to know anything about her mother or her struggles, or the choices Kathryn had made to honor the sacrifices that had been made for her, no matter how badly she'd done at that sometimes. "I do so prefer it when my halo shines, you know."

Luca laughed—and it was *that* laugh. That famous spill of light and life and perfection, illuminating his face and making the air between them dance and shimmer for a long, taut moment before he stopped himself, as if he hadn't realized what was happening.

But she could hoard it anyway, Kathryn thought, feeling dazed. She could hold it close. An unexpected gift she could take out and warm herself with during her next sleepless night—and this was not the time to ask herself why she thought anything this man did was a gift. Not when she knew he'd hate her even more for thinking such a thing.

"And a driving, inescapable passion for a septuagenarian overtook you in this waiting area?" he asked, his voice darker than before, his gaze much too shrewd. "I hear that happens. Though not often to young women in their twenties, unless, of course, you were discussing his net worth."

"I liked him," Kathryn said, and that was the truth about her marriage, no matter the extenuating circumstances. She shrugged. "He made me laugh and I made him laugh, too. It wasn't seedy or mercenary, Luca, no matter how much you wish that it was. He was a good friend to me."

A better friend than most, if she was honest.

"A good friend."

"Yes."

"My father. Gianni Castelli. *A good friend.*"

Kathryn sighed, and set her plate down on the coffee table, her appetite gone. "I take it you've decided in your infinite wisdom that this, too, must be impossible."

Luca's laugh this time was no gift. Not one anyone in her right mind would want anyway.

"My father was born into wealth, and his single goal was to expand it," he told her harshly, the Italian inflection in his voice stronger than usual. "That was his art and his calling, and he dedicated himself to it with single-minded purpose from the time he could walk. His favorite hobby was marriage—the more inappropriate, the better. Do not beat yourself up. Most of his wives misunderstood the breakdown of his affections and attention."

"I don't think you knew your father very well," Kath-

ryn suggested. She lifted up her hands when Luca's
eyes blazed. "Not in the way I did. That's all I mean."

"You're speaking of the two years of your acquain-
tance with him, as opposed to the whole of my life?"

"A son can't possibly know the man his father was."
She lifted a shoulder then dropped it. "He can only
know what kind of father he was or wasn't, and piece
together what clues he can about the man from that.
Isn't that the history of the world? No one ever knows
their parents. Not really."

She certainly didn't know hers. Her father had bug-
gered off before she was born, and her mother had
given up everything that had mattered to her so Kathryn wouldn't have to bear the weight of that. Kathryn
knew the sacrifice. Her mother reminded her of what
she'd left behind for Kathryn's sake at every opportunity, and fair enough. But she still couldn't say she understood the woman—much less the way she'd treated
Kathryn all her life.

A muscle leaped in Luca's lean jaw.

"I knew my father a great deal longer than you did,"
he gritted out after a moment. "He had no friends,
Kathryn. He had business associates and a collection
of wives. Everyone in his life was accorded a role and
expected to play it, and woe betide the fool who did not
live up to his expectations."

"Is that what this has been about all this time? All
the hatred and the nastiness and the threats and so on?"
she asked. She tilted her head to one side and said the
thing she knew she shouldn't. But she couldn't seem to
stop herself. "You…have daddy issues?"

The crack of his temper was very nearly audible.
If the plane itself had been thrown off course and

sent into a spiraling nosedive toward the ocean, she wouldn't have been at all surprised—and it took Kathryn a long, tense, shuddering moment to understand that the jet they sat on was fine. The plane flew on, unaffected by the minor explosion that had taken over the cabin—and the aftershocks that were still rolling through her.

The only steep and terrible free fall was in her stomach as it plummeted to her feet.

Luca hadn't moved. It only felt as if he had.

She watched, as fascinated as she was alarmed, as he tamped that bright current of fury down. He still didn't move. He stared back at her as if he'd very much like to throttle her. One hand twitched as if he'd considered it. This suggested to her that she'd been more on target than she'd imagined when she'd said it.

But then he blinked and the crisis passed. There was only the usual force of his dislike staring back at her. That and the leftover adrenaline trickling through her veins, making her shift against the sofa cushions.

"Why me?" he asked, his dark voice a spiked thing as it slammed into her. "I've made no secret of my opinion of you. What sort of masochism led you to throw yourself in my path when you must know you'd have had a much better time in another branch of the company?"

"Is that a thinly veiled way of asking if I'm pursuing you for my usual gold-digging ends?" she asked, unable to tear her gaze from his and equally unsure why that was. Why did he *invade* her like this? Why did she feel as if he had more control over her than she did?

"Was it veiled, thinly or otherwise?" he asked, his voice soft. If no less harsh. "I must be doing it wrong."

Kathryn's smile felt forced, but she didn't let it fade. She had the wild notion, suddenly, that it was all she had.

"I considered working for your brother, of course," she said quietly. "I doubt he's particularly fond of me, but there's certainly none of...this." She waved her hand between them, in that too-thick air and that taut electric storm that charged it. "It would have been easier, certainly."

"Then, why?" Luca's mouth curled into something much too dark to be any kind of smile, and the echo of it pulsed inside her. "To punish us both?"

"The fact is that your brother maintains the business and he's very good at it," Kathryn said. "He will make certain the Castelli name endures, that no ground will be lost on his watch. He's a very steady hand on the wheel."

"And I am what?" Luca didn't quite laugh. "The drunken driver in this scenario? I drive too fast, Kathryn. But never drunk."

"You're the innovator," she said quietly. It felt... dangerous to praise him to his face. To do something other than suffer through his darkness. "You're the creative force in the company. Never satisfied. Always pushing a new boundary." She shrugged, more uncomfortable than she could remember ever having been around him before, and that was saying something. "My personal feelings about you aside, there's no more exciting place to work. You must know this. I assume that's why all your employees are so—" Kathryn smiled that little bit brighter, and that, too, was harder than it should have been "—fiercely protective."

Luca looked thrown, which she might have considered a victory at any other time—but there was something about the way he gazed at her then. It seemed to sneak into her, wrapping itself around her bones and drawing tight. Too tight.

"Can you do that?" he asked, his voice mild but with that *something* beneath it. "Put your personal feelings aside?"

She met his gaze. She didn't flinch.

"I have to if I want this job to mean something," Kathryn told him, aware as she spoke that this might have been the most honest she'd ever been with him. As if she had nothing to lose, when that couldn't be further from the truth. This was her only chance to prove that she could make something of herself without her mother's input or directives. This was her only chance to honor her mother's sacrifices—and also stay free. "And I do. Unlike you, I don't have a choice."

The Castelli château, the center of Castelli Wine's operations in the States, perched at the top of Northern California's fertile Sonoma Valley like a particularly self-satisfied grande dame. The vineyards stretched out much like voluminous queenly skirts, rolling out over the hills in all directions, seeming to take over this part of the valley all the way to the horizon and back. Tonight the winery gleamed prettily through the crisp winter night, bright lights in every window as a line of cars snaked down the long drive between the marching rows of cypress trees.

Luca loved the unapologetic spectacle of it—the high Italianate drama in every detail, from the epic sweep of the house itself to the grounds kept in a condition to rival the Boboli Gardens in Florence, delighting the tourists on their wine-tasting tours of Sonoma—despite himself.

Tonight was the annual Castelli Wine Winter Ball. This was the reason Luca had flown across the world, landing only a scant hour earlier, which he was sure Rafael would think was cutting it a bit close. He and Rafael needed to make it abundantly clear to all and sundry that nothing had changed since Gianni's passing. That everything was business as usual at Castelli Wine.

And as with most things in life, the more elegant and relaxed and attractive the face of a thing, the more people were likely to believe it.

Kathryn, Luca thought grimly, certainly proved that rule. And so did he. He banked on it, in fact.

He checked his watch for the fifth time in as many seconds, unreasonably irritated that she hadn't been waiting for him when he'd emerged from his bedroom suite, showered and dressed and as recovered from their flight as it was possible to be in such a short time. He could already hear the band in the great ballroom and the sound of very well-heeled enjoyment below, all clinking glasses and graceful laughter, wafting up into the far reaches of the family wing and down the long hall to this remote set of rooms set apart from the rest.

Luca glared at Kathryn's door, as if that might make her appear.

And when it did—when it started to open as if he'd commanded it with that glare—he scowled even more.

Until she stepped out into the hall, and then, he was fairly certain, all the blood in his head sank with an audible thud to his sex.

"What—" and his voice was a strangled version of

his own, even from the great distance that ringing in his ears made it sound "—*the hell* are you wearing?"

Kathryn eyed him with that cool expression of hers that he was beginning to think might be the death of him. It clawed at him. It made him want nothing more than to heat her up and see what lurked beneath it.

"I believe it's called a dress," she said crisply.

"No."

She stood there a moment. Blinked. "No? Are you sure? The last time I checked a dictionary, the word was definitely *dress*. Or perhaps *gown*? A case could be made for each, though I think—"

"Be quiet."

Her mouth snapped closed and she had no idea how lucky she was that he hadn't silenced her in the way he'd much prefer. He could already taste her again, as if he had. Luca pushed off the wall opposite her door, unable to control himself. Unable to *think*.

A red haze of sheer lust kicked through him, making everything else dim.

Yes, Kathryn was wearing a dress. Barely. It was in an off-white shade that should have made her look like a ghost, with that English complexion of hers, but instead made her seem to glow. As if she'd been lit from within by a buttery shimmer. It had a delicate, high neckline and no sleeves, and an elegant sort of wide belt that wrapped around her waist before the full skirt cascaded all the way to the floor.

None of that was the problem. *That* could have been Grace Kelly, it was all so effortlessly tasteful and stylish.

It was the damned cutouts that made his entire body feel like a single, taut ache. Two huge wedges that edged in at sharp angles from the sides, cutting into the lower bodice of the dress and showing sheer acres of her bare skin in that sweet spot below her breasts and above her navel, then flaring out over the curves of her sides.

Luca wanted to taste her everywhere he saw skin. Right here. Right now.

He didn't realize he'd said that out loud until her eyes went wide and turned that fascinating slate-green shade, and then it didn't matter anyway, because he'd lost his mind—and worse, his control. He backed her into her own closed door, bracing himself over her with a hand on either side of her head.

"You can't," Kathryn said. *Whispered*, more like, her voice a rough little scrape that he could feel in the hardest part of him. "Luca. We *can't*."

Luca didn't ask himself what he was doing. He didn't care. That dress pooled around her, seductive and impossible, and he was lost in the elegant line of her neck and the hair she'd swept back into a complicated chignon at her nape.

"Did my father give you these diamonds?" he asked, trying to force this red-hazed lust out of him by any means possible. But it didn't shift at all, not even when he lifted a finger to trace the sparkling stones she wore in both her ears. One, then the next.

All of this was wrong. That pounding ache in his sex. This impossible hunger that stormed through him, casting everything else aside—including his own good intentions. He knew it. He still couldn't seem to care about that as he should. As he knew he would eventually.

"Answer me," he urged her, his mouth much too close to the sweet temptation of that tender spot behind her ear, and he couldn't identify that dark, driving thing that had control of him then. "What did you have to do to earn them, Kathryn?"

She jerked her head to the side, away from his fingers and the way they toyed with the delicate shell of her ear, but it was too late. He could see the way she shivered. He could see the pulse that fluttered madly in her neck. He could see the goose bumps that ran down her bare arms.

There was no ordering himself to pretend he hadn't seen those things. Or that he didn't know what they meant.

"You are meant to be here as my assistant, nothing more," he reminded her, his voice a low throb in the otherwise quiet hallway. "This is not meant to be an opportunity for you to flaunt your wares and pick up new customers."

"You're disgusting."

The icy condemnation in her voice poured over him, gas to a flame.

"That is an interesting choice of words," Luca murmured, his lips the barest breath away from her warm neck, and she shuddered. "What is more disgusting, do you think—the fact that I do not want you parading around the château, contaminating my family home and my father's memory? Or the fact you have no qualms about wearing a dress that makes every man in the vicinity think of nothing but you, naked?"

She turned her head to face him then, and her hands came up, shoving futilely at his chest. Luca didn't budge, and he had the distinct pleasure—or was it pain, he couldn't tell—of watching the color rise in her exquisite cheeks.

"Only you think that," she snapped at him, mutiny

and feminine awareness and something hotter by far in her furious gaze. "Because only you live your life with your head in the gutter. Everyone else will see a lovely dress by a well-known designer and nothing more."

"They will see my father's widow in white, with her naked body on display," he corrected her. "They will see your complete disregard for propriety, to say nothing of the memory of your very dear *friend*."

She laughed. It was a high, outraged sound.

"What should I have worn instead?" she demanded. "A black shroud? What would make you happy, Luca? A tent of shame?"

His hands shook and he flattened them against the wall, because he knew. *He knew.* If he touched her again, he wouldn't stop. He didn't care how much more he'd hate himself for it.

He wasn't sure he'd even try to stop himself.

"You told me your laughable story," he reminded her. "An unlikely friendship struck by chance in a far-off waiting room, between one of the wealthiest men in the world and you, our favorite saint." He studied the way her lush mouth firmed at that, the way her eyes flashed and darkened. "I think I saw the syrupy cable-television movie you based that absurd nursery rhyme on. What is the real story, I wonder?"

"I can't help it if you're so cynical and so jaded that all you see in the world is what you put into it," she threw at him with something more than mere temper in her eyes—and it fascinated him. That was his curse. *She* fascinated him, damn her. Maybe she had from the start. Maybe that was the truth he'd been burying for two years. "Here's a news flash, Luca. If you spend your life looking for ulterior motives and cruelty, that's all you'll ever see. It's a self-fulfilling prophecy."

"Do you know why I hate you, Kathryn?" He didn't wait for her answer. "It's not that you married my father for his money. So did everyone else. It's that you dare to act offended when anyone calls that spade the spade it is. It's that you believe your own tabloid coverage. *Saint Kate* is a myth. You are nothing like a saint at all."

She made a frustrated sound and shoved at him again. "I can't control what you think of me. I certainly can't control what the tabloids say about me. And this might come as a giant shock to you, but I don't *care* if you hate me or not."

Somehow he didn't believe her, and he couldn't have said why that was.

And something inside him cracked. A chain broke, and he shifted, leaning in closer and then reaching down to trace the cutout angle of her dress that was closest to him. He sketched his way from the tender skin at the juncture of her shoulder and chest down, skating around the tempting swell of her breast, then cutting in with the line of the fabric toward her belly.

Her breath came hard. Broken.

But she didn't tell him to stop. She didn't shove at him again. Her hands curled into fists and rested there against his lapels, urging him on.

Luca concentrated on the task of this. Of his fingertip against her insane, impossible smoothness. Of the fire that danced between them, the flames stretching ever higher, until he was wrapped up in the sensation of her skin beneath his and the scent of her besides. The hint of something tropical in her hair and the subtle, powdery notes that whispered of the very expensive perfume he now associated with her so strongly that the hint of it in places she wasn't made his body clench down hard in awareness.

Once in a distant resort in the Austrian Alps. Once in a seaside hotel in the Bahamas. She hadn't been in either place, but she was here. Tonight, she was here.

And this was no different. *This is madness*, he told himself.

He didn't kiss her. He didn't dare risk the possibility that he wouldn't stop this time. But he leaned in closer anyway, until their breaths were the same breath. Until he could see every last thing she felt as it moved through her expressive eyes. Until the fact he *wasn't* taking that mouth with his, that their only point of contact was his finger as it danced along that edge where fabric met skin, became erotic.

It became everything.

And he wanted this too much. He wanted *her*. Luca wanted to lose himself inside her, to hurl them both straight into the heart of this wildfire that was eating them both alive.

"This," he said softly, "is what a whore wears when she wishes to announce she's available again. Discreetly, I grant you. But the message is the same."

He felt the way she stiffened, and then he indulged himself and wrapped the whole of his palm over the exposed indentation of her waist, and, God help him, the smooth heat of her blasted into him. It ricocheted inside him. It lit him on fire.

It made that hunger in him shift from an insistent pulse to a roar.

But even though he could feel the deep, low shudders that moved through her body, that told him she felt the same need that he did, she shoved at him again. Much harder this time, using her fists. He grunted and backed up.

He didn't remove his hand.

"What's your plan, Luca?" Her gaze was dark, and he couldn't read her. Her chin edged higher, and her voice was cool and hard. That was what penetrated the red haze, like shards of ice deep into him. "Are you going to prove I'm a whore by acting like one yourself? Do you think that's how it's done?"

Luca dropped his hand then, with far more reluctance than he cared to examine just then. He stood away from her, lust and longing and that greedy kick of need making him scowl at her. Making him wish too many things he shouldn't.

Making him wonder why she was the only thing he couldn't seem to control—or, more to the point, his reaction to her.

"I don't need to prove the truth," he gritted out. What the hell was happening to him? How had she gotten the better of his control? He tried to shake it off. "It simply is, no matter how you pad it out and pretend otherwise to make yourself look better."

She straightened, only that flush high on her cheeks and the hectic glitter in her too-dark eyes to mark what had happened here.

What had *almost* happened.

"I think you'll find that math doesn't work," Kathryn said crisply, and she might as well have shoved a knife deep into his side. He felt as if she had. "Whorish behavior always adds up to two whores, Luca. Not one dirty whore and an innocent with dirty hands by accident, almost but not quite corrupted by doing the exact same thing. No matter what lies you tell yourself."

And then she pushed past him and started down the hall, her every movement as graceful and elegant as if she was a damned queen, not the grasping little gold digger they both knew full well she was.

CHAPTER FIVE

THE PARTY WAS long and bright and painful.

Of course, it always had been. Kathryn told herself that, really, this was no different than the other times she'd had to parade around the Castelli château in this gorgeous little pocket of the Northern California wine country, acting as if she neither heard nor saw the whispers and the overlong, unpleasantly speculative looks.

This was merely part and parcel of being notorious, she told herself. Something every other member of the Castelli family had found a way to handle. Why couldn't she do the same?

But, of course, she knew.

It was Luca. At every other party she'd ever been to with him, he'd kept as much distance between them as possible, as if he feared too much proximity to her would contaminate him. But this time she was his assistant, no longer his stepmother. That meant her place was at his elbow, no matter what had happened between them in that hallway.

And worse, what had *almost* happened. What she told herself she absolutely would not have allowed to happen—but she could feel the hollowness of that assertion tying her stomach into knots.

He'd caught up to her on the stairs that led down toward the ballroom and had slid a dark, fulminating look her way as he'd fallen into place beside her.

"I think you should leave me alone," she'd told him. Through her teeth.

"With pleasure," he'd replied silkily. "Does this mean you quit?"

She'd glared at him, and he'd caught her by the arm when she'd very nearly missed a step, and then held her fast when she would have yanked herself away from him.

"Careful," he'd warned her. "We are no longer in private. And in public, you are my father's widow and my current assistant."

"That is, in fact, all I am anywhere." She'd shaken her head at him. "Except for the sewer inside your head, of course."

"One scandal at a time," he'd told her, sounding something very much like *grim.* He'd let her go when they'd reached the ground floor. "Tonight I think the fact the Widow Castelli has joined the workforce will have to carry the gossip news cycle, don't you? Unless you'd like to use this opportunity to update your global dating profile by announcing to the world that your hunt for a protector has begun anew."

"And by *hunt,*" she'd retorted icily, "am I to understand you mean something like you manhandling me in a hallway? Was that your version of an audition?"

Luca's mouth had curved in that lethal way that was nothing so palatable as a smile.

"It's a tragedy for you that you can't manipulate me, I'm sure," he'd said, sounding anything but tragic. "Make sure you schedule time in my calendar for me to

care about that. Maybe next month? In the meantime—"
and he'd switched then, from the obnoxious Luca she'd
come to expect into the COO version of Luca that she'd
only ever seen in action over the past few weeks in his
office "—you stay next to me. You do not speak unless
spoken to directly. Just smile and look pretty and make
sure you remember every detail of every conversation
we have so we can compare notes later."

She'd blinked. "Uh, what details am I looking for?"

He'd stared down at her, and it was getting harder
and harder for her to imagine how anyone saw him as
a lazy, lackadaisical playboy when the truth of him
was stark and obvious and stamped right there on his
intensely beautiful face.

"All of them, Kathryn," he said, as if she was an
idiot. She hated that he made her feel like one—and si-
multaneously feel as if she needed to prove him wrong.
Then again, she'd had a great deal of experience with
that feeling. "You never know which little detail will
make all the difference."

And then he'd strode ahead of her straight into the
ballroom, and the moment he'd entered it, become that
other Luca. As if he'd flipped a switch.

Affable and approachable. Quick to make everyone
around him laugh. He always had a drink in his hand
and appeared to be ever so slightly tipsy, though this
close to him, Kathryn discovered that he didn't actually drink much. He slapped backs and kissed cheeks.
He flirted with everybody. He was delightful and about
as unthreatening as a man who looked like him and
moved like him and wore black tie as easily as he did
ever could.

Kathryn didn't have to ask him why he bothered to

put on such an elaborate act. The *why* of it became clear almost instantly.

She'd spent a great deal of time smiling prettily next to Gianni, too, and no one had found him particularly delightful. They'd always been guarded. Distant and cagey. Especially if they were somehow involved in the business.

But it was as if no one could believe that *this* Luca Castelli, who commanded the attention of the whole party simply by entering it, was the same one who ran the Rome office with such a deft hand. This bright, gleaming, careless creature. Even though there was no other name on that door in Rome but his.

Kathryn had heard the rumors. That it was Gianni himself who'd propped up Luca's office—except, of course, for the small problem that an old man with dementia could not possibly have run anything. Perhaps he simply had a particularly good team to support him, the rumor mill had countered. But no matter what people speculated about in private, when they were in Luca's presence, they basked in it. In him. In that effortless sort of sunshine he spread about him so easily.

And they told him everything.

Secrets. Rumors. Things their supervisors—who were often standing across the room—would kill them for saying out loud.

Everyone succumbed to the golden myth of Luca Castelli, Kathryn saw. Everyone. Captains of industry, wine connoisseurs and college-age caterers alike lost in the perfection of his inviting smile.

Watching him in action told her a great many things, but most of all, it made her feel better about herself for falling so completely under his spell every time he got too close to her. It wasn't something fatal in her own design, as she'd imagined. It wasn't that weakness in her that her mother had always despaired of and had gone to such lengths to stamp out of her. It was *him*.

She ducked into the mostly hidden powder room off the main ballroom when Luca got into an intense discussion about a documentary Kathryn had never seen with a handful of very intellectual types who'd made it clear they both recognized her and thought her beneath them. *Far* beneath them. She was happy to let them think so.

Inside the luxurious bathroom suite, she sat down on the couch in the lounge area and took a little breather. Away from the crush of the crowd, most of whom looked at her with nothing but ugly supposition on their faces. Away from Luca, whom she really should hate.

Why didn't she hate him the way she should? The way he unapologetically hated her?

"Being fascinated with him is only making everything worse," she snapped at herself, out loud—and then jumped when the door to the lounge swung open.

"Oh," Lily said. She looked around as if she expected there to be more people in the room—or as if she'd heard Kathryn talking to herself like a crazy person. Kathryn trotted out her smile automatically. "I didn't realize anyone was in here."

"Only me," Kathryn said mildly. "Depending on your point of view, that may or may not count."

Rafael's wife laughed, then smoothed her hands over the swell of her pregnant belly, looking resplendent in a gleaming blue gown. And happy. That it took her a moment to recognize what that expression meant made something inside Kathryn catch. As if happiness was so foreign to her.

"Don't pay any attention to Luca," Lily said, her eyes meeting Kathryn's in the mirror then moving away. "The man is *such* a control freak. He can't stand surprises, that's all."

She ran the water in the sink and then smoothed her damp palms over the coils of heavy braids she wore, all collected into a fat bun at the back of her head. Kathryn had always liked Lily. She was the least judgmental member of the Castelli family. She'd been the most welcoming to Kathryn, and Kathryn had even imagined that under different circumstances they might have been friends. Perhaps that, too, was naive.

She was beginning to realize that *she* was naive, in every possible way—something she'd have thought was impossible, given how hard her mother had worked to wring that out of her. And yet.

"Am I a surprise?" she asked, when she was sure she could keep her voice light and easy. "I don't think that's the word Luca would use."

Lily slanted an amused look at her. "Everything about you is a surprise," she said. "From the day you arrived. You refuse to slot yourself into one of Luca's depressingly functional and supernaturally clean boxes. He hates that."

"He hates surprises?" Kathryn laughed lightly. Very lightly, which was at odds with how her heart punched at her, as if this information about Luca was the most important detail of all she might have collected here tonight. "Here I thought the only thing he hated was me."

It was Lily's turn to laugh, though hers seemed far less for show.

"He hates messes," she said. "He always has. If he hates you? It's because you're messing things up for him, and he doesn't know how to handle something he can't sanitize and shelve somewhere. And between you and me, that's probably a good thing."

Then she smiled her goodbyes and went back out into the crush, leaving Kathryn to mull that over.

But not for long. Her mobile buzzed in her clutch and she knew it was Luca, which got her moving out of the bathroom lounge and back into the party before she even looked at the display.

"Are you taking a holiday?" he growled into the phone when she answered, all spleen and fury. "If not, you'd better be right here when I turn around. I'm not paying you to gallivant around the château like one of the guests."

"Are you paying me at all?" she asked mildly, spotting him several groups away and moving around them as she spoke. "I thought your father set up a trust for me so you couldn't hold a paycheck over my head. Or maybe for other reasons, and that's just a happy accident?"

"I'm turning around now," he said, and she came to a stop before him as he did.

Their eyes met. Held.

It was harder than it should have been to pull herself away. To concentrate on tucking her mobile back in her clutch. To tell herself there was nothing at all in his dark eyes but what there always was: some or other form of fury, brightened up with dislike.

She didn't understand why no one could see the truth about him but her. She told herself she was making it up. That it wouldn't be there when she looked up at him again—that he'd be that half lazy, half obnoxious man he should have been and nothing more.

But it was still there. That fury, that need. That hunger that terrified her and intrigued her in equal measure. A whole world in that gaze of his, and she had no earthly idea what to do about it.

"I think you're being paged," she told him, nodding toward a bejeweled woman in a slinky dress made entirely of sequins, who was bearing down on Luca from afar. "You wouldn't want to disappoint your fans with this show of seriousness, would you?"

"It's not a show. It's business. Not a concept I expect you to comprehend."

"I'm sure that's what you tell yourself," she said unwisely. So very unwisely. "But it's interesting that you're so determined to hide part of yourself away wherever you go, don't you think?"

She had no idea why she'd said that. Luca looked frozen into place for a long, taut moment, an arrested expression on his darkly gorgeous face. Then he blinked, and there was nothing but his usual darkness again, leaving Kathryn faintly dizzy.

"Careful, Stepmother," he said softly. Lethally. "Or I might be tempted to truly give them something to talk about tonight."

She didn't believe he'd do anything of the kind—of course she didn't—but she still had to fight to restrain a shiver at the thought. And she was sure that Luca knew it, that the unholy gleam of something like gold in his dark eyes was that pure male knowledge Kathryn was very much afraid would be her undoing.

But then he turned away, his public smile at the ready, that intensity gone as if it had never been.

And Kathryn reminded herself that it didn't matter what this man's sister-in-law, who had once been his stepsister, had said in the bathroom lounge. It didn't matter what happened in remote hallways in the château. The only truth that mattered was that she was his assistant now, and if she couldn't do that job as well as she should, everything else he'd ever said about her was true. And not just him.

You've had more opportunities than I could have dreamed of having! her mother had said the last time she'd seen her, at Christmas, with that look on her face that had told Kathryn that once again she'd failed Rose terribly, as she'd always managed to do. "And look what you've done with them."

Kathryn hadn't known what to say or how to defend herself. Because Rose had been the one to encourage Kathryn into marrying Gianni in the first place.

"The world is filled with people who marry for far less reason than this," she'd said. "But of course, Kathryn, it's *your* life. You should do what you think is best *for you*, no matter who else might benefit."

And Kathryn hadn't been able to think of a good reason why *not* to marry the kindly old man when her mother had put it like that—especially given what she knew she would gain from it. It would cost her so very little. All *she* had to sacrifice was a couple of years. Not her whole life, as her mother had done, and for far less in return. Though Rose certainly hadn't objected when Gianni's money had allowed Kathryn to buy her a cottage in the sweet Yorkshire village of her choice, and then provide her with live-in care.

She never thanked you, either, a little voice pointed out, deep inside her.

But she felt ungrateful and small even thinking such things. Many women wouldn't have had a baby on their own, with the father adamantly out of the picture. Rose had never faltered.

Which meant Kathryn could do no less—no matter the provocation.

It was time she stopped worrying about Luca Castelli and what he thought about her, and got to work.

One blue-and-gold California day rolled into the next, filled with meetings and vineyard tours and endless business dinners, and Luca found himself more disgruntled than he should have been by the fact Kathryn was…good at the job. More than good, in fact, in the odd role she had to play. Far better at it than the assistant she'd displaced, though he hated to admit it. Marco had been an excellent administrative assistant, but had always been a little too conspicuously himself when out in the field trying to charm potential clients.

Kathryn, on the other hand—who Luca would have asserted could no more *blend* than the sun could rise in the west and was anything but charming besides— did it beautifully.

"No," he barked out one morning, when she'd walked into their shared breakfast room dressed in one of her usual work outfits, a skirt and heels and one of those soft blouses that made him unable to think of anything at all but the breasts pressed *just there* behind the silk.

Kathryn paused, her hand on the back of the nearest chair, her bearing that of slightly offended royalty. It put his teeth on edge.

"You can't wear that," he growled at her, feeling like some kind of sulky child, which was insupportable. He was not one of his nephews, having a tantrum. Why couldn't he control himself around this woman? "We are walking through the vines with one of the accounts today. They find the Castelli family on the verge of being too European for their tastes as is, so we must be certain to impress them with our homespun, regular-person charm."

"I don't think even you can convince someone you are either homespun or regular."

"I'm a chameleon," he said drily. And was uncomfortable with how that sat there on the sunny table like truth, when he hadn't meant it that way. *It's interesting that you're so determined to hide part of yourself away wherever you go*, she'd said, damn her. He scowled at her. "But I doubt you can say the same."

He was wrong. Kathryn turned and left the room and when she reappeared, she'd transformed herself. She wore jeans, a pair of boots and a soft, casual, long-sleeved shirt. She'd let her hair down to pool around her shoulders and had scrubbed the makeup from her face. She looked like a host of fantasies he hadn't realized he had. She looked like an advertisement for healthy Californian living. Like a dream come true.

The emissaries from this tricky account of theirs had agreed, hanging on Kathryn's every word and acting as if Luca was *her* assistant, a state of affairs that didn't annoy him as much as it should have done— because he got to trail behind her, admiring the curve of her bottom in faded denim.

And imagining what it would be like to throw her down in one of the tidy rows between the vines and taste all that sweet, soft skin and that mouth that was driving him to the brink of madness.

When they were finally alone again, having waved off the ebullient account managers who'd doubled their national order based entirely on the force of Kathryn's smile, he found himself watching her much too closely. As if he might pounce.

"I told you I could do the job," she said, and he wondered if she knew how fierce she sounded. "Any job."

"So you did."

"But don't worry, Luca," she said, and he had the sense she'd collected herself—remembered who they were. He hated that he felt it as a kind of loss—and it seemed to collect inside him with all the other things he hated about himself. "I won't let that get in the way of all my whoring around. I know you need that to feel better about yourself and, of course, my only aim is to please you."

He felt his jaw clench and every muscle in his body tense. But there was something about the way she stood there in the bright winter sun, her hands tucked into the back pockets of her jeans and the Sonoma wind toying with her dark hair. He had the strangest sense of tightness around his chest, as if there was a steel band clamping down on him.

He didn't know what to do with it. He didn't know how to handle it. Or her.

Or worst of all, himself.

"Why did you marry him?" he asked.

Her marvelous eyes were dove gray in all that too-blue California light, and she didn't look away from him.

"I don't see why it matters to you."

"And yet it does."

"I think you want there to be some kind of rationale,"

she said quietly. "Something you can point to that makes it all okay in your head. Because otherwise you're just a man who has grabbed his father's widow. Twice."

"Is there one, then? A rationale? Were you a street urchin he saved? Did you personally support a threatened orphanage and his money saved a host of children from eviction?"

She smiled at him, and it wasn't her usual smile. It wasn't that serene, bulletproof smile she trotted out for work and had used on him at least a thousand times in the past three weeks alone. This one hurt. It was sad and it was reflected in her eyes, and he didn't understand what was happening here.

What had already happened, if he was honest with himself.

Luca decided honesty was overrated. But it was too late. She was speaking.

"No," she said. "I married him because I wanted to marry him. He was rich and I was struggling through my degree and some personal issues, and he told me he could make all my troubles go away. I liked that. I wanted that." His mouth twisted, but her smile only deepened, and still it hurt. "Is that what you wanted to hear?"

"It doesn't surprise me."

"What do you think marriage is, Luca?" she asked, and she tilted her head slightly to one side.

He was mesmerized by it, by *her*, and it occurred to him that they'd never actually *talked* before. It had been all insults and glares, that scene in the library or in the hallway between their rooms, what he still thought was just another rehearsed story on the plane. She shook her hair back from her face and he wanted to do that for her. He wanted to touch her, he realized, more than he could recall ever wanting anything else.

And nothing had ever been more impossible.

"Not the transaction it was for you," he said, aware that his voice was too raw, too rough. It gave him away. "Not a bit of cold calculation with a monetized end."

But Kathryn only continued to smile at him in that same way, as if *he* made her sad. As if he was *doing something* to her. That tight band around his chest seemed to pull even tauter. It pinched.

"Who are you to judge?" she asked softly, and it was more of a slap, perhaps, because it lacked heat or accusation. She simply asked. "We were happy with our arrangement. We fulfilled the promises we made to each other."

He couldn't take it. He moved toward her, aware but not caring that they were standing out in front of the château where anyone could see them, and he took her face between his hands. This would be so much easier if she weren't so pretty, he told himself—if she was a little more plastic and a whole lot less polished.

If she didn't short-circuit every bit of control he'd ever had.

"Tell me more about how happy you were," he dared her, aware that he was furious. More than furious. "How perfect your marriage was—a union of two identical souls, yes?"

But she didn't back down. She didn't flush hot or look the least bit ashamed. Her hands came up and hooked around his wrists, but she didn't pull him away.

"Go on, then," Luca urged her, his voice an aching thing that simmered in the scant space between them. "Tell me how you fulfilled those promises to the old man. Were you contractually obligated to kneel before him and pleasure him a certain number of nights per week? Or was he past that point—did he have you tend to yourself while he watched? What promises did you keep, Kathryn?"

Something gleamed in that gaze of hers and turned her eyes a darker shade of gray, but she didn't jerk away from him.

"What amazes me about you," she whispered, "is how you think it's your right to ask these questions. You don't get to know what happened in my marriage. You can drive yourself crazy with all your dark imaginings, and I hope you do. You can whisper your filthy thoughts to anyone who will listen. It doesn't make them true, and it certainly doesn't require me to comment on them. If you want to believe that's what happened between me and your father, then go ahead. Believe it."

There was a resolve in her gaze Luca didn't like, and he didn't know what he might have done then, but down at the bottom of the château's long drive, a busload of wine tasters pulled in and started up the winding way toward them.

And he had no choice but to let her go.

Kathryn woke when the moonlight poured in her windows, making her blink in confusion at the clock. It was just before four in the morning, and that was, she realized after a moment or two of uncertainty, very definitely the moon and not the sun.

Her internal clock was still a mess, even after nearly a week in California, and she only had to lie there a little while before she accepted the reality that she was not going to fall back asleep. Not tonight.

She swung her feet over the side of the tall, canopied bed piled high with soft linens, and dressed quickly in the clothes she'd left draped over her chair, a simple pair of terry lounging trousers and a cashmere hooded top. She twisted her hair back out of her way, tying it in a knot at her nape. She wrapped a long merino wool sweater around her to cut the chill, and then she pushed open the glass doors that led out onto her balcony and stepped outside.

The moon was huge and so bright it lit up the whole of the valley and all Kathryn could see in all directions, pouring over the cypress trees and dancing over the gnarled rows of vines. Making the pockets of night where it didn't touch even darker, and turning the world a spectral silver. The breeze was high, whipping into her, just cold enough to feel like exhilaration.

She closed her eyes and leaned into it.

"Couldn't sleep?" asked a low male voice from far too close. "Perhaps it's your conscience."

Kathryn looked over, as slowly as possible, as a counterpoint to the sudden clatter of her heart. She'd forgotten that the balconies of these rooms all ran together here at the far end of the château, despite half walls between the rooms that were little more than decorative gestures toward privacy and did nothing to conceal her from Luca. Nothing at all.

He was sprawled on one of the soft loungers, wearing nothing but a pair of exercise trousers very low on his hips, as if he was impervious to the winter air around him.

And the moonlight crawled all over him. Sliding across that vast expanse of his chest, cavorting in the ridges and hollows, licking him and writhing over him, illuminating every inch of his shocking male beauty. And doing nothing at all to temper that stark expression on his face or that dark hunger in his eyes.

"Says the man who's clearly been out here awhile," Kathryn replied. Lightly. So very lightly. As if he was nothing to her. As if his voice did nothing to her. As if this was as unremarkable as having any other sort of meeting with him in the broad daylight, surrounded by other people.

But it was as if he knew exactly what she was trying to hide, or perhaps the moon showed him far too much, because he made it worse. He stood.

"What are you doing out here?" she asked.

"I have no idea," he said in a low voice, his gaze still on her. "Something I'm certain I'll regret. But that is nothing new."

The clatter of her heart became a deep bass drumming.

Luca raked back that thick fall of hair, the gesture as lazy as his hot eyes were not. Then he started toward her in that low, rolling gait that marked him as exactly the sort of predator she needed most to avoid.

Kathryn knew she shouldn't try to tough this out. She knew that there was no shame at all in simply turning tail and running, barring herself in her room against a man who looked at her with that much *intent*. But she couldn't bring herself to do it. She couldn't let him see how much he affected her. She couldn't let him know how he got to her. *She couldn't.*

More than that, she couldn't seem to move.

He walked over to the little half wall and then, his eyes never leaving hers, he simply swung himself over it with an offhanded show of male grace that made everything inside Kathryn clench tight. Then run hot, pooling low in her belly and making her think she might simply melt where she stood. Making her think that perhaps she already had.

Luca didn't stop. He walked straight to her and he sank his hands in her hair and he hauled her close to him. To that mouth of his, dangerous and impossible and lush. To his flashing dark eyes that saw too much and condemned too deeply.

"What are you doing?" she asked again.

But her voice was a whisper, not a protest, and he knew it. She could tell by the way his fingers sank deeper into her hair, holding her that much more immobile.

"Sleepwalking, I think," he told her in that low voice of his that wound around inside her, making her burn. "It's a terrible habit. Worse than alcohol. There's no telling what I'll do in the middle of the night and then forget come morning."

"Luca—"

"I'll show you what I mean."

His voice was little more than a growl.

And then he slid his mouth over hers.

CHAPTER SIX

KATHRYN TOLD HERSELF it was a dream.

The moonlight. This man.

It was a dream, that was all, and so it didn't matter if she simply opened to him. If she let him sweep her up his bare chest, cool to the touch but still so hard, like steel. If she made no sign of protest.

If all she did was kiss him back as hungrily and greedily as if she'd been the one to go to him.

And everything was heat. Fire. Need and longing made real in the silvery night.

His hands were big and hard, slipping from her hair to cradle her face, holding her where he wanted her.

And he plundered her mouth, using his lips and his teeth and that clever tongue of his, angling his jaw to take the kiss deeper, wilder.

She felt dizzy again—unmoored and lost—and was only dimly aware that he'd hauled her off the ground and up into his arms. She didn't care. It was a dream, so what did it matter if he was carrying her somewhere, his mouth still fused to hers? He was tall and so very strong, and the feel of him surrounding her made her shake and quiver deep inside.

He walked back through her door and straight to her

bed, laying her across the piled-high linens and following her down into the clutch of all that softness, and it was…astonishing. There was no other word for the press of him against her, so male and darkly perfect, so hard and *Luca.* There was no other way to describe that absurdly sculpted body rubbing all over hers.

Making her feel new. Like a strange creature, red-hot and molten, taking over the body she'd thought until this moment she knew so well.

This is only a dream, she told herself, and so she indulged herself.

He stroked his way deep into her mouth, tasting her deeply, and she met him. She ran her fingers through that thick dark hair of his, crisp and warm to her touch. She traced the magnificent line of his wide, muscled back down to his narrow hips, then worked her way back up those *ridges* on his abdomen that she could admit, here in this dream where nothing counted, fascinated her to the point of distraction.

Beyond that point, perhaps.

He tore his mouth from hers even as his hands moved. He propped himself up on one forearm and smoothed his other hand over her cashmere top, pausing at the top and then tugging—and it was a measure of how dazed she was that she didn't comprehend what he was doing until he'd unzipped her and the cool air teased over her bare breasts.

And she was panting as if she was running. As if she'd been running for miles.

Luca muttered something in Italian that washed over her like a caress, and then he bent his head and took one nipple she hadn't realized had pebbled into a hard point deep into his mouth.

Kathryn heard a noise that could not possibly have been her, so high-pitched and keening, bouncing back from the canopy above them, the ornate ceiling. She felt the dark current of his laughter shake through him and into her, making his shoulders move beneath her hands and shudder against her breasts. The sheer physicality of that stunned her, and then he simply sucked on her, that rich tugging setting off an explosion inside her. It seared its way through her, like a lightning bolt from his mouth straight down the center of her body to kick between her legs.

Hard and something like beautiful, all at once.

And Kathryn didn't know what to do. There was too *much* of him, everywhere. All over her, pressing her down with him into the embrace of her soft, soft mattress, making her wish this mad dream could go on and on forever.

He made a low, greedy sound that she recognized somehow, in a deep feminine place inside her she'd never known was there, and thrilled to at once. She dug her hands in his hair, but not to guide him—only to anchor herself as he smoothed his wicked palm down over her exposed belly, pausing to test the indentation of her navel, then dipping even lower to slip beneath the waistband of her soft trousers.

Kathryn opened her mouth to speak, to say *something*— to *do* something—

But Luca knew exactly what he was about. He didn't pause. He simply slid his hand down, so hot and hard, and then held the core of her, molten and hot and swollen with need, in his palm.

She made a noise, and he laughed again. He used the faint edge of his teeth against her nipple and made that lightning bolt roar through her again, wider and hotter and far more dangerous, and then he ground the heel of his hand against the place she ached most.

And Kathryn disappeared. She went up in a column of flame that tore her apart. She lost herself, shattering into too many pieces to count. She shook and she shook, bucking against him and unable to stop or hold on or do anything but survive the explosion—and when she finally came back to earth it was with a giant thud and a heartbeat so hard against her ribs that it hurt.

It *hurt*.

There was no pretending *that* was a dream.

Luca's hand was still down her trousers, tracing lazy patterns in her wet heat, and he'd propped himself up next to her while he did it. Watching her. Learning her. And Kathryn found she couldn't quite breathe. Something he made that much worse when he shifted from watching his own hand play with her, letting his gaze slam into hers.

His eyes were dark. So very dark. There was something powerful and supremely knowing in the way he looked at her then, and she shuddered again, as if she couldn't keep herself from falling apart. As if now he needed only to look at her to make her crack wide-open.

"Luca..." But she didn't sound like herself. She didn't recognize that small, profoundly needy voice that came out of her own mouth.

And she had no idea what to say.

He murmured something else in Italian, a low string of syllables that danced over her the way he did as he moved down the bed, hooking his fingers in the waistband of her trousers and yanking them down over her hips. He peeled them down her legs and tossed them aside, and Kathryn was shaking. She couldn't stop shaking.

And she was still so hot. So needy. Helpless, somehow, in the face of all that yearning and that intense look on his beautiful face.

"Luca," she said again, forcing herself to speak because this wasn't a dream, and reality was coming at her as hard as if the canopy had collapsed above her, bringing the whole of the château down with it.

"I have to taste you," he growled at her, his voice thicker and rougher than she'd ever heard it before, and that, too, slicked through her like lightning. Then he said something in Italian, and that, somehow, was worse. Or better.

"I don't think…" she tried to say.

"Good. Don't think."

He moved to take her hips in his hands, then settled himself between her legs as if he belonged there. He wedged her thighs open with his sculpted shoulders, and then he made a growling sort of sound that made a wave of goose bumps crash over the whole of her body.

"Bellissima," he murmured, directly into the heart of her need.

And then he simply licked his way straight into her core.

She tasted sweet and hot, the richest cream and all woman, and Luca drank deep.

Kathryn went stiff beneath him, shuddering anew, her hands tugging at him as if she couldn't decide whether to pull him closer or shove him away.

He took her over. He licked and he hummed, throwing her straight back into that fire, until she was rolling her hips to get closer to his mouth, begging him with her body.

He was so hard he thought it might kill him.

He found his way to the hot little center of her and sucked, hard.

And Kathryn made a low sound, long and wild. Then she was bucking against him, her hoarse cry rebounding off the walls, shattering beneath him all over again, and if he had ever seen anything better in all his life, he couldn't recall it.

Luca waited her out. She sobbed something incomprehensible and he liked that. He liked it too much.

He knelt up, letting his gaze trace over her as she lay sprawled there before him, more beautiful than he could have imagined—and the truth was, he'd imagined this very thing far more often than he was comfortable admitting, even to himself.

Her breasts were the perfect small handfuls, tipped in rose, and the center of her femininity was slick and hot. The taste of her poured through him like fire, arousal and need, the spice of a woman and her own particular sweetness besides.

And even here, open and shuddering, splayed out before him, there was something about her. A certain innocence, however impossible that seemed, that made him that much harder—the need in him taking on a near vicious edge.

He shoved his hair back from his face and looked around, wondering where she kept her condoms. Because surely she had some. Or perhaps she dealt with birth control a different way entirely, which meant he could—

And Luca froze then.

Because if Kathryn was on birth control, that would have been to keep herself from getting pregnant *with his father*. To keep herself from giving birth to a child that would have been Luca's own sibling.

Disgust and self-loathing hit him like a blow. Like an attack. He felt dazed.

How could he have forgotten who she was? How could he have let this happen?

You didn't let *this happen, you fool*, he growled at himself. *You did this all yourself.*

Kathryn was a spider at best, and now he knew exactly how sweet her web was, and he was ruined. *Ruined.*

Damn her.

He pushed back, levering himself off the bed and letting the chill of the winter night, even here inside her bedroom, sink into him from his bare feet up. He hadn't been able to sleep. No surprise, given the direction of his thoughts and his knowledge that she'd slept *just there* on the other side of his wall.

He'd tortured himself with the temperature, bathing himself in the winter moon as if it had been a form of cold shower. He had no idea how long he'd been out there, fighting a pitched battle with an enemy that he knew wasn't Kathryn at all. It was him. It was this need in him, gripping him hard and mercilessly even now, making him want to forget all over again and lose himself in that sweet, dangerous oblivion between her thighs.

You are the worst kind of idiot, he told himself harshly.

He watched her come back to herself, flushed and satisfied and more beautiful than any woman should be.

And far more dangerously compelling than *this* woman should be, especially to him.

He hated himself.

He told himself he hated her more.

"Is this how you do it?" he asked, and his voice was as cold as the night outside. *"Stepmother?"*

Kathryn jerked against the pillows as if he'd thrown a bucket of cold water on her. She looked stunned for a moment, and Luca felt something snake through him, hot and low and much too black to bear. It felt a good deal like shame—but he refused to let that stop him.

His breath sawed out of his chest, and Kathryn didn't help things. She sat up slowly, as if she ached. As if she didn't understand what he'd done to her—what he was doing—and he hated that she could keep the act going even now. When he was still so hard it hurt, and worse, he knew how she tasted now. And she was rumpled and flushed from his hands and his mouth—yet looked at him with her gray eyes dark as if she couldn't comprehend how that had happened.

He gritted his teeth as she swallowed, so hard he heard it, and then tugged her clothing back into place. And his curse was that howling thing inside him that wanted to strip her down and worship her, glut himself in her, until this madness in him subsided. Until he could *think*.

"I'm touched by this performance," he told her, his voice a dark thing in the moonlit room. "Truly I am. You look nothing less than ravished and yet innocent besides, as if I didn't just make you come. Twice."

He watched the way she shivered. The way she pulled her longer sweater tighter around her as if it was made of chain mail and could fend him off. The way she didn't quite meet his gaze.

"As a matter of fact," she said, carefully, as if she wasn't sure of her own voice, "I'd prefer not to have this postmortem just now."

"I imagine you don't."

She swallowed again, and there was nothing but shadows in her eyes when she finally looked at him.

"You were sleepwalking," she said softly. "I was dreaming. This never happened."

"Yet it did," he gritted out at her. "I can still taste you."

She pulled her knees up beneath her and hugged them close, and he loathed himself. He did. She looked like a lost little girl, and he was still hard and furious, and beyond all of that, she was still his father's widow.

His father's widow.

"Why did you marry him?"

He didn't mean to ask that again. He didn't know why he had.

But this time, when she gazed back at him, her gray eyes were like storms.

"To torture you," she told him, her voice still hoarse, but something hard beneath it. "Is that what you want to hear?"

"I suspect that's not far from the truth, if likely not so personal."

She made a frustrated sort of noise and rolled off the bed—but kept her distance, he noticed, as she skirted around to its foot.

"I'm taking a bath," she said in a low tone. "I want to wipe this entire night off me." She looked at him over her shoulder. "Torture yourself all you want, Luca. But I'll thank you to do it somewhere else."

And this time when she walked away from him, Luca told himself he was glad of it. That it was better.

No matter that his body still wanted her.

But that was all the information he needed, surely. The things he wanted were always the things that destroyed him—his family being a case in point. That was why, so long ago now he could hardly remember anything else, he'd stopped allowing himself to want anything.

He would conquer this, too.

Kathryn decided to treat the entire situation as if it really had been a dream. Everyone had unfortunately detailed and potentially steamy dreams about coworkers sometimes, surely. The trick was acting as if it had only ever happened inside her head.

She told herself she could do that. Why not? Luca was the master at playing whatever role worked best for his purposes. She could do the same.

Though it was harder than she'd anticipated to walk into that breakfast room the way she'd done every other morning in California and act as if her body didn't flush into shivering awareness at the sight of him.

It was so unfair.

He was gorgeous and terrible, commanding his side of the table with that lazy authority of his that she felt as if his mouth against her center again, bold and insistent. He was dressed in one of his devastatingly perfect suits today, crisp and lethally masculine as if he hadn't been up half the night, and Kathryn forced herself to stand there with her usual serene smile on her face. She was determined to do her best to *look* as calm and un-ruffled as he did.

But there was no controlling that low, wild lick of pure fire that swept through her, curling itself into dark knots deep inside, then blooming into something greedy and consuming in her sex.

You are in so much trouble, a small voice whispered inside her.

Worse, she was sure he knew it. That he could *see* every last thing she tried to hide from him. When all she could see in him was that harsh light in his dark eyes and that dangerous look on his face.

"Don't loom there," he said, all silken threat and a kind of menace that made her pulse pick up. "Sit down. This is meant to be a breakfast meeting to outline my plans for the day, Kathryn." He waited for her to look at him. To meet that awful gaze of his that tore straight through her. "Not agony."

There was absolutely no reason that should make her feel as if she might swallow her tongue. Kathryn ordered herself to pull it together. She pulled out her graceful, high-backed chair and sat down, the same way she had every other morning on this endless trip that she worried would leave her a mere shell of herself before it was done.

Maybe it already had, she thought with a shiver she fought to repress when he did nothing more shocking than fill her cup with coffee, a rich, dark brew that she thought was the precise color of his furious eyes—

She needed to stop.

"Tonight will be a family event," Luca said in a con-trolled sort of way that made the fact of his temper a living thing, dancing there between them. All the more obvious because it was hidden. Controlled. Just as he always had been—except for last night. Kathryn had to conceal the shiver that moved through her then. "Rafael, Lily and I—and therefore you, as my personal shadow—are expected at another winery in Napa."

"The next valley over."

"Yes." He set the silver coffeepot down on the table between them with a hint of something like violence, if carefully restrained. "Your command of geography is impressive."

"As is your use of sarcasm."

"Careful, Kathryn." His voice seemed darker then. Deeper. Infinitely more dangerous. "I know too much about you now. Far too many secrets about what makes you…" He paused, and she flushed then. She couldn't help it, no matter that she saw that gleam of satisfaction in his dark gaze and hated the both of them. "Tick." He eyed her. "You should keep that in mind."

He meant sex. All of this was about sex, the last topic on earth she wanted to discuss—especially with him. But it shot through her anyway, flame and heat, like the word itself was a heavy stone plummeting from a great height. It hit bottom in that molten-hot place between her legs, where she could still feel him. Where no amount of soaking in that bath earlier had managed to wipe away the exquisite feel of his hands or his mouth. She felt branded. Marked.

Though she thought she'd rather die right where she sat than let him know it.

"I'm so glad you brought that up," she said crisply. "Obviously, what happened last night can never happen again. You are my late husband's son and my supervisor, not to mention the fact that you are anything but a fan of mine. I'm appalled that we got as carried away as we did."

"If you plan to clutch at your pearls, you should have worn some." Luca's voice sounded decadent then. Dark and rich, and with that lazy note to it besides, as if he was enjoying himself. "As it is, it's difficult to take anything you say seriously when I can see how hard your nipples are, Kathryn. I don't think the word you're looking for is *appalled*."

Kathryn would never know how she managed to keep herself from looking down at her own breasts then, where she could feel a traitorous tightening that suggested he was right. How she only stared back at him with a faintly pitying air instead.

"It's winter, Luca," she said, almost gently. "You're wearing a suit. I am not. Do you need me to explain how female biology works?"

And that impossibly golden smile of his flashed then, as beautiful and bright as it was totally unexpected.

"Do you?" he asked, and there was that same note in his voice that every part of her recognized, down into her bones. It took her a moment to place it.

I have to taste you, he'd growled at her last night before he'd done just that. In exactly this same way.

Kathryn went very still. Or he did. Or maybe it was the world that stopped for a long, taut moment, as if there was nothing but the pounding of her heart and that betraying *tightening* everywhere else. As if he really could see straight into her. As if he knew. As if, were she to give him the slightest signal, he'd simply sweep all the breakfast things off the table and haul her across it, setting his mouth to her the way he had in all that silvery moonlight.

How could she fear him and want him at the same time?

"Good morning."

Rafael's voice from the doorway cut through the tension between them as if he'd used one of the ceremonial swords that hung theatrically in the château's tasting room in another part of the winery.

Kathryn told herself it was a relief. That it was *relief* that coursed through her, syrupy and thick.

She swiveled to face him, entirely too aware that Luca did the same thing—entirely too aware of Luca, come to that.

Rafael's cool gaze moved between them. From Luca to Kathryn and then back, and Kathryn was suddenly certain that he knew. That he could *see* what had happened between them, that he could hear the echo of those impossible cries she'd made into the night, that she was marked bright red and obvious.

"Lily and I won't be coming with you tonight" was all he said, in that remote way of his that made him such an excellent CEO. "She's having some contractions, and it's better that she stay off her feet."

"Is she all right?" Kathryn asked, frowning. "Isn't it a little bit early?" And then she regretted it when two pairs of dark and speculative Castelli eyes fixed on her in a way she didn't like at all. She forced a smile. "I beg your pardon. Am I not allowed to ask now that I'm merely a Castelli Wine employee?"

"No," Luca said at once. "It makes me question your motives."

"You would do that anyway," she replied smoothly,

without looking at him. "As far as I can tell, it's your favorite pastime."

Rafael smiled, and Kathryn was certain she didn't like the way he did it. "Lily is fine, Kathryn. Thank you for asking. This is nothing particularly worrisome, but her doctor would prefer she put her feet up for a few days, and that means another work event would be too much."

He aimed that smile at his brother then, and it took on a sharper edge that even Kathryn could feel. She was aware of Luca stiffening at his place across the table.

And of Rafael, still there in the doorway, his gaze entirely too assessing. "But it looks as if you have things as well in hand as ever, brother. I leave it to you."

CHAPTER SEVEN

HALFWAY THROUGH THE formal dinner laid out with luxurious attention to detail in one of the Napa winery's private rooms up high on a hillside, every plate and glass and carefully arranged bit of food as choreographed as some refined ballet, Luca was so darkly furious he had no idea how he kept to his seat.

He told himself it wasn't fury. Or it shouldn't have been. That Kathryn was simply doing what she did, what she had always done and always would, and there was no point reacting to it at all—

But that didn't help. Every time her musical little laugh floated across the table, he tensed. Every time that silver-haired jackass to her left with the wandering hands touched her, he thought smoke might pour from his ears.

It was one thing to know that this was what she did. That she was no doubt lining up potential selections for her future wherever she went. He'd never expected anything less. Yet it turned out it was something else to witness her in action.

Particularly when he could still *feel* her. Still hear those cries in his ears. Still taste her, the hard nub of her nipple and that creamy heat below.

Damn her.

He had no memory of the conversations he must have engaged in with the people sitting on either side of him. When the eternal dinner ground to an end at last and he could finally get the hell away, he escorted Kathryn to their waiting car with a hand that was, he could admit, perhaps a little too insistent against the small of her back.

"Is this an attempt at chivalry or are you herding me?" she asked under her breath, that damned smile of hers still welded into place even outside, in the dark, where there was no one to see her but him.

He wanted to mess her up, Luca acknowledged. He wanted to dig his fingers beneath that facade of hers and see what she hid away underneath. He wanted far too much, and all of it wrong. And dangerous, besides.

He was not a man who had ever been interested in entanglements. But *tangled* was the very least of the things he felt around this woman.

Luca held the passenger door of the sleek limousine open as she climbed inside, nodding brusquely at their driver. Then he swung into the limo's hushed interior himself, making no particular attempt to keep to his own side of the wide backseat as he slammed the door shut behind him.

Kathryn was digging in her evening bag. She glanced at him as he came close, then froze.

"What's the matter?" she asked. The faintest frown etched itself between her eyes, where that fringe of hers nearly touched her eyes and drove him utterly crazy with that same sharp longing he was finding it harder and harder—impossible—to control. Just as he could no longer seem to control himself. "What happened?"

"You tell me."

He felt outsized and more than a little maddened. He sprawled there next to her, too close but not quite touching her. Not quite. His blood was pumping through him much too fast. His heart was trying to kick its way out of his chest. He was holding himself back by the smallest thread.

He wasn't sure how he was holding himself back at all.

Her frown deepened, which was at least better than that damned smile.

"I don't know, Luca. I thought that went well enough. I'm not sure what you wanted out of it, but it seems as if every vintner in two valleys is deeply impressed with your varietals. What more can you ask?"

For the first time in his life, Luca did not care the slightest bit about wine or the wine business or anything having to do with his damned vines or vintages or barrels or whatever else.

"I could ask that when we are conducting business, you manage to keep your mind on that," he seethed at her. He didn't even try to contain that tone of his or the simmering outrage in it. "And not on laying your trap for your next victim."

Her gray eyes chilled. "What are you talking about?"

"You weren't particularly subtle," he gritted at her as the car began to move, sweeping them out toward the main road and the mountains to the west. "Everyone at the table got to watch you hang all over that poor man and play your little games with him."

"And by *little games*, I assume you mean the work you and I were there to do? That I was doing while you sulked?"

"You spent a long time off in the bathroom before dessert," he continued, not caring that he could see the effect of his harsh tone in the way she shivered slightly. "What were you doing, I wonder? Your target also disappeared for a similar span of time. And God only knows what you were doing beneath the table where no one could see."

He'd thought of little else. He knew the meal he'd been served had been the finest Californian cuisine, a fusion of the state's rich bounty presented to perfection, and yet it had all been tasteless and pointless to him.

Kathryn shook her head, her lips pressing together. "This is ridiculous. Not to mention offensive in the extreme." Her gray eyes flashed. "Of course, that's your thing, isn't it? The more horrible, the better."

"And here's what I wonder." He shifted so he was closer to her, looming over her, his whole body humming with that darkness, that tension, that driving need he could neither understand nor control. This was what she did to him. She made him lose the tight control he'd always maintained over himself, his world, his life. Always. He found that the most unforgivable. Maybe that was what made him move his face that much closer to hers—so she could *feel* his fury in every word he spoke. "How does a noted whore for hire seal the deal? On your knees or on your back? Does it vary with each mark or do you stick to a set routine?"

He didn't see her move, and that told him more about the blind single-mindedness of that darkness in him than anything else. He felt her palm against his jaw, heard the *crack* of it fill the car's interior with the bright burst of the slap she delivered and he saw the fire and the fury in her dark gray eyes.

The pain came a moment later, sharp and swift.

"You're a vile little man," she threw at him, and he didn't disagree with her. But that was neither here nor there. "The only thing more disgusting than your imagination is the fact you think you can dump it out on me whenever you feel like it, like a toxic spill."

Luca laughed, a darker sound than the night outside the car or the way her breath came out in angry pants, and tested his jaw with his hand.

"That actually hurt." He shifted his gaze to hers, and eyed the way she sat there, clearly trembling with rage. "Is this where you play the outraged and offended virgin? I must tell you, Kathryn. You're not that accomplished an actress."

She paled. He thought she might keel over, or explode, but she pressed her lips together again instead. She lifted a hand, and he thought she might try to hit him once more—and the operative word was *try*—but she only put her palm to her neck. As if she wanted to control her own pulse. Or her own breath.

Or herself.

And he didn't know what to do with that notion that swept over him like heat, that she might find herself as out of control in the middle of this mess as he clearly was.

"If you hit me again," he told her softly, "I'll return the favor."

"You'll hit me?" Her eyes were grim in the dark. "I'm glad your father is dead, Luca. He would have been horrified by you."

He ignored the little flare of something a good deal like shame deep inside him then, even as it knotted itself in his gut.

"Let's be very clear about this," he said, and he was aware on a distant level that the fury that had been riding him all through dinner had eased. Not disappeared, but loosened its hold. He didn't ask himself why. "It will be a very cold day in hell before I worry myself over what my father, of all people, might have thought about anything I do. Much less what you think. That's the moral equivalent of taking lectures on good behavior from the devil himself." He eyed her in the close confines of the car's backseat, where he was still too much in her space, and it still wasn't enough. Not close enough. Not *enough*. "But I don't hit women. Not even when they've hit me first."

She had the grace to look faintly abashed at that, and her gaze dropped to her hand. She flexed her fingers out in front of her, and he wondered if her palm stung as much as his jaw did. The idea didn't make that heavy knot inside him loosen any.

He reached over and took her hand in his, and held on when she tried to jerk it out of his grasp. He ignored the little *huff* of air that escaped her lips, and smoothed his fingers over her palm as if he was tracing it. As if he wanted to rub the sting out.

As if he didn't know what the hell he wanted.

"Hit me again, Kathryn," he said in a low voice, looking at her hand instead of her face, "and I'll take that as an invitation to finish what we started last night. No matter how many old men you make dance to your tune at a dinner table. No matter who you're pretending to be tonight."

Her fingers curled as if she wanted to clench them into a fist.

"I'm not pretending to be anyone," she snapped at

him. "The only person playing a game here is you. And there will never be an invitation to finish anything. That was an aberration. A terrible, horrifying mistake. I have no idea why it happened and—"

"Don't you?"

He hadn't meant to ask that question, but once out, it seemed to hover there between them, threatening everything. Pounding in him so hard it became indistinguishable from his own heartbeat.

"No," she whispered, but her gray eyes were too large and too dark. Her pretty mouth trembled with the lie of it. And he could feel the tremor she fought to repress in that hand he held between his. "I have no idea what you're talking about. I never do."

And Luca smiled. Hard. "Let me give you some clarity."

He let go of her hand and reached for her, wrapping his hands around her waist and lifting her out of her seat and over his lap. He heard her breath desert her as he settled her against him, her legs to one side. Then he simply bent his head and took her mouth with his.

Once again, that maddening fire. Once again, that swift shock, lust and need, greed and hunger, burning him alive.

As hot and as wild as if they were still in her bed. As if they'd never left, never stopped.

And she didn't fight him. She didn't pretend. He felt her give in to this thing that pounded between them, felt the heady rush of her surrender.

She hooked her arms around his neck as if she couldn't control herself any more than he could, then she opened her mouth to him and kissed him back.

And Luca lost track of everything.

That he was trying to make a point. That they were in the back of a moving car. That she was the last woman on earth he should be touching at all, much less like this. That he absolutely should not be doing this.

He simply lost himself in the perfection of her mouth. The sweet heat of the way she kissed him and tangled her fingers in his hair. The weight of her slender body against his and the sheer desperation in the way they came together.

Again and again.

But it wasn't enough.

He groaned against her mouth, and she shifted against him as if he'd lit her on fire, the curve of her hip coming up hard against his aching sex.

And Luca stopped pretending he had any control where this woman was concerned. Or at all.

He shifted her on top of him, swinging her around to straddle him. He shoved the dress she wore up and out of his way, settling her down astride his lap, and he almost lost it when she gasped into his mouth as the softest part of her came up flush against his hardness.

He could feel her shudder all around him, or maybe that was him, as lost in this insanity as she was.

There was no control. There was no hint of it. And the truly scary part of that was how little Luca cared that it was gone.

There was nothing but his hands buried in her hair again and his mouth against hers, feasting on her. Ravishing her. He could feel her wet heat against him and rolled himself into it, aware that only the fabric of his trousers and the insubstantial panties she wore separated them. He let the slick, hot glory of it build.

There was nothing but her taste, an addictive wildness against his tongue. She surrounded him, more beautiful with her dress at her waist and her hair half–falling down from its elegant little knot than any other woman he'd ever seen.

Than anything at all.

And Luca found himself muttering things he knew better than to say out loud, even if he was speaking in Italian.

"Tu sei mia," he told her. *You are mine.* He didn't know where that had come from, what the hell he was doing. Why he meant such things down deep in his bones, when he shouldn't. When he couldn't.

But he found he didn't much care then. He filled his hands with the taut curves of her bottom and guided her against him in an unapologetically carnal rhythm, until she tilted her head back and moaned.

So he did it even harder, watching her face go slack as she rocked against him, driving him crazy, making him so hard and ready for her it bordered on pain. He moved his hand from her gorgeous bottom, sliding it around to find the heat of her with his fingers through the barrier of those soft panties.

"Look at me, Kathryn," he ordered her, his voice little more than a growl.

She obeyed. And her eyes were wide and gray. Slicked hot with desire. Her lips were parted, and her cheeks were flushed. Luca felt something shift inside him, a sharp and uncompromising tilt. He couldn't name it, though there was no pretending he didn't feel it. He only knew that he was no longer the same man he'd been even five minutes before.

There was only Kathryn, arched above him, straining against him, her beautiful eyes locked on to his.

And there is this, he thought, sliding his hands into her panties and slicking his way through the molten wildfire of her sweet core to find the neediest part of her. Then he pressed down, hard and sure, and watched her hurtle over the side of the world.

She bucked against him as her pleasure tumbled through her, making greedy little noises that were almost his undoing, her fingers digging hard into his shoulders, her head thrown back and her lovely back arched like a bow.

And everything shifted again, but this time, all the hunger and greed and sense in his body surged straight to his sex.

Luca needed to be inside her. Right now.

She was still shaking, still astride him. She was still panting as she tipped forward until she could rest her forehead against his shoulder. And now he could feel her harsh little breaths as well as hear them, and somehow, that made everything hotter.

Closer. Crazier. Better.

He reached between them, amazed to find his hand was unsteady as he pulled himself from his trousers at last, so aching and so hard. Kathryn was limp now, still shuddering and gasping, and he simply pulled her panties to one side and lined himself up with her entrance, the scalding heat of her nearly enough to make him lose it right there.

He thought he swore in Italian, or perhaps it was a prayer. She was slick and hot, and he didn't care where else she'd been or with whom. He didn't care why. He didn't care about anything but the way she fit in his arms, his lap.

He didn't care about anything but this.

It had been two years of sheer torment with this woman; he could admit that now, when the truth seemed so obvious at last. He'd wanted her from the moment he'd first laid eyes on her. Perhaps he would always want her. But that wasn't something Luca wanted to think about. Not now when she was everything he'd ever wanted, poised there above him, hot and wet and nearly his.

Nearly.

He moved his hands to her hips to hold her right where he wanted her. He tucked his mouth against her neck, where he could taste her, salt and need.

And then finally, finally, he thrust his way home.

It hurt.

God, did it hurt.

Kathryn felt something tear, felt a shriek of agony sear through her like a burn, and then there was nothing but the hugeness of him. Deep, deep inside her. So deep she found she couldn't breathe, couldn't think, couldn't do anything but freeze there over him, that harsh thrust of his possession like a throbbing brand within her.

Luca swore.

Then again, in both Italian and English, and she scrunched up her face so she wouldn't cry and kept it buried in the crook of his shoulder as if she could hide from this. As if that might make the shuddering, aching heaviness go away.

But it didn't work.

"Look at me," he said, his voice hoarse. "Kathryn. Sit up."

"I don't want to."

He was still buried deep inside her, though he didn't

move. Then the car bumped over a dip in the road and thrust him deeper into her, and she felt the way he braced himself. Heard the small exhalation he made, as if this was no easier for him than it was for her. And that heavy sharpness radiated out from where the length of him was still inside her, making even her breasts feel stung with it.

As if the whole of her body was one giant *ache*.

"Sit up, *cucciola mia*," he said, in a voice she'd never heard him use before, something far warmer and indulgent than any she associated with him. He nudged her with his jaw. "Now, please."

And it seemed the hardest thing she'd ever done, to ease herself back, knowing he could see the panic and the pain and the leftover heat all over her face. To *feel him* lodged *inside* her as she carefully shifted position. To look into his dark eyes, so close to hers, aware that he knew things about her now she hadn't wanted to share.

Too many things.

It had all happened too fast. She'd been lost in another bone-deep, impossible shattering, torn apart into a million little pieces and unable to breathe, and then it had been too late.

Too late, she thought again.

She wasn't sure what that thing was that crept over her, deep in her chest and her gut, a raw sort of hollow. She was terribly afraid it might be a sob.

Luca reached up and smoothed her hair back from her still-flushed face. She squirmed against that thick, hard intrusion that connected them so intimately, and he only watched her do it. He didn't move—though she thought that steel line of his jaw hardened.

"Why didn't you tell me?" he asked, his voice the

quietest she'd ever heard it, and she didn't know what to make of that. She didn't know how to feel.

She moved her hips and didn't understand how people did this, or *why*, when there was no comfortable position and too much of that heavy, aching heat. "I didn't think you'd notice."

"Kathryn," he said, that low voice at odds, somehow, with the very nearly tender way his thumbs brushed over her temples, and her name in his mouth a kind of poetry that made that hollow thing inside her seem to hum. "You went from pleasure to pain in an instant. How could I not notice that?"

She shifted again, still trying to find a way to sit on his lap when he was *inside her*, and this time his eyes darkened. She caught her breath.

The car bumped again and this time, the sensations that spun out from that involuntary thrust were more of a deep spark than anything sharp or painful. The ache inside her...changed. The spark seemed to light it up, infusing it with something else besides the pain. She shifted experimentally, then tugged her bottom lip between her teeth when that *something else* bloomed into something better, and watched that slow hunger burn in his dark eyes.

She felt an answering echo of it in her, as if the heaviness and the stretched ache were connected to all that delicious heat she thought of as his, that she could feel easing back into her the longer they sat like this.

"I wasn't aware that it would matter to you whether or not you hurt me," she said, without meaning to speak.

Luca's hands moved to cup her cheeks, and his dark

eyes met hers, nearly grim in the shadows of this car slipping through the California night.

"It matters," he said gruffly. "You should have told me."

And that hollow thing inside her swelled, crashing over her like a terrible tide. She didn't know what it was. She only felt the sting of tears in her eyes and the throb of something far heavier in her chest.

And Luca deep inside her, hot and still.

"Tell you?" she whispered, because her voice had deserted her. "How could I tell you? You don't just think I'm a whore, Luca. You *know* it. You've never had the slightest doubt."

"Kathryn."

"You wouldn't have believed me." She only realized that her tears had spilled out when he wiped them away with his thumbs, more gentle with her than made any sense. "You would have laughed in my face."

He didn't deny that, though his gaze darkened even further.

He pulled her face to his and kissed her, and it was almost too much. The thrust of him deep inside her body and the impossible sweetness of his lips on hers. It made her brain short out. It made that great rawness inside her glow.

"Ah, *cucciola mia*," he murmured, pulling back from her mouth, still holding her face in his hands—almost as if he found her somehow precious. "I'm not laughing now."

And then he began to move.

CHAPTER EIGHT

KATHRYN TENSED, BUT Luca only pulled out slowly and then pressed back in, far more gently this time.

It didn't hurt. It felt…strange, but that was better than the pain.

"Breathe," he told her, in that bossy way of his that shouldn't have made something ignite inside her. But she did it anyway.

She pulled in a deep breath and let it out, and still he moved inside her. Lazy. Relaxed. An easy sort of rocking.

Slowly, almost despite herself, Kathryn began to anticipate him. She met him when he thrust in, moving her hips in a way that made a low, shimmering thing dance inside her.

His mouth curved, and she thought that later—much later—she would have to examine why it was that it made her flush with so much pleasure.

He maintained that same lazy pace, and let his hands wander where they pleased. He smoothed his way up her back. He tested the thrust of her breasts through the dress that was still bunched around her waist. He reached beneath it and drew patterns on the soft skin of her belly, on the outsides of her thighs.

Kathryn found herself moving more, rolling her hips and testing the depth of his stroke. *This* dragged the center of her against him, and it made everything inside her wind up tight. *That* made a sweet shudder work its way up her spine. She tried different movements, wriggling against him and rocking into him, and he let her, only that heavy-lidded heat in his dark eyes and the faint flush high on his cheekbones a hint that he felt the same fire she did.

And slowly, surely, inevitably, she forgot that anything had ever hurt her. There was nothing but the glide, the pull. The bright heat that expanded the deeper he went into her and the more she met each thrust.

There was a coiling thing inside her, huge and terrifying, and Kathryn didn't know which she wanted more—to hide from it or throw herself straight into its center. And in any case, it didn't matter. Because Luca let out a delicious little laugh as if he knew exactly what she felt, and took control.

He pulled her hips flush with his. He took her mouth in a deep, dark, endless kiss. And he began to move within her in earnest, each slick thrust making that coil wind tighter, making it bigger and wilder and that much more intense.

And she couldn't. She couldn't—

"You can," he said against her mouth, and she realized she'd said that out loud. "You will."

And he shifted beneath her, then ran his clever fingers down to the place they were joined, and rubbed.

The next time he thrust inside her, she imploded. A brilliant, impossible shattering that rolled out from the place where he maintained that demanding pace, tearing her soul from her body and her limbs apart.

She heard him groan out her name, his mouth against her neck, and then he toppled right over that same cliff beside her.

And for a very long time, that was all there was.

When Kathryn came back to herself, she was still slumped against him and still astride him, and the car was slowing to make its final turn into the Castelli vineyard.

She pushed herself back up to a sitting position and climbed off Luca at the same time, feeling the loss of that length of him inside her like a blow. It made her feel even more awkward as she struggled to wriggle her dress back into place. Even more...off center.

He didn't speak. She didn't dare look at him. She heard him zip himself up, and then there was the long drive up from the road to the château to endure in the same heavy silence. Kathryn felt too many things, thought too many things, all of them battering at her like a thousand desperate winds, but she couldn't let herself do that here. Not while he was still beside her, so male and so hard, and now something entirely different than what he'd been even an hour before.

She didn't want to change. She didn't want the shift. She didn't understand how she'd simply...surrendered to him when she was twenty-five years old and hadn't felt the slightest urge to give herself to anyone in all her years.

"You're much too pretty," her mother had told her when she was barely thirteen, with a frown that told Kathryn that this was not a positive thing. "Mind you don't let it make you lazy. *Pretty* is nothing more than a prison sentence. Best you remember that before you let it turn your head."

And she'd tried. She'd buried herself in her studies. She'd run from the slightest hint of male interest or even friendships with girls who had any kind of active social lives, lest she be tempted into joining in. She'd done everything she could think of to prove to her mother that her looks weren't a weakness, that she could take advantage of the gifts Rose had given her with all her scrimping and saving and hard work.

But Rose had never been convinced.

"They'll trap you if they can," she'd told Kathryn again and again throughout her teenage years. "Tell you it's love. There's no such thing, my girl. There are only men who will leave you and babies who need raising once they're gone. A pretty thing like you will be easy pickings."

And Kathryn had resolved that whatever else she was, she wouldn't be *that*.

Even at university she'd been good at holding herself apart, keeping herself safe. She didn't want boyfriends or even supposed male friends who might think they could get to her that way, when her defenses were down. She avoided any scenario that might lead to lowered inhibitions or the slightest hint of danger. No pubs with her classmates. No parties. She'd kept herself in her own little tower, locked safely away, where nothing and no one could ever touch her or ruin her or make her a disappointment to her mother, who had given up so much to make her life possible.

All this time, she thought now, as the limo pulled up to the château's grand entrance, and Rose had been right. It really was a slippery slope, and Kathryn had plummeted straight down it and crashed at the bottom. One single car ride with a man who despised her, and she'd lost a lifetime of her moral high ground, her entire self-definition. She'd become exactly what Luca had always accused her of being, what Rose had always darkly intimated she'd become one day whether she liked it or not.

The whole world was different. *She* was different. And she didn't have the slightest idea how to come to terms with any of it, or what it meant.

The driver opened the door, and Kathryn climbed out too quickly, shocked when she felt twinges in all sorts of unfamiliar places. She might have toppled to the ground, but Luca was there, taking her arm as if he'd anticipated this. Holding her steady.

Though he still didn't say a word.

Kathryn pulled her arm out of his grasp, aware that he let her do it, and felt a rush of sheer, hot embarrassment wash over her. She couldn't read that expression on his face, making him look like granite in the light that beamed out from the château's windows and the moon high above. She couldn't imagine what she must look like—wrinkled and rumpled, used and altered, like a walking neon advertisement for what she'd just done. Was it written on her face? Would the whole world be able to *see* what had happened right there—what she'd done? What she'd let him do?

The notion made her panic.

She all but ran up the steps and threw open the door, relieved that there was no sign of anyone around as she hurtled herself inside the château's ornate entry hall like a missile.

It's fine, she told herself, though she didn't believe it. Though she could hear the drumming panic in her own head. *Everything is perfectly fine.*

She made herself slow down. She was aware of Luca just behind her, a solid wall of regret at her heels, but she told herself to ignore it. To pretend he wasn't there. She forced herself to walk, not run. She headed up the stairs and then down the hall that led to the family wing. She made her way all the way to the far end of the château, and then finally, *finally*, she could see the door to her own room. She couldn't wait to close herself inside and…breathe.

She would take another very long bath. She would scrub all of this away. She would curl herself up into a tiny little ball, and she would not permit herself to cry.

She would not.

Luca said her name when she'd finally reached her door, when she had her hand out to grab the handle and was *this close*—

And Kathryn didn't want this. She didn't want whatever cutting, eviscerating, gut punch of a thing he was about to say. Whatever new and inventive way he'd come up with to call her a whore and make her feel like one.

But she wanted him to know how fragile she was even less, so she turned around and faced him.

He stood much too close, his dark eyes glittering, an expression she couldn't place on his beautiful face. She wished he wasn't so gorgeous, that he didn't make her ache. She imagined that might make it easier— might make that tugging thing near her heart dissipate more quickly.

She should say something; she knew she should. But she couldn't seem to make her mouth work.

"Where are you going, *cucciola mia*?" he asked softly.

She hated him, she told herself. The only thing worse

than his insults was this. That softness she couldn't understand at all.

"I don't know what that means. I don't speak any Italian."

His mouth moved into that curve again, and his dark eyes were much too intense. He reached over and tucked a strand of her hair behind her ear, and Kathryn knew he could feel the way that made her shudder. And her breath catch.

"I suppose it means *my pet*, more or less," Luca said, as if he hadn't considered it until that moment.

And the true betrayal was the warmth that spread through her at that, as if it was that laugh of his, bottled up, pure liquid sunshine starting deep inside her. Because he was dangerous enough when he was hateful. Kathryn thought that this other side of him—what she might have called *affectionate* had they been other people—might actually kill her.

Her throat felt swollen. Scratchy. Because of the noises she'd made in that car that she couldn't let herself think about? Or because of that brand-new rawness lodged inside her now? She didn't know. But she forced herself to speak anyway. "I don't want to be your pet."

That curve of his mouth deepened. "I don't know that it's up to you."

Kathryn felt restless. Edgy. As if she might burst. Or scream. Or simply crumple to the ground—and he seemed perfectly content to stand there forever, seeing things in her face she was quite certain she'd prefer to hide.

She scowled at him. "I don't know what you want from me."

This time, when he reached out, he took her shoulders in his hands and tugged her into his arms, and when he wrapped his arms around her, she melted. God help her, but she simply…fell into him. All that heat and strength, enveloping her like some kind of benediction.

"Come," he said quietly, letting her go. "I'll show you."

Kathryn knew what she needed to do. What her mother would expect her to do. One slip was bad enough. One terrible mistake. There was still time to save herself. There was still the possibility that she could call tonight a lost battle and go on to win the war, surely. She needed only to pull away from him, step inside her room and lock him out, so she could set about the Herculean task of putting herself back together.

But she couldn't make herself do it.

And when Luca opened the door to his bedroom and held out his hand as if he knew exactly what battles she was fighting and, more than that, how to win them, Kathryn ignored the great riot and tumult that shook inside her, and took it.

Luca didn't know how to make sense of any of this.

And that lost look in her too-dark gray eyes, something too close to broken, was too much for him. He had a thousand questions he didn't ask. A thousand more stacked behind them. He had the sense that there was something lying in wait for him, just over his shoulder or perhaps deep inside him, that he didn't care to examine.

Not tonight, when he'd discovered that she was precisely as innocent as she'd sometimes appeared.

It didn't matter how or why. Even the subject of her marriage to his father could wait.

What mattered—what beat in him like a darkening pulse that only got louder and more insistent with every breath—was that whatever else happened, whatever games she played or was playing even now, whatever the hell was going on here in all this California moonlight, she was his.

His.

Luca didn't wish to question himself on that. On why that surge of sheer possession seared through him, as if she'd branded him somehow with the unexpected gift of her innocence. He only knew that she was his. Only his.

And Luca wasn't done with her. Not even close.

She put her hand in his and let him lead her into his rooms, and there was no particular reason that should feel like trumpets blaring, drums pounding, a whole damned parade. But it did.

It should horrify him, he knew, that he had so little control where this woman was concerned—but tonight he couldn't bring himself to care.

He took his time.

He stood her at the foot of the great platform bed and undressed her slowly, not letting her help. He slid her shoes from her feet. He found the hidden side zipper on the bodice of her dress and eased it down, then tugged the whole of it up and over her head. He unhooked the bra she wore and pulled it from her arms, letting it fall to the floor with the rest.

When she stood before him in nothing but those panties he'd shoved out of his way in the car and that uncertain look on her face that he thought might kill him, Luca took a moment to ease his fingers through her hair. He pulled out what remained of that upswept knot she'd worn to dinner. He stroked his hands through the thick, straight strands, comforting them both.

And only when she let out a long breath he didn't think she knew she'd been holding did he finish undressing her, easing her panties down over her hips and then over the length of her perfectly formed legs.

Luca let himself look at her for a long time, indulging that possessive streak he'd never known he had. Because he'd never felt anything like it before tonight. He shrugged out of his jacket and kicked off his shoes. Still he gazed at her, letting her exquisite beauty imprint itself deep inside him. Every part of her was lovely, so astonishingly perfect that something moved in him at the sight, equal parts need and alarm.

He swept her up into his arms, enjoying the tiny noise she made, and then he carried her into the bathroom suite. He set her down next to the tub and ran the water, tossing in a handful of bath salts as it began to fill.

"Are we taking a bath?" Her voice cracked and she flushed, and Luca understood that this was a Kathryn he'd never seen before, this unsteady, uncertain creature who suddenly seemed much younger and far more breakable to him.

Or this has always been Kathryn, a voice in him suggested, more sharply than was strictly comfortable. *And you have been nothing but an ass*.

He shoved that aside, ruthlessly. There would be time enough to address the great mess of things that waited for him with the dawn.

Tonight was about this. Tonight was about her.

Instead of answering her, he stripped, watching her color rise the more he revealed. He was fascinated. Mesmerized by that spread of color, from her cheeks down her neck, to turn even her chest a pale pink, a shade or two lighter than the rose of her upturned nipples.

He wanted to feast on her. All of her.

When they were both naked he urged her into the hot water, settling her in front of him and between his legs with her back to him. He took the heavy mass of her thick dark hair in his hands and carefully made a new knot of it, high on the top of her head, and then wrapped his arms around her and held her there against him.

He didn't let himself think about anything. Just the sheer perfection of her body against his. The silken slide of the salted water, making her skin a smooth caress against his. He waited as she relaxed in increments against him, as she softened and, eventually, sighed. And only then did he begin to wash her.

He took his time. He touched her everywhere. He put his hands on every inch of her skin, saving that slippery heat between her legs for last, and a hard sort of satisfaction gripped him when she let out a hungry little moan at his touch.

Only when he'd made sure she was utterly boneless did he finish, standing her up and toweling her off, then carrying her back into the bedroom to put her in his bed at last. Her gaze never left him, wide and nearly green, and he'd learned her tonight. He knew what that faint quiver in her body meant. How she flushed when he crawled over her, a bright red on top of the pink she'd turned in the heat of the bath.

And when he was fully stretched out above her, skin to skin, he learned her all over again.

With his hands, his mouth. His tongue and his teeth.

He explored her. She'd given him something he could

hardly get his head around, could barely understand, and this was how he expressed his gratitude. His wonder. All those tangled things inside him that he knew better than to look at too closely. He worked them out against her lovely body, inch by perfect inch.

She arched up beneath him and he feasted on her breasts. She rocked against him and he held her down, tracing every muscle and every smooth curve, making her his. Making every last part of her inarguably his.

And this time, when he surged inside her, she was soft and shaking and ready for him.

She cried out his name.

Luca set a more demanding pace, gathering her beneath him, lost in the sleek glory of her hips against his. He built her up high. He made her sob. And then he threw her straight off that cliff and into bliss.

Once, then again.

And only then, when she was shattered twice over, her eyes slate green and filled with him and nothing else, did he follow her over that edge.

CHAPTER NINE

IT WAS NOT until the following morning—after Luca had woken up to discover that none of the previous night had been one of the remarkably detailed dreams he'd had about Kathryn over the past couple of years, because she was still there, sprawled out beside him and wholly irresistible—that he allowed himself to think about what the inescapable fact of her innocence meant.

First, he'd rolled over, instantly awake and aware and as hard for her as if he'd never had her. She'd come awake a moment later, and he'd watched her eyes go from sleepy to pleased to wary in the course of a few blinks.

He'd found he hadn't cared much for *wary*.

So he'd pinned her hands above her head and settled himself between her thighs. He'd expressed his feelings on her tender breasts until she'd been gasping and arching beneath him, and then he'd driven himself home once again, losing himself in all her molten sweetness.

And he'd found the sound of her gasping his name as she convulsed around him far, far preferable to any wariness.

He managed to control himself in the shower they shared—but barely—and maybe the fact that doing so was so much harder than it should have been kicked his brain back into gear.

Kathryn was dressing, her head bent and a certain set expression on her face that he didn't like. He stood in the doorway to the bathroom with only a towel wrapped around his hips and watched her, aware that he should not be feeling any of the things that stampeded through him then. He knew that expression she wore. He usually liked it when the women he bedded showed him that particular blankness, because it meant they planned to walk away from him with no fuss. And quickly.

He didn't want her to walk away.

He wanted her right here, and he didn't care how crazy that was. How insane this entire situation was. That no one but him—that no one, *especially* him—would ever believe that *Saint Kate* had been a virgin until now.

"Kathryn." She didn't precisely jolt when she heard her name, but that wariness was back in her gaze when she lifted it to his. "Why did you marry him?"

She pressed her lips together in that way of hers that he should not find so fascinating. She tugged her bra into place and then bent to pick up her crumpled dress, frowning at it in a way that made something in the vicinity of his heart clench. Luca didn't speak. He swept up his own discarded shirt and prowled over to her, watching the way her eyes widened as he approached. Her lips parted slightly, as if she needed more air, and he couldn't pretend he didn't like that.

He liked entirely too much. Her lush little body, packaged in that lacy bra and matching panties that highlighted parts of her he could never obsess about *enough*. The faint marks from his mouth, his unshaven jaw. He was a primitive creature, he understood then, though he'd never thought of himself in those terms before. When it came to Kathryn, he was nothing short of a beast.

Luca liked his mark on her. He liked it hard and deep, so much it very nearly hurt.

He settled his dress shirt around her shoulders, then tugged her arms through. And then he took his time buttoning it up, fashioning her a dress that was much too big for her frame, but was in its way another mark. Another brand.

The beast within him roared its approval.

"Are you going to answer me?" he asked in a low voice as he rolled up one cuff, then the other, to keep the sleeves from hanging nearly to her knees.

She swallowed, and he saw that her eyes had changed color again, to that slate green that meant she was aroused. *Good*, he thought. He didn't imagine he'd ever be anything but aroused in her presence again. He wasn't sure he ever had been anything else, come to that.

But she blinked it away and took in a shuddering sort of breath.

"He said he could help," she said.

She moved away from him, and the sight of her in his shirt did things to Luca that he couldn't explain. He didn't want to explain them. They simply settled inside him, like light.

"Why did you need help?"

Kathryn worried her lower lip with her teeth, which he felt like her mouth against his sex, but he held himself in check.

"My mother was single when she had me," she said, and Luca blinked. He didn't know what he'd expected, but it wasn't that. Something so…mundane. "She'd never expected or even wanted to have a baby at all, but there she was, pregnant. Her partner made it clear he couldn't be bothered, and in case she'd any doubts about that, moved out of the country straightaway, so no one could expect him to contribute in any way to the life of a child he didn't want."

"He sounds charming."

Kathryn smiled, very slightly. "I wouldn't know. We've never met."

Luca watched as she moved to the bed and climbed onto the mattress, settling herself near the foot with her legs crossed beneath her and his shirt billowing around her slender form. It only made her look that much more fragile.

And made him want to protect her, somehow—even against this story she was telling him.

"My mother had huge dreams," she said after a moment. "She'd worked so hard to get where she was. She wanted a whole, rich life, and what she got instead was a daughter to raise right when she really could have made something of herself."

Something in the way she said that scraped at him. Luca frowned. "Surely raising a child is merely a different rich life. Not the lack of one altogether."

Kathryn's gaze met his for a moment then dropped.

"She'd worked so hard to succeed in finance, but couldn't keep up with the hours required once she had me. And once she left the job she loved, at an investment bank, she couldn't afford child care, so she had to manage it all on her own." She threaded her hands together in front of her. "All of my memories of her were of her working. She usually had more than one job, in fact, so I wouldn't want for anything. She wasn't too proud to do the things others refused to do. She cleaned houses on her hands and knees, anything to make my life better, and despite all of that, I was a terrible disappointment."

Luca had the sense that if he disputed this story, if he questioned it at all—and he couldn't understand why there was that thing in him that insisted this was a story that needed disputing when until hours ago he'd been Kathryn's biggest critic—she would stop talking. It was something in the set of her mouth, the line of her jaw. The stormy gray color of her eyes. So he said nothing. He merely exchanged his towel for a pair of exercise trousers and then crossed his arms over his chest. He waited.

Kathryn let out a breath that was more like a sigh.

"She wanted me to be an investment banker, too. That was always her preference, because she could teach me everything I needed to know and because her experience meant she could direct me."

"I believe that is called living through one's child. Not the best form of parenting, I think."

She frowned at him. "Not in this case. I could never get my head around the math. My mother tried to tutor me herself, but it was a waste of time. I can't think the way she can. My brain simply won't work the way hers does."

"My brain does not work the way my brother's does," Luca pointed out mildly, "and yet we've muddled along, running a rather successful company together for some time."

"That's different." Kathryn lifted a shoulder then dropped it. "I nearly killed myself getting a First in economics. I spent hours and hours torturing myself with the coursework. But I did it. Then I went on to an MBA course because that was what my mother thought was the best path toward the brightest future." She blew out a breath that made her fringe dance above her brow. "But the MBA was beyond torture. I was used to putting the hours in, but it wasn't enough. No matter what I did, it wasn't enough."

She shook her head, frowning down at her hands, and Luca had never wanted to touch another person more than he did then. She looked too small and something like defeated, and it lodged in his chest like a bullet.

It occurred to him that he'd never seen her look like this. That she'd fought him every step of the way, if sometimes only with a straight spine and a head held high. But *defeat* was not a word he'd ever associated with her before.

He found he hated it.

Kathryn met his gaze again then. "And that was when I met your father."

He shifted position and realized he was holding himself back as much as anything else. As if he didn't know what he might do if he stopped—as if he still had that little control, when it still involved Kathryn yet wasn't about sex. He couldn't say he much enjoyed the sensation.

But one great mess at a time, he thought darkly.

"Ah, yes," he said. "In that mythic waiting room, the birthplace of your epic friendship. The only friendship the old man ever had, as far as I am aware."

"You asked me to tell you this story," she pointed out. "You keep asking."

Luca couldn't trust himself to speak, one more novel

experience where this woman was concerned—and one he knew he would have to think about later. He inclined his head, silently bidding her to continue.

"It happened just as I told you," Kathryn said, her gaze reproving. "We started talking. Your father was charming. Funny."

Luca snorted. "Old."

"Maybe everyone is not as ageist as you are," she snapped at him.

He raked his hand through his hair then, annoyed and frustrated in equal measure.

"It is time for the truth, *cucciola mia*," he said then, roughly.

He moved before he knew he meant to, crossing over to place himself directly in front of her, at the foot of the high bed. She tilted up that chin of hers, as if she expected him to take a swing, and Luca was obviously deeply perverse, that such a thing should excite him. Or maybe it was simply that he liked it when she fought. When she stood up for herself, even against him. When she was nothing remotely like *defeated*.

"I'm telling you the truth. I can't help it if it's not the truth you want to hear." She eyed him, as if his proximity bothered her. Luca hoped it did. It would make them even. "I think we've already established that you have a history of believing what you want to believe, no matter what the actual truth might be."

He felt his mouth curve in acknowledgment. "But this is not a question of innocence. This is a question of how a young woman meets a much older man in a medical facility, so she could have no fantasy that there was anything virile about him at all, and decides to marry him anyway. I have no doubt that he proposed to you. That was what he did, always. But what made you agree?"

Kathryn held his gaze, and Luca didn't move. He didn't even blink, aware somehow that she was making a momentous decision. And he needed it to be the right one. *He needed it*—and he wasn't sure he wanted to investigate why that need was so intense. After a long while, she let out a sigh.

"My mother has crippling arthritis," Kathryn explained. "When it flares up she can hardly move. It had become very difficult for her to take care of herself." She shook her head, more as if she was shaking off a wave of emotion than negating anything. "I should have been there to help her, but between the classes for my degree and all the studying I had to do to barely keep up, I couldn't even do that well. I lived with her, which was one thing, but it was all beginning to feel a lot like drowning." She sucked in a breath. "But when my mother came out of her appointment, she recognized your father at a glance. One thing led to another, and we all went out for a meal."

Luca waited.

"Your father is very easy to talk to, actually."

"That was not a common sentiment."

"My mother told him everything. My struggles with my degree. Her battle with her arthritis. He was very kind." Her gray eyes grew distant, and he thought she tipped her chin up that much farther. "And at the end of the evening, he asked if he could see me—just me—again."

"This is where I think I need some clarification," Luca murmured. "Did you date a great deal?"

"I didn't date at all," she retorted, and he almost didn't

recognize that fierce thing that soared in him at that, possessiveness mixed with a kind of triumph.

"But you dated my father."

For the first time she looked uncomfortable. "I didn't necessarily want to *date* him," she said softly. "But he'd been so nice, and so sweet, and I didn't see the harm in having another dinner with him. I thought I was doing a good deed."

"What did your mother think?"

She didn't quite flinch. But he saw the tiny, abortive movement she made, and his eyes narrowed.

"She's always worried that I had more looks than sense," Kathryn said quietly. "Which I'm afraid I proved to her through my failures with my studies."

"A first-class degree is, by definition, not any kind of failure."

"I had to work ten times as hard as she did, and I still only did it by my teeth," she said with a dismissive wave of one hand. "But when we met your father, it seemed a perfect opportunity to stop worrying about the brains part and let the looks do some good for a change."

"What," Luca asked through his teeth, "does that mean?"

"It meant we both knew he liked the look of me," Kathryn said, with an edge to her voice. She sat up straighter on the bed. "And he was just as funny and kind and charming when I went out with him alone. Still, when he asked me to marry him on the third date, I laughed."

Her gaze had gone fierce. Protective, Luca thought.

"He told me that he knew he was a foolish old man, vain and silly, to think a young girl like me would want to shackle herself to a man like him. He knew he didn't have much time left. He assured me that all he wanted was companionship, because he didn't have any of the rest of it in him any longer. He told me I was the most beautiful thing he'd seen in years, and he couldn't think of a better way to go than to have me holding his hand."

"He flattered you."

"He *needed* me," she snapped. "He was old and scared and lonely. He told me that he had sons he wasn't close to and no particular reason to imagine that might change. He didn't want to die alone, Luca. I didn't think that made him a monster."

He felt as if he was nailed to the floor beneath him. As if he'd turned to stone.

"And this is why you married him? Out of pity? Out of the goodness of your heart? To save an old man from loneliness? You are a saint, indeed." Her breath hissed from her mouth. Luca kept going. "But he was a very wealthy man, Kathryn, and he did not traffic much in saints or pity. He didn't have to. He could have bought himself a fleet of nurses to keep him company, if company was what he wanted in his final days. So I'll ask you again. Why did he buy you?"

"He didn't buy me, Luca," she threw at him, sounding as furious as she did vulnerable. "He saved me."

Kathryn wanted to snatch the words back the moment she said them.

They hung there in the air between them, the glare of them enough to cast the rest of the room and even Luca in shadow.

She didn't know what she expected him to do, but it wasn't to simply stand there and gaze back at her, with all of his intensity focused hard on her, in a way she understood differently today.

The truth was, she understood a whole lot of things differently today.

Her own body. His body. The things he could *do* with both. What that look in his dark eyes meant—and more, what it had always meant, all these years, though she hadn't had a clue. Where it had always been leading them, this mad thing between them that not even the night they'd spent together had eased at all.

But she'd never said that out loud before, that little truth about her marriage. She wasn't entirely sure why she had now.

"Go on, then," Luca rumbled at her when it seemed whole ages had passed. When she'd died a thousand deaths, each one of them more disloyal than the last. "Explain that to me."

He stood there like some kind of ancient god of judgment, sculpted and remote, with his arms crossed and that mouth of his in a stern line. And it didn't seem to matter that he'd had that mouth on parts of her body she'd had no idea could be that sensitive. That he knew her now in a way no one else ever had. That he was the only person on the earth who had ever been *inside* her. It all made her dizzy.

And it didn't change the fact that he stared down at her as if he was hewn from rock. Or that compulsion she didn't understand that worked inside her, that wanted to give him anything he asked for, anything at all.

Anything. Even this.

"My mother was thrilled," she said, her voice scratchy, as if her own surrender choked her on its way down. "She got a cottage and her own live-in nurses out of the deal, so she never needs to work again."

Her mother had been something a bit more complicated than simply *thrilled*, Kathryn thought, though she didn't know how to explain that to this man. She didn't quite know how to think about it herself. All these years later.

"Being the wife of a man like Gianni Castelli is a full-time job," Rose had said imperiously, sitting at the kitchen table in their grotty old flat with the real-estate listings spread out before her. She'd had no doubt that Kathryn would accept Gianni's proposal. It hadn't even been a discussion. "It will require study and application, of course, should you want to make it into a career."

"A career?" Kathryn hadn't understood. "He's not well, Mum. He's not likely to last five years."

"You need to view this as an internship, my girl. A stepping stone to bigger and better things." Rose had eyed her up and down then shaken her head. "You're pretty enough, there's no denying it. And while you haven't proved to be as smart as we hoped, I'd imagine you can succeed in *this* arena anyway. The only figure you'll need to know is the size of your allowance."

"Mum," she'd said then, uncertainly. "I'm just not sure…"

"You listen to me, Kathryn," Rose had said, and she hadn't raised her voice. She hadn't needed to raise her voice, not when she used that withering tone. "I sacrificed everything for you. I worked myself into this state. And what would we have done if Gianni Castelli hadn't happened along and gone ass over teakettle for that face of yours? You need to capitalize on that." She'd sniffed. "For my sake, if nothing else. The truth is you've proved yourself unequal to the task of a career in finance. How will we pay the bills without this marriage?"

"But…" She'd felt all the usual things she always had when Rose spoke like this. Shame. Guilt. Despair that she was so deficient. Anguish that she couldn't live up to her mother's expectations. And that sliver of something else, something stubborn and forlorn, that didn't quite understand why nothing she did, no matter how hard she worked, was ever good enough. "It isn't *we*, Mum. It's me. I have to marry a man I don't love—"

"You must be having a laugh." Though the look on Rose's face had indicated there was precious little to laugh about. "Love? This isn't a fairy story, Kathryn. This is about duty and responsibility." She'd brandished her hands in the air, her gnarled and swollen knuckles. "Look at what I did to myself to do right by you. Look at how I ruined myself and threw away everything that ever mattered to me. It's between you and your conscience how you want to repay me."

And put that way, Kathryn hadn't had a choice.

"It sounds as if your mother got the better part of the bargain," Luca said quietly, snapping her back into the present.

"She got what she deserved after all she did for me," Kathryn said stoutly. "And I certainly couldn't give it to her. Thanks to your father, she can live out the rest of her days in peace. She's earned that."

There was a certain tightness to Luca's expression that suggested he didn't agree, and she tensed, instantly on the defensive, but he didn't pursue it. He cocked his head slightly to one side.

"And what did you earn?" he asked. "How did saving your mother save you?"

"I got to quit my MBA course," she said in a rush, and she felt the heat of that admission wash over her like some kind of flu. "I walked away and I never had to go back, and it didn't matter that we were out of the tuition money. The whole slate was wiped clean. All that struggle, all those years of never living up to expectations, gone in an instant and forgiven completely, simply because your father wanted to marry me."

And maybe, just maybe, she'd enjoyed a little holiday from her subservience to her mother's wishes. Maybe she'd liked having someone treat her like some kind of prize for a change.

"Kathryn," Luca said, his voice so gentle it made her shiver, "you must know—"

But she didn't want to hear whatever it was he was going to say. She didn't want whatever devastation that was lurking there in his dark eyes, lit now with something very much like compassion.

She lurched forward instead, coming up on her knees before him and throwing out her hands to catch herself against the wall of his chest. He didn't so much as rock on his feet with the impact. He simply studied her.

"Listen to me," Kathryn said, aware that she sounded desperate. "You can think whatever you like about your father's intentions. But to me, he was a dream come true. You don't have to like that," she said hurriedly when the edges of his mouth turned down, "but it's the truth. It's a fact."

And she was so close to him then. Touching him again. Her palms were propped against the sculpted perfection of his pectoral muscles, and that delirious heat of his poured into her, making her flush all over again.

But this fever she recognized.

Kathryn didn't want to talk about her marriage. She didn't want to talk about their complicated families. She didn't know what that dark thing was that lurked there in the way he was looking at her then, and she didn't want to know.

She did the only thing she knew to do. The only thing that made sense.

She tipped herself forward and pressed her mouth to his.

And it felt artless and silly, nothing like the way he'd kissed her—and for a shuddering moment that felt like forever he merely stood there, as if he was stunned—but then he moved. He took the back of her head in his palm and he opened his mouth, driving into hers and taking complete and delicious control.

He kissed her and he kissed her. He kissed her until she was wound around him, pressing herself against him, desperate and wild—because now she knew. Now she knew what else there was. Where else they could go.

All the magical things he could do.

But Luca pulled away, still curving that big hand of his over the back of her head, his dark eyes glittering.

"Did you do that to distract me?" he asked, his voice gruff. His breath not entirely steady—which made a whole different fire ignite within her.

"Yes," she said. Her mouth felt swollen again. And even though she wore his shirt and it covered more of her than some of her own clothes, she felt stripped bare. Naked and vulnerable and wide-open to him in every way.

"Is that the only reason?" If possible, his voice was even rougher.

Kathryn shifted on her knees. She slid her hands up,

over his jaw, holding his face between her palms, the way he'd done before to her. And she was so close that she could feel that shake in him, low and deep. So close she could feel that he was unsteady, too.

It made her feel as if she was made of light. As if she was filled with power.

"You might have noticed that I like kissing you, Luca," she said, and her voice was solemn. Because somehow everything between them had shifted, and there was something much too serious in his eyes. "You're my first."

"Your first in bed."

She waited, still holding him. She saw the exact moment he understood. The very second it crashed through him, leaving him stunned. And then something far darker, hungrier and indescribably male, lit him up. It made his dark eyes gleam. It made him tighten his grip.

"Cucciola mia," he murmured, his mouth against her lips, "we might kill each other."

And then he bore her back down to the bed and showed her exactly what he meant.

CHAPTER TEN

A WEEK LATER they concluded their business in California and flew back to Italy with Rafael, Lily and a private nurse for Lily and her unborn baby in tow.

Luca could have done without the crowd.

It had been a week of abject torture, having claimed Kathryn in private yet having to act as if nothing had changed between them in public. That she was the assistant he hadn't wanted, and he the Castelli who had always hated her the most. Luca had found that his much-vaunted control had deserted him almost entirely, making him uneasy about where this madness was leading him—but he couldn't stop.

Any moment of privacy they had, he exulted in her. Cars. Alcoves. Out walking the property. He kept waiting for this grip she had on him to ease, for the wildfire only she had ever stirred in him like this to abate—but it still hadn't. If anything, it grew stronger. Every day brighter and hotter than the day before.

It would be different once they were back in Rome, he told himself. There would be no sneaking around to avoid his brother, or at least, far less of that kind of thing. With no element of the forbidden, he was certain the hunger would ease. It always did. He was not the kind of man who formed attachments, and he knew better to want things he couldn't have. He'd learned that as a child, and he'd never forgotten it.

In truth, it had never been an issue before.

But first they had to make it to Rome, and separate themselves from his brother and Lily, who would be flying on to the family seat in the Dolomites. Several hours into their nighttime flight, only Rafael and Luca remained awake in the lounge area of the jet, the others having long since headed to the jet's stately guest rooms.

Rafael was talking about their next steps as a company and how best to capitalize on the goodwill they'd sown about the accounts in the wake of the annual ball. Luca, meanwhile, had spent longer than he cared to admit imagining Kathryn spread out against the pillows just down the plane's narrow hall, her long dark hair—

"Kathryn," Rafael said, intoning her name as if he could read Luca's dirty mind.

Luca eyed his brother across the width of the lounge and maintained his infinitely lazy position, stretched out on one of the couches like some kind of *dauphin*.

"Yes," he said. "Kathryn. My personal assistant, in fulfillment of our beloved patriarch's will. I haven't complained, have I?"

"You have not," his brother agreed. He looked so stern and austere as he sat there, his bearing far more dignified than Luca's had ever been. "That is what concerns me."

Luca forced a laugh he didn't feel. "I am nothing if not adaptable. And obedient."

"But that is the point." Rafael raised his brows. "You are neither one of those things, despite the great joy it gives you to pretend otherwise."

"You are mistaken, brother. I am nothing but a jumped-up playboy with excellent staff, all of whom are well paid to cover for my incompetence. The tabloids have decreed it, therefore it must be true."

Rafael said nothing for a moment that dragged on too long. Luca found himself clenching his jaw and forced himself to stop.

"I expected you to run her off within the week."

Luca shrugged. "She proved somewhat more tenacious than anticipated."

Rafael considered him. "She was also a surprising asset these past two weeks. The accounts adored her. I suspect half of them raced to the tabloids to submit their own *Saint Kate* stories within hours of meeting her." He stretched his legs out before him. "Needless to say, this has put a rather positive spin on things. I had more business associates than I can count commend me— us—on our magnanimity in hiring her. She might as well be the mascot of the company."

Luca didn't remember moving, but there he was, sitting up and glaring at his older brother.

"This is a temporary situation," he said, his voice clipped. "We agreed on that."

"Maybe we should reconsider." Rafael shrugged when Luca continued to glare at him. "If using Saint Kate boosts our profile, I don't see why we *wouldn't* use her as long as possible."

"Perhaps," Luca said coolly, "the lady no longer wishes to be used. It's possible she had her fill of it during her commercial transaction of a marriage. Maybe all she wants to do is her job."

That was, of course, a huge mistake. He knew it the moment he spoke without thinking—as it was the first time he could remember doing so to a family member since he was a child.

Rafael blinked. "I don't care what she wants, as long as it benefits the company," he said in a low voice.

"The company," Luca muttered, again without thinking. Almost as if he couldn't control himself at all. "Always the company."

He didn't much care for the way his brother looked at him then.

"Have our objectives changed without my knowledge, Luca?" Rafael let that sit there for a moment, and the expression on his face was far too shrewd for Luca's peace of mind. "Have yours?"

It was not until she was safely barricaded in her little Italian flat that Kathryn really breathed.

And moments after that first, deep, full-bodied breath, she simply sank down on the soft carpet in her cozy lounge, as if the knees that had somehow carried her all the way through her trip to California and the long flight back were no longer up to the task. As if everything that had happened in the past two weeks finally caught up with her.

With a wallop.

She found herself looking around her flat, the morning light streaming in from the high windows that had sold her on the place, as if she'd never seen it before. It was hard to imagine the person she'd been when she'd left here. The person she'd left behind her in Sonoma somewhere.

How could her whole world change so quickly?

Her marriage to Gianni had been a change, certainly, but it had been a change of circumstances, not of who she was inside. She had merely swapped one set of duties and obligations for another, and the truth was, she'd found caring for Gianni infinitely more pleasant than statistics. Or tending to her difficult mother, if she was brutally honest with herself.

This was different. *She* was different.

And she had no idea if she needed to set about putting herself back together somehow, or if she needed to figure out a way to simply accept who she'd become. Whoever the hell that was.

Kathryn breathed in, deep. Then out again. She did it a few more times, and then she climbed back to her feet and decided that a cup of tea was all the answer she needed just now. Everything else would wait.

She was just finishing that same cup, sitting out on her small balcony with her view over the red-tipped Roman rooftops that made her heart sing a little in her chest, when she heard the banging on her front door.

Luca, she thought at once. Because who else could it be?

And the fact that her heart echoed that pounding told her more than she needed to know about those feelings that the tea hadn't suppressed at all.

She considered not answering it—but dismissed that thought in an instant. This was Luca. It wasn't as if he'd simply shrug and wander off.

Kathryn padded to the door in her bare feet and swung it open, not at all surprised to find him braced there against the doorjamb, one arm over his head and a scowl on his face.

"Where did you go?" he demanded.

"Home," she replied. "Obviously."

He ignored that. "Why did you race off like that? I looked around and you'd disappeared."

She didn't want to let him inside her flat, and she couldn't have said why. She crossed her arms over her chest and stood in the doorway instead.

"I came home," she said, very distinctly. "You told me I didn't have to go into work today. Has something changed?"

Something ignited in those dark eyes of his, and he pushed himself off the doorjamb. Technically, he'd moved back, and yet he still seemed to fill the doorway. The narrow hallway behind him. The whole of her flat he hadn't even entered.

"What do you think is happening here, Kathryn?" he asked softly.

She refused to show him her uncertainty. That had been situational, she assured herself. She'd lost her virginity to this man, and he was a very demanding, very detail-oriented lover. Anyone would have trouble finding her footing after that kind of combination.

But she was standing just fine now.

"What's happening is that after a long, two-week business trip, my boss is standing at my door," she said crisply. "If you don't have an assignment for me, I think you should leave."

She expected his temper, braced herself for it. Luca looked astounded for a beat, but then, impossibly, he laughed. And it was that same delighted, beautiful laugh of his that rivaled the Italian scenery itself and did far worse things to her poor heart. It made her scowl at him, so determined was she to ward him off. To keep that laughter from sinking in deep beneath her skin.

But it was like fighting off sunlight. No matter what she wanted, no matter what she did, it filled her.

"Come here, *cucciola mia*," he said when the laughter faded away.

He crooked his finger at her, and she wanted to bite him. He was a foot away at most. He was already too close.

"I'm right here," she told him. "I don't need to come any closer, and I'm not your pet."

"That's where you're wrong," he said in that dark voice of his that made need roll through her like a terrible thirst. "Come, Kathryn. Put that mouth on me. It will feel much better than using it as a battering ram when I can see you don't mean it."

"I do."

"You do not," he corrected her. He moved toward her then, advancing on her with that intense gleam in his dark gaze that she knew now was hunger. And the remains of that laughter that made him seem even more beautiful than he already was. "You're afraid."

"I most certainly am not," she said, but then she couldn't move any farther.

He'd backed her up into her flat and straight into the wall of the small foyer, and she hadn't even noticed. She swallowed, hard.

"I'm not afraid," she told him, very distinctly. "But I need some time to clear my head."

"Why?"

"I don't have to justify how I spend my free time to you."

"You don't. But you could spend it beneath me, driving us both insane with the way you move those hips of yours. You can see why I'd agitate for that option."

Her jaw worked, but no words came out. Luca grinned.

"We can't just…have sex all the time," she protested, but even she could hear that her voice was weak. Reedy.

This time that marvelous laughter stayed in his eyes, making them gleam gold and shiver straight through her.

"Why ever not?"

"Sex is a weakness," she told him, very seriously, the words coming from some part of her she hadn't known was there. "A weapon."

"That sounds like the ravings of someone who isn't very good at it, *cucciola mia*, and therefore doesn't enjoy it," he said with another laugh, obviously unaware that he'd just dismissed one of her mother's favorite sayings so easily. "A description that does not fit you at all."

She didn't know what expression she wore then, but his hard face softened, and he pulled her against him as if she was a fragile little thing, made of spun glass. He smoothed her hair back from her face, as she'd already discovered he loved to do. And when he gazed down at her there was something so bright in his eyes that it made her shake.

And her heart broke open inside her, telling her things she didn't want to accept. Making her feel things she'd never thought she'd feel for anyone, and certainly not for him. But she might have been a virgin before she'd met Luca, and she might have been completely untouched until he'd handled that, too, but she wasn't an idiot.

Only an idiot would tell Luca Castelli she was falling in love with him, she scolded herself. *He doesn't want to know.*

"I can't think around you," she whispered, though she knew she shouldn't. That it was far too close to a truth even she wanted to pretend wasn't real. "Sex only makes it worse."

She felt his chest move against her as if he was laughing, though he didn't make a sound. Slowly, slowly, his perfect mouth curved.

"I know," he said, and he ran his hands down the length of her spine, then over the curves of her bottom, pulling her flush against him. "Sex makes everything terrible."

He was hot and hard against her belly, and she thought he knew the precise moment when she simply... melted. Kathryn thought he always knew.

Luca smiled then. "But then it makes it much, much better."

And when he set about proving it, Kathryn surrendered.

Because she wanted him more than she wanted to resist him.

And she thought he knew that, too.

Some ten days after their return from California, Luca paused at his office door after finishing a round of calls to the States and frowned. It was late in the evening, and his staff had long since departed for the day—all except Kathryn.

She sat at her desk in the open space outside his office, where she was meant to act as his guard and first line of support, furiously typing—which didn't make any sense. He hadn't given her any work that needed finishing at this hour.

"You should have left hours ago," he said, and the beast that still paced inside him when it came to her growled in approval when she jolted at the sound of his voice, then melted into a smile. "Didn't I mention something about swimming naked beneath the stars? That happens upstairs, Kathryn. Away from the computer."

"I have to finish this," she said, her fingers flying over the keys. "Then we can stargaze all you like."

"It's the naked part that interests me, *cucciola mia*. The stars are a ploy. You may not have noticed this, but we're in the middle of the city."

She wrinkled her nose at him, which he found tugged at him in ways that he wasn't entirely comfortable exploring, but she typed on. He moved to stand behind her, smoothing his hands over her shoulders and tugging gently on the end of her fashionably sleek ponytail. She sighed happily enough, but she didn't stop, and he read over her shoulder.

And this time, he scowled. "This is Marco's report. He told me he'd have it in to me tomorrow morning."

"And so he will," Kathryn said, her voice even. "Just as soon as I finish it."

Luca pulled her chair back from the desk, forcing her to stop, then swiveled it around so he could look her in the eyes. Hers were gray and far too calm when they met his.

"You are not Marco's assistant," he told her, perhaps more harshly than necessary. "You are mine."

Kathryn was far more than that, though Luca knew he didn't have the words to tell her that. She was that pounding in his heart. She was that heat that never left him. And all of that was wrapped up in those cool gray eyes, that serene little smile, the entire package that was Kathryn. *His*.

"Perhaps you're unaware that it's part of your assistant's job to pretty up all the reports that make it to your desk," Kathryn said mildly.

"It is not."

"How strange," she murmured. "I have been assured by no less than six different members of the team that it is."

Of course she'd been told that—and who knew what else? He'd essentially declared open season on her when he'd brought her on board. How had he managed to forget that? But of course, he knew how. Because all he thought about was getting his hands on her—and she never, ever complained. She smiled instead.

He shoved his hair back with an impatient hand. "I will speak to them."

"No," she countered, "you will not."

"They cannot continue to abuse you in this fashion."

She leaned back in her chair and crossed her arms. "You can't interfere. It will work itself out."

"This is not a cause worth martyring yourself for," he told her. "I put this target on your back. I'll take it off."

"And if you do that, you might as well shoot me yourself," she said, with an edge to her voice. "I don't need you to give me special treatment. Everyone knows you were forced to hire me. You stepping in now will only make it worse."

"Kathryn—"

"I told you I'd be good at this and I am," she said, her voice low and her chin high. "My work speaks for itself. It will win over your team, and if it doesn't, doing all the work they don't want to do means I'll know their jobs as well as mine. It all only helps me."

"You don't need any help."

"I couldn't do the job I trained my whole life to do,"

she threw at him fiercely. And he knew she meant the job her mother had wanted for her. "This is my chance. I'm not going to waste it, and I'm not going to let you save me, either. I'll succeed or fail on my own."

He stared down at her, a kind of battle inside him that he didn't understand. Maybe he didn't want to understand it. Maybe what was shaking through him was so outside his experience, understanding the truth of it might break him in two.

"You let my father save you once," he said quietly.

She didn't flinch from that. She held his gaze, though he could feel the way it burned, and hers was solemn.

"And now I want to save myself," she said with soft determination. "And I want you to let me."

CHAPTER ELEVEN

ANOTHER WEEK EASED BY, then another, and Luca was forced to face the fact that his driving need for Kathryn wasn't going anywhere.

He'd spent more time with her than any other woman he'd ever been with. She worked with him. She traveled with him. She slept with him. He would have imagined that such familiarity could only breed the swiftest contempt, but Kathryn was a revelation. Daily. She fascinated him, from her cool competence in the office that even his staff had been forced to heed to her uninhibited delight in all they did together in bed.

It was too perfect. Too good. And he had learned the hard way that there was no such thing as "too good to be true." There was only paying for it.

His childhood had taught him well.

He remembered it all too vividly, the various ways he'd acted out in the vain hope of getting his father's attention. The commotion he'd caused. The precious objects he'd broken. The tantrums, the running away, the back talk. All so someone who was actually related to him would show him that they'd cared about him—but that had never happened.

And Luca was no longer an abandoned boy. He'd

long since forgiven his brother, who had handled their family situation in the best way he'd known how—and had then embroiled himself in a mad relationship with Lily. His mother had killed herself—he didn't care that the hospital had claimed it had been an accident, he'd never doubted what she'd done—rather than face the children she'd made. And Gianni had never paid the slightest attention to Luca. His heir apparent had been one thing, but Luca had merely been the forgotten spare.

He didn't know how to believe in the possibility that Kathryn could truly want him. That she'd chosen him to work with. That all of this wasn't a giant ploy.

"What reaction are you looking for?" one of his stepmothers had asked him years ago, when Luca had broken all the dishes at dinner one night. Gianni had merely exited the room, as if Luca was an animal far beneath his notice. His stepmother had remained, brittle and cold.

"I hate you," Luca had shouted at her, with all the fury in his ten-year-old heart.

"No one hates you," she'd replied, her gaze bland on his. "No one cares either way. The sooner you recognize that, the happier you'll be."

He'd never forgotten it. And he'd never begged for attention again.

Today was a lazy Sunday that hinted of spring. He breathed it in, hard. He'd woken Kathryn in his usual fashion while it was still dark, left her quivering in his bed and had gone out for a long run around his beautiful city while it was still shaking off the last of the night before. He ran through piazzas that were famed for their crowds, past famous fountains and monuments, all deserted this early in the day, as if Rome was entirely his.

He was waiting for the other shoe to drop and crush him where he stood. He told himself he expected it, so it couldn't possibly be too bad. Even if he couldn't quite imagine what that might be. He ran faster. Harder.

It was his favorite time to run, these early mornings that were all his. He usually took his time, doing lazy loops through places usually too packed to navigate. But he found that today, knowing Kathryn waited in his penthouse for his return, he ran even faster on his way back home.

She wasn't on the first level of the penthouse when he returned, as she often was, usually making coffee or putting together something to eat in his kitchen. He climbed the spiral stairs from his vast living area up to his rooftop bedroom, expecting to find her still sprawled in his bed. But that was empty, too, the duvet tossed back and the pillows still dented.

Luca peered out through the windows and saw her on the farthest part of the roof, her back to him, her eyes on the city laid out at her feet. He took a quick detour into his bathroom, showering off his run, then pulled on the pair of trousers he'd left at the foot of the bed before he went outside.

She didn't turn as he closed the great glass door behind him, or even when he skirted the pool. She stayed as she was, her back perhaps *too* straight, he thought, as he drew close.

"I hope you're not thinking of jumping," he said as he came up behind her. "I would not find that amusing at all." Kathryn didn't respond, not even when he came to stand beside her at the balustrade. She looked pale. Almost…scared, he would have said, if she'd been anyone else. If that made any sense. "Has something happened?"

She swallowed, and he saw she was hugging herself, wrapped up tight in one of the draped sweaters she preferred, as if she needed armor. Slowly, much too slowly, she turned to face him.

"I don't know how to tell you this," she said, and even her voice didn't sound like hers.

Her eyes were dark gray, the darkest he'd ever seen them. Her lovely mouth was pressed into a vulnerable line. And when Luca reached out to touch her face, she jerked away.

"I suggest you do it fast," he said, frowning, as something cold washed over him.

She looked lost for a moment. Then she seemed to collect herself.

"After you left," she said, still in that strangely disembodied voice, as if she was speaking to him from a great distance, "I was sick."

"Then, what are you doing out here?" he demanded, a protective impulse he hadn't known he possessed roaring inside him. "Come. We'll put you back in bed."

"I've had this strange stomach thing for a while now," she told him, not moving at all. "It comes and goes. I thought maybe it was anxiety." He waited. Sheer misery washed over her face, and she pressed her lips together, hard, as if she was holding back a sob. "But today something else occurred to me. So I went to the supermarket and I got a test. And I had my answer in an instant."

Luca felt as if he'd been frozen solid where he stood. He was aware of everything. The breeze with its hints of spring that danced between them and toyed with her hair. The way the old gold of the sun made the city gleam all around them. The clatter of traffic in the distance and bells ringing out on the wind.

And the thing she was about to say, that made all of this—all he'd felt and all that had happened since that night in the car in California—a lie. A scam. That other shoe he'd been expecting all this time, kicking him straight in the face. The ultimate act of a creature who had deceived him completely, snowed him utterly. Made him believe he could be a different man. Made him imagine for an instant that he could live a different life. Made him forget all the truths he knew about this one.

But he had always known better. He had never given up his control, not ever, until her. He had never begged for anyone's attention. He had never wanted a damned thing.

And this was why.

Luca thought what he would find most unforgivable when the dust cleared was that even now, even in this sharp, unbearable instant when he understood exactly how expertly he'd been played for a fool, he would have given anything at all for her to say something else.

Anything else.

Anything that would allow him to keep pretending he could be this other, softer version of himself—

But that was not his fate.

And she was an illusion.

He should have known that from the start.

Even then, he hoped. God, how he hoped.

"Luca," she said, his name in her mouth like a blow. The final betrayal in a war he hadn't realized she'd been fighting all this while. A war he understood, at last, he'd lost the moment he'd stopped viewing her as his enemy, when she'd never been anything but. *Never.* And that meant he would hurt her in any way he could. In every way. "I'm pregnant."

Kathryn found she was clenching her hands together in front of her, and she couldn't seem to stop it, no matter how revealing that was. No matter that the man she'd fallen in love with despite herself had gone so still he could have been part of the stone wall that surrounded his rooftop terrace. Just another Roman statue, and about as approachable.

She didn't know what she expected. Luca to grow pale. To shout. To keel over or stagger about dramatically. To react in some over-the-top and awful way, as she'd imagined he would and had braced herself against—because she'd spent a deeply unpleasant hour or so since she'd taken that test imagining all the various horrible ways Luca might take this news, and panicking about each and every one of them in turn.

He did none of those things.

Instead, he stared.

His gaze dropped from her face to her belly, where he should know perfectly well there would be no sign of anything. Not this soon. It took him a long time to drag that dark gaze of his back up. He stared at her far past the point where it could be considered anything but aggressive, while a muscle clenched in his lean jaw, and every nerve in Kathryn's body tied itself into a painful knot.

And yet when Luca finally spoke, his voice was something like lazy. Ripe with disinterest and bland insult.

She recognized that voice instantly. She'd forgotten how much she hated it.

"You have the necessary paperwork, I assume, to support this claim."

Kathryn blinked. "Paperwork? I took a pregnancy test. It's a…stick, not paper."

Luca's dark eyes gleamed, and not in a nice way.

"Kathryn, please," he said, with a little laugh that was like sandpaper against her skin. "Surely you cannot imagine that you are the first woman to share my bed and then decide she'd quite like to nurse at the Castelli teat for the rest of her life." He shrugged. Horribly. "I like sex, as you have discovered, and in these things there is always risk. I would never dismiss a paternity claim out of hand." His dark gaze hurt as it bored into her. "But I do insist that it be proved beyond any doubt."

She realized her hands had balled into fists. "Do you have a great many accidental children, then?"

"I have none, in fact," Luca said viciously. As if he meant it to be a blow. "Such is the perfidy of the average woman."

"You mean the average woman you choose to sleep with," Kathryn threw at him, because she couldn't seem to help herself. When he'd left this morning to go on his run she'd been toying with the idea of telling him how she felt, because it was so huge, so overwhelming, she didn't think she could keep it to herself. Now she rather thought she'd prefer to die. "Maybe the common denominator is less their treachery and more you."

He eyed her from his place a foot or so away with that same searing fury and simmering dislike that had always made her feel…restless before. When she hadn't known him. When she hadn't understood what that thing was between them.

Now it simply made her feel sick.

"I will assemble the usual team of lawyers and doctors," Luca said, sounding deeply bored. "I'll inform them you'll be in tomorrow for the typical workup." Despite that tone, there wasn't a trace of boredom in the searing fury of those dark eyes of his. Not the faintest hint. "Does that suit your schedule? You'll have a great deal of free time, if that helps. My father's will means I can't fire you, but I think you'll find you'll work better as a distant telecommuter from here on out."

"I…" Kathryn shook her head again, refusing to succumb to the wave of dizziness that buffeted her. She shouldn't have been surprised by this, either. When had she ever had the upper hand with Luca? Why had she foolishly held out some kernel of hope that he'd react better? She hadn't realized *how much* she'd been holding on to that hope until now, she realized. When he'd crushed it. "But…"

"I'm sorry if this does not live up to your fantasies of melodrama, *Stepmother*," he said, his voice like steel and that word as harsh as if he'd backhanded her with it. Kathryn fell back a step as if he really had. "You should be aware that eighty percent of the women who make these claims do not return for the appointment that would prove them liars. The other twenty percent must imagine that I'm kidding when I say I'll run these tests. I'm not. Which will you be, I wonder?"

Kathryn felt off balance and worse, something like half hollow, half sick. And beyond that, she had the sickening sense that this had all happened before. Not to her, but because of her. Her own mother had been forced to have a conversation just like this one. Kathryn, too, had been an accident. She found she couldn't get her head around that—it was too much déjà vu to take in at once.

But one thing was perfectly clear. She'd failed her mother. Again. And this time, in the one way she knew Rose could never forgive. That was fair enough. Kathryn was quite sure she'd never forgive herself, either.

"Luca," she said, and she didn't care that her voice shook, that her eyes were blurry with tears, "you don't have to do this."

He laughed. The derisive note in it scraped at her, as she supposed it was meant to do. "Your acting skills are impressive, Kathryn. Maybe far more impressive than I realized."

Her teeth ached. She realized she was gritting them. "You know perfectly well I was a virgin."

"I know that's what you wanted me to think," he threw back at her, his tone mild and unperturbed, though his eyes blazed. "But who can say what is true and what is one more bit of theater from one such as you? A DNA test is far more straightforward."

She shook her head at him, furious with herself that she was so susceptible to him. Furious that he always won. *Always*.

Furious that despite everything, she'd forgotten that deep down, this man hated her. Everything else was sex. The truth was that Luca had always hated her and always would. And they'd made a child out of that. Out of her profound stupidity in the face of the one temptation she hadn't denied herself.

It only takes one mistake, her mother had always told her.

And Kathryn had made it. But that didn't mean she

had to make another one. She'd told Luca she wanted to save herself. Now she had someone else to think about, and the best thing she could do for her baby was keep it the hell away from Luca Castelli and all that hate that burned in him like coals and never, ever went out.

It didn't matter that she thought she loved him. Maybe she did. But what mattered was what kind of life she could provide for the baby she carried. That swept over her with all the grace and conviction of a plan, as if this hadn't been a mistake at all. As if she'd made this decision instead of having it thrust upon her.

Kathryn supposed it didn't matter either way. None of this mattered. Someday her child would tell the story of his or her father with a shrug, just as Kathryn did, and the world would go right on turning.

Her broken heart didn't matter to anyone. It never had.

She cleared her throat and got on with it. "Let me make this simple, then," she said, pleased her voice sounded, if not quite even, like hers again. "I quit. I'll contact Rafael and let him know I'd prefer the bulk sum your father left me, and you'll never see me again. Are you happy now?"

If possible, his gaze got darker. More intense. The blast of his temper scorched her, the fire of it crowding her as if it had eaten the whole of Rome alive, the flames licking over her skin. She braced herself as if she expected him to haul off and hit her, because his gorgeously elegant fingers curled up into fists right there at his sides—

But he didn't hit her. Of course he didn't hit her.

That would have been easier to bear.

Instead, Luca reached over, curled a hard hand around her neck and hauled her mouth to his.

He tasted like sin and redemption, fury and betrayal, and Kathryn was a fool.

An inexcusable fool, but she couldn't stop kissing him back. Even if this was the last time.

Or especially because it was the last time.

He angled his jaw, taking her mouth as if he owned her, and the burn of it flooded through her. He hauled her even closer, so her breasts were crushed against his chest, and she arched into him despite herself.

Her heart kicked at her, a wild and desperate drumming.

He sank his hands into her hair and he devoured her, kissing her again and again. Until she was pliant against him. Until she was kissing him back with the same wildfire, the same mindless need.

And only then did he let her go.

"Luca…" she whispered.

But his face twisted with dislike and disillusion, and something so harsh it made her stomach ache.

"Get out," he told her, in a stranger's pitiless voice that rocked through her like a terrible hurricane, destroying everything in its path. She knew she'd bear the mark of it forever, her own, secret scar. "And, Kathryn…"

She waited, unable to see through the misery that clouded her eyes. Aware that she was trembling, and not sure she'd ever stop. The look he gave her ripped her apart, but when he spoke, his voice was arctic.

"Don't come back here. Ever."

Three days later, Luca was seething his way through a meeting in his conference room when every mobile phone in his office blew up with texts and calls.

His particularly.

He grimly ignored it, gesturing for the man in front of him to continue his presentation. But as the meeting droned on, he saw entirely too much activity on the other side of the glass. His mobile kept buzzing.

And finally, his senior PR person came and stood at the door with an expression on her face that boded nothing but ill.

"Excuse me," Luca said. "It appears I am needed."

He swiped his mobile from the tabletop and stepped out into the office, scowling at Isabella.

"What is it?"

"Ah, well." She actually backed away from him. "The tabloids. I think you'd better look."

He refused to think her name, even though it burst through him then like a song. He felt that like another betrayal. His mobile vibrated in his hand, but he didn't glance at it. Not with every person in his office trying so hard not to stare at him.

He made his way toward his office, past her empty desk that he hadn't been able to make himself fill yet because she'd ruined him, she truly had, and he closed himself inside.

He went to his computer to find his inbox full. Gritting his teeth, he clicked on the links that so many people had helpfully sent him. And there it was.

SAINT KATE IN SEX ROMP WITH GIANNI'S PLAYBOY SON!
SAINT KATE UPGRADES FROM FATHER TO SON!
SAINT KATE STEPMAMA DRAMA!

And underneath the shrieking headlines were the pictures. Kathryn on his roof. More to the point, Luca on his roof with her, half-naked, kissing her as if his life depended on it. As if she hadn't just revealed herself as the traitorous, mercenary bitch she was. As if that wasn't a scene of desperation and betrayal, and nothing more.

Next to him, his mobile buzzed again, this time with a text from Rafael.

Fix it, it read.

It was succinct and to the point, and did nothing at all to soothe the raging thing inside Luca that was too angry, too ferocious to be a simple beast. This thing wanted blood. This thing wanted payback.

This time, he vowed, he wouldn't rest until he'd destroyed her, too.

CHAPTER TWELVE

KATHRYN NOTICED THE sleek black luxury car, entirely too flashy for the quiet English country lane it blocked, the moment she came around the bend on her walk back from the shops.

It had been twelve days since she'd dragged herself out of Rome and back to England. Twelve days since she'd gotten on the next flight back home. She'd never been so pleased to return to her native Yorkshire in all her life. The wolds and the country lanes. The clouds and the green. The redbrick houses that lined this small village, just over five miles outside Hull's city center.

Even her prickly mother, she told herself, was a vast improvement over anyone named Castelli.

She slowed her pace as she drew closer to the car, parked as it was at a sharp angle directly in front of the cottage. Her carrier bag *thwacked* against her thigh. High above, plump clouds scudded across the winter sky, some thick with rain, some as wispy as cotton.

And then Luca threw open the low-slung driver's door and climbed out, unfolding himself onto her remote little lane like a nightmare come to life.

A nightmare, she told herself firmly, as her heart squeezed tight in her chest. *Definitely a nightmare.*

She couldn't pretend she was entirely surprised. She'd seen all the papers. So had everyone else in this tiny little village—and most of England, for that matter. To say nothing of all the world.

Kathryn had told herself that if she could weather a tabloid storm in a village this small, she could do anything. Including having a second generation of illegitimate children, like her mother before her. She'd imagined that when her pregnancy eventually became impossible to conceal, it would seem unworthy of comment in comparison.

"It's like you to give up, isn't it?" her mother had sniffed when Kathryn had made it home. "I think we both know that's your father's blood in you. Making you as weak as he was."

There'd been no point replying to that. Or to the far more unkind things Rose had said when the tabloids had splashed those pictures everywhere.

She'd decided that was all fine, too. She could stomp around in the chilly Yorkshire lanes wrapped up in concealing coats and heavy boots and pretend she was invisible, until she wasn't.

Luca, by contrast, looked lethal. Not invisible at all. He wore a pair of casual trousers and a shirt that would have looked unremarkable on any of the men Kathryn had just seen down on the high street, but this was Luca. He somehow looked as powerful, as darkly ruthless, as he had when he'd been wearing a bespoke suit. His hair was in its usual tousled state that somehow softened the austere male beauty of his hard face, making him that much more stunning. And no matter that he was scowling at her.

The difference was that today Kathryn didn't give a toss. He couldn't break what was already broken.

What he'd stomped into pieces himself on that rooftop far away.

"Oh, lovely," she said coolly as she drew closer. She didn't smile at him, not even a forced rendition of one, and she told herself it was a bit sad that felt like a rebellion. "Does this mean it's my turn to fling horrid accusations at your head and shred your character at will? I've been saving up insults, just in case."

"You took your turn in the tabloids," he bit out. "So here I am, and no matter that it took me over a week to track you down to this godforsaken place. What do you want?"

Kathryn blinked. "I don't want anything. I might have liked some compassion when I told you some startling news, but that ship sailed."

"What game is this?" His voice was soft, but Kathryn could hear the thunder in it. It rolled off him like electricity and deep into her, setting off a different set of explosions. "What can you possibly hope to win?"

Kathryn shifted her weight back on her heels and studied him, shoving her hands deep into her coat pockets as she did. He looked...unhinged, she thought. She'd never seen that wild look in Luca's dark eyes, nor that tension that seemed to grip him.

Luca slammed the car door shut with more violence than was necessary, rocking the magnificent sports car where it sprawled there, as muscular and dangerous as he was. Kathryn thought he might reach for her then, and braced herself against it—but he only eyed her in that predatory way of his that made her blood feel spiked in her veins.

Then he leaned back against the car, crossing one boot over the other and his arms over his chest as if he was not only wholly at his ease, but also impervious to the Yorkshire winter wind that whipped down the lane in irregular bursts to shake the trees and slap at them. As if he would stand there forever if she didn't answer him.

"I don't want anything from you." Kathryn met his dark gaze and felt that same old heavy, edgy thing flip over deep inside her. Maybe she would always have this odd yearning, this bizarre hope that he might prove himself a different man. But he wasn't. And she didn't have to tolerate the way he spoke to her. "I told you that you're going to be a father. What you choose to do with that information is entirely up to you."

"And this independent stance has nothing to do with the fact that if I fail to claim this child you can try to pass it off as my father's, I'm sure." Luca's eyes blazed, though he still stood there as if he was relaxed. "And in so doing, potentially win yourself a conservatorship of one-third of the Castelli fortune my brother and I now share between us. That is quite the luxurious life you've plotted out for yourself, *Stepmother*. Let me guess. You spent your entire marriage trying to get pregnant, but failed. Then when my father died, you realized you had one shot left. Rafael has never had eyes for any woman but Lily, not even when he thought she was dead, which left me."

She wished she could run him over with his own ridiculous car.

"Right," she said in a flat voice. "You've figured me out. Except for the fact that I was a virgin, as you know very well."

"There are words for what you are," he retorted, in that hard-edged way that slapped at her the same way it had in Rome. "But I don't think *virgin* is one of them."

"Yes," she said, scathingly. "You saw to that."

"You can't lose, can you?" He was seething, she realized. So furious that the only thing containing him was the way he held himself there, so rigid and still. "If I do nothing, the way I would with any other woman who tried to claim I'd impregnated her, the world will assume the child is my father's. You've guaranteed yourself a payday for the rest of your mercenary little life."

Kathryn opened her mouth to throw something back at him, to defend herself somehow, but instead found herself swamped by a tide of heavy emotion, as deep and as dark as the North Sea. She tried to fight it off. She'd sworn to herself that this man would never see her cry again, that he didn't deserve it—

But it was no use.

It rushed over her. It betrayed her as surely as he had.

Entirely against her will, Kathryn sobbed.

All the things he'd called her over these past two years, and the past twelve days in particular. All those vicious lies in the paper. All the nasty things her mother had said to her about history repeating itself, but much dumber this time. And the way Luca had turned on her so completely. So certain she was every terrible thing she'd been called.

So certain that he'd called her some of them himself, this same man who had tended to her so gently that night in Sonoma. Held her against him and bathed her himself.

She sobbed and she sobbed.

"How could you?" she demanded, when she could

talk—or try—through the flood of tears. "You were there, Luca. You know perfectly well this baby is no-body's but yours!"

"Why?" he threw right back at her, and he wasn't standing there so languidly any longer. He didn't sound like himself, either. Not lazy or amused in the least. He moved toward her, wrapping his hands around her upper arms and pulling her face to his. "You held on to your virginity against all odds for twenty-five years, even made it through an entire marriage with it intact, then threw it away in the back of a car with a man who used to be your stepson? Why would anyone do that without an ulterior motive? How could it be anything but a plot?"

Kathryn shook with all the huge and unwieldy things inside her. She didn't know when she'd dropped the car-rier bag. Or when she started pounding her fists against his impervious chest.

"Because I love you, you jackass!" she cried.

He closed his hands over her fists and held them away from him, and something in the expression on his beautiful face made her still. She stopped trying to hit him. She stopped fighting. All she could hear was her own ragged breathing, and everything else was that raw thing in his eyes.

And the foolishness in her, that still hurt when he did.

"Then, you are the only one who ever has," Luca said, matter-of-fact and quiet.

And it turned out a broken heart could break again, after all.

Luca felt outside himself. He let go of Kathryn's hands, and she wiped at her face. And he didn't understand how he could feel turned inside out, a stranger to himself, and still enjoy it when she straightened and fixed him with that fierce scowl of hers.

Had he really come here to hurt her? He'd been lying to himself. He understood that he'd have taken any excuse at all to hunt her down. Any reason in the world to see her again. Anything to shift this darkness off him—and only she could do that, though Luca couldn't think of a single reason in the world she'd want to do anything of the kind.

"That's ridiculous," she said crossly now. "Of course you're loved. The whole world loves you. You are beloved wherever you go."

"I am known. It's not the same thing."

"Your family—"

"Listen to me," Luca said, his voice darker than he meant it to be and far more urgent. "My father loved his money and his search for new wives. My mother loved her own illness. Rafael loves Lily. I decided early on that I wanted no part of any of that, because there was no room for me anyway. I wanted control, not love. I wanted to make sure nothing and no one could hurt me the way all of them either hurt others or were hurt themselves. Maybe the truth is I don't know how. It isn't in me."

Her scowl deepened. "Luca—"

"And then came you," he gritted out. "You got under my skin from the first. You spent two years married to my father and still, you drove me crazy. I've never met anyone who bothered me more."

"You've mentioned that. At length."

"But I couldn't stay away from you, Kathryn. I couldn't stop." He shook his head. "And then, when I touched you, I didn't want to stop. I thought that maybe I'd finally found the thing that brought down every other member of my family. I thought maybe I could be different." He blew out a breath. "Then you betrayed me, and I knew."

Her gray eyes were dark and solemn. "You knew what?"

"That it's no more than what I deserve," he said harshly. "I don't blame you for wanting to do this on your own. You shouldn't want me, Kathryn, and you certainly shouldn't want me near any child. What would I teach it? To be like me?"

"Stop," she commanded him.

"I'll support you in any way you want me to," he said gruffly. "But I won't be surprised if you think that's a terrible idea."

Kathryn stared at him for a long moment, then made a low, hard sort of noise. She surged forward, wrapping her arms around him. And he couldn't seem to keep himself from folding his own over her, to keep her there.

"My mother lives her whole life in the past, Luca," she whispered fiercely. "Nothing is ever good enough for her, certainly not me." She reached over and took his hand then dragged it to her still-flat belly. "But this baby won't live like that. This baby will be loved. It already is."

He shook his head. "You're both better off without me."

"Luca," she whispered, her voice just as ferocious, "I love you. That isn't going to go away, no matter what you do."

"I don't know what that is," he threw at her. "You should pay attention. I'm a terrible man, Kathryn. Terrible enough to let you take me back, because I want you too much. Terrible enough to keep you when I know I should let you go. What would you call that if not crazy?"

"Love, you idiot," she told him, tears falling down her cheeks again. "I'd call it love."

Luca reached over then and cupped her face between his hands, drawing her closer. Drawing her in, where he'd never thought he'd have her again. Where he would do his best to earn her.

"I think," he said, right there against that mouth of hers, "that you're going to have to show me what you mean. And it might take a while."

And he could feel her smile, right there against his own, and it was like coming home.

"I have a lifetime," she told him.

Which, Luca decided as she pressed her mouth to his at last, was a very good start.

The second time she married a Castelli, it was a bright June day with an achingly beautiful English summer sky arched blue and impossible above them that no one had to tell Kathryn was its own miracle.

She was beginning to depend on miracles.

Kathryn hid her pregnancy, early in its second trimester, behind the grand white dress she hadn't worn to her first wedding. The bells rang out, and the hordes that Luca had insisted upon inviting packed the village church and spilled out into the lane. It was a far cry from the quick trip to the registry office that had comprised her first set of wedding vows.

The paparazzi had hounded them after those pictures, after Luca had come to Yorkshire and they'd worked things out between them. That hounding had taken on the edge of hysteria when Luca had only shrugged one day at the usual set of shouted questions and announced that he and Kathryn Castelli, yes, the widow of his father formerly known as Saint Kate, were engaged.

They'd been back in Rome by then, tucked away in the penthouse he'd insisted she live in with him, and she'd taken it upon herself to warm up a little bit. She'd started with flowers. Lots and lots of flowers. Acrobatic and colorful, splashing warmth and cheer throughout the stark, steel and crisp-lined space.

"How many flowers are too many?" he'd asked the other day, turning in a circle in the center of the massive space.

"They're a metaphor," she'd replied tartly, typing on her tablet. "The more color in this flat, the more love in your cold, cold heart."

"Then, you'd better call the florist and have more delivered," he'd told her, that simmering look in his dark eyes that still made her own heart flip in her chest. "I feel almost empty."

Then he'd showed her how much of a lie that was, right there on the sleek sofa.

"You haven't asked me to marry you, I note," she'd pointed out after the engagement announcement had spilled all over the papers.

"I'm getting around to it," Luca had said, watching her arrange another dramatic bouquet. He'd been cooking dinner, something Kathryn would have said was entirely beneath him.

"Just as you were getting around to telling me you were a gourmet cook?" she'd asked.

"I am a man of intense mystery and many facets,

cucciola mia," he'd told her. "And I cannot eat in restaurants every night of my life."

"This has nothing to do with you and your control issues, I'm sure," she'd replied, and then laughed so hard it had made her ache when he'd thrown a handful of chopped nuts at her.

The paparazzi had carried on chasing them around Rome, until the day Luca had actually paused while out on one of his runs and had answered one of their salacious, impertinent questions.

"How can you live with yourself now that you've seduced your father's wife?" the man had shouted at him.

Luca had smiled. That glorious smile.

"Have you seen her?" he'd asked. "I live with myself just fine."

Kathryn had only rolled her eyes at that one. She'd been far more concerned that she be able to continue working, and to do the things she wanted to do in the company. And she hadn't been above winning that argument by using the heavy artillery.

When she'd finished with Luca, he'd laughed and told her he'd give her anything if she knelt before him just like that and did all of it over again, her mouth and her hands, every day.

"All I want is my own marketing campaign," she'd told him. "This is merely a side benefit."

"Keep this up," he'd replied lazily, "and I'll give you the whole damned company."

She won the respect of most of her coworkers eventually. And the ones who couldn't handle her presence in the office stopped mattering to her and usually stopped working there, too. The day Luca smiled at her across the conference room table after a presentation she'd slaved over and called her brilliant was all that mattered.

Because she'd been right. This was what she'd been meant to do.

Luca had been the one to book the church and take care of all the wedding details.

"You could participate, *cucciola mia*," he'd said once, on a trip to Australia to tour the Barossa Valley. "It's your wedding, too, I hesitate to remind you."

"Wedding?" she'd asked mildly. "What wedding? No one has proposed to me. How could there be a wedding?"

He'd only grinned.

Rose, of course, had been her usual vicious self. But on one of her visits to the little cottage in Yorkshire, Kathryn had abruptly cut her off when she'd started to spew her usual venom.

"You sacrificed for me, Mum," she'd said, holding her mother's gaze so there could be no mistake. "I can never thank you enough for that. That's what mothers do. And I did my best to do my part, too." She'd waved her hands at the cottage where they'd stood. "You'll never want for anything again. I'll always take care of you."

"Aren't you high and mighty now that you've lain with not one but two—"

"Careful," Luca had warned from his position in the far doorway, where he liked to stand while she visited her mother—like her very own emotional bodyguard. "Very, very careful, please."

And Kathryn had understood that it was Luca who had given her the strength to do this at last. To understand that she didn't have to suffer through her mother's rages and nastiness. That she didn't have to participate in this dysfunction. Luca loved her. He wanted to marry her. They were having a baby, and most of the time they were happy together.

She had nothing to prove to anyone, least of all to this angry, bitter woman who should have loved her most.

"If you can't learn to keep a civil tongue in your head, you'll never see your grandchild," Kathryn had told her. "I might choose to subject myself to this out of obligation and devotion, but I'll never let you tear into my baby the way you do me." Rose had sputtered about threats. "That's a promise, Mum. Not a threat. The choice is yours."

And then later, Luca had held her tight and hadn't judged her at all for crying over the childhood she'd never had with Rose.

Kathryn thought she could do no less for him.

She'd gone out of her way to make sure that they spent as much time with Raphael and Lily as possible, because they were the future of the Castelli family, not the grim past that Luca had already survived. She'd come to understand that no matter how lovely Gianni had been to her, he'd been a neglectful father to Luca. But Luca and Rafael were brothers, and they owned the company together, and they loved each other. That was what mattered now.

They'd gone up shortly after Lily had given birth to little baby Bruno, another dark-eyed, dark-haired Castelli male, and stayed at the old manor house for a few days to marinate in the new shape of their family.

"I hate it here," Luca had told her when she'd woken one night to find him standing by the window instead of in bed. "I've always hated it here."

He'd told her of his lonely childhood, of all the ways he'd tried to get his family's attention. Of all those sad years where he'd been left to his own devices, or the tender mercies of the staff, or the frustrations of his stepmothers.

"You're not a child any longer," she'd told him, rolling out of the bed to go to him. She'd sneaked her arms around him and pressed her cheek to his back. "This house is what you make it. It's only a house."

"It always seemed like a curse."

"You can break the curse," she'd promised him. "All you have to do is love me."

"That, *cucciola mia*, is no trouble at all."

And they'd broken more than a few curses that night, driving each other blissfully mad in that great big bed.

In the morning they'd gathered in the library with Rafael and Lily and the small boys, all of them bursting with pride over the new addition. This was the new version of the Castellis, Kathryn had thought. Not the stiff, formal way things had been the first time she'd come here with Gianni. No furious, horrible Luca. None of that pounding confusion because she'd been with the wrong man.

Nothing but love. So much love, in so many forms.

"Are you truly marrying in June?" Lily had asked as they'd sat together on one of the sofas, watching Rafael hold his brand-new son, that Castelli smile of his lighting up the whole of Northern Italy. "That's only a month away."

"Luca is planning a huge wedding to someone," Kathryn had replied with a laugh. "But he has yet to ask anyone in particular, as far as I know. It's very mysterious."

"About that," Luca had said.

She'd looked up to find him standing before her, the whole world in his dark eyes. Then he'd dropped to his knees, and she'd clapped her hands over her mouth. Kathryn had heard Lily's gasp from the sofa beside her, and had sensed more than seen the way Raphael had turned that smile of his their way.

"I love you," Luca had said. "I want to give you the world. I want this baby and I want you, Kathryn, *cucciola mia*, to be my wife and the mother of my children and the best thing in my life, forever. Will you marry me?"

"I don't know," she'd said, looping her arms around his neck and smiling at him with everything she was. "I've grown so fond of you calling me Stepmother. How can I give that up?"

"You won't regret it," he'd promised her, his hard mouth curving and so much light in his dark eyes. "I have far better names for you."

"I love you," she'd whispered. "I think I always have."

"You are the love of my life," he'd said as he'd tugged her hand down from his neck and slipped a ring onto her finger, where it sparkled so brightly it made her feel dazzled. Or perhaps that was him. "You are the reason I know that such things exist. You are my heart, Kathryn."

"Yes," she'd whispered, tears flowing freely down her cheeks. "Always yes, Luca. Always."

And she married him with his brother at his side and her new sister-in-law at hers, because family was what mattered. Their family. The one they'd made, taking what they needed from what they'd been given and leaving the rest behind, where it belonged.

"This life is too beautiful," she told Luca that night,

their first night together as husband and wife. "How can it ever get better than this?"

Four months later, they found out together, when Kathryn gave birth to a marvelous little creature the Castelli family hadn't seen in generations.

A little girl.

"Hold on tight, *cucciola mia*," Luca told her as they sat together on their first night as their own little nuclear family at last.

He held their perfect daughter in his arms, his dark eyes filled with love and light and the whole of their future, right there within reach.

Theirs for the taking, Kathryn thought happily. Theirs, always.

Luca's smile then was big enough to light up the night. "It's only going to get better from here."

And it did.

* * * * *

'We don't marry for love or companionship, as other people do. We marry for the good of our island. Think of my betrothal as a business arrangement. But *you* are my lover. You are the woman I *want* to be with.'

For an age Amy didn't say anything. She simply looked into Helios's eyes, searching for something—she didn't know what.

He brought his face down to meet her lips, which had parted.

'I mean it, Helios, we're finished. I will never be your mistress.' Her words were but a whisper.

'You think?'

'Yes.'

'Then why are you still standing here? Why is your breath still warm on my face?'

Brushing his lips across the softness of her cheek, he gripped her bottom and ground her to him, letting her feel his desire for her.

The tiniest of moans escaped her throat.

'See?' He trailed kisses over her delicate ear. 'You do want me. But you're punishing me.'

HELIOS CROWNS
HIS MISTRESS

BY
MICHELLE SMART

Published in Great Britain 2016
By Mills & Boon, an imprint of HarperCollins*Publishers*
1 London Bridge Street, London, SE1 9GF

© 2016 Michelle Smart

ISBN: 978-0-263-92100-7

Our policy is to use papers that are natural, renewable and recyclable
products and made from wood grown in sustainable forests. The logging
and manufacturing processes conform to the legal environmental
regulations of the country of origin.

Printed and bound in Spain
by CPI, Barcelona

Michelle Smart's love affair with books started when she was a baby, when she would cuddle them in her cot. A voracious reader of all genres, she found her love of romance established when she stumbled across her first Mills & Boon book at the age of twelve. She's been reading (and writing) them ever since. Michelle lives in Northamptonshire with her husband and two young Smarties.

Books by Michelle Smart

Mills & Boon Modern Romance

The Russian's Ultimatum
The Rings That Bind
The Perfect Cazorla Wife

The Kalliakis Crown

Talos Claims His Virgin
Theseus Discovers His Heir

Society Weddings

The Greek's Pregnant Bride

The Irresistible Sicilians

What a Sicilian Husband Wants
The Sicilian's Unexpected Duty
Taming the Notorious Sicilian

Visit the Author Profile page at millsandboon.co.uk for more titles.

This book is for Aimee—
thank you for all the support and cheerleading
over the years. You're one in a million.

This book is also dedicated to Hannah and Sarah—
the mojitos in this are for you!

xxx

CHAPTER ONE

'Do YOU REALLY have to shave it off?' Amy Green, busy admiring Helios's rear view, slipped a cajoling tone into her plea.

Helios met her eye in the reflection of the bathroom mirror and winked. 'It will grow back.'

She pouted. Carefully. The clay mask she'd applied to her face had dried, making it hard for her to move her features without cracking it. Another ten minutes and she would be able to rinse it off. 'But you're so sexy with a beard.'

'Are you saying I'm not sexy without it?'

She made a harrumphing sound. 'You're always sexy.'

Too sexy for his own good. Even without a beard. Even his voice was sexy: a rich, low-pitched tone that sang to her ears, with the Agon accent which made it dance.

Impossibly tall and rangy, and incredibly strong, with dark olive colouring and ebony hair, currently tousled after a snatched hour in bed with her, Helios had a piratical appearance. The dangerous look was exaggerated by the slight curve of his strong nose and the faint scar running over its bridge: the mark of a fight with his brother Theseus when they were teenagers. Utterly without vanity, Helios wore the scar with pride. He was the sexiest man she'd ever met.

Soon the hair would be tamed and as smooth as his face would be, yet his innate masculinity would still vibrate through him. His rugged body would be hidden by a formal black evening suit, but his strength and vitality would permeate the expensive fabric. The playful expression emanating from his liquid dark brown eyes would still offer sin.

He would turn into Prince Helios Kalliakis, heir to the throne of Agon. But he would still be a flesh and blood man.

He lifted the cut-throat blade. 'Are you sure you don't want to do it?'

Amy shook her head. 'Can you imagine if I were to cut you? I would be arrested for treason.'

He grinned, then gave the mirror a quick wipe to clear away the condensation produced from the steam of her bath.

Smothering a snigger, she stretched out her right leg until her foot reached the taps, and used her toes to pour a little more hot water in.

'I'm sure deliberately steaming up the bathroom so I can't see properly is also treasonous,' he said with a playful shake of his head, striding lithely to the extractor fan and switching it on.

As with everything in his fabulous palace apartment it worked instantly, clearing the enormous bathroom of steam.

He crouched beside the bath and placed his gorgeous face close to hers. 'Any more treasonous behaviour, *matakia mou*, and I will be forced to punish you.'

His breath, hot and laced with a faint trace of their earlier shared pot of coffee, danced against her skin.

'And what form of punishment will you be forced to give me?' she asked, the desire she'd thought spent bubbling back up inside her, her breaths shortening.

Those liquid eyes flashed and a smirk played on the bowed lips that had kissed her everywhere. It was a mouth a woman could happily kiss for ever.

'A punishment you will never forget.' He snapped his teeth together for effect and growled, before throwing her a look full of promise and striding back to the mirror. Half watching her in the reflection, Helios dipped his shaving brush into the pot and began covering his black beard with a rich, foamy lather.

Amy had to admit watching him shave as if he were the leading man in a medieval film fascinated her. It also scared her. The blade he used was sharp enough to slice through flesh. One twitch of the hand...

All the same, she couldn't drag her eyes away as he scraped the cut-throat razor down his cheek. In its own way it had an eroticism to it, transporting her to a bygone time when men had been *men*. And Helios was all man.

If he wanted he could snap his fingers and an army of courtiers would be there to do the job for him. But that wasn't his style. The Kalliakis family were direct descendants of Ares Patakis, the warrior whose uprising had freed Agon from its Venetian invaders over eight hundred years ago. Agon princes were taught how to wield weapons with the same dedication with which they were taught the art of royal protocol. To her lover, a cut-throat razor was but one of many weapons he'd mastered.

She waited until he'd wiped the blade on a towel to clean it before speaking again. 'Do I take it that despite all my little hints you haven't put a space aside for me tonight?'

Her 'little hints' had taken the form of mentioning at every available opportunity how much she would love to attend the Royal Ball that was the talk of the entire island, but she hadn't seriously expected to get an invitation. She

was but a mere employee of the palace museum, and a
temporary employee at that.

And it wasn't as if they would be together for ever, she
thought with a strange stab of wistfulness. Their relationship had never been a secret, but it hadn't been flaunted
either. She was his lover, not his girlfriend, something she
had known from the very start. She had no official place
in his life and never would.

He placed the blade back to his cheek and swiped, revealing another line of smooth olive skin. 'However much
I adore your company, it wouldn't be appropriate for you
to attend.'

She pulled a face, inadvertently cracking the mask
around her mouth. 'Yes, I know. I am a commoner, and
those attending your ball are the *crème de la crème* of
high society.'

'Nothing would please me more than to see you there,
dressed in the finest haute couture money can buy. But
it would be inappropriate for my lover to attend the ball
where I'm to select my future wife.'

The deliciously warm bath turned cold in the beat of
a moment.

She sat up.

'Your future wife? What are you talking about?'

His reflected eyes met hers again. 'The underlying reason for this ball is so that I can choose a wife.'

She paused before asking, 'Like in *Cinderella*?'

'Exactly.' He worked on his chin, then wiped the blade
on the towel again. 'You know all of this.'

'No,' she said slowly, her blood freezing to match the
chills rippling over her skin. 'I was under the impression
this ball was a pre-Gala do.'

In three weeks the eyes of the world would be on Agon
as the island celebrated fifty years of King Astraeus's

reign. Heads of state and dignitaries from all around the world would be flying in for the occasion.

'And so it is. I think the phrase is "killing two birds with one stone"?'

'Why can't you find a wife in the normal way?' And, speaking of normal, how were her vocal cords performing when the rest of her body had been subsumed in a weird kind of paralysis?

'Because, *matakia mou*, I am heir to the throne. I have to marry someone of royal blood. You know that.'

Yes, that she *did* know. Except she hadn't thought it would be now. It hadn't occurred to her. Not once. Not while they were sharing a bed every night.

'I need to choose wisely,' he continued, speaking in the same tone he might use if he were discussing what to order from the palace kitchen for dinner. 'Obviously I have a shortlist of preferred women—princesses and duchesses I have met through the years who have caught my attention.'

'Obviously...' she echoed. 'Is there any particular woman at the top of your shortlist, or are there a few of them jostling for position?'

'Princess Catalina of Monte Cleure is looking the most likely. I've known her and her family for years—they've attended our Christmas Balls since Catalina was a baby. Her sister and brother-in-law got together at the last one.' He grinned at the scandalous memory. 'Catalina and I dined together a couple of times when I was in Denmark the other week. She has all the makings of an excellent queen.'

An image of the raven-haired Princess, a famed beauty who dealt with incessant press scrutiny on account of her ethereal royal loveliness, came to Amy's mind. Waves of nausea rolled in her belly.

'You never mentioned it.'

'There was nothing to say.' He didn't look the slightest bit shamefaced.

'Did you sleep with her?'

He met her stare, censure clear in his reflection. 'What kind of a question is *that*?'

'A natural question for a woman to ask her lover.'

Until that moment it hadn't been something that had occurred to her: the idea that he might have strayed. Helios had never promised fidelity, but he hadn't needed to. Since their first night together their lust for each other had been all-consuming.

'The Princess is a virgin and will remain one until her wedding day whether she marries me or some other man. Does that answer your question?'

Not even a little bit. All it did was open up a whole heap of further questions, all of which she didn't have the right to ask and not one of which she wanted to hear the answer to.

The only question she *could* bring herself to ask was 'When are you hoping to marry the lucky lady?'

If he heard the irony in her voice he hid it well. 'It will be a state wedding, but I would hope to be married in a couple of months.'

A couple of months? He expected to choose a bride and have a state wedding in a few months? Surely it wasn't possible...?

But this was Helios. If there was one thing she knew about her lover it was that he was not a man to let the grass grow beneath his feet. If he wanted something done he wanted it done now, not tomorrow.

But a couple of months...?

Amy was contracted to stay in Agon until September, which was five whole months away. She'd imagined... Hoped...

She thought of King Astraeus, Helios's grandfather. She had never met the King, but through her work in the palace museum she felt she had come to know him. The King was dying. Helios needed to marry and produce an heir of his own to assure the family line.

She *knew* all this. Yet still she'd shared his bed night after night and allowed herself to believe that Helios would hold off his wedding until her time on Agon was up.

Gripping the sides of the free-standing bath, she got carefully to her feet and stepped out. Hands trembling, she pulled a warm, fluffy towel off the rack and held it to her chest, not wanting to waste a second, not even to wrap it around herself.

Helios pulled his top lip down and brought the blade down in careful but expert fashion. 'I'll call you when the ball is finished.'

She strode to the door, uncaring that bathwater was dripping off her and onto the expensive floor tiles. 'No, you won't.'

'Where are you going? You're soaking wet.'

From out of the corner of her eye she saw him pat his towel over his face and follow her through into his bedroom, not bothering to cover himself.

She gathered her clothes into a bundle and held them tightly. A strange burning buzzed in her brain, making coherent thought difficult.

Three months. That was how long she'd shared his bed. In that time they'd slept apart on only a dozen or so occasions, when Helios had been away on official business. Like when he'd gone to Denmark and, unbeknownst to her, dined with Princess Catalina. And now he was throwing a ball to find the woman he would share a bed with for the rest of his life.

She'd known from the start that they had no future, and

had been careful to keep her heart and emotions detached. But to hear him being so blasé about it…

She stood by the door that opened into the secret passageway connecting their apartments. There were dozens and dozens of such secret passageways throughout the palace; a fortress built on intrigue and secrets.

'I'm going to my apartment. Enjoy your evening.'

'Have I missed something?'

The fact that he looked genuinely perplexed only made matters worse.

'You say it isn't appropriate for me to come tonight, but I'll tell you what isn't appropriate—talking about the wife you're hours away from selecting with the woman who has shared your bed for three months.'

'I don't know what your problem is,' he said with a shrug, raising his hands in an open-palmed gesture. 'My marriage won't change anything between us.'

'If you believe that then you're as stupid as you are insensitive and misogynistic. You speak as if the women you are selecting from are sweets lined up in a shop rather than flesh and blood people.' She shook her head to emphasise her distaste, watching as her words seeped in and the perplexity on Helios's face darkened into something ugly.

Helios was not a man who received criticism well. On this island and in this palace he was celebrated and feted, a man whose words people hung on to. Affable and charming, his good humour was infectious. Cross him, however, and he would turn with the snap of two fingers.

If she wasn't so furious with him Amy would probably be afraid.

He strode towards her, magnificently naked. He stopped a foot away and folded his arms across his defined chest. A pulse throbbed at his temple and his jaw clenched tightly.

'Be careful in how you speak to me. I might be your lover, but you do not have a licence to insult me.'

'Why? Because you're a prince?' She hugged the towel and the bundle of clothes even tighter, as if their closeness could stop her erratically thumping heart from jumping out of her chest. 'You're about to make a commitment to another woman and I want no part of it.'

Benedict, Helios's black Labrador, sensed the atmosphere and padded over to her, his tongue lolling out as he sat on his haunches by her side and gave what looked like a disapproving stare at his master.

Helios noticed it too. He rubbed Benedict's head, the darkness disappearing as quickly as it had appeared, an indulgent smile spreading over his face as he looked at Amy. 'Don't be so dramatic. I know you're premenstrual, and that makes you more emotional than you would otherwise be, but you're being irrational.'

'Premenstrual? Did you really just say that? You really are on a different planet. God forbid that I should become "emotional" because my lover has had secret dates with other women and is about to take one of them for his wife and still expects me to warm his bed. But don't worry. Pat me on the head and tell me I'm premenstrual. Pat yourself on the back and tell yourself you've done nothing wrong.'

Too furious to look at him any more, she turned the handle of the door and pushed it open with her hip.

'Are you walking away from me?'

Was that *laughter* in his voice? Did he find this *amusing*?

Ignoring him, Amy raised her head high and walked up the narrow passageway that would take her to her own palace apartment.

A huge hand gripped her biceps, forcing her to twist around. He absolutely dwarfed her.

Regardless of the huge tug in her heart and the rising

nausea, her voice was steady as she said, 'Get your hands off me. We're over.'

'No, we're not.' He slid his hand over her shoulder to snake it around her neck. His breath was hot in her ear as he leaned down to whisper, 'While you're sulking tonight I will be thinking of you and imagining all the ways I can take you when the ball's over. Then you will come to me and we will act them all out.'

Despite her praying to all the gods she could think of, her body reacted to his words and to his closeness the way it always did. With Helios she was like a starved child, finally allowed to feast. She craved him. She had desired him from the moment she'd met him all those months ago, with a powerful need that hadn't abated with time.

But now the time had come to conquer the craving.

Pressing a hand to his solid chest, resisting the urge to run her fingers through the fine black hair that covered it, she pushed herself back and forced her eyes to meet his still playful gaze.

'Enjoy your evening. Try not to spill wine down any princess's dress.'

His mocking laughter followed her all the way to the sanctuary of her own apartment.

It wasn't until she arrived in her apartment, which was spacious compared to normal accommodation but tiny when compared to Helios's, and caught a glimpse of her reflection that she saw the clay mask was still on her face.

It had cracked all over.

Helios led his dance partner—a princess from the old Greek royal family—around the ballroom. She was a very pretty young woman, but as he danced with her and listened to her chatter he mentally struck her off his list. Whoever he married, he wanted to be able to hold a conversation with them about something other than the latest catwalk fashions.

When the waltz had finished he bowed gracefully and excused himself to join his brother Theseus at his table, ignoring all the pleading female eyes silently begging him to take their hand next.

Amy's words about him treating the women here as sweets in a shop came back to him. He was man enough to admit they held the ring of truth. But if he had to choose someone to spend the rest of his life with and to bear his children, he wanted a woman as close to being perfect on his palate as he could taste.

If Amy could see the ladies in question and their eager eyes, the way they thrust their cleavages in his direction as they passed him, hoping to garner his attention, she would understand that they *wanted* to be tasted. They wanted him to find them exactly to his taste.

Theseus's gaze was directed at their younger brother, Talos, who was dancing with the ravishing violinist who would play at their grandfather's Jubilee Gala in three weeks.

'There's something going on there,' Theseus said, swigging back his champagne. 'Look at him. The fool's smitten.'

Helios followed his brother's gaze to the dance floor and knew immediately what he meant. The other couple of hundred guests in the room might as well not have been there for all the attention Talos and his dance partner were paying them. They had eyes only for each other and the heat they were producing…it was almost a visible entity. And strangely mesmerising.

Not for the first time Helios wished Amy could be there. She would adore waltzing around the great ballroom. For a conscientious academic she had a fun side that made her a pleasure to be with.

Theseus fixed his gaze back on Helios. 'So what about you? Shouldn't you be on the dance floor?'

'I'm taking a breather.'

'You should be taking it with Princess Catalina.'

Helios and his brothers had discussed his potential brides numerous times. The consensus was that Catalina would be a perfect fit for their family.

Only a generation ago, the marriages of the heirs to the Agon throne had been arranged. His own parents' marriage had been arranged. It had been witnessing the implosion of their marriage that had led his grandfather King Astraeus to abandon protocol and allow the next generation to select their own spouses, providing they were of royal blood.

For this, Helios was grateful. He was determined that whoever he selected would have no illusions that their marriage would be anything but one of duty.

'You think…?' he asked idly, while his skin crawled at the thought of dancing another waltz with any more of the ladies in attendance, no matter how beautiful they were. Beautiful women were freely available wherever he went. Women of substance less so.

He glanced at his watch. Another couple of hours and this would be over. He would call Amy and she would come to him.

Now, *she* was a woman of substance.

A frisson of tension raced through him as he recalled their earlier exchange. He'd never seen her angry before. There'd been a possessiveness to that anger too. She'd been jealous.

Usually when a lover showed the first sign of possessiveness it meant it was time for him to move on. In Amy's case he'd found it highly alluring. Her jealousy had strangely delighted him.

Helios had long suspected that she kept parts of herself

hidden from him. She gave her body to him willingly, and revelled in their lovemaking as much as he did, but the inner workings of her clever mind remained a mystery.

She'd been different from his usual lovers from the very start. Beautiful and fiercely intelligent, she held his attention in a way no other woman ever had. Her earlier anger hadn't repelled him, as it would have done coming from anyone else; it had intrigued him, peeling away another layer of the brilliant, passionate woman he couldn't get enough of. When he was with her he could forget everything and live for the moment, for their hunger.

The seriousness of his grandfather's illness clung to him like a barnacle, but when he was with Amy it became tamed, was less of a thudding beat of pain and doom. When he was with her he could cast aside the great responsibilities being heir to the throne brought and simply be a man. A lover. *Her* lover. She was a constant thrum in his blood. He had no intention of giving her up—marriage or no marriage.

'Has anyone else caught your attention?' Theseus asked him.

'No.'

Helios had always known he would have to marry. There had never been any question about it. He had no personal feelings about it one way or another. Marriage was an institution within which to produce the next set of Kalliakis heirs, and he was fortunate to be in a position where he could choose his own bride, albeit within certain constraints. His parents hadn't been so lucky. Their marriage had been arranged before his mother had been out of nappies. It had been a disaster. His only real hope for his own marriage was that it be *nothing* like theirs.

Princess Catalina, currently dancing with a British prince, caught his eye. She really was incredibly beautiful. Refined.

Her breeding and lineage shone through. Her brother was an old school friend of his, and their meals together in Denmark had shown her to be a woman of great intelligence as well as beauty, if a little serious for his taste.

She had none of Amy's irreverence.

Still, Catalina would make an excellent queen and he'd wasted enough time as it was. He should have selected a wife months ago, when the gravity of his grandfather's condition had been spelt out to him and his brothers.

Catalina had been raised in a world of protocol, just as he had. She had no illusions or expectations of love. If he chose her he knew theirs would be a marriage of duty. Nothing more, nothing less. No emotional entanglements. Exactly as he wanted.

Making a family with her would be no hardship either. He was certain that with some will on both their parts a bond would form. Chemistry should ensue too. Not the same kind of chemistry he shared with Amy, of course. That would be impossible to replicate.

A memory of Amy heading barefoot down the dimly lit passageway, her clothes and towel huddled to her, her dark blonde hair damp and swinging across her golden back, her bare bottom swaying, flashed into his mind. She'd been as haughty as any princess in that moment, and he couldn't wait to punish her for her insolence. He would bring her to the brink of orgasm so many times she would be *begging* him for release.

But this was neither the time nor the place to imagine Amy's slender form naked in his arms.

With titanium will, he dampened down the fire spreading through his loins and fixed his attention on the women before him. For the next few hours Amy had to be locked away in his mind to free up his concentration for the job in hand.

Before he could bring himself to dance again he beckoned a footman closer, so he could take another glass of champagne and drink a large swallow.

Theseus eyed him shrewdly. 'What's the matter with you?'

'Nothing.'

'You have the face of a man at a wine-tasting event discovering all the bottles are corked.'

Helios fixed a smile on his face. 'Better?'

'Now you look like a mass murderer.'

'Your support is, as always, invaluable.' Draining his glass, he got to his feet. 'Considering the fact I'm not the only Prince expected to marry and produce heirs, I suggest you get off your backside and mingle with the beautiful ladies in attendance too.'

He smirked at Theseus's grimace. While Helios accepted his fate with the steely backbone his upbringing and English boarding school education had instilled in him, he knew his rebellious brother looked forward to matrimony with all the enthusiasm of a zebra entering a lion enclosure.

Later, as he danced with Princess Catalina, holding her at a respectable distance so their bodies didn't touch—and having no compulsion to bridge the gap—his thoughts turned to his grandfather.

The King was not in attendance tonight, as he was saving his limited energy for the Jubilee Gala itself. It was for that great man, who had raised Helios and his brothers since Helios was ten, that he was prepared to take the final leap and settle down.

For his grandfather he would do *anything*.

Soon the crown would pass to him—sooner than he had wanted or expected—and he needed a queen by his side. He wanted his grandfather to move on to the next life at peace, in the knowledge that the succession of the Kalliakis line was secure. If time was kind to them his grandfather might just live long enough to see Helios take his vows.

CHAPTER TWO

WHERE THE HELL was she?

Helios had been back in his apartment for fifteen minutes and Amy wasn't answering his calls. According to the head of security, she had left the palace. Her individual passcode showed that she'd left at seven forty-five; around the time he and his brothers had been welcoming their guests.

Trying her phone one more time, he strolled through to his bar and poured himself a large gin. The call went straight to voicemail. He tipped the neat liquid down his throat and, on a whim, carried the bottle through to his study.

Security monitors there showed pictures from the cameras that ran along the connecting passageways. Only Helios himself had access to the cameras' feeds.

He peered closely at the screen for camera three, which faced the reinforced connecting door. There was something on the floor he couldn't make out clearly...

Striding to it and unbolting the door, he stared down at a box. Crammed inside were bottles of perfume, jewellery, books and mementos. All the gifts he had given Amy during their time together as lovers. Crammed, unwanted, into a box and left on his doorstep.

A burst of fury tore through him, so sudden and so powerful it consumed him in one.

Before he had time to think what he was doing he raised his foot and brought it slamming down onto the box. Glass shattered and crunched beneath him, the sound echoing in the silence.

For an age he did nothing else but inhale deeply, trembling with fury, fighting the urge to smash what was left of the box's contents into smithereens. Violence had been his father's solution to life's problems. It was something Helios had always known resided inside him too but, unlike in his father's case, it was an aspect of himself he controlled.

The sudden fury that had just overtaken him was incomprehensible.

Acutely aware of how late she was, Amy slammed her apartment door shut and hurried down the stairs that led to the palace museum. Punching in her passcode, she waited for the green light to come on, shoved the door open and stepped into the private quarters of the museum, an area out of bounds to visitors.

Gazing longingly at the small staff kitchen as she passed it, she crossed her fingers in the hope that the daily pastries hadn't already been eaten and the coffee already drunk. The *bougatsas*, freshly made by the palace chefs and brought to them every morning, had become her favourite food in the whole world.

Her mouth filled with moisture as she imagined the delicate yet satisfying filo-based pastries. She hoped there were still some custard-filled ones left. She'd hardly eaten a thing in the past couple of days, and now, after finally managing to get a decent night's sleep, she'd woken up ravenous. She'd also slept right through her alarm clock, and the thought made her legs work even quicker as she climbed another set of stairs that led up to the boardroom.

'I'm so sorry I'm late,' she said, rushing through the door, a hand flat on her breathless chest. 'I over...' Her words tailed off as she saw Helios, sitting at the head of the large round table.

His elbows rested on the table, the tips of his fingers rubbing together. He was freshly shaven and, even casually dressed as he was, in a dark green long-sleeved crew-neck top, he exuded an undeniable power. And all the force of that power was at that very moment aimed at her.

'Nice of you to join us, Despinis Green,' he said. His tone was even, but his dark brown eyes resembled bullets waiting to be fired at her. 'Take a seat.'

Utterly shaken to see him there, she blinked rapidly and forced herself to inhale. Helios was the palace museum's director, but his involvement in the day-to-day running of it was minimal. In the four months she'd worked there, he hadn't once attended the weekly Tuesday staff meeting.

She'd known when she'd stolen back into the palace late last night that she would have to face him soon, but she'd hoped for a few more days' grace. Why did he have to appear today, of all days? The one time she'd overslept and looked awful.

Unfortunately the only chair available was directly opposite him. It made a particularly loud scraping sound over the wooden floor as she pulled it back and sat down, clasping her hands tightly on her lap so as not to betray their tremors. Greta, one of the other curators and Amy's best friend on the island, had the seat next to her. She placed a comforting hand over hers and squeezed gently. Greta knew everything.

In the centre of the table was the tray of *bougatsas* Amy had hoped for. Three remained, but she found her appetite

gone and her heart thundering so hard that the ripples spread
to her belly and made her nauseous.

Greta poured her a cup of coffee. Amy clutched it grate-
fully.

'We were discussing the artefacts we're still waiting
on for my grandfather's exhibition,' Helios said, looking
directly at her.

The Agon Palace Museum was world-famous, and as
such attracted curators from across the world, resulting
in a medley of first languages amongst the staff. To sim-
plify matters, English was the official language spoken
when on duty.

Amy cleared her throat and searched her scrambled
brain for coherence. 'The marble statues are on their way
from Italy as we speak and should arrive in port early tomorrow morning.'

'Do we have staff ready to welcome them?'

'Bruno will message me when they reach Agon wa-
ters,' she said, referring to one of the Italian curators accompanying the statues back to their homeland. 'As soon
as I hear from him we'll be ready to go. The drivers are
on call. Everything is in hand.'

'And what about the artefacts from the Greek museum?'

'They will arrive here on Friday.'

Helios *knew* all this. The exhibition was his pet project
and they'd worked closely together on it.

She'd first come to Agon in November, as part of a team
from the British Museum delivering artefacts on loan to the
Agon Palace Museum. During those few days on the island
she'd struck up a friendship with Pedro, the Head of Museum. Unbeknownst to her at the time, he'd been impressed
with her knowledge of Agon, and doubly impressed with
her PhD thesis on Minoan Heritage and its Influences on

Agon Culture. Pedro had been the one to suggest her for the role of curator for the Jubilee Exhibition.

The offer had been a dream come true, and a huge honour for someone with so little experience. Only twenty-seven, what Amy lacked in experience she made up for with enthusiasm.

Amy had learned at the age of ten that the happy, perfect family she'd taken for granted was not as she'd been led to believe. *She* wasn't what she'd been led to believe. Her dad was indeed her biological father, but her brothers were only half-brothers. Her mum wasn't her biological mother. The woman who'd actually given birth to her had been from the Mediterranean island of Agon.

Half of Amy's DNA was Agonite.

Since that bombshell discovery, everything about Agon had fascinated her. She'd devoured books on its Minoan history and its evolution into democracy. She'd thrilled at stories of the wars, the passion and ferocity of its people. She'd studied maps and photographs, staring so intently at the island's high green mountains, sandy beaches and clear blue seas that its geography had become as familiar as her own home town.

Agon had been an obsession.

Somewhere in its history was *her* history, and the key to understanding who she truly was. To have the opportunity to live there on a nine-month secondment had been beyond anything she could have hoped. It had been as if fate was giving her the push she needed to find her birth mother. Somewhere in this land of half a million people was the woman who had borne her.

For seventeen years Amy had thought about her, wondering what she looked like—did she look like *her*?—what her voice sounded like, what regrets she might have. Was she ashamed of what she'd done? Surely she was? How could anyone live through what Neysa Soukis had done and *not* feel shame?

She'd been easy to locate, but how to approach her...? That had always been the biggest question. Amy couldn't just turn up at her door; it would likely be slammed in her face and then she would never have her answers. She'd considered writing a letter but had failed to think of what she could say other than: *Hi, do you remember me? You carried me for nine months and then dumped me. Any chance you could tell me why?*

Greek social media, which Greta had been helping her with, had proved fruitful. Neysa didn't use it, but through it Amy had discovered a half-brother. Tentative communications had started between them. She had to hope he would act as a conduit between them.

'Have you arranged transport for Friday?' Helios asked, the dark eyes hard, the bowed, sensual mouth tight.

'Yes. Everything is in hand,' she said for a second time, as a sharp pang reached through her as she realised she would never feel those lips on hers again. 'We're ahead of schedule.'

'You're confident that come the Gala the exhibition will be ready?'

His voice was casual but there was a hardness there, a scepticism she'd never had directed at her before.

'Yes,' she answered, gritting her teeth to stop her hurt and anger leeching out.

He was punishing her. She should have answered one of his calls. She'd taken the coward's way out and escaped from the palace in the hope that a few days away from him would give her the strength she needed to resist him. The best way—the only way—of beating her craving for him would be by going cold turkey.

Because resist him she must. She couldn't be the other woman. She couldn't.

But she hadn't imagined that seeing him again would physically *hurt*.

It did. Dreadfully.

Before her job had been rubber-stamped, Helios had interviewed her himself. The Jubilee Exhibition was of enormous personal importance to him and he'd been determined that the curator with the strongest affinity to his island would get the job.

Luckily for her, he'd agreed with Pedro that she was the perfect candidate. He'd told her some months later, when they'd been lying replete in each other's arms, that it had been her passion and enthusiasm that had convinced him. He'd known she would give the job the dedication it deserved.

Meeting Helios... He'd been *nothing* as she'd imagined: as far from the stuffy, pompous, 'entitled' Prince she'd expected him to be as was possible.

Her attraction to him had been immediate, a chemical reaction over which she'd had no control. It had taken her completely off guard. Yet she hadn't thought anything of it. He was a prince, after all, both powerful and dangerously handsome. Never in her wildest dreams had she thought the attraction would be reciprocated. But it had been.

He'd been much more involved with the exhibition than she'd anticipated, and she'd often found herself working alone with him, her longing for him an ever-growing fire inside her that she didn't have a clue how to handle.

Affairs in the workplace were a fact of life, even in the studious world of antiquities, but they were not something she'd ever been tempted by. She loved her work so much it took her entire focus. Her work gave her purpose. It grounded her. And working with the ancient objects of her own people, seeing first-hand how techniques and social mores had evolved over the years, was a form of proof that the past didn't have to be the future. Her birth mother's actions didn't have to define her, even if she did feel the taint of her behaviour like an invisible stain.

Relationships of any real meaning had always been out of the question for her. How could she commit to someone if she didn't know who she truly was? So to find herself feeling such an attraction, and to the man who was effectively her boss, who just happened to be a prince... It was no wonder her emotions had been all over the place.

Helios had had no such inhibitions.

Long before he'd laid so much as a finger on her he'd undressed her with his dark liquid eyes, time and again. Until one late afternoon, when she'd been talking to him in the smaller of the exhibition rooms, she on one side, he on the other, and he'd gone from complete stillness to fluid motion in the beat of a heart. He'd walked to her with long strides and pulled her into his arms.

And that had been it. She'd been his for the taking. And he'd been hers.

Their three months together had been a dream. Theirs had been a physically intense but surprisingly easy relationship. There had been no expectations. No inhibitions. Just passion.

Walking away should have been easy.

The eyes that had undressed her a thousand times now flickered to Pedro, giving silent permission for him to move the discussion on to general museum topics. There might be a special exhibition being organised, but the museum itself still needed to be run to its usual high standards.

Clearly unnerved—Helios's mood, usually so congenial, was unsettling all the staff—Pedro raced through the rest of the agenda in double-quick time, finally mentioning the need for someone to cover for one of their tour guides that Thursday. Amy was happy to volunteer. Thursday was her only reasonably quiet day that week, and she enjoyed taking on the tours whenever the opportunity arose.

One of the things she loved so much about the museum was the collaborative way it was run, with everyone helping each other when needed. It was a philosophy that came from the very top, from Helios himself, even if today there was no sign of his usual amiability.

Only at the very end of the meeting did Pedro say, 'Before we leave, can I remind everyone that menus for next Wednesday need to be handed in by Friday?'

As a thank-you for all the museum staff's hard work in organising the exhibition, Helios had arranged a night out for everyone before the summer rush hit, all expenses paid. It was a typically generous gesture from him, and a social event Amy had been very much looking forward to. Now, though, the thought of a night out with Helios in attendance made her stomach twist.

There was a palpable air of relief when the meeting finished. Today there was none of the usual lingering. Everyone scrambled to their feet and rushed for the door.

'Amy, a word please.' Helios's rich voice rose over the clatter of hurrying feet.

She paused, inches from the door, inches from escape. Arranging her face into a neutral expression, she turned around.

'Shut the door behind you.'

She did as she was told, her heart sinking to her feet, then sat back in her original place opposite him but also the greatest distance possible away.

It wasn't far enough.

The man oozed testosterone.

He also oozed menace.

Her heart kicked against her ribs. She clamped her lips together and folded her arms across her chest.

Yet she couldn't stop her eyes moving to his, couldn't stop herself gazing at him.

His silver chain glinted against the base of his throat. That chain had often brushed against her lips when he'd made love to her.

And as she stared at him, wondering when he was going to speak, his eyes studied her with the same intensity, making her mouth run dry and her hammering pulse race into a gallop.

His fingers drummed on the table. 'Did you have a nice time at Greta's?'

'Yes, thank you,' she replied stiffly, before she realised what he'd said. 'How did you know I was there?'

'Through the GPS on your phone.'

'What? You've been *spying* on me?'

'You are the lover of the heir to the throne of Agon. Our relationship is an open secret. I do not endanger what is mine.'

'I'm not yours. Not any more,' she spat at him, running from fear to fury in seconds. 'Whatever tracking device you've put in my phone, you can take it out. Now.'

She yanked her bag onto the table, pulled out her phone and threw it at him.

His hand opened to catch it like a Venus flytrap catching its prey. He laughed. But unlike on Saturday, when he'd thought he'd been indulging her, the sound contained no humour.

He slid the phone back to her. 'There's no tracking device in it. It's all done through your number.'

'Well, you can damn well *un*track it. Take it off your system, or whatever it's on.'

He studied her contemplatively. His stillness unnerved

her. Helios was *never* still. He had enough energy to power the whole palace.

'Why did you leave?'

'To get away from you.'

'You didn't think I would be worried?'

'I thought you'd be too busy cherry-picking your bride to notice I'd gone.'

Finally a smile played on his lips. 'Ah, so you were punishing me.'

'No, I was not,' she refuted hotly. 'I was giving myself space away from you because I knew you'd still expect to sleep with me after an evening of wooing prospective brides.'

'And you didn't think you'd be able to resist me?'

Her cheeks coloured and Helios felt a flare of satisfaction that his thoughts had been correct.

His beautiful, passionate lover had been jealous.

Slender, feminine to her core, with a tumbling mane of thick dark blonde hair, Amy was possibly the most beautiful woman he'd ever met. A sculptor wouldn't hesitate to cast her as Aphrodite. She made his blood thicken just to look at her, even dressed as she was now in an A-line navy skirt and a pretty yet demure lilac top.

But today there was something unkempt about her appearance that wasn't usually there: dark hollows beneath her taupe eyes, her rosebud lips dry, her usual glowing complexion paler than was normal.

And he was the cause of it. The thought sent a thrill through him. Whatever punishment she had hoped to inflict on him by disappearing for a few days, it had backfired on her.

He would never let her know of the overwhelming fury that had rent him when he'd seen the box she'd left by his door.

Which reminded him...

He slid the thick padded envelope he'd placed on the table towards her. Smashing the box when his anger had got the better of him had caused the perfume bottles to spill and ruin the books, but the jewellery had been left undamaged.

Her eyes narrowed with caution, she extended an elegant hand to it and opened it gingerly. Her mouth tightened when she saw what was inside.

She dropped the envelope back on the table and got quickly to her feet. 'I don't want them.'

'They're yours. You insult me by returning them.'

She didn't blink. 'And you insult me by giving them back when you're about to put an engagement ring on another woman's finger.'

He got out of his chair and stalked over to her. With the chair behind her she had nowhere to retreat. He pulled her to him, enfolding her in his arms so that her head was pressed to his chest. He was too strong and she was too slender for her to wriggle out of his hold, and in any case he knew her attempts didn't mean anything.

He could feel her heat. She *wanted* to be in his arms.

Her head was tilted back, her breaths quickening. He watched as the pupils of her eyes darkened and pulsed, as the grey turned to brown, with a passionate fury there that set his veins alight.

'There is no need to be jealous,' he murmured, pressing himself closer. 'My marriage doesn't change my feelings for you.'

Her left eye twitched, an affliction he'd never seen before. Her top teeth razed across her full bottom lip.

'But it changes my feelings for you.'

'Liar. You can't deny you still want me.' He brushed his cheek against hers and whispered into her ear, 'Only a few days ago you screamed out my name. I still have your scratches on my back.'

She reared back. 'That was before I knew you were looking for an immediate wife. I will not be your mistress.'

'There is no shame in it. Generations of Agon monarchs have taken lovers after marriage.' His grandfather had been the exception to the rule, but only because he'd been fortunate enough to fall in love with his wife.

Of the thirty-one monarchs who'd ruled Agon since 1203, only a handful had found love and fidelity with their spouses. His own father, although he'd died before he could take the throne, had had dozens of lovers and mistresses. He'd revelled in waving his indiscretions right under his loving wife's nose.

'And generations ago your ancestors chopped your enemies' limbs off but you've managed to wean yourself off that.'

He laughed at her retort, running a finger over her chin. Even with her oval face free of make-up Amy was beautiful. 'We don't marry for love or companionship, as other people do. We marry for the good of our island. Think of it as a business arrangement. *You* are my lover. You are the woman I *want* to be with.'

His mother had been unfortunate in that she'd already loved his father when they had married, and it was that love which had ultimately destroyed her, long before the car crash that had taken both his parents' lives.

He would never inflict the kind of pain his father had caused, not on anyone. He had to marry, but he was upfront about what he wanted: a royal wife to produce the next generation of Kalliakis heirs. No emotions. No expectations of fidelity. A union founded on duty and nothing more.

Amy stared at him without speaking for the longest

time, searching for something. He didn't know what she hoped to find.

He brought his face down to meet her lips, which had parted, but she pulled back so only the faintest of touches passed between them.

'I mean it, Helios. We're finished. I will never be your mistress.' Her words were but a whisper.

'You think?'

'Yes.'

'Then why are you still standing here? Why is your breath still warm on my face?'

Brushing his lips across the softness of her cheek, he gripped her bottom and ground her against him, letting her feel his desire for her. The tiniest of moans escaped her throat.

'See?' He trailed kisses over her delicate ear. 'You do want me. But you're punishing me.'

'No, I…'

'Shh…' He placed a finger on her mouth. 'We both know I could take you right now and you would welcome it.'

Heat flared from her eyes but her chin jutted up mutinously.

'I am going to give you exactly five seconds of freedom. Five seconds to leave this room. If after those five seconds you are still here…' he spoke very quietly into her ear '…I will lift up your skirt and make love to you right here and now on this table.'

She quivered, a small tell but one so familiar he knew the expression that would be in her eyes when he looked into them.

He was right. The taupe had further darkened; the pupils were even more dilated. The tip of her pink tongue glistened between her parted lips. He knew that if he placed his hands over her small but beautifully formed breasts he would feel her nipples strain towards him.

He released his hold on her and folded his arms across his chest.

'One.'

She put a hand to her mouth and dragged it down over her chin.

'Two.'

She swallowed. Her eyes never left his face. He could practically smell her longing.

'Three… Four…'

She turned on her heel and fled to the door.

'One week,' he called to her retreating back. She was halfway out of the room and made no show of listening to him, but he knew she heard every word. 'One week and you, *matakia mou*, will be back in my bed. I guarantee it.'

CHAPTER THREE

AMY GAZED AT the marble statues that had arrived on Agon by ship that morning and now sat in the grand entrance hall of the museum on their plinths. Three marble statues. Three kings at the height of their glory. All named Astraeus. The fourth, specially commissioned for the exhibition, would be transported from the sculptor's studio in a week's time. It would depict the current monarch, the fourth King Astraeus, as a young man in his prime.

Helios had personally commissioned it. She didn't want to think of Helios. But she couldn't stop.

He was everywhere. In every painting, every sculpture, every fragment of framed scripture, every piece of pottery. Everything was a reminder that this was all his. His people. His ancestors. Him.

Her attention kept flickering back to the statue of the second King Astraeus, a marble titan dating from 1403. Trident in hand and unashamedly naked, he had the same arrogant look with an underlying hint of ferociousness that Helios carried so well. If she had known nothing of the Agon royal dynasty, she would have known instinctively that her lover was a descendent of this man. Agon had been at peace for decades but their warrior roots dated back millennia, were ingrained in their DNA.

Helios had warrior roots in spades.

She had to stop thinking about him.

God, this was supposed to be easy. An affair with no promises and no need for compromise.

She'd been so tempted to stay in the boardroom with him. She'd *ached* to stay. Her body had been weighted down with need for him. But in the back of her mind had been an image of him exchanging his vows with a faceless woman who would become his wife.

Amy couldn't be the other woman. Whatever kind of marriage Helios had in mind for himself, it would still be real. He needed an heir. He would make love to his wife.

She could never allow herself to be the cause of pain and humiliation in another. She'd seen first-hand the damage an affair could cause. After all, she was the result of an affair herself. She'd spent seventeen years knowing she was the result of something sordid.

She was nothing but a dirty secret.

Helios's driver brought the car to a stop at the back of the palace, beside his private entrance. Dozens and dozens of schoolchildren of all shapes and sizes were picnicking on the lawn closest to the museum entrance: some playing football, some doing cartwheels and handstands. In the far distance a group were filing out of the Agon palace's maze, which was famed as one of the biggest and tallest mazes in the world.

Helios checked the time. He was always too busy to spend as much time with the palace visitors as he would like.

He had a small window before he was due at a business meeting he'd arranged with his brothers. His brothers ran the day-to-day side of their investment business, but he was still heavily involved. Then there were his royal duties, which had increased exponentially since the onset of his grandfather's illness. He was in all but name Prince Regent, the highest ranking ambassador for his beloved island. It was his duty to do everything he could to bring investment and tourists to his island, to spread his country's influence on the world's stage and keep his islanders safe and prosperous.

As he neared the children, with his courtiers keeping a discreet distance, their small faces turned to him with curiosity. As often happened, it took only one to recognise him before his identity spread like wildfire and they all came running up. It was one of the things he so liked about children: their lack of inhibition. In a world of politeness and protocol he found it refreshing.

One thing he and Catalina were in agreement about was the wish for a minimum of two children. They agreed on many things. Most things. Which was a good omen for their forthcoming marriage. On paper, everything about their union appeared perfect. But...

Every time he tried to picture the children they would create together his mind came up blank. The picture just would not form.

Despite her ravishing beauty, his blood had yet to thicken for her. But this was only a minor issue, and one he was certain would resolve itself the more time he spent with her. Tomorrow he would fly to Monte Cleure so he could formally ask her father for Catalina's hand in marriage. It was only a formality, but one that couldn't be overlooked.

At least times had moved on from such issues as a dowry having to be found and trade alliances and so on being written into the contract of any royal betrothal. Now all he had to worry about was his bride having blue blood.

He'd always found blue so cold.

He turned his attention on the English children and

answered a host of questions from them, including, 'Is it true your toilet is made of gold?'

His personal favourite was 'Is it true you carry a sub-machine gun wherever you go?'

In answer to this he pulled from his pocket the pen-knife his grandfather had given him on his graduation from Sandhurst; an upgraded version of the one he'd been given on his tenth birthday. 'No, but I always carry *this*.'

As expected, the children were agog to see it. It was termed a penknife only in the loosest sense; on sight any-one would recognise it for the deadly fighting instrument it truly was. Children loved it when he showed it to them. Their basic human nature had not yet been knocked out of them by the insane political correctness infecting the rest of the Western world.

'Most Agonites carry knives with them,' he said to the enthralled children. 'If anyone wants to invade our island they know we will fight back with force.'

Their teacher, who had looked at the knife as if it had come personally from Eurynomos himself, looked most relieved as she glanced at her watch. Immediately she clapped her hands together. 'Everyone into their pairs—it's time for our tour.'

Today was Thursday… Amy was taking on some of the tours…

The hairs on the back of his neck lifted. He looked over at the museum entrance. A slender figure stood at the top of the steps. Even though she was too far away for him to see clearly, the increasing beat of his heart told him it was her.

He straightened, a smile playing on his lips. Only two days had passed since she'd called his bluff and walked out of the boardroom, leaving him with an ache in his groin he'd only just recovered from. He would bet anything she had suffered in the same manner. He would bet she'd spent the past two days jumping every time her phone rang, waiting for his call.

Her pride had been wounded when she'd learned he was taking a wife, but she would get over it. She couldn't punish him for ever, not when she suffered as greatly as he did. Soon she would come crawling back.

After a moment's thought, he beckoned for one of his courtiers and instructed him to pass his apologies to his brothers. They could handle the meeting without him.

The time was ripe to assist Amy in crawling back to him.

The Agon palace dungeons never failed to thrill, whatever the visitor's age. Set deep underground, and reached by steep winding staircases at each end of the gloom, only those over the age of eight were permitted to enter. Inside, dim light was provided by tiny electrical candles that flickered as if they were the real thing, casting shadows wherever one stood. Unsurprisingly, the children today were huddled closely together.

'These dungeons were originally a pit in which to throw the Venetian invaders,' Amy said, speaking clearly so all twenty-three children on the tour could hear. 'The Venetians were the only people to successfully invade Agon, and when Ares the Conqueror, cousin of the King at the time, led the uprising in AD 1205, the first thing he ordered his men to do was build these pits. King Timios, who was the reigning King and whom the Agonites blamed for letting the Venetians in, was thrown into the cell to my left.'

The children took it in turns to gawp through the iron railings at the tiny square stone pit.

'The manacle on the right-hand wall is the original manacle used to chain him,' she added.

'Did he die in here?' a young boy asked.

'No,' said a deep male voice that reverberated off the narrow walls before she could answer, making them all jump.

A long shadow cast over them and Helios appeared. In the flickering light of the damp passageway in which they stood his large frame appeared magnified, as if Orion, the famously handsome giant, had come to life.

What was he *doing* here?

She'd seen him only an hour ago, standing in the gardens talking to the school parties, as at ease with the children as he was in every other situation. That had been the moment she had forgotten how to breathe.

It will get better, she kept assuring herself. *It's still early days and still raw. Soon you'll feel better.*

'King Timios was held in these cells for six months before Ares Patakis expelled him and, with the consent of the people, took the crown for himself,' Helios said to the captivated children. 'The palace was built over these dungeons so King Ares could have personal control over the prisoners.'

'Did he kill anyone?' asked the same bloodthirsty boy.

'He killed many people,' Helios answered solemnly. 'But only in battle. Prisoners of war were released and sent back to Venice.' He paused and offered a smile. 'But only after having their hands chopped off. King Ares wanted to send a warning to other armies wishing to invade—*Step on our shores and you will never wield a weapon again.* That's if they were lucky enough to live.'

The deeper they went into the dungeons, which were large enough to hold up to three hundred prisoners, the more questions were thrown at him as the children did their best to spook each other in the candlelit dimness.

It was with relief that Helios handled everything asked

of him—his presence had made her tongue tie itself into a knot.

'Have *you* ever killed anyone?' an undersized girl asked with a nervous laugh.

He shook his head slowly. 'But since I could walk and talk I've been trained to use knives, shoot arrows and throw a spear. My brothers and I are all military trained. Trust me, should any other nation try to invade us, Agonites are ready. We fight. We are not afraid to spill blood—whether it's an enemy's or our own—to protect what's ours. We will defend our island to the death.'

Utter silence followed this impassioned speech. Twenty-three sets of wide eyes gazed up at Helios with a mixture of awe and terror. The teacher looked shell-shocked.

It had had the opposite effect on Amy.

His words had pushed through her skin to heat her veins. It had never so much been his looks, as gorgeous as he was, that had attracted her. It had been his passion. The Kalliakis family was a dynasty whose blood ran red, not blue. And no one's blood ran redder than Helios's. On the outside he was a true prince. Beneath his skin lay a warrior.

'And that, children, proves that it's not only Ares the Conqueror's blood Prince Helios has inherited from his ancestor but his devotion to his homeland.' Amy spoke quickly, to break the hush and to distract herself from the ache spreading inside her. 'Now, who here would like to be adopted by the Prince? Any takers? No? Hmm… You surprise me. Come on, then, who wants to visit the museum gift shop?'

That brought them back to life; the thought of spending their money on gifts for themselves.

'It's a good thing you'll never have to be a tour guide as your day job,' Amy couldn't resist saying to Helios as she climbed the stairs a little way behind the school party. 'They'll all have nightmares.'

He followed closely behind her. 'They're learning my family's history. I was putting it into the context of the present day for them.'

'Yes. They were learning about your *history*. There's a big difference between hearing about wars and blood-spilling from centuries ago and having it put into the here and now, especially in the dungeons, of all places. They're only ten years old.'

'The world is full of bloodshed. That's never changed in the history of mankind. The only way to stop it creeping to our shores is through fear and stability.'

Her hand tightened on the railing as she carried on climbing. 'But Agon *is* stable. You have an elected senate. You are a democracy.'

'The people still look to us, their royal family, for leadership. Our opinions matter. Our actions matter even more so.'

'Hence the reason you're marrying Princess Catalina,' she stated flatly.

'We are a prosperous, stable island nation, *matakia mou*, and it's the hard work of generations of my family that has made it so. Until the entire world is stable we are vulnerable to attack in many different forms. We lead by example, and as a people we are united as one. Stability within the royal family promotes stability for the whole island. My grandfather is dying. My marriage will bring peace to him and act as security to my people, who will be assured that the future of my family is taken care of and by extension their own families too. They know that with a descendant of Ares Patakis on the throne their country is not only ready to defend itself but able to weather any financial storm that may hit our isles.'

Somewhere during his speech they'd both stopped climbing. Amy found herself facing him from two steps above, coming to eye level with him. His eyes were liquid, the shadows dancing over his features highlighting the strength of the angles and planes that made him so darkly handsome. Her fingers tingled with the urge to reach out and touch him...

'I need to catch up with the children,' she breathed, but her rubbery legs made no attempt to move.

'They know where they're going,' he murmured, placing a hand on the damp wall to steady himself as he leaned in close.

His other hand caught her hip, jerking her to him. Delicious heat swirled through her; moisture pushed out the dryness in her mouth. Her skin danced and her lips parted as she moved her mouth to meet his...

She only just pulled away in time.

Swiping at his hand to remove it from her hip, she said, 'I haven't said goodbye to them.'

'Then say your goodbyes.' His eyes were alight with amusement. 'Keep running, *matakia mou*, but know you can't run for ever. Soon I will catch you.'

She didn't answer, turning tail and racing to the top of the steep staircase, gripping tightly onto the rail, and then out into the corridor.

At least in the corridor she could breathe.

What had just happened? She'd been a breath away from kissing him. Did she have no pride? No sense of preservation?

She wanted to cry with frustration.

Whether Helios believed it or not, they were over. He was marrying someone else. It was abhorrent that she still reacted so strongly towards him.

There was only one thing she could do.

She had to leave.

As soon as the exhibition was officially opened, to coincide with the Gala in just over a fortnight, she would leave the palace and never come back.

After a long day spent overseeing the arrival of artefacts from the Greek museum Amy should have been dead on her feet, but the email she'd just received had acted like a shot of espresso to her brain.

After months of searching and weeks of tentative communication, Leander had agreed to see her. Tomorrow night she would meet her half-brother for the first time.

She looked at her watch. If she moved quickly she could run to Resina and buy herself a new dress to wear for their meal, before late-night shopping was over. She wouldn't have time tomorrow, with Saturday being the museum's busiest day.

After hurriedly turning her computer off and shuffling papers so her desk looked tidy, and not as if she'd abandoned it whilst in the middle of important work, she rushed out of her office and headed downstairs to see if Pedro was still about and could lock up.

She came to an abrupt halt.

There, in the museum entrance, talking to Pedro, stood Helios.

She wasn't quick enough to escape. Both of them turned their faces to her.

'Speak of the woman and she shall appear,' said Pedro, beaming at her.

'What have I done?' she asked, squashing the butterflies in her stomach and feigning nonchalance.

Pedro grinned. 'Don't look so worried. Helios and I have been discussing your future.'

Within the confines of the museum the staff addressed
Helios by his first name, at his insistence.

'Oh?' Her gaze fell on Helios. 'I thought you were going
to Monte Cleure,' she said before she could stop herself.

'My plane leaves in an hour.'

Her chest compressed in on itself. Stupidly, she'd looked
up the distance between Agon and Monte Cleure, which
came in at just over one thousand two hundred miles. Just
over two and a half hours' flying time. With the time difference factored in he would be there in time to share an
intimate dinner with the Princess.

She pressed her lips together to prevent the yelp of pain
that wanted to escape and forced her features into an expression of neutrality. Helios had so much power over her
she couldn't bear for him to know how deeply it ran.

Oblivious to any subtext going on around him, Pedro
said, 'I was going to leave this until tomorrow, but seeing
as you're here there's no time like the present—'

'We were saying how impressed we are with your handling of the exhibition,' Helios cut in smoothly. 'You have
exceeded our expectations. We would like to offer you
a permanent job at the museum when your secondment
finishes.'

'What kind of job?' she asked warily. A week ago this
news would have filled her with joy. But everything was
different now.

'Corinna will be leaving us at the end of the summer.
We would like you to have her job.'

Corinna was second only to Pedro in the museum
hierarchy.

'There are far more qualified curators than me working
here,' she said non-committally, wishing Pegasus might
fly into the palace at that very moment and whisk her
away to safety.

'Pedro is happy to train you in the areas where you lack experience,' said Helios, a smile of triumph dancing in his eyes. 'The important thing is you can do the job. Everyone here likes and respects you...curators at other museums enjoy collaborating with you. You're an asset to the Agon Palace Museum and we would be fools to let you go.'

If Pedro hadn't been there she would have cursed Helios for such a blatant act of manipulation.

'What do you think?' he asked when she remained silent. His dark eyes bored into her, a knowing, almost playful look emanating from them. 'How do you like the idea of living and working here permanently?'

She knew exactly what he was doing and exactly what he was thinking. He knew how much she loved her job, his island and its people. Helios was working tactically. He thought that if he threw enough incentives at her she would be so overcome with gratitude she would allow him back into her bed.

She'd entered their relationship without any illusions of permanency. It had suited her as much as it had suited him. Desire was what had glued them together, and it scared her to know that despite all the protective barriers she'd placed around herself he'd still slipped inside. Not fully, but enough for pain to lance her whenever she thought of him and the Princess together. When she thought of her own future without him in her life.

How could she continue to be his lover feeling as she did now, even putting aside the fact of his imminent engagement?

His engagement had hammered home as nothing else could that she was good enough to share his bed but not good enough for anything more.

She knew she was being unfair—Agon's constitution and Helios's position in life were not his fault or within his control—but for the first time she felt the reality on an emotional level and that terrified her.

In her heart of hearts she'd always longed to meet someone she could trust with the truth about her conception and not fear they would turn away in disgust or believe that the fruit never fell far from the tree. To meet someone who could love her for herself.

During their time together she had come to trust Helios. He was a man she'd thought she could confide the truth to, and she was almost certain he wouldn't turn away in disgust. But still she'd kept her secrets close. He couldn't give her the other things she'd always secretly craved but had never quite believed she deserved. Love. Fidelity. Commitment. It had been wiser to keep her heart as close as her secrets.

She considered her words carefully, although her head swam. 'I'm going to need time to think about it.'

'What is there to think about?' he asked, his dark eyes narrowing slightly.

'My life is in England,' she said evenly, although she knew there was really nothing to think about. He could offer to quadruple her salary and the answer would be the same.

She was saved from elaborating by Helios's phone ringing.

'My cue to leave,' he said, flashing her a grin. 'We can continue this discussion another time soon.'

She knew what 'soon' meant. He meant to visit her on Sunday evening, when he returned.

With Pedro there she was in no position to refuse or challenge anything. And even if she'd wanted to Helios didn't give her the chance, wishing them both a good weekend before striding off and out of the museum. On his way to Monte Cleure to spend his weekend with the Princess and her family.

And she...

As soon as she returned from her last-minute shopping trip she would write her resignation letter. She would give it to Pedro tomorrow, safe in the knowledge that Helios would be over a thousand miles away.

CHAPTER FOUR

AMY PUT THE lip gloss tube to her mouth, but before she could squeeze the gel-like substance on, a loud rap made her jerk her hand back. The banging had come from the door outside her bedroom that connected the passageway between her apartment and Helios's.

She pressed her hand to her pounding heart.

What was he doing here?

He was supposed to be spending the whole weekend in Monte Cleure, using his time there to officially ask Princess Catalina's father's blessing for their marriage. He should still be there, celebrating their forthcoming union, not here on Agon, banging on his ex-lover's door.

Breathing heavily, she closed her eyes and willed him away.

Another loud rap on the door proved the futility of her wish.

Suddenly galvanised into action, she dropped the lip gloss into her handbag and slipped out of her room, hurrying past the connecting door as another knock rang out. Snatching her jacket off the coat stand, she left her apartment through the main exit and hurried down the narrow stairs. With her heart battering against her chest she punched in the code that opened the door and stole outside into the warm spring evening air.

She felt like an escaped convict.

Security lights blazed everywhere, and she kept as close to the palace wall as she could for as long as she could until she had to dart out to cross into the courtyard used by the palace staff. The car she'd ordered earlier was already waiting for her. She jumped straight into the passenger side, making Eustachys the driver, who was busy on his phone, jump.

'You're early,' he said with a grin, before adding, 'Where do you want to go?'

She forced a smile. Whenever she needed one of the pool of cars and drivers that were on permanent standby for the palace staff she was invariably given Eustachys, who spoke excellent English. 'Resina, please.'

She gave him the name of the restaurant she was dining at and tried not to betray her impatience as he inputted it into his satnav, especially as she was perfectly aware that he knew every inch of the island and had no need for it.

A minute later they were off, starting the twenty-minute drive to Agon's capital, a cosmopolitan town rich in history and full of excellent shops and restaurants.

She didn't want to think of Helios, still standing at her door demanding entry. She didn't want to think of him at all.

All she wanted at that moment was to keep her composure as she met the man who shared her blood for the first time.

When Eustachys collected her from the restaurant later that evening Resina's streets were full of Saturday night revellers and stars were twinkling down from the black sky above them.

Amy's head throbbed too hard for her to want to be out amongst them.

Although not a complete disaster, her meeting with Leander had been much more difficult than she'd anticipated. It hadn't helped that she'd still been shaken from Helios's unexpected return to Agon and that she'd been half expecting him to turn up at the restaurant. Discovering where she'd gone would have been as easy for him as buttoning a shirt.

Leander hadn't helped either. She'd already gathered from his social media profile and his posts that he wasn't the most mature of men, but now, reflecting on their meal together—which she had paid for with no argument from him—she came to the sad conclusion that her newly found half-brother was a spoilt brat.

He'd been honest as far as he'd wanted to be. He'd told his mother—Amy's birth mother—about their meeting. He'd made it clear to Amy that it would be his judgement alone that would determine whether Neysa would meet the child she'd abandoned, and that power was a wonderful thing for him to crow about.

Scrap being a spoilt brat. Her half-brother was a monster.

Through all the crowing and the sniffing—she was almost certain he was on drugs—Amy had gleaned that his wealthy father had no idea of her existence. The Soukises had a nice, cosy life, and Amy turning up was in none of their interests. As far as Leander was concerned, Amy was a can of worms that was one twist of the can opener away from potentially destroying his comfortable life.

So, their meeting hadn't been a *complete* Greek tragedy. But not far off.

After being dropped back in the courtyard she made her way on weary legs to her apartment, removing her heels to walk up the staircase to her apartment.

She couldn't elicit the tiniest bit of surprise at finding Helios on her sofa, feet bare, in snug-fitting faded jeans and a black T-shirt, his muscular arms folded in a manner she knew meant only one thing—trouble.

'How did you get in here?' she asked pointlessly. This was his palace. He could go where he pleased.

'With a key,' he answered sardonically, straightening up and rolling his shoulders. 'Where have you been?'

'Out.'

Helios threw her a stare with narrowed eyes, taking in the pretty mint-green dress that fell to her knees, the elegantly knotted hair and the hooped earrings. It was an outfit he'd never seen her wear before. 'Have you been on a date?'

She gazed at him with tired eyes. 'It doesn't matter where I've been. Shouldn't you be with your fiancée? I assume she *is* your fiancée now?'

'Her father gave his blessing. We will make the official announcement during the Gala.'

'So why aren't you in Monte Cleure, celebrating?'

'Some unwelcome news was brought to my attention, so I came back a day early.'

A flicker of alarm flashed across her pretty features. 'Has something happened to your grandfather?'

'My grandfather's fine.' As fine as an eighty-seven-year-old man riddled with cancer could be.

He visited his grandfather every day that he was in the country, always praying that a miracle had occurred and he would see signs of improvement. All he ever saw was further deterioration. The strong, vibrant man who'd been not just the head of his family but the very heart of it was diminishing before his eyes.

Helios and his brothers' business interests had been so successful that their islanders no longer had to pay a cent of tax towards the royal family's upkeep and security. They had enough money to keep their people afloat if the worst economic storm should hit. But not even their great wealth was enough to cure the man who had given up so much to raise them, and it hadn't been enough to cure their beloved grandmother of the pneumonia that had killed her five years ago either. Her death was something their grandfather had never recovered from.

But for once, this evening, he had hardly thought of his grandfather. He'd been sitting rigidly on Amy's hard sofa, trying to keep a lid on his temper as the hours had passed and he'd waited for her to return.

And now here she was, dressed for a romantic night out *with someone else*. It was the final punch in the guts after what had been a hellish day.

The straightforward task of asking the King of Monte Cleure for his daughter's hand in marriage had turned into something infinitely more stomach-turning. The King had received him as if he were a long-lost son, his pride and happiness in his daughter's choice and her future prospects evident.

Throughout the entire private audience a bad taste had been lodged in Helios's throat. Words had formed but he'd spoken them as if they were being dragged over spikes. And throughout all the formalities his brain had been ticking over Amy's less than enthusiastic response to his offer of a permanent role at the palace museum.

To Helios it had been the perfect solution—a way to prove to Amy that she still had a role to play in his life for as long as she wanted, and that he wasn't throwing away what they had for the sake of a piece of paper tying him to another woman. And, besides, she'd earned the job offer. All his reasoning, everything he'd said to her, had been the truth.

Her response had grated on him.

And then he'd received that message from Pedro and taken his jet straight back to Agon.

'Where have you been?' he asked for a second time, noting the way she avoided his gaze at the question.

She sank onto the armchair in the corner, put a palm to her eye and rubbed it, smearing a trail of smoky-grey make-up across her cheek. 'You have no right to ask. Who I see and what I do with my time is my own business.'

'If you have taken another lover then I have every right to question you about it,' he retorted, smothering the nausea roiling in his guts. If she'd taken another lover...

'No, you *don't*,' she said hotly. 'You're the one marrying someone else, not me. That makes me a free agent. I don't owe you anything.'

Staring at her angry face, it struck him for the first time that Amy was serious about their relationship being over. Until that precise moment he'd assumed her pride and jealousy had been speaking for her. That she'd been punishing him.

'Who have you been with?' he demanded. 'Was it a man?'

She met his eyes and gave a sharp nod.

'Is it someone I know?'

'No.'

'Where did you meet him?'

'That doesn't matter.' She sucked in a breath. 'Look, Helios—please—leave me alone. What we had...it's over...'

'So you've jumped straight into bed with another man? Is this your way of punishing me for doing my duty to my family and my country?'

The distaste that flashed over her face answered for her. 'That's disgusting.'

He hid the immediate rush of relief that she hadn't been intimate with this elusive man. The relief died as quickly as it had been born.

'If you're not punishing me then why were you out with someone else? Are you so keen to prove your point that we're finished that you'd humiliate me?'

'How is me dining with someone else humiliating? And how can you dare say that when you're the one *marrying* someone else?'

'And how can *you* dare think I'll let you walk away?'

She stilled, her eyes widening, the flicker under her left eye returning.

'The reason I came back early from Monte Cleure is because Pedro called to inform me that the curator in charge of my grandfather's Jubilee Exhibition—a woman who, may I remind you, was taken on despite her lack of experience, because Pedro and I were both convinced she had the knowledge and enthusiasm to pull it off—has decided to quit five months early.'

His anger burned, enflaming him. He would never have believed Amy could be so underhand.

'Helios…' She reached out a hand, then dropped it back to her side with a sigh. 'What other choice do I have? I can't stay here now.'

'You're not the heroine of some old-fashioned melodrama,' he said scathingly. 'What did you think would happen? That I would hear you had resigned and shrug my shoulders and say that it's okay? Or that I would be so upset at the thought of you leaving my life permanently I would abandon my plans to marry Catalina, renounce my claim to the throne and marry you?'

She clutched at the knot of hair at the nape of her neck. 'I hoped you would accept it and at least try to understand where I'm coming from.'

'Well I don't understand or accept it. Your resignation has been refused. You will stay until your contracted period is up or I will sue you for breach of contract.'

Her shock was visible. 'You wouldn't...'

'Wouldn't I? Leave before September and see for yourself.'

'The exhibition is almost complete,' she said, breathing heavily, angry colour heightening her cheeks. 'Come the Gala and we'll be ready for visitors—my job will be done. Anyone else can carry on.'

'"Anyone else" will not have the breadth of knowledge you've developed about my grandfather and our ancestors. You signed that contract and you will damn well fulfil it.'

She jumped to her feet, her hands balled into fists. 'Why are you doing this? Why can't you just let me go?'

'Because we belong together,' he snarled. 'You're mine—do you understand that?'

'No, the *Princess* belongs to you. Not me. I belong only to myself. You can insist I work the rest of my contract—that's absolutely within your rights—but that doesn't change anything else. I will work out the contract if I must, but I will not share your bed. I will not be your mistress.'

Helios could feel the blood pumping in his head. His veins were aflame; needles were pushing into his skin. Deep in his gut was something he couldn't identify—but, *Theos*, whatever it was, it hurt.

He'd known from the outset that Amy was a woman of honour. Her excitement at his job offer had been so evident it had been contagious, but she'd refused to agree or to sign the contract until she'd spoken to her bosses at the British Museum face-to-face. If there had been any hesitation from them in letting her take the role she would have refused it, even though it was, by her own admission, a dream come true.

If it was such a dream then why was she prepared to walk away from it now?

And if she was so honourable how could she already be actively seeking a new lover?

He needed to get out of this apartment before he did something he would regret. So many emotions were riding through him it was impossible to distinguish them. He only knew his fists wanted nothing more than to smash things, to take every ornament and piece of furniture in this apartment and pulverise it.

For the second time in as many weeks the violence that lived in his blood threatened to boil over, and he despised himself for it almost as much as he despised Amy right now for seeking to leave him. But, unlike his violent father, Helios knew his own temper would never be directed at a woman. It was the only certainty he could take comfort from.

Striding over to her, he took her chin in his hand and forced her to look at him. *Theos*, she had such delicate features and such gorgeous skin. He didn't think there was an inch of her he hadn't stroked and kissed. He refused to believe he would never make love to her again. He *refused*.

'If you understand nothing else, understand this—you will *always* belong to me,' he said roughly, before dropping his hold and walking out of her apartment.

Amy's phone vibrated, breaking her concentration on the beautiful green sapphire ring she was supposed to be categorising but instead could only stare at with a lump in her throat.

This ring had belonged to Helios's mother. This ring would one day soon slide onto Princess Catalina's finger.

The message from Leander was simple and clear.

She doesn't want to meet you. Do not contact me again.

She read it a number of times before closing her eyes

and rubbing at the nape of her neck. A burn stung the back of her retinas.

She had never expected her birth mother to welcome her long-abandoned daughter with cheers and whistles, but she had expected *something*. Some curiosity, if nothing else. Did she not even wonder what Amy looked like? Or who she had become?

But there was too much shame. To Neysa Soukis, Amy was nothing but a scar on her memories; a scar that had to remain hidden.

If Amy were a different person she would force the issue. She would stalk Neysa at her house until she was browbeaten into seeing her. But even if she was capable of doing that what would it accomplish? Nothing more than Neysa's further contempt and probably a restraining order to boot.

All she wanted was to talk to her. Just once. But clearly she wasn't worth even that.

'Are you ready to go yet?'

Blinking rapidly, she looked up and found Greta standing in the doorway.

Amy turned her phone off. 'She doesn't want to meet me.'

At least with Greta she didn't have to pretend.

Greta came over to her and put an arm around her back. 'I'm sorry.'

Amy sniffed. 'I just thought...'

'I know,' said Greta softly. 'But learning you were here probably came as a big shock to her. She'll change her mind.'

'What if she doesn't?'

'She will,' Greta insisted. 'Now, turn your computer off. We've a night out to get ready for.'

'I'm not going.'

'You are. A night out is exactly what you need.'

'But Helios will be there.'

'So what? This will be your chance to let him see you having a great time and that you're completely unaffected by your break-up.'

Amy gave a laugh that came out as more of a snort than anything else. Thank God for Greta. Without her cheering friendship and positive attitude life on Agon would be unbearable right now.

Was it only four months ago that she'd arrived on this island full of excitement for what the future held? With a handsome prince as her boss and the opportunity to find the woman who'd given birth to her?

Now she was stuck here for another five months, and she would have to watch the handsome prince marry his princess and her birth mother wanted nothing to do with her.

She wished she'd never come to Agon.

Greta rubbed her arm in solidarity. 'Let's get your dress and go back to my flat. There's a bottle of ouzo waiting for us.'

'But…'

'Are you going to give that man so much power over you that you'd give up a free night out with all your friends and colleagues?'

Amy sighed and shook her head. Greta was right. She'd spent the past four days hiding away, mostly holing herself up in the museum's enormous basement, on the pretext of categorising artefacts, desperate to avoid bumping into Helios. And she'd been successful—other than one brief glimpse of him in the palace gardens she'd not had any dealings with him. Of course he was incredibly busy, with the Gala being only ten days away.

'Maybe he won't come,' she said with sudden hopefulness.

'Maybe…' Greta didn't look convinced.

But the thought of him not coming made her feel just as rotten as the thought of him being there.

If he did come, she had to pray he didn't bring the Princess as his guest.

To meet his future wife in the flesh would be one wound too many.

CHAPTER FIVE

THE MAIN REASON Helios had chosen Hotel Giroud for the staff night out was because his staff deserved to enjoy themselves in the most exclusive hotel on Agon. The fact its gardens led to a private beach was a plus.

Owned by Nathaniel Giroud, an old friend from his schooldays, it was the sister establishment of Club Giroud, the most exclusive and secret club on the island. The hotel was only marginally more inclusive, provided one had the funds and the connections. The quality of Helios's connections went without saying, and of course he had the funds, more than he could ever spend. He didn't begrudge spending a cent of his money on the staff who worked so hard for him.

He took his museum staff out twice a year: once at the beginning of the summer season, and once right at the end. Although the events weren't compulsory everyone attended, even those curators and conservators who would live in the museum basement if he'd let them. Most of his museum staff were a breed unto themselves, deeply dedicated to their work. He'd never imagined he would *desire* one of them.

And yet he had. He did.

During what was possibly the busiest time of his life, he couldn't flush Amy from his mind. Even after the news his brother Theseus had given him a couple of days ago he couldn't rid himself of her. Here he was, wrestling with the bombshell that Theseus had a secret child, a Kalliakis heir, and still she remained at the forefront of his mind.

It was taking everything he had to keep away from the museum. There was far too much going on for him to spend any time there, but knowing Amy was within its spacious walls meant the place acted like a magnet to him.

There were only ten days now until the Gala, and he had a mountain of work to do for it. He was determined to make it a success for his grandfather and for all his people.

On Agon, heirs traditionally took the throne at the age of forty. His father had died a few years short of that age and so his grandfather—without a word of complaint—had abandoned his retirement plans to hold the throne for Helios. His grandparents had sacrificed their dreams of travelling the world and his grandmother had put aside her thoughts of returning to her first love of performing as violin virtuoso. Those dreams had been abandoned so they could raise their orphaned grandchildren and mould them into princes the whole of Agon could be proud of. They had sacrificed everything.

There was no person on this earth Helios respected more or felt a deeper affection for than his grandfather. He would do anything for him. And, out of everything, it was marriage he knew his grandfather wanted the most for him. King Astraeus the Fourth wanted to leave this world secure in the knowledge that his lineage would live on and that the monarchy was in safe hands.

Although his engagement was now an open secret, the official announcement would bring his grandfather peace. That more than anything was Helios's overriding concern. He didn't like to think what it would bring for his own state of mind.

Catalina wouldn't return to Agon until the Gala. He'd dissuaded her from coming any earlier, using his busyness as an excuse to keep her away. A shudder ran through him as he recalled her obvious disappointment when he'd left Monte Cleure a day early. When he'd said goodbye she'd raised her chin in anticipation of his kiss. The most he'd been able to do was brush his lips against her cheek. She'd smelled fantastic, and she'd looked beautiful, but he might as well have been dead from the waist down for all she did for him.

Catalina knew what she was marrying into, he reminded himself. She had no illusions that their union would ever be about love. She'd assured him of that herself. But now he wondered if mutual respect would be enough when he couldn't even bring himself to kiss her.

He stood in the hotel lobby, personally greeting his staff and their partners. In all, over one hundred people were expected. He always enjoyed seeing their transformation, enjoyed seeing the back-room staff, who tended to live in jeans and baggy tops, and the front-line staff, who wore smart uniforms, all dressed to the nines in smart suits and cocktail dresses.

As each person entered he welcomed them with an embrace while Talia, his private secretary, handed them all an envelope.

Soon the lobby was full and waiting staff with trays of champagne were circulating. Conversation was stilted, as it always was at the beginning of such evenings, but he knew that wouldn't last long. Once everyone had had a drink or two their inhibitions would fall away and they would enjoy themselves properly. They all worked so hard they deserved to let their hair down.

Through the lobby's wide glass doors he saw two figures approach, their heads bent close together, laughing. His heart jolted, making him lose the thread of the conversation he'd struck up with one of the tour guides. Closer they came, until they reached the doors and showed their identification to the guards on duty, who inspected them closely before standing to one side to admit them.

The doors opened automatically and in they walked.

He greeted Greta first, with the same kind of embrace he'd shared with everyone else. She returned it warmly, gushing about how excited she was. And then it was time to greet Amy.

The same smile she'd entered the lobby with stayed fixed on her face, but her eyes told a different story.

His throat ran dry.

He'd seen her dressed up on a few occasions before: when he'd taken her out on dates away from the palace, and last weekend for her 'date' with someone else, but tonight...

Theos. She looked stunning.

She wore a sleeveless navy blue chiffon dress that floated just above her knees, with silver diamond-shaped beads layered along the hem and across the high round neckline. On her feet were simple high-heeled black shoes that showcased her slender legs. She'd left her dark blonde hair loose, so that it fell across her shoulders and down her back. Her large taupe eyes were ringed with dark grey eyeshadow and her delectable lips were painted nude.

He couldn't drag his eyes away.

For what had to be the first time ever he found himself at a loss for words.

Judging by the expression in her wide eyes, pain emanating from them as she gazed back at him, she was struggling to form words on her own tongue too.

It was Greta who broke the silence, with a shout of, 'Champagne!' She grinned at Helios, slipped her arm through Amy's and whisked her off to find them a glass each.

'Thanks,' Amy muttered the second they were out of

his earshot. Her heart was hammering so hard she could swear she was suffering from palpitations.

'You're welcome. Here,' said Greta, thrusting a glass into Amy's hand. 'Drink this.'

'I've had enough already.' They'd had a couple of shots of ouzo each in Greta's flat, before the car had arrived for them, and while not drunk she definitely felt a little light-headed.

Greta shook her head. 'You're going to need a lot more than this to get through the night without throwing yourself at him.'

'I'm not going to throw myself at him.'

'You could have fooled me from the way you were just staring at each other.'

'We're over,' Amy stated flatly.

'So you keep telling yourself.'

'I mean it.'

'I know you do. The problem is I don't think your heart believes it.' Greta squeezed her hand. 'Don't worry. I'll stop you from entering the big bad wolf's clutches again.'

Fighting to stop her gaze flickering back to him, Amy nodded and swallowed half of her champagne.

'Let's see what's in these envelopes,' Greta said, ripping hers open.

Amy followed suit and found inside a personalised card, thanking her for all her hard work since joining the museum, and two hundred euros to spend in the casino.

'Last year we spent a day on Helios's yacht,' Greta confided, fingering her own pile of notes lovingly. 'It was amazing—when we got back to shore Talia was so drunk Pedro had to carry her off.'

Her words did the trick, making Amy laugh at the image of Helios's prim private secretary, brought along to keep events ticking along smoothly, losing control of herself in such a manner.

Some of her angst loosened and she made a pledge to enjoy herself. At some point just about *everyone* who'd had a work-based affair had to deal with an ex being present. She didn't have to make a big deal of it. If she stuck to Greta's side and avoided even looking at Helios she would be fine.

But stopping herself from staring became harder when they were taken through to the restaurant, which had been put aside for their private use. The seating plan meant she had an excellent view of the top table, where Helios was seated. So good was her view that the moment she took her seat his eyes found her.

She cast her eyes down to her menu, ostensibly familiarising herself with her selections. When she dared to look back up he was engaged in conversation with Jessica, an American curator who had worked at the museum for two decades.

'You're staring,' Greta hissed.

Smiling tightly, Amy forced small talk from her lips, taking a small breath of relief when the starters were brought out.

Her plate was placed before her, and the waiter removed the silver lid with a flourish to release the beautiful aromas of roast sea scallops and smoked celeriac purée sitting in a shellfish broth. It tasted as wonderful as it smelled, and she wished she could appreciate it more, but as hard as she tried her awareness of Helios two tables away was all-consuming.

She was powerless to stop her eyes flickering to him, taking in the strong brown throat exposed by his unbuttoned white silk shirt—all the other men wore ties—and the way his dark blue dinner jacket emphasised the breadth of his chest. If she could only ever stare at one thing for the rest of her life it would be him.

He was laughing at something Jessica had said, his generous smile wide, his liquid eyes lively. A burst of jealousy ripped through her to see him enjoying Jessica's company so much, a totally irrational feeling, considering that Jessica was old enough to be his mother, but real nonetheless.

It was some consolation that he hadn't brought the Princess with him. If she'd had to watch him talking and laughing with her, Amy was certain she would have been sick.

And then his gaze found hers again and her stomach somersaulted. He raised his glass of wine slowly and took a long swallow.

An elbow in her ribs brought her back to earth.

'Stop it!' Greta whispered fiercely.

But she couldn't.

Even when her main course of fillet of beef and truffle mash was brought out to her she couldn't stop her eyes from constantly darting to him.

There was nothing wrong in looking, she told herself helplessly. So long as she kept away from him she could look. She just couldn't touch.

After what felt like hours the meal was over. Before she could flee into the casino, away from the magnetism of Helios's stare, he was on his feet and making a speech, which ended with him raising his glass and offering a toast to them all.

'If you'd all make your way to the private beach at midnight you'll find a last surprise for you,' he finished with a grin. 'Until then, enjoy the casino and the music and most of all have fun—you've earned it.'

Keeping herself glued to Greta's side, Amy headed into the casino, which was every bit as opulent as she'd expected and very busy. However, Helios had arranged for them to

have their own private poker, blackjack and roulette tables.
She had no interest in playing but it was fun to observe,
especially to watch Jessica, who seemed to be cleaning up
on the blackjack table, to everyone's amazement. There
was soon a crowd forming around her.

The only blot on the landscape was a prickle on her
neck: the weight of Helios's stare upon her. It took everything she had not to return it. Without the dining tables
separating them she felt vulnerable. It was only a matter
of time before he sought her out.

Except it never happened. From out of the corner of
her eye she watched him make his way around the casino
and the adjoining dance room, speaking to all his staff in
turn, his easy smile evident.

So many free drinks were being pressed into their hands
that Amy felt herself becoming more light-headed by the
minute. Soon it was enough to make herself switch to
coffee.

She couldn't stop her heart from jolting every time Helios moved away from one person and on to another. Ir-
rationally, she longed for him to bestow his attentions on
her. But other than with his eyes he made no such attempt.
She must be the only member of staff he hadn't made an
effort to speak to. Apart from Greta, who hadn't let Amy
out of her sight all evening.

Maybe he'd finally accepted that they were over, despite
his proclamation that she would always be his. Maybe their
short time apart had convinced him she had been right to
end things between them.

A dagger speared her stomach at the thought of never
feeling his strong arms around her again, or the heat of
his kiss.

She needed to get out of there, to go back to her apartment and lick her wounds in peace before she gave in to

the howl building in her throat. She'd done her best tonight, but not even the alcohol had numbed the ache pounding beneath her ribs. If anything, it had got worse.

But what peace could she find in her apartment when Helios was only the other side of a secret passageway? How could she survive another five months of living so close to him? With her resignation rejected and his threat of legal action if she left hanging over her head, her choices were limited. Her career would be ruined. Who would trust her if she were to breach her contract and be sued by the heir to the throne of Agon?

Because she believed that if she were to leave now he *would* carry out his threat.

He wasn't a cruel man, but when provoked Helios was hot-tempered, passionate and filled to the brim with pride. Her attempted resignation had punctured his ego.

But then, if he had finally accepted they were finished maybe he'd be more understanding and amenable to her leaving if she broached the subject again, once the Gala was over.

She wished so hard that she could hate him, but she couldn't. How could anyone hate him?

'It's nearly midnight,' Greta said animatedly. 'Let's go to the beach.'

Amy nodded. The low buzzing noise of all the surrounding chatter was making her head ache. Some fresh sea air would do her good. She'd go out and watch the last of the entertainment and then she would slip away and lick her wounds in earnest.

The hotel's curved private beach brought gasps of delight from everyone. Helios was pleased by their reaction. Indeed, the whole evening had been a marked success. He was sure there would be plenty of foggy heads in the morning, but he doubted anyone would regret them.

Rows of wooden tables with benches had been set along the sand, and gas lamps had been placed on them for illumination under the moonless sky. The hotel's beach bar was open and cocktails were being made.

To get to the beach you had to cut through the hotel's garden and follow a gentle, meandering trail, then take half a dozen steep steps down to it. It wasn't until the tables were half-full that he spotted Amy, making her way down with Greta, whom she'd clung to like a shield for the entire evening.

He knew why.

Amy didn't want to be alone because she was scared he would pounce the second he had the chance. And if she was scared of him pouncing there could only be one reason— she knew she would struggle to resist.

Her eyes had followed him everywhere that evening. She might try, but she could no more deny the chemistry between them than he could. Soon she would realise resistance was futile. Did the tide resist the pull of the moon? Of course not. Nature worked in perfect harmony, just like the desire that pulled him and Amy together.

And yet… Shadows darkened her eyes. There was pain there, the same pain he'd seen when she'd arrived at the hotel. Seeing it had made him…uneasy. It disturbed him in ways he couldn't explain, not even to himself.

It had made him think twice about approaching her. Could *he* be the cause of that pain?

When she got to the bottom of the pathway she held Greta's arm while she took her shoes off, then the pair of them took themselves to a table where some of their fellow curators were seated. Within moments of her sitting down her eyes roamed until they found him.

Even with only the soft glow of the lamps to illuminate her face he could see her yearning. He could sense her resistance waning. The uneasiness that had pulled at him all evening abated. He'd been imagining it.

With all the stress in his life—from his grandfather's deteriorating health, Theseus's shocking news, the forthcoming Gala, his own engagement and everything in between—it was no wonder his mind was playing tricks on him and making him see things that weren't there.

Music from the DJ's deck began to play; a soft dance beat for everyone to tap their bare feet to, its pulse riding through his veins.

Soon Amy would be his again. And when he got her back in his bed he was never going to let her go.

CHAPTER SIX

DESPITE HER LONGING to be away from the hotel, far from the pull of Helios, Amy was enchanted by what surrounded her. The beach, under the light of the twinkling stars, was the most perfect scene imaginable. The noise of the lapping waves mingled with the dance beat playing behind them and gave her a sense of serenity that had been missing from her life since Helios had announced his intention to marry.

'I need to use the bathroom,' Greta murmured, rising from the table. 'Are you coming?'

'I don't think you need me to hold your hand, do you?' Amy said drily.

Greta laughed and set off into the hotel on decidedly unsteady feet.

Amy shook her head with a smile. Greta had been enjoying the steady stream of free cocktails even more than Amy had enjoyed the steady stream of free coffee.

No sooner had Greta gone than two men with matching goatee beards and dreadlocks pulled back into ponytails appeared. Both were dressed in black outfits that brought to mind samurai warriors crossed with pirates. These men were Agonites; Amy would bet her savings on it.

With interpreters translating from their Greek, the two men insisted that the table Amy was seated at be moved back ten feet. As soon as that was done they drew a line in the sand, marking a semicircle which they made clear no one should cross.

Curiosity drove everyone to their feet. Without her heels on Amy had trouble seeing anything, so she ducked out of the crowd to stand at the top of the steps leading down to the beach. The extra height and distance allowed her to see unhindered.

As the men set themselves up, removing objects she couldn't see from two huge crates, Greta came out of the bathroom and made her way to the semicircle of people crowding around them.

The sun had long gone down and standing alone, without the shared body heat of the people below, Amy felt the slight chill in the air. Rubbing her arms for warmth, she kept her gaze on the men, pretending to herself that she hadn't seen Helios step out from the bar with two large cocktail glasses in his hands...

'I thought you looked thirsty,' he said, climbing the steps to stand with her.

Her heart and throat catching, she shook her head. Deep down she'd known that separating herself from the group would be perceived as an open invitation.

His smile was knowing as he handed her one of the drinks. 'Try this. I think you'll like it.'

The glass was full of crushed ice, and the liquid within it was pink. Fresh strawberries had been placed around the rim, and sprigs of mint laced the cocktail. Wordlessly, she took it from him and placed the straw between her lips.

He knew her tastes too well. 'It's delicious. What is it?'

'A strawberry mojito.'

'Did you make it?'

He laughed lightly and shook his head. 'I wouldn't know where to begin.'

She took another sip. The combination of fresh mint and crushed strawberries played on her tongue, as did the taste of rum.

'What are you drinking?'

'A Long Island iced tea. Try some?'

She shouldn't. Really, she shouldn't.

With the moonless sky filled with twinkling stars, the scent of the sea, the background throb of music, the laughter coming from the crowd of people before them…it was a scene for romance, one she should turn and run away from.

Yet her hand disobeyed her brain, reaching out to take the glass from him, bringing the straw his own lips had wrapped around to her mouth so she could take a small sip.

Her eyes widened. 'That packs a punch!'

He grinned and took the glass back from her, brushing his fingers against hers for a second too long.

Little darts raced through her hand and up her arm. She took another sip of her mojito, fighting desperately to stop herself from leaning forward and into him. He was so close…

'I found out the other day that I'm an uncle,' Helios said, making conversation before she could remember to flee again. Besides, this was something he really needed to talk about, before his head exploded with the magnitude of it all.

'Really?'

Her shock mirrored his own initial reaction to the news. 'Theseus. He had a one-night stand with a woman he met on his sabbatical.'

'Wow. That was a few years ago, wasn't it?'

'The boy is four. His name's Toby. Theseus only found out by accident and a quirk of fate—he lied about his identity to the mother, so she was never able to tell him. And then she turned up at the palace to work on the official biography.'

'That really *is* a quirk of fate. Is he going to recognise him?'

'Yes. And he's going to marry the mother to legitimise him.'

She took another long sip of her mojito, her eyes wide as she finally met his gaze. 'Does your grandfather know?'

'Theseus is going to tell him after the Gala. We've agreed it's best to let that day be for our grandfather.'

She looked down at the ground. He wondered if she was thinking the same thing, that he was using the Gala to make the announcement of his marriage. But his announcement was different—for his grandfather it would be the pinnacle of the day, confirmation of the security that would come with knowing his heir was going to embark on matrimony.

'Theseus's relationship with my grandfather is complicated. Being a Prince of Agon is not something he's ever liked or adjusted to. It's the reason why he's been working so hard on the biography, to prove that he is ready to embrace who he is.'

'Whereas you've always embraced your destiny?' she said softly.

'I am who I am,' he answered with a shrug, not admitting that for a fleeting moment his brother's news had given him pause for thought. Theseus had a ready-made heir and a fiancée he certainly was not indifferent to...

But, no, the thought had been pushed aside before he'd allowed it to float too far into his mind. The throne would be his. It was his destiny. It was his pride. Being King was a role Theseus would hate with every fibre of his being.

Seeing Amy using her straw to fight through the ice to

the liquid left in the bottom of her glass, he signalled to a passing bartender for two more drinks.

'The news about Toby is confidential, of course,' he said, once the man had returned to the bar. 'Only you and I and Theseus's private staff know.'

'Which means half the palace knows.'

He laughed. 'The palace grapevine has a life of its own, I admit, but I hadn't heard anything before Theseus told me, so I don't think word has got out yet.'

'No one will hear anything from me.'

'That goes without saying.' In their time together he had learned to trust Amy completely. He'd never had to watch what he said to her... Apart from the time he'd failed to tell her about the real purpose behind the pre-Gala ball.

Something glistened in her eyes, a spark that flew out to touch him and cut the last of the smile from his face. Had it not been for the bartender, carrying their fresh drinks up the steps, he would have leaned in to kiss her.

Amy blinked herself out of the minor stupor she'd been in danger of falling into and took a grateful sip of her fresh mojito.

It was crazy, but Helios's news about his nephew had brought a spark of hope within her. If there was a ready-made heir in the family...

But, no. Such hopes were futile. Helios had been born to rule this great nation with a royal bride at his side. It was his destiny. And she, Amy, was a nobody.

'The entertainment's about to begin.'

'Sorry?'

That knowing smile spread once again over his handsome face. He nodded at the crowd on the beach.

Following his gaze, she saw the two piratical men standing side by side in the semicircle they'd created, their legs parted in a warrior stance. What ensued was an acrobatic

display of perfect synchronicity that on its own would
have been marvellous but which then switched to a whole
new level.

The men ducked out of Amy's eyesight before reappear-
ing with thick, long sticks, the ends of which were ablaze.
Her mouth opened in awe as she watched them dancing
and twirling and leaping and whirling whilst the fire made
patterns in the darkness, bringing the very air to life.

'You look cold,' Helios murmured, stepping behind her
and wrapping an arm around her waist to secure her to
him.

Transfixed by what was happening on the beach, her
skin dancing with something like the same flames that
were playing out before her, Amy didn't resist, not even
when he brought his mouth down to nuzzle into her hair.
Her insides melted and despite herself she leant back into
his hardness, dizzying relief rushing through her at the
sensation of being back where she belonged. In Helios's
arms.

She gasped as she felt his hand slide over her stomach
and drift up to rest under her breasts. She knew she should
throw off his hand and walk away, that allowing herself
to be held like this was the height of stupidity and danger,
but no matter how loudly her brain shouted at her feet to
start walking her body refused to obey.

A thumb was raised up to brush against the underside
of her breast and he pressed his groin into the small of her
back, letting her feel his arousal. The fire-wielding acro-
bats became a blur in her vision as her senses all turned
inwards to relish the feel of Helios against her.

She should be like a marble Minoan statue. Unrespon-
sive. Cold. But his touch turned her molten.

Send her to hell, but she rubbed against his arousal.
He hissed in her ear, dropping his hand to her hip and

gripping it tightly. She could feel his racing heart beating against her back.

Only the loud sound of applause cut through the sensuous fog she'd fallen into.

The show had finished.

The crowd was dispersing.

Blinking hard, aware of Greta searching for her, Amy finally managed to make her body obey, grabbed Helios's hand and pushed it away.

She took a step to distance herself from the security of his hold and drank the last of her mojito.

'Come back with me,' he said. For once, there was no arrogance in his voice.

She kept her eyes from his, not wanting him to see the longing she knew would be written all over her face. 'I can't.'

'You can.'

Greta had spotted them and was heading for them, or rather weaving unsteadily towards them.

'Come back with me,' he repeated.

'No.' She propelled herself down the steps, desperate to be away from him before her vocal cords said the *yes* they so yearned to speak.

He followed her, grabbing her hand when she reached the bottom step and spinning her around.

She waited breathlessly for him to say something, but all he did was stare at her as if he was drinking her in, his thumb brushing little swirls over the inside of her wrist. The message he was sending didn't need words.

Tugging out of his hold, she hurried away before she could respond to his silent request.

Helios pressed a hand to his forehead and growled to his empty bedroom. He'd been back for over an hour and not even his two Long Island iced teas, which had virtually every spirit imaginable in them, had numbed his brain enough to allow him to sleep.

His body still carried remnants of the arousal that had been unleashed by holding Amy in his arms. One touch was all it had taken. One touch and he'd been fit to burst.

If he'd been one of his ancestors from four hundred years ago he would have marched down the passageway, broken down her door and demanded she give herself to him. As he was a prince of these lands she wouldn't have been allowed to refuse him. She would have had to submit to his will.

But good Queen Athena, Agon's reigning monarch from 1671, had been at the forefront of the abolition of the law which had allowed women to be little more than chattels for the royal family's pleasure.

And even if he could he wouldn't force Amy into his bed. If she came back to him he wanted it to be under her own free will.

He knew she'd returned to the palace. After the fire show she'd disappeared into the throng, and then the last he'd seen of her had been when she'd climbed into one of the waiting palace cars with some of the other live-in staff.

Why was she doing this to him? To *them*? She was as crazy for him as he was for her, and he struggled to understand why she was resisting so hard.

He knew that she wanted to punish him because he had to marry someone else—if he were in her shoes he would probably feel the same way. The mere idea of her with another man was enough to make his blood pressure rise to the point where his veins might explode.

As ashamed as he was to have done so, he'd got his security team to find out who she'd dined with on Saturday night. Leander Soukis, a twenty-two-year-old layabout from a small village on the outskirts of Resina. How Amy had met this man was a mystery. And there was something about their meeting that ground at him.

Never mind that Leander was five years younger than Amy, when Helios distinctly remembered her saying she couldn't relate to younger men, he was also a slight, skinny thing, with a bad reputation. He came from a wealthy family, but that counted for nothing—Leander had been kicked out of three schools and had never held a job for longer than a week. Indeed, he was an ideal candidate for his brother Talos's boxing gym, which he'd opened in order to help disaffected youths, teaching them to channel their anger and giving them a leg up in life.

Why had she gone on a date with him of all people? Had it been her way of proving to Helios that she was serious about their relationship being over? Maybe he should have accepted her resignation rather than let his pride and ego force her into staying. If she was gone from Agon he wouldn't be lying in his bed with a body aching from unfulfilled desire.

But he knew such thoughts were pointless. Amy didn't need to be in his sight to be on his mind. She was there constantly.

And he would bet the palace that right at that moment she was lying in her bed thinking of him.

A soft ping from the security pad on his wall broke through his thoughts.

Jumping out of bed, he pressed a button on it, which brought up the screen issuing the alert. It was from the camera and the sensors in the secret passageway.

Peering closely, he saw a figure moving stealthily along the passageway, getting closer and closer to his room. With his heart in his mouth he watched as she hesitated, and willed her to take the final step and knock on the door.

* * *

Amy stared at Helios's door, not quite certain what she was doing or how she had got to this point.

Knowing she was vulnerable to temptation, she'd accepted an invitation to go to one of the other curator's apartments for a drink: a mini-soirée she would usually have loved attending. She'd tried so hard to pull herself out of the trance she'd fallen into, but her contribution to the conversation had been minimal. She couldn't remember a word of it. It was as if she'd been floating above it all, there in body but not in spirit.

She wanted to blame the alcohol, especially the mojitos Helios had given her, but that would have been a lie. It was all down to him.

She'd gone back to her own apartment after just one drink, but before she'd even stepped into her bedroom she'd stopped and stared at the door that led to the secret passageway. Her breaths had shortened as a deep yearning had pulled at her.

Impulse had overridden common sense. She'd unlocked the connecting door and stepped into the passageway in the same dreamlike state she'd ridden back to the palace in, not consciously thinking about where she was going. But now, standing at his door, sanity had pushed its way back through into her mind.

She couldn't do this. It was all wrong.

Closing her eyes, she pressed the palm of her hand to his door, holding it there.

This was as far as she dared go. If she were to knock and he were to answer...

She heard the telltale click of the lock turning.

She snatched her hand away, her breath catching in her throat.

The door opened.

Helios stood in the doorway, naked, nonchalant, as if Amy sneaking up to his room and doing nothing but touch his door was an everyday occurrence. Except the nonchalance was only on the surface. His chest rose and fell in tight judders. His jaw was taut; his nostrils flared. His eyes bore through her as he did nothing but stare.

And then he moved, sending out a hand to wrap around the nape of her neck and pull her to him and over the threshold. As soon as they were in his room he held her firmly and pushed the door shut. He pressed her against it, trapping her.

'Why are you here?' he asked roughly, leaning close enough for his warm, faintly minty breath to touch her skin.

'I don't know,' she whispered.

She *didn't* know. The closest she could come to describing it was her subconscious overriding her resolve. Now, though, the opposite was true. The sensations darting through her had overridden her subconscious and every inch of her had sprung into life. There was not a single atom of her body that wasn't tilting into him, yearning for his kiss, his touch.

'*I* know.'

Then, with a look that suggested he wanted to eat her alive, he brought his mouth to hers and caught her in his kiss.

CHAPTER SEVEN

IF HIS KISS had been the demanding assault she'd anticipated Amy would have been able to resist and push him away. But it wasn't. His lips rested against hers but he made no movement, stilling as if he was breathing in her essence. Amy inhaled deeply in turn, letting the warmth of his breath and the scent of him creep through her pores and inhabit her.

It was as if everything that had happened in the past ten days had been blown away, and with it all the reasons why being alone with him in his apartment and in his arms was all wrong. This was everything she wanted, everything she needed. How could something so wrong feel so *right*?

And now she didn't even want to think about right and wrong. All she wanted was to be in his arms. For ever.

She was the one to part her lips, to dart her tongue into the darkness of his mouth, to wind her arms around his neck and press into him. She was the one to break the kiss and drag her lips over his stubble-roughened cheeks and jaw and down the strong length of his neck, to run her tongue over the smooth skin, tasting his musky, masculine scent. And she was the one to draw her tongue back up his throat, dig her nails into his scalp and capture his lips with her own.

A tiny sob escaped her mouth when Helios growled and drew his arms around her. He crushed her to him. His lips parted and he kissed her so deeply and so thoroughly that in the breath of an instant she was lost in him.

A large hand dived into her hair whilst his other hand roamed down her back to clutch her bottom, which he squeezed before spreading his palm over her thigh and lifting it. He ground into her and she gasped to feel him huge against her, her underwear the only barrier to stop him entering her there and then.

In a mesh of lips and tongues he pushed her back against the wall, kissing her as if she were a banquet to be feasted on, before pulling away, tugging at her bottom lip painlessly with his teeth as he did so. His chest rising and falling in rapid motion, the palm of one hand held against her chest to still her, Helios lowered himself, pinched the hem of her dress and slowly raised it up. He kissed her stomach as he lifted the dress to her abdomen, his tongue making a trail upwards, through the valley of her breasts, into her neck, until he'd pulled it over her head and thrown it onto the floor.

Amy dug her toes into the hard flooring, her head spinning. Everything inside her blazed as fiercely as the whirling fires she'd seen on the beach. Her skin was alive to his touch. *She* was alive to his touch. Her senses had sprung to life from the very first moment she'd looked at him all those months ago and since then she'd been helpless to switch them off.

He straightened to his full height and stared down at her, his throat moving as his liquid eyes took in her semi-nakedness. He clasped her cheeks in his hands and brought his nose to hers. 'Not being able to touch you or make love to you has driven me crazy,' he said hoarsely. '*You've* driven me crazy.'

She pulled at his hair, wanting to hurt him, wanting him to experience the pain she'd gone through at the separation she'd had no choice but to force upon them. 'It's hurt me every bit as much as you,' she whispered, bringing her mouth back to his.

Holding her tightly, Helios lifted Amy into his arms, staring at her as he carried her through to his bedroom, delighting in the heightened colour of her cheeks and the dilation of her pupils.

All his dreams and fantasies had come true.

She'd come to him.

He hadn't realised how badly he'd prayed for it until he'd opened the door to her.

But he could still see the last vestiges of doubt and fear ringing in her eyes and he was determined to drive them away.

How could she not know that *this*, here, being together, was exactly how it was supposed to be?

Laying her down on his bed, he kissed her rosebud mouth and inhaled the sweet scent he had come close to believing he would never delight in again. All that separated them was her pretty black underwear. He remembered how once he'd peeled it off with his teeth, in those early hedonistic days when the desire between them had been so great he'd been certain it would *have* to abate. But it had only developed into something deeper, something needier.

Whatever it took, he would keep her in his bed.

As he gazed down, seeing the pulse beating in the arch of her neck, the way she stretched out her legs before raising her pelvis, the urgency grew. *Theos*, but he needed to be inside her.

She raised a lazy hand and pressed it to his chest, then spread her fingers over him, touching him in the way that always filled him with such gratification, as if he were one of the Seven Wonders of the World.

The knowledge that she would explore him in the same manner with which he delighted in exploring her had always been indescribable. There was not a fraction of her he had not tasted and not a fraction of him she had not touched. He would *never* tire of tasting her and making her his.

He slipped a hand behind her back and unclasped her bra, then carefully pulled the straps down her arms, kissing the trail they made and throwing it onto the floor with a flick. With her delectable breasts now bare, the dusky nipples puckered in open invitation, he dipped his head to take one tip in his mouth, groaning as she immediately arched her back to allow him to take more of her in.

Her fingers tugged through his hair as she twisted and writhed beneath him, the urgency in her movements matching the urgency flowing through his veins. She skimmed a hand down over his back before slipping it across his stomach, reaching for him. His attentions now on her other breast, he raised himself a little to make it easier for her to take his erection into her hand, groaning again as she held it in the way she knew he adored, rubbing her thumb over the head and guiding him to the apex of her thighs.

Gritting his teeth and breathing heavily, he kissed her neck and moved her hand away, squeezing her fingers between his own. Immediately she raised her thighs and rubbed against his length, moaning, begging him with soft murmurs.

But there was still the final barrier of her underwear between them.

He kissed her hard on the mouth, then pulled back, drifting his lips down the creaminess of her neck and breasts until he reached her abdomen. There, he pinched the elastic of her underwear between the fingers of both hands and tugged it down, past her thighs and calves and delicate ankles, until she was fully naked before him.

'Please...' she beseeched him, raising her thighs higher and reaching out a hand to touch him. *'Please.'*

Swallowing hard at the sight of her, so full of desire and need for him it made him heady, he guided his erection into her welcoming heat.

He pushed himself in with one long drive and buried his face in her neck, biting gently into the soft skin. And as she gripped him tightly within her he knew without a shadow of a doubt that *this* was where he belonged.

Skin against skin, heartbeat to heartbeat, arms and legs entwined, he made love to her.

And she made love to him.

He could sense the tension within her building, could hear it in the shortening of her breaths, the shallowness of her moans, feel it in the way she gripped his buttocks, deepening his thrusts. And then he felt her pulses pulling at him, pulling him even deeper inside her, her slender frame stilling, her teeth biting into his shoulder.

He didn't want it to end. He wanted it to last for ever, to be locked in her tight sweetness with her legs wrapped around him and her nails digging into his back for eternity...

And then there was no more consciousness. His own climax surged through him, tipping him over a precipice he hadn't known he was on the edge of and exploding in a wash of bright colours that took him to a place he'd never been before.

Amy awoke in the comfort of Helios's embrace, her face pressed against his chest, his arm hooked across her waist, his thigh draped heavily over hers.

Remorse flooded her in an instant.

What had she done?

Everything she'd sworn she wouldn't do had been ripped away in one moment of madness.

She should go. She had to go. She couldn't stay here.

How many times had she awoken in the night in his arms and felt the stirring to make love to him all over again? How many times had she lifted her head a touch and met his kiss? Had him fully hard and inside her in an instant? Too many to count. Sometimes she would wake in the morning and wonder if she'd dreamt their lovemaking in the early hours.

But at this moment Helios's breathing was deep and even. If she was careful she might be able to sneak out without him waking. Then she could flee to her apartment, pack a suitcase and check into a hotel. That was it. That was what she had to do.

Because she couldn't stay here—not now when she knew how hopeless she was at resisting him.

She'd tried so hard to stay away.

Oh, God, what had she *done*?

She could dress it up any way she liked but she'd given in to temptation, and now the ecstasy of being back in his arms had gone, replaced with an acrid taste in her mouth and a gutful of guilt.

She had to leave. Right now.

Carefully, after stealthily slipping out of his arms, she edged her way out of the bed, holding her breath until her feet touched the floor.

Scrambling, half-blind in the dark, she found her dress thrown across an armchair. She had no idea where her underwear had got to and was in too much of a panic to escape to hunt for it for long. She shrugged her dress on and, fearful of choking on the swell rising in her chest, tiptoed to the door.

'You wouldn't be running away, would you?'

Helios watched as Amy's silhouette froze at the bedroom door. Switching on the bedside light, he propped himself up on an elbow as she slowly turned around to face him with wide, pain-filled taupe eyes. To see her mussed-up hair and her beautiful face contorted in such misery... Something sharp pierced him.

'I'm sorry,' she whimpered. 'I know it's cowardly to sneak away.'

'Then why are you?'

'I shouldn't be here. We shouldn't have...' Her voice tailed away and she looked down at the floor.

'Made love?' he supplied.

She gave a tiny nod. 'It was wrong. All wrong.'

'It felt damn right to me.'

'I know.' She gave a sudden bark of harsh laughter and her eyes flashed. 'It's what I keep thinking. How can something so wrong feel so right?'

'If it feels so right then how can it be wrong?' he countered.

'It just is. You're getting *married*.'

That little fact was something that constantly played on his mind. Only being in Amy's arms had driven it and the accompanying nausea away.

Tightness coiled in his stomach. Throwing off the covers, he climbed out of bed and strode over to her, slamming his hand on the door to prevent her from escaping.

He spoke slowly, trying to think the words through before he vocalised them, knowing that one wrong word would make her flee whether or not he barricaded the door. 'Amy, I might be getting married, but it's *you* I want.'

'We've been through this before. It doesn't matter what you want or what I want. It doesn't change the reality of the situation. Tonight was a mistake that can't be repeated.'

'Running away won't change anything either. Admit it, *matakia mou*. You and I belong together.'

Her jaw clenched in response.

'So what are you going to do?' he asked scathingly, leaning closer to her ashen face. 'Run away and start a relationship with Leander? Is that how you intend to prove we're over?'

'How do you know about Leander?' She shook her head and took a deep inhalation. 'Don't answer that. I can guess.'

He felt no guilt for seeking information about her date. Helios looked out for those he cared for. 'He's too young for you. I know you, Amy. You don't need a boy. You need—'

'He's my brother,' she snapped suddenly, angry colour flushing her cheeks.

Her declaration momentarily stunned him into silence. Stepping back to look at her properly, he dragged a hand through his hair. 'But Leander is from Agon. Your brothers are English, like you...'

'I'm only half-English.'

'Your parents are English.' *Weren't* they? Wasn't this something they had talked about...?

'My father's English. Elaine—my mum—didn't give birth to me. My birth mother's from Agon.'

How had he not known this?

Amy must have sensed the direction his mind was travelling in. 'Do you remember once asking me how I'd developed such an obsession and a love for your country?'

'You said it was... You never gave a proper answer...'
Realisation dawned on him as he thought back to that

conversation, months ago, when they had first started sleeping together. She'd brushed his question aside.

'And you never pursued it.' She shook her head in a mixture of sadness and anger.

'I didn't know there was anything to pursue. I'm not a mind reader.'

'I'm sorry.' She gave a helpless shrug. 'A huge part of me wanted to tell you, and ask for your help in finding her, but I knew that confiding in you would change the nature of our relationship.'

'What would have changed?' he asked, completely perplexed.

From the first the chemistry between them had been off the charts. Making love to Amy had always felt different from the way it had felt with his other lovers. He'd never felt the urge to ask her to leave at night—he liked sharing his space with her, this incredibly sexy woman with a brain the size of a watermelon. He loved it that she could teach him things he didn't know about his own country.

To learn now that she had *roots* in his country...

'I didn't keep any secrets from you,' he added, his head reeling.

'Apart from throwing a party to find a wife?'

He inhaled deeply. Yes, the real purpose of the ball *was* something he'd kept from her for as long as he could. But this information was on a different scale. He'd known Amy had kept a part of herself sheltered from him, but he'd had no idea it was something so fundamental.

Her eyes held his. 'I was scared.'

Another stabbing pain lanced him. 'Of me?'

'Of what you would think of me. At least I was in the beginning.' Her voice lowered to a whisper. 'And I was scared because you and I came with time constraints. We had a fixed marker for when we would end, we both knew that. We both held things back.'

'I never held anything back.'

'Didn't you?' There was no challenge in her eyes, just a simple question. 'Helios, I couldn't take the risk of what we had developing into something more—of us becoming closer. We can't be together for ever. I was trying to protect myself.'

For an age he stared at her, wishing he could see into her mind, wishing he could shake her…wishing that everything could be different.

'Do not go anywhere,' he said, turning his back to her and striding to his dressing room. 'You and I are going to talk, and this is not a conversation to have naked. We're long past the point of keeping secrets from each other.'

While Helios slipped on a pair of boxers Amy used the few moments alone to catch her thoughts before he reappeared.

It wasn't long enough.

She pressed her back tightly against the door, her vocal cords too constricted for speech.

'I mean it, Amy,' he said with a hard look in his eye. 'You're not going anywhere until we've talked this through.'

'What's the point?' she asked, her voice hoarse.

'If your history is what's stopping us from being together then I damn well deserve to know the truth.' He strolled back to the bed and sat in the middle of it, his back resting against the headboard. 'Now, come here.'

What an unholy mess. It had never been supposed to end like this. Her memories of her time with him were supposed to be filled with wonder, not sorrow and despair. Losing him wasn't supposed to *hurt*.

She perched on the end of the bed and twisted to face him. Blowing out a puff of air, she gazed at the ceiling.

'My father had an affair with the au pair. She dumped me on him when I was two weeks old and has wanted nothing to do with me since. Her husband and her parents don't know I exist.'

CHAPTER EIGHT

Other than a slight shake of his head and a tightening of his lips, Helios gave no response.

'My birth mother had me when she was nineteen. I know very little about her—she didn't work for them for long.'

'When you say *for them*…?'

'My parents. My mum—as in the woman who raised me—was pregnant and had a three-year-old son when they employed Neysa, my birth mother, as an au pair. She quit after a couple of months but then turned up at my dad's workplace seven months later and left me with the receptionist.'

Amy studied Helios's reaction carefully. She no longer really feared, as she had at the beginning of their relationship, that he would think any less of her, but nagging doubts remained. Cruel words spoken in the playground still haunted her, clouding her judgement.

'You must have been one ugly baby for your own mum to dump you.'

'Do you have 666 marked on the back of your head?'

'Your real mum's a slut.'

She'd had to force herself to rise above it and pretend the taunts didn't affect her when in reality they had burned. For years she had tortured herself, wondering if the taunts held the ring of truth. For years she'd tried to live a life as pure as the driven snow to *prove* she wasn't intrinsically bad.

For years she'd wondered how Elaine—to her mind, her mum—could even bring herself to look at her.

Helios stared at her as if she'd just told him that all the scientists and even physics itself were wrong and the world was actually flat.

'Did she leave a note?' he asked quietly. 'Give a reason?'

'Her note to my father said only that I was his and that she couldn't keep me.'

'So your father had an affair with the au pair when your mum was pregnant? And they're still together?'

She nodded. 'God knows how Mum found it in her to forgive him but she did, and she raised me as her own.'

Helios shook his head, amazement in his eyes. 'She raised you with her own children?'

'Yes. Danny was born five months before me. We were in the same school year.'

He closed his eyes with a wince. 'That must have been difficult.'

'At times it was horrendous—especially at secondary school. But we coped.'

Amy's existence could have caused major friction between her and her siblings, but both Danny and their older brother, Neil, had always been fiercely protective of her, particularly during their teenage years.

'Did you always know?'

'Not when I was a young child. My family was my family. Danny being five months older than me…it was just a fact of our lives. Neil always knew I was only his half-sister but, again, it was just a fact of our lives and something he assumed was normal. My parents never mentioned it so he didn't either. Then we got older and other kids started asking questions… Mum told me the truth when I was ten.'

She shuddered at the memory of that sudden realisation that her whole life had been a lie.

'She'd been waiting until I was old enough to understand.'

It had been the most significant moment of Amy's life. It would have been easy to feel as if her whole world had caved in, but Danny and Neil had simply shrugged it off and continued to treat her as they always had—as their sister. That, more than anything, had made it easier to cope with.

'Did you not have *any* idea you weren't hers?'

'Not in the slightest. She loved me. Any resentment was hidden.'

'What about your father? Where does he fit in with all this?'

'He left it to my mum to tell me. When it came out he carried on as normal, trying to pretend nothing had changed.'

But of course everything had changed. *She'd* changed. How could she not? Everything she'd thought she knew about herself had been a lie.

She looked back at Helios, wanting him to understand. 'When I was told the truth it became important, I guess, to pretend that nothing had changed. They still treated me the same. They still scolded me when I was naughty. My mum still tucked me up in bed and kissed me goodnight. Outwardly, nothing did change.'

'And how does she feel about you being here now, trying to find your birth mother?'

'She understands. She's adopted herself—I think that's why she was able to raise me without blaming me for the sins of my birth mother. She knows what the urge to find out who you really are is like.'

Her mum had encouraged Amy's quest to learn all there was to know about Agon. She'd been the one to take her to the library to seek out books on Agon and Minoan culture and to record any television documentary that featured the island. So encouraging had she been that a part of Amy had been scared her mum *wanted* her to go to Agon and stay there. She'd been afraid that she wanted to get rid of the living proof of her husband's infidelity, that all the love she had bestowed on Amy had only been an act.

But Amy couldn't deny that she'd seen the apprehension in her mum's eyes when she'd left for Agon. Since she'd been on the island she'd received more daily calls and messages than she had when she'd first left home for university. Was she secretly worried that Amy would abandon her for Neysa...?

Secretly worried or not, wanting to get rid of her or not, being adopted herself meant her mum had first-hand experience of knowing what it was like to feel a part of you was missing. Helios had always known exactly who he was. There hadn't been a single day of his life when he hadn't known his place in the world or his destiny.

'She sounds like a good woman.'

'She is. She's lovely.' And she was. Loving and self-less. Amy knew her fears were irrational, but she had no control over them. They were still there, taunting her, in the deepest recesses of her mind.

'So why do you want to meet your birth mother?' Helios asked, puzzled that Amy could want *anything* to do with someone who'd caused such pain and destruction. 'She abandoned you and destroyed your mum's trust.'

She looked away. 'I don't want a relationship with her.

I just… I want to know what she looks like. Do I look like her? Because the only thing I've inherited from my dad is his nose. And I want to know why she did what she did.'

'Even if the truth hurts you?' If her birth mother was anything like her layabout son, he would guess she'd abandoned Amy for purely selfish reasons.

'I've been hurt every day of my life since I learned the truth of my conception,' she said softly. 'I know there are risks to meeting her, but I can't spend the rest of my life wondering.'

'Has your father not been able to fill in any of the gaps for you?'

'Not really. He doesn't like to talk about her—he's still ashamed of his behaviour. He's a scientist, happily stuck in a laboratory all day, and what he did was completely out of character.' She gave a sad smile. 'Even if he did want to talk about it there's not much for him to say. He hardly knew her. She was hired on a recommendation from one of Dad's colleagues who left his research company before I was dumped on him. All he and my mum knew was that Neysa—my birth mother—was from Agon and had come to England for a year to improve her English.'

And so the Greens had allowed a stranger into their home, with no foreknowledge of the havoc that would be wreaked on them.

'Everything else I've learned since I came here,' she added wistfully. 'Greta has helped me.'

But she hadn't confided in *him* or approached him for help.

Helios tried to imagine the pain and angst she'd been living with during all the nights they'd shared together. She hadn't breathed a word of it, although she must have known he was in the best position to help her.

'How's your parents' marriage now?'

Amy shrugged. 'When it all happened I was still a new-born baby. They patched their marriage up as best they could for the sake of us kids. They seem happy. I don't think my dad ever cheated again, but who knows?'

'My mother was a good woman too,' he said.

He was realising that Amy was right in her assertion that they had both kept things hidden. Both of them had kept parts of their lives locked away. And now it was time to unlock them.

'And my father was also a philanderer. But, unlike your father, mine never showed any penitence. The opposite, in fact.'

Her taupe eyes widened a touch but she didn't answer, just waited for him to continue in his own time.

'My father was hugely unfaithful—to be honest, he was a complete bastard. And my mother was incredibly jealous. To shut her up when she questioned him about his infidelities he would hit her. She deserved better than him.'

This was not a subject he'd ever discussed with anyone outside of his family. His father's infidelities were well documented, but his violence...that was something they'd all closed ranks on. Being the sons of such a vicious, narcissistic man was not something any of the brothers had found it easy to reconcile themselves with.

'I'm sorry,' Amy said, shaking her head slowly as if trying to take in his words. 'Did you know it was going on? The violence, I mean?'

'Only on an instinctual level. It was only ever a feeling.'

'How was *your* relationship with your father?' she asked quietly.

He grimaced as decades-old memories flooded him. 'I was the apple of his eye. He adored me, to the point that he excluded my brothers. It felt good, being the "special" one, but I also felt much guilt about it too. He was cruel—especially to Theseus. My mother struggled to make him treat us all fairly.'

Amy didn't say anything, just stared at him with haunted eyes.

'I was a child when they died. My memories are tainted by everything I learned after he'd gone, but I remember the looks he would give my mother when she stood up for Theseus or made a pointed remark about his other women. I would feel sick with worry for her, but he was always careful to make sure I was out of sight and earshot before hitting her. It got worse once I left for boarding school,' he continued. 'With me gone, he didn't have to hide it any more.'

'You surely don't blame yourself for that?'

'Not any more. But I did when I first learned the truth.' He met her gaze. 'It took me a long time to truly believe I couldn't have stopped him even if I had known. But, like you when your life fell apart, I was a child. Talos tried to stop it—that last day, before my parents were driven to the Greek Embassy and their car crashed, Talos was there, right in the middle of it. He got hurt himself in the crossfire.'

'Oh, the poor boy. That must have been horrendous for him.'

'It screwed up his ideas of marriage. He has no intention of ever marrying.'

'Not an option for you,' she said softly.

'No.' He shook his head for emphasis. 'Nor for Theseus. The security of our family and our island rests in our hands. But I swear this now—my parents' marriage will not be mine.'

'What if it was an option?' she asked suddenly, straightening. 'What if you'd been born an ordinary person? Who would you be now?'

'I don't know.' And he didn't. 'It's not something I've ever thought about.'

'Really?'

'Theseus spent most of his life fighting his birthright and all it brought him was misery. Why rail against something you have no control over? I had no control over my conception, just as I had no control over my parents' marriage or their deaths. My destiny is what it is, and I've always known and accepted that. I am who I am and I'm comfortable with that.'

It was only in recent weeks that the destiny he'd always taken for granted had gained a more acrid tang.

During their conversation Amy had moved fully back onto the bed and was now facing him, hugging her knees. Reaching forward, he took her left foot into his hands and gently tugged at it so it rested on his lap.

A strange cathartic sensation blew through him, and with it a sense of release. His father's violence and complete disrespect to his mother were things that he'd locked away inside, not wanting to give voice to the despicable actions he and his brothers felt tainted by. But Amy was the last person who would judge a child for the sins of its parents. In that respect they shared something no other could understand.

'The main reason I selected Catalina is because she has no illusions about what our marriage will be,' he said, massaging Amy's foot. 'She has been groomed from birth to marry someone of equal stature. I will be King, but I will never be like my father. Marrying Catalina guarantees that she will never expect more than I can give.'

'But your mother was a princess before she married your father.'

His mouth twisted. 'Their marriage was arranged before she could walk. She grew up knowing she would marry my father and she built an ideal in her head of what their marriage would be like. She loved him all her life and, God help her, she was doomed to disappointment. The only person my father loved was himself. Catalina doesn't love me any more than I love her. There will be no jealousy. She has no expectations of fidelity.'

'Has she said that?' Amy asked doubtfully.

'Her only expectation is that I be respectful to her and discreet, and that is something I will always be. Whatever happens in the future, I will *never* inflict on her or on anyone the pain my father inflicted on my mother.'

'I know you wouldn't hurt her intentionally. But, Helios, what she says now…it doesn't mean she'll feel the same way once you've exchanged your vows.' Amy closed her eyes and sighed. 'And it doesn't change how I feel about it. I won't be the other woman. Marriage vows should be sacred.'

Helios placed her foot gently onto the bed before pouncing, grabbing her hands and pinning her beneath him.

Breathing heavily, she turned her face away from him.

'Look at me,' he commanded.

'No.'

'Amy, look at me.' He loosened his hold only when she reluctantly turned her face back to him. 'You are not Neysa—you are Elaine's daughter, with all *her* goodness. Catalina is not your mother. Nor is she mine. And I am *not* my father. The mistakes they all made and the pain they caused are not ours to repeat. That's something neither of us would ever allow to happen.'

He came closer so his lips were a breath away from hers.

'And I'm not married yet.'

Her eyes blazed back at him, desire and misery fighting in them. He leaned down and placed a kiss to her neck, smoothing his hand over her breasts and down to her thighs. He inched the hem of her dress up and slid between her legs.

'Neither of us are ready for this to end. Why deny ourselves when my vows are still to be made and we're not hurting anyone?'

Amy fought the familiar tingles and sensations spreading through her again as the need to touch him and hold him grew stronger than ever. How was it possible to go from wanting to wrap him in her arms, to chase away what she knew were dreadful memories for him, to sensual need in the blink of an eye?

She writhed beneath him. Her words came in short breaths. 'I can't think when you're doing this to me.'

'Then don't think. Just feel. And accept that we're not over.'

In desperation she grabbed at his hair, forcing *him* to look at *her.* 'But you've made a commitment.'

'A commitment that won't be fulfilled for two months.' He slid inside her, penetrating as deep as he could go.

She gasped as pleasure filled her.

'Until then,' he continued, his voice becoming heavy as he began to move, 'you are mine and I am yours.'

Amy tightened her hold around Helios, wishing she didn't feel so complete with his weight upon her and his steadying breaths softly tickling the skin of her neck. She was a fool for him. More so than she could have imagined.

They'd laid their pasts bare to each other and the effect had been the very thing she'd been scared of. She felt closer to him, as if an invisible emotional bond had wrapped itself around them.

He finally shifted his weight off her and she rolled over and burrowed into his arms.

'Don't even think about trying to sneak out,' he said sleepily.

'I won't.' She gave a soft, bittersweet laugh. Her resolve had deserted her. Those bonds had cocooned her so tightly to him she could no longer envisage cutting them. Not yet. Not until she really had to. 'You and I…'

'What?' he asked, after her words had tailed off.

'No one can know. Please. Everyone who knew we were together knows we split up. I couldn't bear for them to think we're having an affair behind the Princess's back.'

When they'd been together originally Helios had made no secret of her place in his life. She might not have accompanied him to official functions, or been recognised as his official girlfriend, but she had been his almost constant companion within the palace.

She'd spent far more time in his apartment than she had in her own, and whenever he had come into the museum he would seek her out. He would touch her—not sexually… he at least had a sense of propriety when it came to *that* in public…but he would rest his hand in the small of her back, lean close to her, all the little tells of a possessive man staking his claim on the woman in his life. And if work or duty took him away from the palace she would be the one to look after Benedict.

It had only been on the inside, emotionally, that they had been separated. But not any more. At this moment she didn't think she had ever felt as close to anyone in her life.

'Discretion will be my new name,' he acquiesced.

'And when you marry you will let me go.'

He stilled.

Watching for his reaction, she saw his eyes open. 'That gives you two months to find my replacement,' she whispered. 'I want to know that you'll release me from the palace and from your life. I appreciate it means bringing my contract to an early end, but I don't think I'll be able to cope with living and working here knowing it's the Princess you're sleeping with.'

When he married their bonds would be destroyed.

He breathed deeply, then nodded. 'I can agree to that. But until then…'

'Until then I am yours.'

CHAPTER NINE

HELIOS CLICKED ON Leander Soukis's profile and stared hard at it. There was something about the young man's chin and the colouring of his hair that reminded him of Amy, but that was the only resemblance he could see. How could Amy share half her DNA with this layabout? Amy was one of the hardest workers he'd ever met, which, in a palace and museum full of overachievers was saying something.

And how she could be from the loins of Neysa Soukis was beyond his comprehension. Helios had done his homework on Amy's birth mother and what he had learned had not given him hope of a happy ending.

Neysa was a social climber. Approaching fifty, she still had a refined beauty. She had a rich older husband, who doted on her, and a comfortable lifestyle. Helios vaguely recalled meeting her husband at a palace function a few years back. Neysa had married him when she was twenty-one, less than two years after having Amy. Why she hadn't confessed to having had a child he could only speculate upon, but his guess was that it had nothing to do with shame and everything to do with fear. No doubt she'd been scared of losing the wealth that came with her marriage.

Neysa had put money before her own flesh and blood. If Helios had his way Amy wouldn't be allowed within a mile's radius of the woman. But he understood how deep blood could go. That morning he'd met his nephew for the first time. He'd felt an instant thump in his heart.

This little boy, this walking, talking dark-haired creation was a part of *him*. His family. His bloodline. He was a Kalliakis, and Helios had felt the connection on an emotional level.

It might break her heart in the process, but Amy deserved to know her bloodline too.

Whether the Soukis family deserved *her* was another matter...

If they did break her heart he would be there to pick up the pieces and help her through it, just as Amy had been there with a comforting embrace whenever the pain of his grandfather's illness had caught him in its grip.

Thinking quickly, Helios drafted a private message. If having a decree from the heir to the throne didn't motivate Leander to bring his mother and half-sister together, nothing would.

'Amy, you're late for your meeting.'

'What meeting?' she asked Pedro in surprise, looking down at him from her position on a stepladder, from where she was adjusting the portraits lining the first exhibition room. She wanted them to be hung perfectly, not so much as a millimetre out of alignment.

The museum and the palace tours had been closed to visitors all week in order to prepare for the Gala. As a result the palace and its grounds were in a state of absolute frenzy, with helicopters landing on the palace helipad on a seemingly constant basis. And the Gala was still a day away!

She'd never known the palace to be such a hive of activity. There was a buzz about the place, and information and gossip were being dripped in from so many sources, including the more serious museum curators, whose heads were usually stuck in historical tomes, that it seemed like a spreading infection.

The Orchestre National de Paris had arrived to great fanfare, a world-famous circus troupe had been spotted lurking in the grounds, the gardens had been closed off to allow even more blooms to be planted... Everywhere Amy went something magical was occurring.

The exhibition was to all intents and purposes ready for the *very* exclusive private tour that would be conducted after the pre-Gala lunch. Another, less exclusive tour would take place on Sunday, and the museum and exhibition would open to the public on Monday. From then on it really would be all systems go. Ticket demand had exceeded expectations.

She wanted it to be perfect—not just because of her professional pride, but also for Helios, his grandfather and his brothers.

'Your meeting with Helios,' Pedro said. 'He's waiting for you in his private offices.'

'Oh.' She rubbed at her lips, avoiding Greta's curious stare, willing them both not to notice the flames licking at her face.

Helios had been as good as his word. No one knew they were sharing a bed again, not even Greta. It wasn't just guilt preventing Amy from confiding in her friend, but the feeling that what she and Helios had now was just too intimate to share.

'Yes. Yes, I remember.'

Excusing herself politely, still not meeting their eyes, Amy hurried away. When she'd kissed Helios goodbye that morning, before coming to work, she'd assumed that he would be flat-out busy all day. His itinerary had given her a headache just looking at it. A frisson ran up her spine as she imagined what he might be wanting from her. She doubted very much that it had anything to do with the museum.

Helios's private offices were attached to his private apartment. Getting there was a trek in itself. She could cut through her own apartment and use their secret passageway, but during daylight hours it wasn't feasible, not when this was an 'official' meeting, even if it would shave ten minutes off her walk.

The usual courtiers guarded his quarters. They were expecting her and opened the door without any questions. She stepped inside, into a large reception area. The door to the left led to his apartment. She turned the handle of the door to the right.

Talia, Helios's private secretary, rose to greet her, a pastry in her hand. 'Hello, Amy,' she said with a welcoming smile. Usually immaculately presented, today Talia had a wild-eyed, frazzled look about her. 'He's expecting you.'

Did Talia suspect Amy and Helios had resumed their relationship? Did *anyone* suspect?

Amy smiled back politely. 'How are things?'

Talia crossed her eyes and pulled a face. 'Busy. This is the first time we've stopped all day.' She pressed a key on one of her desk phones. 'Despinis Green is here,' she said.

'Send her in,' came the response.

Amy found Helios sitting behind his sprawling desk with Benedict, his black Labrador, snoozing beside him. Benedict cocked an ear and opened his eyes when she walked into the office, then promptly went back to sleep.

'Take a seat,' Helios said politely, his eyes following her every movement with a certain knowingness.

As soon as the door was closed and they had some privacy he rose from his chair and stepped round the desk to take her in his arms.

'Was there a reason you made up a non-existent meeting

other than to make out with me in your office?' she asked
with bemusement when they came up for air.

His hands forked through her hair and he kissed her
again. 'The French Ambassador's flight was slightly de-
layed, giving me an unexpected half-hour window.'

'It took me that long to get here,' she said teasingly.

'I know.' He gave a mock sigh. 'I suppose a few kisses
are better than nothing.'

She laughed and rested her head against his chest.
'Should I go now?'

He looked at his watch. 'Five minutes.'

'That's hardly any time.'

Not that she could do anything more than share a few
kisses with him in his office, with Talia on the other side
of the door and the palace full of Very Important People
who all demanded his time. How he kept his good humour
was a mystery...

'There's always time for kissing,' he said, tilting her chin
up so he could nuzzle into her cheek. 'Especially as I won't
get the chance to touch you again for at least another ten
hours...' Before she could get too comfortable, however,
he stepped away. 'To answer your original question—yes,
I did have an ulterior motive for seeing you other than the
insatiable need to kiss you.'

She rolled her eyes.

'Before I tell you... I don't want you to think I've been
interfering.'

'What have you interfered with?'

'I told you, I'm not interfering. I'm helping,' he added,
with a deliberate display of faux innocence.

'What have you done?'

His features became serious. 'I've been in contact with
your birth mother.'

Her heart almost stopped. 'And?' she asked breathlessly.

'She has agreed to meet you in a neutral place on Monday.'

She shook her head, trying to clear the sudden buzzing that had started in her brain at this unexpected development.

'Are you angry with me?'

'No. Of course not.' She wrapped her arms around him and breathed him in. His scent was so very reassuring. 'It's in your nature to take charge and boss people around.'

He laughed and rubbed his hands down her back. 'I wrote to her in my capacity as your boss. And in my capacity as her Prince.'

'It's amazing how people are able to do an about-turn on the basis of a simple word from you.'

'It certainly is,' he agreed cheerfully.

'If I were a princess I would throw my weight around everywhere.'

He pulled back and tapped her on the nose. 'No, you wouldn't… And I don't throw my weight around,' he continued, feigning injury.

She grinned. 'You don't need to.' Stepping onto her toes, she pressed a kiss to his lips. 'Thank you.'

'Don't thank me yet—there are no guarantees the meeting will go well.'

She shrugged. 'Having met Leander, I have no expectations. I don't want to be part of her family or cause trouble for her. I just want to meet her.'

'Just…be careful. Don't build your hopes up.'

'I won't,' she promised, knowing his warning came from a place of caring, just as his interference had. If their roles had been reversed she would be warning him too.

'Good. I'll email you the details.'

'Thank you.'

One of the landlines on his desk buzzed. Sighing, Helios disentangled his arms from around her and pressed a button. 'Yes?'

'The French contingent have landed and are expected in twenty minutes.'

'Thank you. I'll leave in a moment to greet them.' Disconnecting the call, he shook his head and grimaced. 'One more kiss before duty calls?'

Obliging him, Amy leaned closer, raised herself onto the tips of her toes and brought her mouth to his, giving him one last, lingering kiss before he broke away with a rueful smile.

'I'll see you later and we'll do a *lot* more than kissing,' he said, then strode to the office door and opened it.

'The Koreans will be arriving within the hour,' Talia called as he walked past her.

He shook his head. 'Whose idea was it to have so many guests arrive a day early?'

'Yours,' Talia said, her expression deadpan.

'The next time I come up with such an idea you're welcome to chop my hands off.'

Hoping her demeanour was as nonchalant as his, Amy said goodbye to Talia. When she stepped out into the corridor Helios had already gone.

Gala day had arrived.

If Helios had been busy the day before, it was nothing compared to today. His whole morning had been spent meeting and greeting guests and making sure everything was running perfectly.

This was a day he'd looked forward to. No one could organise an occasion better than the Agon palace staff and he always enjoyed celebrating the events they hosted. He was immensely proud of his family and his island, and never turned down an opportunity to discuss its virtues with interesting people.

With his grandfather's situation as it was, he'd expected

the day to feel bittersweet, with the joy of celebrating the great man's life certain to be shadowed by the knowledge that it would soon be ending.

What Helios hadn't expected was to feel flat.

There was a strange lethargy within him which he was fighting against. Merely shaking hands and making eye contact felt like an effort. His mouth didn't want to smile. He hadn't even found the energy to be disappointed by the news that the solo violinist Talos had been working so closely with would not be able to perform due to severe stage fright.

One bright spot had been the unveiling of his grandfather's biography, which he and his brothers had looked through with their grandfather privately before the pre-Gala lunch. To see the man who'd raised them make his peace with Theseus had warmed him. And King Astraeus had surprised them all by revealing that he knew about Theseus's son and his plans to marry the boy's mother, and had given his blessing.

These were all things that should have had Helios slapping his brothers' backs and calling for a glass of champagne.

They'd gone through to the lunch together. Again, he should have revelled in the occasion, but the food had tasted like cardboard, the champagne flat on his tongue.

His fiancée, who'd arrived with her father and her brother, Helios's old school friend, had sat next to him throughout the lunch. He'd had to force the pleasantries expected of him. When Catalina's father, the King of Monte Cleure, had commented about the announcement of their engagement it had taken all his willpower not to slam his knife into the table and shout, *To hell with the announcement!*

And now, with the lunch over, the clock was ticking

furiously fast towards the time when he would make his engagement official to the world.

First, though, it was time for his grandfather to have a very exclusive viewing of his exhibition. It would include just the King and his three grandsons. Above everything else occurring that day, taking his grandfather to the exhibition created in his honour was the part Helios had most been looking forward to. The biography was the culmination of Theseus's hard work—a tangible acknowledgement of his love and pride—and this exhibition was the pinnacle of his own.

With his brothers by his side, Helios and a couple of courtiers now led his grandfather out into the palace grounds and along the footpath that led to the museum.

The joy and pride he'd anticipated feeling in this moment had been squashed by a very real sense of dread. And when they arrived at the museum doors he understood where the dread had come from.

Amy, Pedro and four other staff members closely involved in the exhibition were there to greet them at the museum's entrance. All were wearing their official uniforms and not a single hair was out of place. This was their big moment as much as his.

Talos wheeled their grandfather up to the line of waiting staff so they could be spoken to in turn. When they reached Amy the thuds in Helios's heart became a painful racket.

This was the first time she would meet his family. It would also be the last.

Bracing himself, he said, 'This is the exhibition curator, Amy Green. She's on secondment from England to organise it all.'

Not looking at Helios, Amy curtsied. 'It is an honour to meet you, Your Majesty.'

'The honour is mine,' his grandfather replied with that

wheeze in his voice Helios didn't think he would ever get used to. 'I've been looking forward to seeing this exhibition. Are you my tour guide?'

Her eyes darted to Pedro, who, as Head of Museum, was supposed to take the role of the King's guide.

Sensing her dilemma, Helios stepped in. 'Despinis Green would be delighted to be your guide. Let's get you inside and we can make a start.'

Inside the main exhibition room the four King Astraeus statues were lined up on their plinths. The sculptor of the fourth, which was covered and ready for unveiling, awaited his introduction to the King. When that was done, and the official photographers were in position, in a hushed silence the cover was removed and the King was able to see his own youthful image portrayed in marble for the first time.

For the longest, stillest moment the King simply stared at it, drinking in the vibrant, enigmatic quality of his statue. There was a collective exhalation of breath when he finally spoke of his delight and reached out a wizened hand to touch his own marble foot.

It was a moment Amy knew would be shown in all the world's press.

From there, the group progressed through to the rest of the exhibition.

The thought of being the King's personal tour guide should have had Amy in fits of terror, but it was a welcome relief. She had to concentrate so hard to keep up with etiquette and protocol that she could almost act as if Helios meant nothing to her other than as her boss.

But only almost.

After the King had examined and admired all of the military exhibits, they moved through to the room dedicated to his marriage to Queen Rhea, who had died five years previously. It was heartbreaking and yet uplifting to see the King's reaction first-hand.

Their wedding outfits had been carefully placed on mannequins and secured inside a glass cabinet. Queen Rhea's wedding dress was one of the most beautiful creations Amy had ever been privileged to handle, covered as it was with over ten thousand tiny diamonds and crystals.

King Astraeus gazed at it with moist eyes before saying to her, 'My Queen looked beautiful that day.'

Amy murmured her agreement. On the opposite wall hung the official wedding portrait. Queen Rhea had been a beauty by anyone's standards, but on that particular day there had been a glow about her that shone through the portrait and every photo that had been taken.

What would it be like to have a marriage such as theirs? Her own parents' marriage had seemed mostly happy, but once Amy had learned of her true parentage her memories had become slanted.

Her father's infidelity, although mostly never spoken of, remained a scar. Danny knew their father had cheated on his mother whilst she'd carried him. Neil knew their father had cheated on his mother back when he'd still been talking in broken sentences. They might love Amy as a true sister, and have nothing to do with anyone who saw things differently, but their relationship with their father bordered on uncomfortable. They didn't trust him and neither did Amy. She loved him very much, but the nagging doubts remained. When they'd still been living at home, and he'd been kept late at work, although they'd never said anything they'd all wondered if his excuses were true. And as for her mum...

To anyone looking in, their marriage would seem complete. They laughed together and enjoyed each other's company. But then Amy thought of the times she'd caught her mum going through her father's phone when she'd thought no one was looking and knew the pain she'd gone through had never fully mended. Once trust had been broken it was incredibly hard to repair.

King Astraeus and Queen Rhea's marriage had bloomed into that rarest of things: enduring, faithful love. The kind of love Amy longed to have. The kind of love she could never have when the man she loved was going to marry someone else...

The truth hit her like a bolt of lightning.

She *did* love him.

And as the revelation hit her so did another truth of equal magnitude.

She was going to lose him.

But he'd never been hers to lose, so she already had.

There was nothing for her to hold on to for support. All she could do was keep a grip on herself and wait for the wave of anguish to pass.

The only man she could ever be happy with, the only man she could ever find enduring love with, the only man she had trusted with the truth of her conception... He was marrying someone else. The happy ending she'd always hoped she would one day have would never be hers.

When she dared to look at Helios she found his gaze on her, a question resonating from his liquid eyes. He was as sensitive to her changes of mood as she was to his.

She forced a smile and straightened her posture, doing her best to resume her professional demeanour. Whatever personal torment she might have churning inside her, she still had a job to do.

This was King Astraeus's big day, one he'd spent eighty-seven years of duty and sacrifice working towards. This was his moment. It was also Helios's and his brothers' moment too. The three Princes loved their grandfather, and this day was as much for them to show their appreciation of him as to allow their great nation to celebrate. She wouldn't do anything to detract from the culmination of all their hard work.

Amy kept her head up throughout the rest of the tour, but as soon as it was over she fled, using the pretext of needing to change her outfit for the Gala. Thankfully all the other staff wanted to change too, so saw nothing strange in her behaviour.

Finally alone in her apartment, she sank onto the edge of her bed and cradled her head in her hands. The tears that had threatened to pour throughout the exhibition tour had now become blocked. The emotions raging inside her had compacted so tightly and painfully that the release she needed wouldn't come.

The truth of her feelings and the hopelessness of her love had hit her so hard she had shut down inside.

CHAPTER TEN

FIVE THOUSAND PEOPLE were settled in the amphitheatre, watching the Gala, enjoying the multitude of performances taking turns on the stage, the glorious sunshine, the food and the drink.

Amy, sitting with the rest of the museum staff, tried to enjoy what was a truly spectacular occasion. A world-famous operatic duo from the US had just completed a medley of songs from *The Phantom of the Opera*, and now a Russian ballet troupe had taken to the stage, holding everyone spellbound.

When they were done, the compère came bounding back on. 'Ladies and gentlemen, boys and girls, in a small addition to our official programme, I am proud to welcome to the stage His Royal Highness, Prince Helios.'

Huge cheers broke out around the amphitheatre as the crowd rose to their feet to applaud the popular Prince.

Amy's stone-filled feet moved of their own accord and she stood too. The coldness rippling through her was such that it felt as if someone had injected ice into her veins. All the hairs on her arms had sprung upright. Nausea didn't churn—no, it turned and twisted, as if her stomach had been locked in a superfast waltzer. And yet the tightness in her chest remained, coiling even tighter if that were possible.

Helios started his address by thanking everyone for attending, then launched into a witty monologue about his grandfather, which led him neatly into entreating the audience and the hundreds of millions of worldwide viewers to visit the exhibition of the King's life now being held in the palace museum.

And then he cleared his throat.

Amy's own throat closed.

'I would also like to take this opportunity to confirm the speculation about my private life that has been documented in the world's press for these past few weeks. I am honoured to announce that Princess Catalina Fernandez of Monte Cleure has consented to be my wife.'

Such raucous cheers broke out at the news that they drowned out the rest of his speech. The crowd was still whooping when Helios bowed to them all and left the stage, with a grin on his handsome face that looked to Amy's eyes more like a grimace.

Looking around the crowd, blinking to clear the cold fog enveloping her mind, Amy saw that the happiest faces were those of the Agonites who'd been lucky enough to get tickets for this event.

So now it was official.

Helios and the Princess were betrothed. There could be no backing out of the marriage now; not when the pride of two nations was at stake.

And the tiny spark of hope she hadn't even realised she carried in her extinguished into nothing.

Helios shook the hand of yet another post-Gala party guest and silently cursed Talos for disappearing with the violinist, who'd overcome her stage fright and wowed everyone that evening. His grandfather had retired to bed, exhausted after such a full day, leaving Helios and

Theseus to welcome all the people on the three-hundred-strong guest list.

Thank goodness protocol dictated that his fiancée acted in no official capacity until their nuptials had been exchanged. He still couldn't imagine her by his side. Or in his bed.

For the first time he accepted that Amy leaving Agon when he married would be a good thing. The best thing. For all of them.

All he knew was that he wouldn't be able to commit himself to Catalina as a husband if Amy resided under the palace roof and worked in the palace museum.

He'd thought when she had come back to him that everything would be all right and they could return to the way they'd been. But everything was not all right. Everything was worse.

His feelings for her...

There was a trapdoor looming in front of him and every step he made took him closer to falling through it. But he couldn't see in which direction the trapdoor lay. He just knew it was there, readying itself to swallow him whole.

As was normal at a Kalliakis party, none of the guests was in a hurry to leave. But, as was not normal, Helios was in no mood to party with them.

He did his duty and danced with the Princess. Again he felt nothing. His body didn't produce the slightest twinge. Nothing.

When Catalina finally left to catch her flight back to Monte Cleure with her father and brother Helios sought out Theseus, who was still going through the motions with the last of the straggling guests, and bore him away to his apartment.

From the look on his brother's face he needed a drink as much as Helios did.

For someone with a newly discovered son he adored, and a wedding to the boy's mother on the horizon, Theseus was acting like someone who'd been told he was to spend the rest of his life locked in the palace dungeons.

Much as Helios himself felt.

He'd never thought of alcohol as a tool for making problems better—on the contrary, he knew it tended to make matters worse. But he wasn't trying to make himself feel better. That wouldn't be possible. All he wanted was a healthy dose of numbness, even if only for a short time.

Was Amy waiting up for him?

They hadn't made their usual arrangement. It had been on the tip of his tongue to say his customary 'I'll come to you when I'm done' that morning, but this time something had stopped him. A sense of impropriety. Indecency. To parade the news of his fiancée to the world, then expect to slip between the covers with his mistress...

An image flashed into his mind of Amy standing in the cathedral in a wedding dress, of his mother's sapphire ring sliding onto her finger... It was an image he'd been fighting not to see for weeks.

He closed his eyes and breathed deeply.

This was madness.

He took another swig of neat gin and said without thinking, 'Those people watching the Gala. They have no idea of our sacrifices.'

'What?' Theseus slurred, staring at him with bloodshot eyes Helios knew mirrored his own.

'Nothing.'

Even if he'd wanted to confide in his brother, Theseus was clearly in no state to listen. He knew he should ask him what was wrong, but the truth was he was in no state of mind to listen either.

Moody silence followed, both brothers locked in their

own thoughts. The anticipated numbness failed to materialise. All the gin had brought on was the monster of all headaches.

Helios slammed his glass on the table. 'It's time for you to crawl to your own apartment—I'm going to bed.'

Theseus downed his drink without a murmur of protest and got to his unsteady feet. At least his brother was drunk enough to pass out without any problems, he mused darkly.

As Theseus staggered out Helios promised himself that he would leave Amy to sleep. It was long past midnight. Soon the sun would rise. To wake her would be cruel. To go to her at all, tonight of all nights, would be the height of crassness.

Dammit. He'd just become officially engaged. Couldn't he show some decorum for *one* night?

But the memory of Amy's ashen face during the exhibition tour refused to leave him and he knew he had to go to her. He had to see for himself that she was all right.

He walked down the passageway, promising himself that he would leave if there was no answer. When he reached her bedroom door, he rapped on it lightly.

Within seconds he heard the telltale turning of the lock.

When she'd opened the door Amy gazed up at him with an expression he couldn't distinguish. One that combined anguish, desire and need in one big melting pot.

And as he stepped into her welcoming arms he realised that, for all his talk of sacrifice, he didn't yet know how great his biggest sacrifice would be.

With the early-morning sunlight peeking through the curtains, Amy gazed at Helios's sleeping form.

Hours after the post-Gala party had finished he'd come to her. And for the first time since they'd started their relationship all those months ago, nothing physical had happened between them.

Until he'd quietly knocked on her door she'd been trying to sleep, without any luck. She hadn't wanted to stay awake for him. She'd been scared that he wouldn't come to her and equally scared that he would.

Images had tortured her: thoughts of Helios and the Princess dancing together, becoming an official couple, discussing their wedding plans, showing the world how perfect they were for each other. Her stomach had ached so much it had been as if she'd swallowed a jug of battery acid.

With the hours ticking down until morning, she'd assumed the worst. She'd seen the helicopters and limousines taking their honoured guests away from the palace and had been unable to stop herself from wondering which of them carried the Princess.

Then, just as any hope that he would appear had gone, Helios had arrived at her door with bloodshot eyes, exhaustion etched on his face. He'd stripped off his clothes, climbed into her bed, pulled her into his arms and promptly fallen asleep.

How many more nights would he do this? How many more nights would they have together?

The official announcement had set off an alarm clock in her battery-acid-filled stomach and its persistent tick was excruciating.

Careful not to wake him, she sat up, doing nothing but drink him in.

How many more nights could she do this? Simply look at him?

Later that day he would be flying to the US for the start of an official state visit.

In her heart she knew that now, this moment, truly was the beginning of the end for them.

She reached out a hand and gently palmed his cheek. He nuzzled sleepily into her hand and kissed it. Lightly, she began to trace her fingers over the handsome face she loved so much, from his forehead—over which locks of hair had fallen—to his cheekbones, then over the bump on his nose, the bow of his lips, the jawline where thick stubble had broken out, and down his neck. She took his silver chain between her fingers and then touched the mandarin garnet necklace around her own neck.

It had been a birthday present from him, one he'd given her shortly after they'd started sleeping together. Of all the gifts he'd bestowed upon her, it was the one to which she felt the closest. The meaning behind it, the fact Helios had gone out of his way to find an item of jewellery made with her birthstone, meant that she'd swallowed her guilt and taken it out of the padded envelope where the rest of the jewellery he'd given her remained.

Whatever lay in the future, she knew she would never take it off again.

Slowly she explored his naked body, trailing her fingers over his collarbone and shoulder, down his right arm, lacing them through the fine black hair covering his forearm. When she reached his hand and took each finger in turn, gently pressing into them, he gave a light squeeze in response but otherwise remained still.

After repeating her exploration down his left arm, she moved to his chest. Helios's breathing had changed. It no longer had the deep, rhythmic sound of sleep. A heavier, more ragged sound was coming from him.

Over his pecs she traced her hands, encircling his dark brown nipples, catching the dark hair that was spread finely across his chest, pressing her palm down where the beat of his heart was strongest, then moving them across his ribcage and down to his abdomen...

His erection stopped her in her tracks.

Sucking in a breath, she ignored it, outlining the smooth skin on either side and drawing her fingers over his narrow hips. Gently spreading his muscular thighs, she knelt between them and carried her exploration down his left leg, tracing the silvery scar on his calf—the result of being thrown from a horse at the age of nine—and down to his feet. Then she moved to his right leg, this time starting from his toes and making her way up...all the way to the line where his thigh met his groin.

Helios's hand dug into her hair, spearing it, his breaths now erratic. Still only using her fingers, she traced the long stretch of his erection, cupping him, delighting in his tortured groans, before she put him out of his misery and ran her tongue along its length, then took him into her mouth.

For an age she moved him with her hand whilst licking and sucking. His hand cradled her scalp, massaging it, but he let her set the pace. Heat bubbled deep inside her, burning her from her core outwards, enflaming her skin. Giving him pleasure gave her as much joy as when he pleasured her.

When she sensed him getting close to breaking point she pulled away, unable to give him the playful smile she would normally give. She had never felt less playful when making love to him.

Moving up to straddle him, she gazed into his eyes, thrilling to see the heady desire ringing in them. He cupped her neck and pulled her down to meet his mouth. His tongue swept into hers, his kiss full of all the dark, potent neediness flowing through her own veins.

Slowly, with their lips and tongues still entwined, she sank onto him until he was fully sheathed inside her.

Breaking the kiss, she pulled back to sit atop him, needing to look at him.

As his groans became louder he placed one hand flat on her breast, whilst his other hand held tightly to her hip, steadying and supporting her. Then, with her hands resting lightly on his shoulders, she began to move. The feel of him deep inside her, the friction of their movements, it all built on the sensations already whirling inside her.

She could make love to this man every day for the rest of her life and it still wouldn't be enough. She would always want—need—more. Even if they had all the time in the world it wouldn't be enough time for her to look at his face, to touch him, to hear his voice, to witness his smile.

But there was only now, this moment in time when it was just them. There was no palace, no duty...

Just them. One man. One woman.

She wished she could hold on to it for ever.

She tried to hold back the climax growing within her, tried to blunt her responses, but it was all too intoxicating. With a cry that was as much dismay as it was delight, the pulsations swept through her, starting deep in the very heart of her and rippling out to embrace her every atom.

She threw herself down to bury her face in his neck and his arms immediately wrapped around her. A strangled groan escaped his mouth and he gave one last thrust upwards as his own climax tore through him with the same strength as her own. Both of them rode it for as long as they could until there was nothing left but their breaths, burning heavily into each other's necks.

The hotel, arranged by Talia under Helios's instructions, had a charming air to it, an ambience that carried through inside, through the cosy lobby and into the even cosier restaurant.

It was Agon's oldest hotel and a favourite on the tourist trail. It was guaranteed to be busy, whatever the time of year. Thus, two women could meet and dine together during the lunchtime rush without attracting any attention. It was safe for Amy's birth mother here. No one would know who she was. No one would report back to her husband. Ignorance would continue to be bliss for him.

As strange as she knew it to be, Amy would have recognised Neysa even if she hadn't known who she was. Her heart stuttered as she was caught in the gaze of eyes that were identical to her own.

This was the woman who had carried her in her womb for nine months.

This was the woman who had abandoned her.

Neysa Soukis hesitated before asking, 'Amy…?'

'Neysa?' Calling her Mum or Mother was *not* an option.

Grasping the outstretched hand, Amy marvelled at how it was an identical size to her own. It was like seeing a model of herself twenty years from now, although she doubted she would ever be as well groomed. Neysa was expensively dressed and immaculately coiffured.

After ordering drinks and some mezzes Neysa gave a brittle smile, opened her mouth and then closed it again.

Amy filled the silence. 'Why didn't you want to meet me?'

Fingers similar to her own but older, and with buffed nails, drummed on the table. 'You are a stranger to me.' Her English accent was heavy and unpractised.

'You carried me. You gave birth to me.' *You abandoned me.* 'Weren't you curious?'

'I have a life now. Husband. A son.'

Yes… Her son. Leander. The man-child Neysa doted on.

'What made you change your mind?'

She gave a harsh bark of laughter. 'The threat that my husband would learn of you.'

That would be Helios's doing. He was not a man one could say no to. Neysa was here because Helios had effectively blackmailed her, not because she wanted to meet the child she'd given up.

'Leander could tell your husband.'

'Leander would never tell.'

Neysa's confidence in this statement didn't surprise her. Helios had done some more digging into the mother-son relationship and discovered that Leander's father had all but given up on him. Neysa was the one to lavish him with love and the all-important money. He was dependent on her. If she withdrew her funds he would, heaven forbid, have to get a job and keep it.

If her husband was to learn that Neysa had been keeping such a monumental secret from him throughout their twenty-five-year marriage who knew how he would react? Both Neysa and Leander might be thrown off the gravy train they worshipped so much.

A waiter appeared with a tray of drinks.

'Did you ever think of me?' Amy asked when they were alone again.

A flicker of something she couldn't decipher crossed Neysa's face. 'Many times.'

She was lying. Amy didn't know how she could be certain of this, but certain she was. Neysa had forged a new life for herself, with a rich husband two decades her senior. Amy was a dirty little secret she couldn't afford to let anyone find out about. She had no interest in her child. Her only interest was in protecting her secret.

'I knew your father would take good care of you,' Neysa explained earnestly. Too earnestly.

She had known nothing of the sort, and neither had she tried to find out. For all she knew Amy might have been dumped in an orphanage. She'd had no way of knowing that Elaine—the woman who had taken Neysa into her home and trusted her with her young son, the woman Neysa had betrayed in such a heinous way without one word of remorse—had raised Amy as her own.

Amy had spent seventeen years hoping that it had been shame which had kept Neysa away. That she'd acknowledged that what she'd done to the Green family had been so great a sin that she couldn't bring herself to face Elaine and say sorry.

She couldn't have been more wrong.

At least her father had been genuinely remorseful. Her mum had promised her that. *He'd* acknowledged the terrible deed he'd done and had spent twenty-seven years trying to make amends for it. One mad weekend alone, without his wife and with a hot young woman parading herself around the house before him… He'd been too weak not to take advantage and he'd paid the price every day of his life since.

Looking at her birth mother now, Amy couldn't believe her mum had been able to love her the way she did. Amy was the image of Neysa. Every time her mum had looked at Amy's face she must have seen the image of the woman who had betrayed her and the living proof of her husband's infidelity.

How could Amy even be in the same room as this woman? Neysa hadn't cared that she'd almost destroyed Amy's mum—her *real* mum…the woman who had loved her every day of her life from the age of two weeks.

And she'd been scared that her mum secretly wanted to get rid of her? Never. Not her loving, generous mum.

The waiter returned to the table with their food.

Amy waited until he'd laid everything out before getting to her feet and hooking the strap of her handbag over her shoulder.

'You have nothing to fear from me,' she said slowly. 'I want no part of your life. I wanted to see you. And now I have.'

'You are going?'

'I shouldn't have come. Goodbye, Neysa.'

Leaving her birth mother open-mouthed in shock, Amy made her way out of the hotel and into the warm spring street brimming with tourists.

She stood for a moment, breathing in the sweet scent. She hadn't found a single place in Agon where the air didn't smell good. And yet an acrid odour lingered around her from her encounter.

Breathing heavily, Amy raised her eyes to the sky and thanked whatever benevolent being that was up there for allowing Neysa to abandon her.

Who would she be if she'd been raised on Agon under Neysa's narcissistic hand? If she'd grown up with Leander? If she'd lived without Danny and Neil's fierce protection, her mum's loving guidance and her dad's silent but constant presence?

And she thanked Helios too. His interference had allowed her to put to bed one of the biggest questions in her life: who had made her?

That *'who'* was someone she had no wish to see again. But at least she knew that now. Thanks to Helios she could move on and stop wondering *what if...?*

As she thought his name her phone buzzed. It was a brief message from him, checking that everything was okay. Her darling Helios was on a state visit to America and had still found the time to think of her and send her a message.

But how could she be okay? she thought as she replied, saying that she was fine and that she would explain everything to him later, when he called. Which he would. He called her every night when he travelled abroad.

How could everything be okay when very soon she would have to say goodbye to the one person who *did* make everything okay?

CHAPTER ELEVEN

AMY CARRIED ON as best she could over the next few days, never letting her smile drop or her shoulders slouch. She was determined that no one looking at her would have reason to suspect that she was suffering in any way.

The entire island was aflame with gossip following the confirmation of Helios's engagement to the Princess. Naturally this enthusiasm was tripled in the palace itself. Everywhere she went she heard excited chatter. It had got to the stage where, even if she didn't understand what was being said, she imagined it was all about the forthcoming wedding.

The date had been set. In six weeks and one day Helios would marry. It was going to happen sooner than she had thought. She had forgotten about all the work for the wedding that had been going on behind the scenes. Helios had wisely never mentioned it in any of their calls.

Other than in the privacy of her apartment, the only place she found any crumb of solace was amongst the staff in the museum. Whereas the visitors—whose numbers were daily in the thousands—kept up a non-stop commentary about the wedding, the staff took a different approach. They knew Amy had been Helios's lover. *Everyone* had known. So when she was in the same room conversation was kept as far away from matrimony as it was possible to get. But she caught the pitying, often worried glances that were thrown her way.

Her colleagues were a good, kindly, close-knit bunch who supported and looked out for each other. It was in this vein that Claudia, one of the tour guides, approached her in the staff room during Amy's break on the Friday after the Gala.

'I'm sorry to disturb your lunch, but Princess Catalina is here.'

Amy immediately froze, as if a skewer of ice had been thrust into her central nervous system. Somehow she managed to swallow her mouthful of tomato and feta salad, the food clawing its way down her numbed throat.

The tour guide bit her lip. 'She is asking for you.'

'For *me*?' she choked out.

Claudia nodded. 'She wants a tour of the King's exhibition and has asked for you personally.'

It was on the tip of her tongue to ask if Helios was with her, but she stopped herself in time. If Helios was with the Princess they wouldn't need Amy. Helios could do the tour himself.

She didn't even know if he was back from his trip to America. She'd thought he was due back sometime that afternoon.

She'd spent five nights without him.

It had been much harder than any of their other separations. She'd missed him desperately, as a small child missed home.

It was a pain she would have to get used to.

Her main source of comfort had come from Benedict, who had stayed in her apartment during Helios's absence. The lovable black Labrador had seemed to sense Amy's despondency and had kept close to her. Their evenings together had been spent on the sofa, watching films, Benedict's head on her lap.

When she returned to England she would get her own Labrador for company.

Blowing out a long breath of air, Amy closed the lid of her salad box and forced herself to her feet. She couldn't manage another bite.

'Where is she?'

'In the entrance hall.'

'Okay. Give me two minutes to use the bathroom.'

Concentrating on her breathing, Amy took her handbag and locked herself in the staff bathroom. She took stock of her reflection in the mirror and pulled a face. Hastily she loosened her hair from its ponytail, brushed it and then tied it back again. From her handbag she pulled her compressed face powder and a make-up brush and applied a light covering. She would have added eyeliner and lip gloss but her hands were shaking too much.

As a means of buying time for herself, her trip to the bathroom was wasted. The hopes she'd had of making it through the next few months without having to meet the Princess had been blown to pieces.

Why *her*? Why had the Princess asked for her by name? How did she even know who she was?

Terror gripped her, but she forced herself to straighten up and pushed air into her cramped lungs.

The Princess was an honoured guest, she reminded herself. It was natural she would ask for the exhibition's curator to be her guide. *Just be professional,* she told herself as she left her sanctuary.

The Princess awaited her in the entrance hall, flanked by two huge bodyguards.

She was the epitome of glamour, wearing skintight white jeans, an off-the-shoulder rose-pink top, an elegant pale blue silk scarf and blue high heels. Her ebony hair was loose around her shoulders, and an expensive pair of sunglasses sat atop her head.

But there was more to her than mere glamour; a beautiful, almost ethereal aura she carried effortlessly. She was a princess in every sense of the word. If she slept on a hundred mattresses no doubt she would still feel the pea at the bottom.

Swallowing down the dread lodged like bile in her throat, Amy strode towards her with a welcoming smile. 'Your Highness, I am Amy Green,' she said, dropping into a curtsy. 'It is an honour to meet you.'

The Princess smiled graciously. 'Forgive me for disturbing your break, but I wanted a tour of the exhibition. I've been told you're the curator and that you have a wealth of knowledge about my fiancé's family. I couldn't think of a better person to show me around.' All of this was delivered in almost faultless English.

'I am honoured.' And it *was* an honour. A true honour.

They went slowly around the exhibition rooms, with Amy politely discussing the various artefacts and their context in the Kalliakis family's history. She answered the Princess's questions as best she could whilst all too aware of her constantly clammy hands.

Princess Catalina might look as if she would feel the pea through a hundred mattresses, but she was so much more than a princess from the realms of fairy tales.

She was a flesh and blood human.

It wasn't until they entered The Wedding Room, with the bodyguards keeping a close but respectable distance, that the Princess showed any real animation. She was immediately drawn to Queen Rhea's wedding dress, staring at it adoringly for long, excruciating seconds before she turned to Amy.

'Isn't this the most beautiful dress?' she said with her gaze fixed on her, her eyes searching.

Amy nodded, the bile in her throat burning.

'The dressmaker who made this has agreed to come out of retirement to make mine. I'm having my first fitting tomorrow—did Helios tell you I will be staying at the palace for the weekend?'

'I've heard it mentioned,' she whispered. She'd overheard a couple of the tour guides discussing the visit. They'd been wondering whether the Princess would bring her fabulous Vuitton bag with her. She had.

The Princess smiled. Despite her amiability, sadness lurked behind her eyes. It filled Amy with horror.

'There isn't much that happens within the palace that's kept secret, is there?'

Flames licked her cheeks. It took all her willpower for her not to cover them with her hands.

The Princess seemed not to want a response of the verbal kind. Her sad, probing eyes never left Amy's face, but she smiled. 'I thank you for your time.'

'Do you not want to see the other exhibition rooms?' Caught off guard, Amy took the Princess's hand; a major breach of protocol. She had the softest skin imaginable.

The Princess's squeeze of her hand was gentle and... forgiving? The smile thrown at her was enigmatic. 'I have seen what I came to see.'

Nodding at her bodyguards, she glided away, tall, lithe and poised.

Amy stared at the retreating figure and rubbed the nape of her neck, feeling as if all the wind had been knocked out of her.

The Princess knew.

Dear God, the Princess *knew*.

* * *

Her concentration lost, Amy wandered around the exhibition rooms, praying no one would ask her anything that required any thought to answer. Feeling nauseous to the bone, she eventually settled in the entrance hall, trying her hardest to keep herself together.

But all too soon the influx of guests had reduced and reality was given space to taunt her.

The marble sculptures of the four Kings kept drawing her attention, and as much as she knew she shouldn't she went and stood before them.

King Astraeus the Third had been famed for his wisdom. She wished he could transmute some of it to herself. But it was King Astraeus the Second she couldn't tear her eyes away from. His resemblance to Helios was so strong she could fool herself into thinking it *was* him.

One day, decades from now, a statue much like this would be made of him. If she closed her eyes she could see it, could envisage every inch of the ten-foot marble figure. If the sculptor were to show her the block of stone she would be able to tell him where every line and sinew should go.

It came to her then what she'd been doing that night after the Gala—or early morning—when she'd touched every part of him. She'd been committing him to memory. She hadn't been able to face the truth at the time, but it hit her now. She'd imprinted him on her mind because her subconscious had known that it would be their last time.

Their time together was truly over.

The walls of the great exhibition room suddenly loomed large over her, swallowing her. The statues and the other exhibits blurred. She needed air. But to flee outside would mean risking seeing the Princess or, worse, Helios. She couldn't face him with an audience watching. The next time she saw him she had to be alone with him.

Pulling her identity card from around her neck and stuffing it in her pocket, she walked into the main museum, hurrying through the crowds of visitors until she found Claudia.

'I've got a migraine coming,' she said. 'I need to rest—can you give my apologies to Pedro?'

'Sure.' Claudia looked at her with concern Amy knew she didn't deserve. 'Can I get you anything?'

'No, thank you. Please, I just need to get some sleep in a darkened room.'

Not waiting for a response, Amy wove her way through the remaining people to the private staff entrance to the palace, then hurried up the stairs to her apartment, kicked off her shoes and threw herself onto the bed.

She might not really have a migraine, but her head pounded as if a dozen church bells were ringing inside it. Let it pound. Let the bells clang as loudly as they could and the decibels increase.

She deserved nothing less.

Helios stood in the green stateroom, holding discussions with a group of German business people who wanted to invest considerable sums in Agon's infrastructure and, naturally, recoup their investment with considerable profit. With them was Agon's Transport Minister.

Agon had its own senate, and committees which decided on issues such as outside investors, but an endorsement from one of the royal Princes meant this would be as good as a done deal. Helios knew his opinions carried a great deal of weight and did his utmost to use his influence wisely.

When his phone rang he was tempted to ignore it, but

it was his personal phone and only the most important people in his life had been given the number. He frowned when he saw Amy's name on the screen.

He hadn't had a chance to call her and let her know he was back from his trip to the US. In any case he'd assumed she would be busy at the museum… She hardly ever called him and *never* out of the blue.

'Excuse me,' he murmured to the delegation, stepping away from the group with an apologetic smile. He swiped the screen to answer. 'Amy?'

'I'm sorry to disturb you,' she said, her usual soft tones sounding strangely muffled. 'I know you're busy, but I wondered if you're coming to me tonight.'

Not only did she never call him, she never questioned his movements either. A dark sense of foreboding snaked up his spine. 'Is something the matter?'

He heard her hesitation.

'I just need to see you.'

He looked at his watch. 'Where are you?'

'In my apartment.'

'Are you ill?'

'No. Not really. Not ill, ill.'

He wanted to pump her for information but, aware of the delegation, Talia and all the courtiers eyeing him with curiosity, he resisted.

'I'll be with you as soon as I can,' he said, before hanging up.

He'd be with her as soon as he could politely extricate himself. Something was wrong. The cold dread wedged in the marrow of his bones told him that.

It was half an hour before he was able to extract himself from the group, saying he had some personal business to catch up with and that he would see them at the dinner being held in their honour. He then told Talia that she could leave early. Talia didn't argue the matter—in fact he would swear she left so quickly she left a trail of dust in her wake. He didn't blame her. It had been a long few weeks and she must be exhausted.

When he reached his office he cut through to his apartment and slipped through the passageway into Amy's apartment. She answered his knock quickly, with a startled expression on her face.

'I didn't think I would see you until much later,' she said wanly. 'I hope I haven't put you out.'

'You could never put me out.' He studied her carefully. Her face was grey, her eyes were bloodshot and her hair looked unkempt. 'Have you been crying?'

She bit her lip and took a shuddery breath. Closing the door, she rested her hand on the handle. 'The Princess knows.'

'Catalina? What does she know?'

'About us.' She met his gaze. 'She came to the museum. She wanted me, personally, to give her a tour of the exhibition.'

'You're the exhibition's curator,' he pointed out.

She shook her head. 'It was more than that. She knows, Helios. I think… I think she's heard rumours about us. Maybe someone saw me walking Benedict… I think she was looking for confirmation. Whatever I did, I don't know, but I'm sure something confirmed her suspicions.'

He ran a hand through his hair. 'Even assuming you're right, there is nothing for you to worry about. Catalina isn't stupid. She knows there will be other women.'

It was the wrong thing to say. Amy looked as if he'd slapped her.

'I didn't mean it like that,' he added hastily. 'All I meant was that Catalina has no illusions of fidelity. You know there is no love between us.'

There was nothing between them. Not the smallest twinge.

Shaking her head again, Amy sidestepped past him and went through to her kitchen. 'You're a fool if you believe that. She *wants* it to be a love match.'

'No…'

'Yes,' she said through gritted teeth. 'She does. Whatever you think you know about her, you've got it wrong.'

'She does not love me.'

'Not yet.'

Her eyes bored into his as her words hung in the air between them, then she turned sharply and pulled a bottle of white wine out of the fridge.

'Glass?' she asked.

'You're drinking already?' A trace of his bemusement cut through the darkening atmosphere.

'Right now I need it.'

She leant against the work surface and closed her eyes briefly, then poured them both some wine. When she passed his glass to him she snatched her hand away before there was any chance of their fingers brushing.

She went to take a sip from her own, but as she brought it to her mouth her face crumpled.

Stepping quickly to her, Helios took the glass from her shaking hand and placed it with his own on the counter, then wrapped his arms around her.

At first she resisted, but then she gave in to it, almost burying her head in his chest. Within seconds his shirt was wet with her tears.

'Don't cry, *matakia mou,*' he whispered, stroking her hair. 'It will all work out. I promise.'

'How?' she asked between sobs. 'How can it ever work out? We're breaking her heart.'

'No, we're not.'

'We *are*. Maybe she doesn't love you yet, but she wants to. She wants your marriage to work. Have you even seen her since you got back from America?'

'I've been busy.'

Disentangling herself from his hold, Amy grabbed a handful of tissues from a box. The tears kept falling.

'Helios, the Princess is your fiancée. She's come all this way to see you. You should be with her. This time before your marriage should be spent getting to know each other...'

'We do know each other.'

'Do you?' She raised her shoulders. 'Then tell me this—what are her dreams? What are her fears? Can you answer any of that? You're going to be spending the rest of your life with her.'

'Yes,' he agreed tightly. 'The rest of my life. But the rest of my life hasn't started yet.'

'It started the minute you put an engagement ring on her finger.'

The engagement ring. He'd told Catalina to choose her own, with the excuse that she would be the one wearing it and so she should have something that was to her own taste. He hadn't been able to bring himself to do the deed himself.

He knew she coveted his mother's sapphire ring. Growing up, he'd always known that ring would be given to the woman he made his wife. He'd had the ready-made excuse that it was a feature of the exhibition to stop him sliding it onto Catalina's finger yet, but he'd promised that when the exhibition was over it would be hers.

'I can't do this any more,' Amy said, her voice choking on the words. 'What we're doing to the Princess is abhorrent. She's a princess but she's *real*, not a fairy-tale creation. She's human, and the guilt is eating me alive.'

He moved to take her back into his arms but she held up a hand to him and shook her head.

'We can't. *I* can't. I won't be the cause of someone else's misery. How can I when I've seen first-hand the damage it causes?' Wiping away a fresh batch of tears, she swallowed before saying, 'When I came to Agon and I wanted to find my birth mother, it wasn't because I wanted to form a relationship with her. I wanted to know my other family and my roots, yes, and I was *desperate* to see what she looked like. But what I really wanted from her was to know why.'

'Why she abandoned you?' She had told him on the phone about the meeting. How she had left within minutes, abandoning the mother who'd abandoned her.

'Partly. What I really wanted to know was how she could have done what she did to my mum. She was her au pair— Mum had trusted her with her child and welcomed her into her home. My mum is the most loving woman in the world. There is no way she would have treated Neysa with anything but kindness. How could she sneak around behind her back with her husband? What kind of evil selfishness makes a person act like that?'

'Did you ask her that?'

'No. I was so desperate to get away from her that I didn't ask her any of the questions I'd been storing up for seventeen years.' She gave a half-hearted shrug. 'And now I don't want to know. I don't want to hear her excuses because that's all they'll be. I don't think she feels any remorse.'

'Amy, our situation is very different. How Neysa and your father behaved…it's not like for like.'

'You might not be married yet, but the intention and commitment are still there. The agony my mum must have gone through… She never got over it. She forgave my father but she's never forgotten, and she's not been able to trust him properly since.'

More tears fell, harder now, turning her face into a torrent of salt water.

'I can't live with the guilt. I've spent my entire life, through no fault of my own, being a person people point at and whisper about. I've had to work so hard to make myself believe that I didn't deserve it and that I was innocent. But how can I be innocent when *I'm* the one now causing someone's misery? I don't want to be the selfish woman Neysa is. I don't want to hurt anyone. The Princess is a good and lovely person and she doesn't deserve this—no one does. Whatever she's been raised to be, she's still human.'

The depth of Amy's guilt and misery stabbed at him, right in his guts, evoking a wave of shame that came rushing through him, a wave so powerful that he reeled and held on to the small kitchen table for support.

'Listen to me,' he said urgently. 'The very fact you feel such guilt proves you are *nothing* like Neysa, so put such thoughts from your mind. You would never hurt anyone, not on purpose.'

'But that is what I've been doing!' she cried. 'I'm *exactly* like her.'

'No! All you inherited from Neysa was her looks. Everything else came from Elaine and the rest of your English family and the goodness that is *you*. You are a good person—the best I know.'

She didn't look the slightest bit convinced by anything he'd said. Helios's mind worked frantically as he tried to think of a solution whereby Amy's guilt could be obliterated. But nothing came to him. He *had* to marry someone of royal blood to secure the Kalliakis line.

He was hurting her, the last thing he'd ever wanted to do. Not Amy. Not her. Not ever.

His father had done more than hurt his mother physically; the destruction had been emotional too. Helios had always known he would never follow his footsteps on the physical side, but to discover he was guilty of an emotional destruction every bit as great...

Something that felt suspiciously like panic clawed at him, biting and contracting through every part of him, converging in his stomach into a pain so acute he wanted to shout out with the agony of it all.

His relationship with Amy was long past being the light, playful interlude it had begun as. Along the way it had developed into something so deep he feared he would no longer be able to see the light if they went any further.

If he had the slightest ounce of decency he would let Amy go before he destroyed her completely.

CHAPTER TWELVE

FOLDING HIS ARMS across his chest, Helios stared at Amy, wondering how he was going to cope without seeing her beautiful face every day and making love to her every night. She was so much more to him than just his lover. She was his best friend, the first true friend he'd ever had. She'd been brought into his life not through her own wealth or social standing but simply by being Amy.

Amy gazed back at him with the same intensity and attempted a brave smile. 'Do you think there's a parallel world out there, where we can be free to be together and love each other?'

Love?

She must have registered the shock in his eyes at her use of the *L* word for she laughed wanly. 'Oh, I do love you. Very much. More than I ever knew was possible.'

He stepped out of her reach, backing himself against the kitchen door. He didn't know how to answer. He couldn't think.

His private phone buzzed in his pocket. He pulled it out and rejected the call without looking at it.

'Love is not something I have ever required,' he finally said, his brain reeling as much as his body.

'I know that.' Her chin wobbled and she took deep breaths, raising her eyes to the ceiling.

'*Theos*, Amy, you...' He blew out a long breath as his brain scrambled to unravel itself. 'I've always known I must marry for duty. Love isn't something I've ever expected or thought about. It has no place in my life, you must see that?'

'Yes, I do.'

Of course she did. Amy knew his full ancestral history better than she could ever know her own.

'If you love me then how can you leave me?' he asked, still shell-shocked at her declaration but grasping at straws.

'Because I want to be able to look at my reflection every day and not throw darts at it,' she answered with a choked laugh. 'And my leaving isn't just to do with Catalina.'

There. She'd finally uttered the Princess's name aloud.

'I might have been made from a dirty secret but I don't want to live my life as one. You're right that I'm not Neysa, and I will not allow myself to be like her. Even if you wanted it—even if you loved me—you're not in a position to give me the commitment and fidelity I need. I want to be yours. Just yours. Openly yours. With the whole world knowing we belong together. I can't make love with you while you're sleeping in the bed of another, and I can't make love knowing I'm good enough for sex but not good enough for for ever.'

What she didn't say was that Helios had lodged himself so deeply into her heart she doubted there was room left in there for any other man to find an opening. Her heart belonged to him now.

She should have left weeks ago. The physical pain she'd experienced when he'd told her of his intention to marry as soon as possible should have acted as a warning. If she'd gone then she would have left with her pride intact and her heart would still have enough room for someone else.

His face contorted. 'Don't you *ever* say you're not good enough.'

'But that's how I feel,' she said, shrugging her shoulders helplessly. 'I know that's not your intention, and that you don't think or believe that—I *know*—but I've spent most of my life feeling like a dirty secret. For us to carry on, even if it's only until you marry, will *make* me one.'

He didn't say anything, just stared at her as if he were seeing her for the first time.

'Helios, when you marry the Princess be faithful to her. Give your marriage a chance. She deserves that and so do you.'

'You sound like you're planning to leave now...' A strange look flashed in his eyes and suddenly he sprang to life like *Galatea*, the statue created with such love by Pygmalion.

He strode out of the kitchen and into her bedroom, taking in the suitcases on the bed, half-filled with clothing.

His face contorted and he shook his head. 'No.'

'Helios...'

'No.' His hands clenched into fists.

She could see him fighting the urge to throw her cases out of the window.

His phone buzzed again, the third time it had rung in as many minutes.

'Answer it,' she insisted. 'It might be important.'

'*This* is important.' After a moment's pause he swore and pulled the phone to his ear. 'Yes?'

After a few moments his demeanour changed. As he listened he straightened his neck and rolled his shoulders, breathing deeply. His only contribution to the conversation was a few short words of Greek.

'I need to go,' he said when he'd finished the call. 'My

grandfather's suffering from a mild infection and is fighting with the doctors over his treatment.'

'I hope it's nothing too serious,' she said, immediately concerned.

'Just my grandfather being a stubborn old man.' He rubbed his chin and glared at her with his jaw clenched. 'I'll be back later. Don't even *think* of going anywhere.'

She didn't answer.

'I need to hear it, Amy. Tell me you won't go anywhere or do anything until I get back. Promise me.'

Knowing even as she spoke them that her words were a lie, she said, 'I'll be here.'

His shoulders loosened a little. Pacing over to her, he took her face in his hands and crushed her lips with his mouth, kissing her as if he'd been starved of her kisses for ever. And then he dropped his hold on her and walked out of her bedroom.

She heard the slam of the interconnecting door as he left.

Theos, his grandfather had to be the most stubborn man alive. He was refusing the intravenous drugs his doctors wanted to give him.

What could he do? He couldn't force him. The King wasn't a baby to be coaxed into doing his elders' bidding.

That hadn't stopped Helios from trying to make him see reason. Now he wanted to tear his hair out, to claw at his scalp and draw blood.

'At least he's not in pain,' Talos said quietly.

Their grandfather hadn't resisted painkillers for the pain racking his body. The cancer, kept at bay by months of chemotherapy, was making another, deadlier assault on his body. No one would say it, but time was slipping away from them.

One good thing to come out of the mess this day had turned into was the news from Theseus, who had gone tearing after Jo, the mother of his child, a couple of days ago. The fool had realised when it was almost too late that he truly did love her, and luckily it seemed Jo loved him too and had agreed to marry him.

No coercion, no thoughts of duty. They were marrying for love. Helios had never heard his brother sound so happy.

Both his brothers were marrying.

As Talos—who was marrying his violinist—had chosen someone not of royal blood, any child he had would not be in the line of succession to the throne, but Toby, Theseus's beautiful son, had already secured the throne for the next generation. Until Helios's own children were born.

Helios sighed and got to his feet. 'I need to change for dinner.'

He wished he could pull out of it, but it was a matter of honour amongst his family that personal matters never got in the way of duty. And this dinner was duty.

Nausea fermented in him as he remembered that Catalina would be attending. She was already there in the palace. He still couldn't bring himself to call her.

As much as he wanted to, there wasn't time to make a diversion to Amy's apartment and check that she was okay. Instead he fired off a quick message to her before showering and changing into his dinner jacket. He put his cufflinks on during his walk to the designated dining room for the evening, his courtiers struggling to keep up with his long strides.

Forcing bonhomie, Helios plastered a smile on his face and entered the dining room, where the delegation was waiting for him. Catalina was already there, holding court like a professional. When she saw him she excused herself to join him.

If she really did suspect him and his relationship with Amy, she covered it well.

'I understand your grandfather is unwell?' she said quietly.

'He's been better.' It was all he could bring himself to answer with.

Why couldn't he feel anything for her? Here was a beautiful, compassionate woman of royal blood and all he felt when she touched him was cold.

He tried again, using a milder tone of voice. 'He has an infection.'

She smiled sympathetically. 'I hope he recovers quickly.'

'So do I.'

But he didn't hold out much hope. These past five months had been a battle to keep him alive long enough for him to see the Gala. That was all his grandfather had been focusing on. Now, with the Gala over, his grandsons all paired off and the succession to the throne secured, King Astracus was preparing to die.

His duty was done. His grandfather wanted to be with the woman he'd loved for his entire adult life.

And Amy had said she loved *him*.

Helios wished he could unhear those words.

What kind of selfish monster was he to tie her to him when he knew doing so was destroying her?

It was possibly the longest meal of his life. For once, the power of speech had deserted him. He couldn't think of a single witty remark or any of the tales that usually had guests enthralled.

Throughout the meal disquiet grew within him, a foreboding which came upon him from an unseen direction.

As soon as the coffee had been cleared away he cleared

his throat. 'My apologies, ladies and gentlemen, but I need to retire for the evening. I know I haven't been very good company this evening—I think exhaustion has crept up on me—but be assured that I am very impressed with everything you've told me and will give my recommendation to the committee early next week.'

When he'd finished speaking he glanced at Catalina. She was staring at him with a cool, thoughtful expression.

It took fifteen minutes, time spent saying goodnight to everyone individually, before he was finally able to leave the dining room.

Catalina made no effort to follow him.

The disquiet in his chest grew with every step he took towards his apartment. By the time he reached his door and was able to shake off the courtiers, perspiration had broken out on his brow and his pulse had surged.

He headed straight down the passageway and rapped on Amy's connecting door.

No answer.

He banged again, louder.

No answer.

'Amy?' he shouted, pounding on the door with his fist.

On impulse he tried the handle, even though Amy always kept the door locked...

The door opened.

His heart thundering painfully beneath his ribs, he stepped into her apartment.

'Amy?' he called into the silence.

His heart knew before his head could comprehend it.

On legs weighted down with lead, he stepped into her bedroom.

The room was spotless. And empty.

All that lay on the dressing table, which was usually heaped with cosmetics and bottles of perfume, was a large padded envelope he recognised as the one he'd given to her all those weeks ago, containing the jewellery he'd bought her. Next to it lay a scrap of paper. Written on it were two words.

Forgive me.

'You look troubled, Helios,' his grandfather said, in the wheezing voice Helios hated so much.

They were playing chess, his grandfather's favourite game. The King was in his wheelchair, an oxygen tank to his right, a nurse set back a little to his left.

'I'm just tired.' Helios moved a pawn two spaces forward, unable to stop his stomach curdling with the fear that this might be the last game they played together.

'How are the wedding preparations going?'

'Well.'

Not that he was having anything to do with them. The palace staff were more than capable of handling it without his input. And without Catalina, who seemingly had as much interest in the preparations as he had. None at all.

His grandfather placed the oxygen mask on his face for a minute, before indicating for the nurse to take it off.

'I remember my own wedding day well.' The misty eyes grew mistier. 'Your grandmother looked like an angel sent from heaven.' Then the old eyes sharpened. 'Your mother looked beautiful on her wedding day too. It is my eternal sorrow that your father couldn't see her beauty. Your mother was beautiful, inside and out.'

Helios's spine stiffened. His parents' marriage was a subject they rarely touched upon other than in the most generic terms.

'The biggest regret of my life—and your grandmother's, rest her soul—was that your father couldn't choose his own wife. Would it have made a difference if he'd been able to choose?' He raised a weak, bony shoulder. 'We will never know. Despite our best efforts he was a vain and cruel man. He thrived on power. Your mother didn't stand a chance.'

He moved his castle forward with a quivering, gnarled finger.

'We pushed through the changes in law that would allow you and your heirs to select your own spouses in the hope that your parents' marriage would never be repeated.' His voice weakening with each word he said, the King turned his gaze to Helios again. 'However important duty is, marriage to someone you feel no affection for can only bring misery. And for ever is a long time to be miserable.'

The nurse, attuned to his weakening, placed the oxygen mask back over his face.

Helios waited for him to inhale as much as he needed, all the time his mind was reeling over what it was, exactly, that his grandfather was trying to tell him. Was it a reproach that he wasn't spending enough time with Catalina and that his indifference to her was showing?

But how could he feel anything *but* indifference when his head was still consumed with thoughts of Amy? She'd left the palace a week ago but she was still *everywhere*.

He moved his knight, then opened his mouth to pose the question, only to find his grandfather's head had lolled to one side and he'd dozed off mid-game and mid-conversation.

He looked at the nurse, who raised her shoulders sympathetically. Helios exhaled and gazed at his sleeping grandfather, a huge wave of love washing through him.

Whatever his grandfather had tried to tell him, it could wait.

'I'll put him to bed tonight,' he told the nurse, whose eyes immediately widened in fright.

'It's okay,' he assured her with a wry smile. 'I know what I'm doing. You can supervise if you want.'

Half an hour later the King was in his bed, his medication having been given and the oxygen mask attached to his face. His gentle snores were strangely calming.

Helios placed a kiss to his grandfather's forehead. 'I love you,' he said, before leaving him to sleep.

Movement beside her woke Amy from the light doze she'd fallen into. Since returning to England a week ago she'd slept a lot. She liked sleeping. It was the perfect route to forgetting. It was waking that was the problem.

Her mum handed her a cup of tea and sat in the deck-chair next to her.

When she'd returned to England she'd given the taxi driver directions to her childhood home rather than the flat she shared in central London. Sometimes a girl just needed her mum. Her *real* mum. The woman who'd loved and raised her since she'd barely been able to open her eyes.

And her mum had been overjoyed to see her.

Amy's last lingering doubts had been well and truly banished.

A late-night confession between them had culminated with the admission that her mum had been terrified that Amy would forge a relationship with Neysa.

'Never,' Amy had said with a firm shake of her head. 'You're my mum. Not her.'

'Good.' Ferocity had suddenly flashed in her mum's usually calm eyes. 'Because you're *my* daughter. Not hers.'

'Then why did you encourage me to learn about my roots?' she'd asked, bewildered.

'We all need to know where we come from. And I was scared that if I discouraged it you would do it in secret and one day you'd be gone and I would lose you.'

'You will never lose me.'

The tears had flowed easily that night.

Now they sat in companionable silence in the English sun, the only sound the chirruping of fledgling birds in the garden's thick hedges. It was a quintessentially British beautiful late-spring day.

'Are you ready to talk now?' her mum asked.

A lump forming in her throat, Amy shook her head. For all their late-night talks, she hadn't been able to bring up the subject of Helios.

To even think of him was too painful.

She'd had only one piece of correspondence from him since she'd left—a text message that said: I do.

He forgave her for running away.

Judging by his silence since, he'd accepted it too. She had no right to feel hurt that he'd made no further attempt to contact her.

'What's that you keep fingering around your neck?'

Wordlessly, Amy leaned forward to show her the garnet necklace.

Her mum took it between her fingers and smiled. 'It's lovely.'

Amy couldn't find the words to answer. When her mum let the necklace go Amy clasped it in her own hand and held it close.

'Broken hearts do mend,' her mum said softly.

Amy gave a ragged nod and swallowed, terrified of crying again. 'It hurts,' she choked out.

Her mum took her hand and squeezed it. 'Do you know what to do when life gives you lemons?'

'Make lemonade?'

'No. You throw them back and get yourself an orange.'

Amy spluttered, laughing. 'I haven't the faintest idea what that means.'

'Neither do I! It was something my mother used to say when I was a child.'

Still holding on tightly to each other's hands, they settled back in their deckchairs, sunglasses on, and basked in the sun.

After a while, her mum spoke again. 'I think what my mother was trying to say is that, whatever life throws at you, there are always choices and options other than the obvious ones. When your father first brought you home the obvious solution for me would have been to throw him out, and you with him. That would have been me making lemonade. But when I looked at you all I saw was an innocent, helpless newborn baby—a sister to the child I already had and a sister to the child I carried in my belly. So I chose to get myself an orange instead. I kept you— *you* were my orange. And I have never regretted it. My only regret is that I never carried you in my womb like I did your brothers.'

She took her sunglasses off and smiled the warm, motherly smile Amy loved so much.

'This man who's broken your heart…is he a good man?'

'He's the best,' she whispered.

'Is he worth the pain?'

She jerked a nod.

'Then you have to decide whether you're going to make lemonade or find an orange. Are you going to wallow in your pain or turn it into something constructive?'

'I wouldn't know where to start.'

'You start by accepting the pain for what it is but refusing to let it define you.'

Amy closed her eyes. If anyone knew how to cope with pain it was her mum. She'd handled a mountain of it and had never let it define her.

Compared to her mum she had nothing to complain about. Her mum had been innocent. She, Amy, had brought her misery upon herself.

Helios stood at the door to his grandfather's apartments and braced himself for the medicinal odour that would attack his senses when he stepped over the threshold.

Inside, all was quiet.

Stepping through to what had once been the King's bedroom and now resembled a hospital ward, he found his grandfather sleeping in his adjustable medical bed, with an oxygen mask over his nose and mouth.

At his side sat Helios's brothers. A nurse read unobtrusively in the corner.

'Any change?' he asked quietly. He'd only left the room for an hour, but the speed of his grandfather's deterioration over the past couple of days had been frightening. They all knew it wouldn't be long now.

Talos shook his head.

Taking his place on the other side of the bed from his brothers, Helios rolled his shoulders. Every part of his body felt stiff.

Theseus was holding their grandfather's right hand. Leaning forward, Helios took the left one, assuming the same position his grandfather had taken when his Queen had lain in an identical bed in the adjoining room, the life leaching out of her.

After a few long, long minutes their grandfather's eyes fluttered open. 'Water…' he croaked.

With Helios and Theseus working together from separate sides of the bed to raise him, Talos brought a glass to his mouth and placed the straw between his lips.

When he'd settled back the King looked at his three

grandsons, his stare lingering on each of them in turn, emotion ringing the rapidly dulling eyes.

The pauses between each of his inhalations grew. Then the corners of his lips twitched as if in a smile and his eyes closed for the last time.

CHAPTER THIRTEEN

AMY SAW THE announcement on the morning news.

'A statement from the palace said, "His Majesty King Astraeus the Fourth of Agon passed away peacefully in his sleep last night. His three grandsons were at his side."'

There then followed some speculation by the presenters and royal correspondents about what this meant for the island nation.

Without warning a picture of Helios and Catalina flashed onto the screen. It was an unofficial shot taken at the Gala. And then there was an off-screen voice saying, 'It is believed the heir to the throne will marry the Princess before taking the crown.'

Amy switched off the television, grabbed a pillow and cuddled into it, her head pounding.

Helios's grandfather, the King, had *died*.

She'd known it was coming, but still it hit her like a blow. She'd created his exhibition. During those happy months of curating that tribute to his life and the ancestors closest to him she'd felt as if she'd got to know him. Somehow she'd fooled herself into believing he was immortal. He had been a proud, dutiful man and she'd been privileged to meet him.

And then she thought of his eldest grandson, who had revered him.

Her phone lay on the floor beside her and she stared at it, wishing with all her heart that she could call Helios.

Would he even want to hear her condolences? The condolences of the woman who had sneaked out of the palace while he was dining with potential investors, supporting the island he loved?

She'd told him she would stay.

He'd forgiven her lie, but he had Catalina now. Without Amy's presence there, distracting him, he would turn to the Princess for comfort. Just as he should. Maybe grief would bring them together properly.

And as she prayed for a happy ending for her Prince and his Princess, hot tears spilled out of her eyes. She brought her knees to her chest and cried her broken heart out for the happy ending that would never be hers.

The funeral, a full state affair, was a sombre occasion.

People lined the streets in tens of thousands, all there to bow their heads in silence and pay their respects to the man who had served them with such dedication for fifty years.

The wake was an entirely different matter.

Out on the streets the atmosphere changed markedly. Television coverage showed military re-enactments from throughout the ages, even children dressed in loincloths and armed with plastic tridents. Barbecues lit up Agon's famous beaches, music played on every corner and there was food, drink and dancing everywhere in abundance.

Agon was putting on a show in the only way it knew how.

In the blue stateroom of the palace solemnity had given way to merriness too. The King was with his Queen. His suffering was over. His country and his family had laid him to rest and now they could celebrate his life.

For Helios, the occasion brought no joy. He accepted

that his grandfather had moved on to a better place, but
the hole in his heart felt so great he didn't know how it
would ever heal.

To know he would never talk to him again, dine with
him, play chess… All the things he'd taken for granted
were all gone. The man he'd worshipped, a man ten times
the man his own father had been, was gone.

Helios watched his brothers, stuck like glue to the sides
of their respective fiancées, and smiled for them. Their parents' marriage had been the worst template a child could
have asked for. That his brothers were heading into marriages that would be more like their grandparents' gave
him much hope. They would be happy.

He was under no illusions that he would follow suit.

Although he had seen little of her since his grandfather's
death, Catalina had been at his side throughout the funeral
service, a calm presence who had known exactly what to
say in all the right moments.

But, however perfect she might be, he knew that fifty
years of marriage wouldn't bring them the bond Talos and
Theseus shared with their fiancées.

That last smile his grandfather had given them was a
white shadow in Helios's mind. It gave him comfort. His
grandfather had welcomed death. He'd left the world knowing his grandsons—all of them—would take care of his beloved island, freeing him to move on to his beloved Rhea.

His *three* grandsons.

Three boys raised to be princes.

Catalina came to stand by him. He stared down at her
and met her thoughtful gaze.

*'Marriage to someone you feel no affection for can
only bring misery.'*

Those were the words his grandfather had said the last
time they'd spoken lucidly together. And in that moment

he knew those words hadn't been a reproach. They'd been a warning from a man who knew how powerful love could be and had witnessed the destructive nature of his son's contempt for the wife he didn't love.

And in that instant everything became clear.

He couldn't marry Catalina.

If he'd never met Amy everything would be different. *He* would be different.

If he'd never met Amy he would be marrying Catalina with no expectations or knowledge of how things might be. He would be King. She would be Queen. Their only bond would be of duty. He wouldn't know what it felt like to love or be loved.

Love.

The one word he'd never expected to apply to himself other than in an abstract form. Familial love he'd felt and believed in, but romantic love…? That was not something he'd ever been able to hope for, so not something he had ever allowed himself to think about. And, if he was being honest with himself, it was something he'd hidden away from. The scars of his parents' marriage ran so deep that what he'd convinced himself was rational acceptance of his future union was in fact a mask to hide the real truth—that love in all its forms was the most terrifying emotion of all.

But also the most wonderful.

Because, *Theos*, he loved Amy. With everything he had.

Try as he might, he couldn't get used to walking into the museum and not seeing her there. He couldn't get used to being in his apartment and seeing the connecting door, knowing she wasn't at the end of the passageway.

Not a second of his waking day was spent without him wondering where she was and what she was doing.

After his grandfather's death had been announced he'd

kept staring at his phone, willing it to ring. Knowing it wouldn't. Knowing she was right not to call him.

But his intellectual acceptance that she was gone and that it was all for the best wasn't something his heart had any intention of agreeing with.

He'd long trusted Amy with his confidences. Now he understood that he'd also trusted her with his heart, and that a relationship with any other woman was doomed to failure because he belonged to Amy. All of him.

When the day of his own death came the last thing his conscious mind would see would be her face.

Three weeks without her.

The time had dragged like a decade.

How could he think straight without her?

How could he breathe without her when she was as necessary to him as air?

He loved her.

He cast his eyes around the room until he found Theseus, deep in conversation with his fiancée, Jo, and a Swedish politician the three Princes had been at school with. Theseus was settled. He had a child. His marriage would be taking place in a week.

Helios took a deep breath. Before he spoke to his brother there was someone else who needed to be spoken to first.

He looked at her, still by his side, the silence between them stark.

'Catalina…'

'We need to talk, don't we?' she said quietly.

'Yes.'

Weaving their way through the crowd, they walked through a corridor, and then another, and then stepped out into the palace gardens.

'Catalina, I'm sorry but I can't marry you.'

She closed her eyes and breathed deeply.

'I've been grossly unfair to you. I'm not...' It was his turn to take a breath. 'I'm in love with someone else.'

She bowed her head and eventually met his gaze. 'Thank you for finally being honest with me—and with yourself.'

'I never meant to hurt you.'

Her smile was stoical. 'All you have hurt is my pride.'

He opened his mouth to speak further but she raised a hand to stop him.

'It would never have worked between us. I've known it for a while now, but I didn't want to add to the burden you've carried with your grandfather's illness.' She sighed. 'I will get my people to issue a press release in a couple of days, saying I have called the engagement off due to an incompatibility between us.'

It was the least he could let her do. 'Catalina, I am sorry. I never wanted...'

'No. Do not say anything else.' She lifted her chin. 'Let me leave here with *some* dignity.'

For a moment Helios did nothing but stare at the woman he had intended to spend the rest of his life with. Then, taking her shoulders, he pulled her into his embrace. It warmed his heart to feel her arms wrap around his waist.

'You will find a better man than me,' he whispered.

'I doubt that,' she answered drily. 'But perhaps I will find a man whose heart is free to love me.'

'I hope that for you too.'

Pulling apart, they kissed each other on both cheeks and smiled.

The weight he carried on his shoulders lifted a fraction.

'I expect an invitation,' she said as she walked away.

'An invitation to what?'

'To your wedding to your English curator. Your mother's ring will look wonderful on her finger.'

With one final wink she sashayed into the palace, not looking back.

Alone in the gardens Helios did a slow turn, taking in the verdant lawns, the sweet-scented flowers in bloom, the distant maze. It was a paradise of nature and life. Whether he became custodian of it all, as he'd spent his entire life believing he would, or not, the flowers would continue to bloom. That he knew with absolute certainty.

His heart beating loudly, echoing through every chamber of his body, he took his phone out of his pocket and dialled the number he had spent the past three weeks fighting not to call.

It went straight to voicemail.

He tried again.

The same thing happened.

Back in the palace, he entered the stateroom and found the person he was looking for.

'I need to borrow you,' he said to Pedro, interrupting his Head of Museum's conversation with a person he did not recognise.

'Where are we going?' Pedro asked.

'To the museum. I need to get something.'

The museum was closed out of respect for his grandfather and to allow all the staff to pay their respects too.

With long strides they followed the corridors into the museum's private entrance and cut through the large exhibition rooms until they reached the rooms that mattered to Helios at that moment. The Kalliakis Family exhibition rooms.

After he'd explained to Pedro what he wanted, a thought struck him.

'Do you know where Amy's working now?'

'She's back at the British Museum.'

No wonder she'd turned her phone off. She would be working. 'Do you have the number?'

Pedro scrolled through his phone until he found the relevant number and thrust the phone at him.

Helios put it to his ear whilst indicating that Pedro could start on the task he'd set for him. It rang a couple of times, a passage of time that to Helios's ears was longer than for ever, before it was answered.

'Put me through to Amy Green,' he said.

'One moment, please.'

There followed a merry little game in which he was routed to varying offices until a voice said, 'Ancient Greece Department.'

'I wish to speak to Amy Green.'

'I'm sorry, sir, but Amy is on leave. She'll be back on Monday.'

'Do you know where she's gone?'

'As far as I'm aware she's attending a funeral.'

'Thank you.'

Disconnecting the call, his brain reeling, Helios rubbed the nape of his neck.

Now what?

And as he wondered what the hell his next step should be his heart went out to her. To think she too had lost someone important... She would be in need of comfort just as he—

And in the space of a heartbeat he knew whose funeral she'd attended.

Hope filled him, spreading from his toes right to the roots of his hair.

He put a call through to his private secretary. 'Talia,' he said as soon as she answered, 'I need you to find Amy Green for me. She's in the country. Go through to Immigration and take it from there.'

To her credit, Talia took his instructions in her stride. 'The Immigration Minister is here.'

'Good. Speak to him. Now.'

While all this was going on Pedro had completed the task he'd been set and so the pair of them reset the alarms, closed the museum and went back to the wake.

Helios found Talia in a quiet corridor, with her phone pressed to her ear by her shoulder, writing information on her hand. She gave him a thumbs-up and carried on her conversation.

'She's at the airport,' she said without preamble a few minutes later. 'Her flight back to England leaves in forty-five minutes. The passengers for her flight will be boarding any minute.'

'I need to get to the airport.'

A tremor of fear flashed over Talia's face. 'All the roads are blocked. You'll never make it in time.'

'Watch me.'

With that, he headed back into the stateroom and, ignoring everyone who tried to speak to him, found the butler of Theseus's private villa, Philippe, a man who looked as if he should be catching the surf, not running a Prince's household.

He pulled him aside to speak to him privately.

'You have a motorbike, don't you?'

'Yes, Your Highness.'

'Is it here at the palace?'

'It's in the staff courtyard.'

'I need to borrow it.'

'Now?'

'Now.'

'Do you know how to ride?'

'You have the time it takes us to walk there to teach me. Let's go.'

* * *

Amy stared out of the oval window with a heavy heart.

She was glad she'd come.

It had been a snap decision, driven by a sense of certainty that she had to go, to pay her respects to the man for whom she'd devoted almost six months of her life to creating an exhibition of *his* life.

Watching Helios and his brothers walking with military precision in front of the coffin, their gazes aimed forward, knowing how they must be bleeding inside...

The crowds had been so thick there had been no chance of Helios catching sight of her, but even so she hadn't taken any chances, keeping a good distance from the barrier.

What good would it have done for him to see her? The Princess had been there for him, just as Amy had known she would be, travelling in an official car with Theseus's and Talos's fiancées.

A steward made his sweep down the aisle, checking everyone's seat belts were fastened. The plane began to move. Over the speakers came the sombre voice of the captain, welcoming them all to this flight to London.

The ache in her chest told her she'd been wise to get a return flight home straight after the funeral. Any longer and the temptation to call Helios and seek him out would have become too great to resist. One night on Agon was as much as she'd been prepared to risk.

She'd taken her mother's advice to heart, and God knew she was trying to get herself an orange.

She'd taken up her old job at the museum and enrolled in a postgraduate course on the Ancient Romans, which she would start in September. She figured she might as well expand her knowledge so that her life wasn't all about Agon and its people, whether from history or the present. There was a big world out there to explore and learn about.

She'd kept herself busy, working by day and socialising by evening. It was the nights that were unbearable. Despite the mild heatwave sweeping through the UK, her nights were always cold.

Somehow she would find a way to forget him.

The plane had reached the place where it would turn around and face the runway.

The woman sitting beside her gripped the armrests, her knuckles turning white in anticipation of take-off.

But no sooner had the plane started its journey down the runway than it was brought to a stop.

It took a while before the passengers realised something was wrong, and then low murmurs began spreading throughout the plane.

The voice of a stewardesses came over the speaker. 'Could passenger Miss Amy Green please make herself known to a member of the cabin crew?'

Amy barely heard, her attention caught by a motorcyclist, speeding over the tarmac, heading towards them. Behind him was a buggy, with two men in orange high-visibility jackets towing metal steps. There was something about the figure riding the motorbike…

'Amy Green? Miss Amy Green—please make yourself known to a member of the cabin crew.'

With a jolt she realised it was *her* they were asking for. Tearing her gaze away from the window, she raised a hesitant hand.

A stewardess bustled over to her, looking harassed. 'Amy Green?'

Amy nodded, bemused and not a little scared.

'I need you to come with me.'

'Why?'

'We've been asked to escort you off this flight.'

'But *why*? Have I done something wrong?'

The stewardess shook her head. 'I don't know why.'

The couple she was sitting next to had to get out of their seats to let her pass, but it wasn't long before she was trailing the stewardess to the exit, her face burning with mortification, her brain burning with confusion.

What the hell was going on...?

At the rear exit of the plane the crew were all staring at her unabashedly, no doubt wondering if she was some kind of fugitive.

Was she a fugitive? Had she unwittingly committed a crime that necessitated her being escorted off a plane and arrested?

And then the door opened, the metal stairs were hastily bolted on and she stood at the threshold, looking to see if a dozen police officers were waiting at the bottom to take her into custody.

The only person waiting for her was the motorcyclist she'd spotted. He sat astride the bike, his helmet resting under an arm...

CHAPTER FOURTEEN

AMY'S HEART LEAPT so hard it almost jumped out of her mouth.

Behind her came a collective sigh from the crew. One of them squeezed her shoulder. 'Go to him.'

But she couldn't. Her legs had turned to jelly.

She covered her mouth, unable to believe her eyes.

What was he doing here?

His handsome face immobile, he got off his bike, placed the helmet on the seat and climbed the stairs with heavy treads.

It was only when he was at eye level with her and she was able to gaze into the liquid dark brown eyes she loved so much that Amy dared to breathe.

'Helios,' she whispered, raising a hand to brush it against his cheek, to feel for herself that he truly was there and that this wasn't some dream she'd fallen into.

But no. No dream.

His cheek was warm and smooth, his jawline rough, at the stage where stubble was just starting to poke through the skin. His warm, familiar scent played under her nose.

'Sneaking away again?' he asked, in a voice that was meant to be humorous but that cracked on the last syllable.

'What...? What are you doing here?'

His eyes bored into her, emotion seeping out of them.

'I'm taking you home.' Then he took the final step up and lifted her into his arms. 'I'm taking you home,' he repeated.

Another collective 'Ooh…' sounded from behind her, and as Helios carried her down the steps a round of applause broke out. One of the men in high-visibility jackets, who was waiting by the buggy, wolf-whistled.

Amy heard it all, but none of it penetrated. All her senses were focused so intensely on her lover that everything else had become a blur.

At the bottom of the steps Helios placed her carefully on her feet.

Suddenly the biggest, widest grin spread over his face. 'Would Despinis Green like a ride on my bike?'

Laughter bubbled up in her throat and broke through her daze. She flung her arms around him. 'Yes. Please. Take me anywhere.'

Amy kept a tight hold on Helios as he drove them through the streets of Resina. She didn't *have* to hold him tightly—the dense throng of partying people meant he had to ride at a snail's pace—but she needed to. Keeping her cheek pressed into the solidity of his back and her arms around his waist grounded her, helped her accept the reality of what had just happened.

Soon they had passed through the capital and were out in the verdant countryside, with Agon's mountains looming before them. Helios found a road that took them up Mount Ares, the rockiest of Agon's mountains, past goats casually chewing grass by sheer drops, taking them higher and higher until they arrived at a clearing.

He turned the engine off and clicked the stand down to keep the bike upright before helping her off.

She looked at him, laughing as she properly noticed for the first time that he'd ridden with her up a mountain

in a pair of handmade black trousers, black brogues, now
covered in dust, and a white shirt with the sleeves rolled
up that had probably been as crisp as freshly baked pie
earlier but was now crumpled and stained.

'Your clothes are ruined.'

He shrugged, his eyes sparkling. 'I couldn't care less.'

Taking her hand, he led her to a flat grassy area and sat
down, enfolding her in his arms so her back rested against
his chest and her head was tucked beneath his chin.

'When I was a child my brothers and I would race to the
top of this mountain. When we'd all reached the summit we
would come down to this clearing and eat our picnic. This
spot has the best view of the sunset on the whole of Agon.'

The sun was already making its descent, causing a
darkly colourful hue to settle over the island.

'How did you know I was here?' she asked eventually.

'Your museum told me you'd gone to a funeral. I guessed.'

'But how did you know what plane I was on?'

'Do you really need me to answer that?' he said with
bemusement.

She smiled to herself, tightening her hold on his hands,
which were still wrapped around her waist. And then she
remembered *why* she had come to Agon today.

'I'm so sorry about your grandfather,' she said softly.

He kissed her head. 'He was ready to go.'

'I wanted to call you.'

'I know you did. And you were right not to.'

She sighed. Now that she had come to her senses, reality
was poking at her painfully.

'How did you manage to sneak out without your bodyguards?'

'Simple. I didn't tell them what I was doing. The palace
was so busy with the wake it was easy. Talia will have told
them by now.'

'She knows you came for me?'

'Yes. So does Pedro.'

'How long do we have? Here, I mean?'

'As long as we want.'

'But you'll be missed,' she said with another sigh, thinking that, however wonderful it was to be sat in his arms again, she would be dragged away from him again soon.

She was here now, though. A short interlude. Two lovers snatching a few minutes together to watch the sunset. One final sweet goodbye.

'I have done my duty by my grandfather today. And, *matakia mou*, he would want me to be here with you.'

'He would?'

'My grandfather was a great believer in two things—duty and love.'

Her heart gave a little skip at his words, a skip she tried frantically to dampen.

'Please, Helios, don't say things like that. It isn't fair.'

He caught her chin and turned her face to look at him. 'How can the truth not be fair? You are my whole world. I love you.'

'Please, stop,' she beseeched, clutching at his shirt. 'Don't speak of love to me when you will be marrying Catalina—'

'I'm not marrying Catalina,' Helios interrupted, castigating himself for being foolish enough to believe Amy was a mind reader who would have known the truth from the minute she'd seen him from her plane window. 'The wedding is off.'

Her eyes widened into huge round orbs. 'It is? Since when?'

'Since about three hours ago, when I realised I couldn't live another day without you. Catalina and I had a talk.' Knowing Amy would be concerned for the Princess, he took pains to reassure her. 'She will be fine. She's as good a woman as you always told me, and I promise you we have her blessing.'

'But…' Nothing else came. Her mouth was opening and closing as if her tongue had forgotten how to form words.

He pressed his lips to hers, inhaling the warm, sweet breath he had believed he would never taste again.

'I love you,' he repeated, looking at her shocked face. 'It's you I want to marry. Just you. Only you.'

'I want that too. More than anything in the world.'

'Then why do you look so sad?'

'Because I know it can never be. You aren't allowed to marry a commoner.'

He took hold of her hand and pressed it to his chest. 'Listen to my heart,' he said quietly. 'I knew I had to find a wife when my grandfather was given his diagnosis, but I put it off and put it off because deep down I knew it would mean losing you. My heart has been beating for you from the very start.'

Her breath gave a tiny hitch.

'You asked me what I would have been if I hadn't been born heir to the throne and I had no good answer for you, because it wasn't something I had ever allowed myself to think about. The throne, my country…they were my life. I didn't expect love. My only hope for marriage was that it would be better than what my parents had. However it panned out I would do my duty and I would respect my wife. That was the most I hoped for. I didn't *want* love. I saw the way my father abused the power of my mother's love and I never wanted to have the power to inflict such hurt on a woman. That's why Catalina seemed so perfect— I thought she was emotionally cold.'

Amy shivered.

Helios tightened his hold and gently kissed her. 'I know

I have the power to hurt you, *matakia mou*, and I swear on everything holy that I will never abuse it. But you need to understand one thing.'

'What's that?' she whispered.

'You have equal power to hurt me.'

'I do?'

'Living without you… It's been like living in an emotional dungeon. Cold and dark and without hope.' He brushed his thumb over her soft cheek. 'If spending the rest of my life with you means I have to relinquish the throne, then that's the price I'll pay and I'll pay it gladly.'

Her hold on his shirt tightening, her eyes wide and fearful, she said, 'But what about the throne? What will happen to it?'

'I don't know.' He laughed ruefully. 'Theseus is next in line. That's one of the things that struck me earlier—my grandparents raised *three* princes. It doesn't have to be me. We're all capable and worthy of taking the throne. Except Talos,' he added as an afterthought. 'Never mind that he's marrying a commoner too. He can be particularly fierce. He'll probably scare more people away from our country than attract them.'

She managed a painful chortle at his attempt at humour. 'But what if Theseus doesn't want it?'

'He probably *won't* want it,' he answered honestly. 'But he understands what it's like to be without the one you love. His fiancée has royal blood in her. It should be enough.'

'And if it isn't?'

'Then we will work something out. Whatever happens, I swear to you that we will be together until we take our dying breaths and that the Agon monarchy will remain intact. Have faith, *matakia mou*. And to prove it…'

Disentangling himself from her arms, he dug into his

pocket and pulled out the object Pedro had set about retrieving a few short hours ago.

Dumbstruck, she simply stared at it as he displayed it to her.

'This, my love, belongs to you.' He took her trembling left hand, slid the ring onto her engagement finger, then kissed it. 'One day the eldest of our children will inherit it, and in turn they will pass it to the eldest of their children—either to wear themselves upon marriage or for their wives to wear.'

'Our *children*?'

'You do want them, don't you?' he asked, suddenly anxious that he might have made one assumption too many. 'If you don't we can pass the ring to Theseus…'

'No, no—I *do* want your children,' she said. And then, like a cloud moving away from the sun, the fear left her eyes and a smile as wide as the sunset before them spread across her cheeks, lighting up her whole face. 'We're really going to be together?'

'Until death us do part.'

Such was the weight of her joy that when she threw herself into him he fell back onto the grass, taking her with him, and her overjoyed kisses as she straddled him filled him with more happiness than he had ever thought possible.

She was *his*. He was hers.

And as they lay on the grass, watching the orange sun make its final descent through the pink sky, he knew in his heart that the rest of his life would be filled with the glorious colours of this most beautiful of sunsets.

EPILOGUE

Six months later

THE RED DOME of the Aghia Sophia, the cathedral located in the exact central point between the Agon palace and the capital, Resina, gleamed as if it were burnt liquid gold under the autumn sky.

As Amy was taken through the cheering crowds on a horse-drawn carriage she turned her face upwards, letting the sun's rays warm her face, and sighed with contentment. Unlike many brides on their big day, she had no fear or apprehension whatsoever.

Beside her sat her father, who would be walking her down the aisle, and little Toby, proud as Punch to have been given the important role of ring bearer. In the carriage ahead of them sat her three bridesmaids: her soon-to-be sisters-in-law, Amalie and Jo, and Greta. Ahead of them were seven mounted military guards, in all their ceremonial attire, with the front rider holding the Kalliakis Royal Standard. More guards rode alongside the carriages, and there were a dozen at the rear.

It was pure pageantry at its finest. Triple the number of military guards were scheduled for a fortnight's time, when she and Helios would return to the cathedral to be crowned King and Queen of Agon.

In the sky were dozens of helicopters, sent from news outlets across the world to film the event.

Unbelievably she, Amy Green—a woman abandoned as a two-week-old baby by her birth mother, a woman who had never been quite sure of her place in the world—was going to be Queen of Agon.

Helios would be King. And it was the woman who'd abandoned her who'd made it all possible.

According to Helios, Theseus had turned the colour of puce when he'd sat his two brothers down and explained the situation to them. As Helios had suspected, Theseus had reluctantly agreed he would take the throne but only if all other avenues had first been explored.

Constitutional experts had been put on the case, to no avail, until Talos had come up with the bright idea of changing the constitution, rightly pointing out it had been changed numerous times before.

A meeting with the Agon senate had been arranged, and there the president, who, like all the members of the senate, was sympathetic to the Crown Prince's plight, had murmured about how much easier it would be to bring about the constitutional change if the bride were of Agon blood…

A referendum had taken place. Of the ninety per cent turnout, ninety-three per cent had voted for changing the constitution to allow a person of non-royal blood to marry into the royal family, provided that she was of Agon blood.

And now, as the carriage pulled up at the front of the cathedral, where the cheers from the crowd were deafening, Amy was helped down. She stepped carefully, so as not to trip over the fifteen-foot train of her ivory silk dress, handmade by Queen Rhea's personal designer, Natalia.

How she loved her dress, with its spaghetti straps and the rounded neck that skimmed her cleavage, the flared skirt that was as far from the traditional meringue shape as could be. Simpler in form and design than both Queen Rhea's dress and Helios's mother's dress, it was utterly perfect for her. And it was lucky she had insisted on something simpler considering they'd had to expand the waistline at the last fitting, to take into account the swelling of her stomach...

She and Helios had taken the decision a couple of months ago for Amy to come off the contraceptive pill, both of them figuring that it would take a good few months for the hormones to get out of her system. The hope had been that she would conceive after their coronation.

Whoops.

A month after taking her last pill Amy's breasts had suddenly grown in size. Their baby—the new heir to the throne—was due in six months, something they had decided not to make public until after their coronation. Naturally half the palace knew about it.

Greta had been given Corinna's job at the museum and was thoroughly enjoying bossing Amy about. Amy had gone back to curating King Astraeus's exhibition and then, when the exhibition had closed, she'd taken on the role of museum tour guide. It was a job she would be able to fit around the royal duties she would have to take on when she was crowned Queen.

Helios still thought it appropriate to give bloodthirsty Agon history lessons to children in the dungeons.

In all, everything had worked out perfectly, as if the stars had aligned for them.

Jo stepped forward to adjust Amy's veil, having to stretch to accommodate her own swollen stomach, which was fast resembling a beach ball, and then it was time.

When her arm was held tightly in her father's, the doors of the cathedral were thrown open, the music started and Amy took the first step towards the rest of her life.

The congregation rose as one, every head turning to stare. The first face she saw was that of Princess Catalina, who, as gracious as ever, smiled at Amy with both her lips and her eyes. When the press had bombarded her with questions about Helios and Amy's marriage her statement of support for them had been heartfelt and touching.

Surely somewhere in this packed cathedral stood a prince in need of a beautiful, elegant princess to make his own?

In the back row was the woman who had made all this happen—Neysa Soukis, there with her husband, and their son, Leander. It was amazing how the thought of being Queen Mother had spurred Neysa to recognise Amy as her child with enthusiasm and thus proclaim her a child of Agon blood. No doubt Neysa had imagined this moment many times, had thought she would be sitting in the front row of the congregation.

Alas, Neysa had soon learned that the only place she had in Amy's life was as a name on a piece of paper. Elaine—her mum, the woman who had raised and loved her—would be the officially recognised Queen Mother.

And, thinking of her mum, there she stood in the front row, beautiful in a pea-green skirt suit and an enormous hat, beaming with pride. Next to her stood Amy's *real* brothers, Neil and Danny, with identical grins on their faces. Both of them had been fit to burst with pride when Helios had appointed them as his ushers. Their wives had a dazed, 'someone pinch me to prove this is really happening' look about them.

And best of all, standing at the front, beside the altar, his brothers by his side, stood Helios; her lover and her best friend all rolled into one.

The three Princes were dressed in their military uniforms: the Kalliakis livery complete with sashes. They all looked magnificent, like three benevolent giants.

Helios might not be able to see her face through her veil, but she could see his, and see the full beard he'd grown especially for her. The expression in his eyes made every step she took closer to him feel as if she were bouncing on the moon.

When she reached him Helios took her hand, and together they knelt at the altar to pledge their lives, fidelity and love to each other for ever.

They were pledges neither of them would ever break.

* * * * *

MILLS & BOON®

MODERN™

POWER, PASSION AND IRRESISTIBLE TEMPTATION

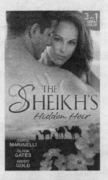

MILLS & BOON®

Why shop at millsandboon.co.uk?

Each year, thousands of romance readers find their perfect read at millsandboon.co.uk. That's because we're passionate about bringing you the very best romantic fiction. Here are some of the advantages of shopping at www.millsandboon.co.uk:

* **Get new books first**—you'll be able to buy your favourite books one month before they hit the shops

* **Get exclusive discounts**—you'll also be able to buy our specially created monthly collections, with up to 50% off the RRP

* **Find your favourite authors**—latest news, interviews and new releases for all your favourite authors and series on our website, plus ideas for what to try next

* **Join in**—once you've bought your favourite books, don't forget to register with us to rate, review and join in the discussions

Visit **www.millsandboon.co.uk**
for all this and more today!